
★

This wasn't hunting season, Jean told herself. And the shape in the shadows wasn't that of a deer.

The faraway voices were all chattering brightly now. The sound faded in and out as though she turned a volume knob up and down. The pipes skreeled, but nowhere near as loudly as her brain. Her stomach clenched. The shape was an optical illusion. Please let it be an optical illusion.

She already knew, though, that it was no such thing. Groping alongside the door, she found a light switch and pushed at it blindly.

The dangling man's head was tilted to one side, as though delicately averting his gaze. But there was nothing delicate about his face, slightly swollen and ash-pink, his tongue a purplish bulge between blue lips, his eyes slits showing flat, ghastly whites.

George Lovelace. Unrecognizable. Perfectly recognizable.

★

THE SECRET PORTRAIT

LILLIAN STEWART CARL

TORONTO • NEW YORK • LONDON
AMSTERDAM • PARIS • SYDNEY • HAMBURG
STOCKHOLM • ATHENS • TOKYO • MILAN
MADRID • WARSAW • BUDAPEST • AUCKLAND

THE SECRET PORTRAIT

A Worldwide Mystery/May 2008

First published by Five Star.

ISBN-13: 978-0-373-26637-1
ISBN-10:   0-373-26637-5

To

Jared Sullivan Carl and his bride,
Shirisha Reddy, M.D.

We haven't lost this son, either;
we've gained another doctor.

ONE

JEAN FAIRBAIRN SAT ON the stone windowsill of her office, if hardly
in command then at least in admiration of all she surveyed.

The bloodstained walls of Edinburgh Castle loomed over a row
of modern shops. The dour medieval houses of the Old Town
turned their backs on the sprightly Regency façades of the new.
Car parks overlooked cemeteries. Businesspeople carrying cell
phones and briefcases threaded their way among tourists dawdling
over their maps, all pretending not to see the homeless.

Edinburgh itself, Jean thought with a smile, should have been
the protagonist of native son Robert Louis Stevenson's *Dr. Jekyll
and Mr. Hyde*. It was an appropriate place for her to either find
herself or lose herself, depending on her mood of the moment. And
right now her mood was upbeat, confident, eager to explore. She
must be getting in touch with her feline side, and not only in posture.

"You'll have me barring the window," said a voice behind her. "We
can't have you falling out and scaring away the paying customers."

Jean looked around to see Miranda Capaldi, her friend of twenty
years and business partner of four months, peering into the room.
Jean's smile grew into a grin. "Funny how the tourist brochures
never show the throngs of tourists. It's quantum travel. The act of
looking at the sites changes the nature of the sites you look at."

"Oh aye. The cafe up at the Castle is serving iced tea. Seems
you Yanks can't leave home without bringing your bad habits
along with you. That much for their authentic Scottish experience."
Laughing, Miranda strolled across to the window and sat down on
the other half of the sill.

Jean gathered in her denim skirt, not that Miranda's svelte
figure needed much room. The subtle fragrance of her Chanel
moderated the odors of diesel and frying food rising from the
street four stories below. Jean's perfumes usually evaporated into
a brown sludge, sour with reproach, before she remembered to use

them. Speaking of odors, she said, "Two hundred years ago people were emptying chamber pots out this very window. If tourists want authenticity…."

"Authenticity? Not a bit of it. They come here chasing romantic fantasies. Like you, I'm thinking."

"Me? I'm a hard-bitten old cynic. Look at the articles I was doing for the magazine even before I moved here, about legends hitting the road and blowing a tire. Playing reality off illusion."

Miranda cocked a tweezed eyebrow.

"Okay, okay." Jean raised her hands in surrender. "I wouldn't have moved here if I didn't think the grass was greener or the tartan brighter, whatever. It's merciful fantasy that keeps you going. Still, I maintain that anyone who moves to Scotland in January isn't chasing illusions, romantic or meteorological."

"Oh aye, the winter was dreadful, right enough. But look now, a May afternoon with sunshine enough to warm the cockles of your heart."

Yes, just as the sunlight transformed Edinburgh's Calvinist gray to cosmopolitan color, some similar alchemy was going on in that part of Jean's psyche known as "heart," whether that included the ambiguous "cockles" or not. Home is where the heart is, she thought. Heart of Midlothian. My heart's in the Highlands. Queen of…

"Is living here what you were expecting, then?" Miranda, as always, cut to the chase.

"Scotland is. Owning half the magazine is. Living alone, that still seems strange."

"Just you wait, you'll meet someone new."

"No way," stated Jean. That was the last thing she needed, another man to complicate the life she'd gone to such lengths to simplify.

Miranda's other brow rose to meet its mate, but she held her tongue. A soft knock on the door announced Gavin, the teenager who minded the reception desk. "Ms. Fairbairn, you've got a visitor."

An elderly gentleman peered around Gavin's shoulder. His diction betrayed his national origin south of Hadrian's Wall. "I wasn't quite sure I should call in, I suppose I should have rung for an appointment…."

"Come on in." Jean stood up.

Miranda sauntered away, her murmured, "I'll leave you to it, then," pierced by a curious backward glance.

"Good of you to see me. I'm George Lovelace, Leicester University, retired." The old man extended his hand.

Jean took it. "No problem."

While many old men had a handshake that felt like an empty glove, his was firm, almost fierce. He stood so ramrod straight his ivory-headed walking stick must have been not support but swagger stick. Maybe his gray regimental moustache, thick glasses, and tweed suit—sturdy old-fashioned tweed, not today's lighter fabric—boded less an hour of polite boredom than an interesting new story-quest to complement the day's sunlit affirmations.

"Please, sit down. What can I do for you?" Adjusting her own glasses, Jean maneuvered around the corner of the desk and into her chair.

Lovelace took the other chair in the room, a straight-backed number that belonged in a collection of torture devices, and looked vaguely around at Jean's books and papers before looking somewhat less vaguely at her. "Miss Fairbairn. Dr. Fairbairn, rather."

Her doctorate had been awarded to Jean Inglis. Just because the marriage was over didn't mean the degree wasn't valid. Still, she defaulted to, "It's Jean."

"I've been enjoying your articles in *Great Scot,* er, Jean. Fine magazine, that. Miss Capaldi has made a good fist of bringing it to life again. It was one of my childhood favorites, Scotland being another world to me as a lad in the Home Counties. Happy days, those, when I'd play at Arthur and his knights or William Wallace or Bonnie Prince Charlie in the heather. Not that we had heather in Orpington."

Jean had seen Orpington. It was a suburb of London teeming with traffic. She suspected Lovelace would not agree with those who thought the change meant progress.

"Well now." He leaned forward, focusing. "I most especially enjoyed your article about Prince Charles. Not the present one, of course. The Young Pretender, the Bonnie Prince of the seventeen forty-five rebellion. History creates different versions of such figures, doesn't it?"

"Like running them through a hall of mirrors."

"Quite right. That's how history is transmuted to legend. Not that I mean to disparage legend. As you said yourself, legend is the yeast that makes history rise. Nice turn of phrase, that."

Miranda had wanted to edit out that flight of verbosity. Jean decided Lovelace was a charming old gentleman.

"I understand," he went on, "that you had a most distinguished career at a university in America."

Her biography was printed in the back of the magazine. The fact that her academic career was dead, buried, and eulogized was not. She said neutrally, "I taught British history for almost twenty years. What's your field?"

"Eighteenth-century literature, specializing in first editions, ephemera, arcana, curiosa, and marginalia."

"Love letters, diaries, political pamphlets, penny dreadful novels, and menus from the *Titanic*—well, not in the eighteenth century. Menus from the *Bounty,* maybe. Historical gossip columns."

"Very much so. Fascinating, but quite tiring to the eyes, which is why I took to watching birds. I spent many a holiday in the Western Highlands, and finally moved house there. Mind you, I was stationed at Achnacarry for a time during the war. That was a shocker, coming to such rough country after my youth in Kent. Although that's the point of commando training, to toughen you up. They used live fire in those days, mind you, none of this limp-wristed please-and-thank-you business you see today. But our backs aren't against the wall today, thank God. We lost too many young people then, too many who gave their todays for our tomorrows.... Well, I'm sure old soldiers since Marathon have been uttering the same sentiments."

"It comes with the territory, yes."

"So does my bewilderment with today's culture, I suppose. Music, clothes, the telly—not mine to criticize, though. Must keep up with the times. But oh dear, this modern food, a few stunted vegetables in a pool of muck with some contrived bit of protein perched on top. What happened to the good honest chop, potato, and veg, I ask you?"

He shouldn't ask Jean. She was grateful for the proliferation of exotic foodstuffs like nachos and Thai curry on menus all over Scotland, let alone in sophisticated Edinburgh. But food, like humor, was a very personal subject.

Lovelace's watery blue eyes blinked rapidly. "I'm rambling. Old men have a tendency to ramble. Too many memories stored in the gray matter, I expect; can't quite lay your hand on the point of the exercise."

"I'm still with you," she assured him, although as yet she had no idea where they were going.

"Well then." Reaching inside his jacket, he produced a flat white box and set it on the desk. He whisked away the lid like a magician pulling a rabbit from a hat.

Good Lord. Jean's eyes bulged. Without looking away, she fumbled for the desk lamp and turned it on.

Inside the box, on a bed of white cotton, lay a massive coin. Its surface blazed a fiery gold. Every mound and furrow of the face stamped on it was finely etched: the double chin, the long, sloping forehead.

From a long way away Lovelace's voice said, "Have a look at the reverse."

She reached out, mentally slapped her own hand, and instead opened the desk drawer where she kept her supply of tissues—in Edinburgh in the spring, you soaked the rain up through your feet and blew it out your nose.

The tissue covering her fingertips, Jean gingerly picked up the coin. Yes, it was heavy, and even through the tissue ice-cold. On the back was a design of the Palace of Versailles, every window so finely detailed she expected to see Madame de Maintenon pull aside the drapes.

She turned the coin face-up again. The words surrounding the haughty, regal visage—*grace a dieu*—yes, they were in French. Exhaling through pursed lips, she settled the coin back into its cotton bed and looked up. "That's a Louis d'Or. King Louis the Fourteenth in gold."

Lovelace was staring at her, no longer blinking. "An excellent specimen. Almost three hundred years old, and bright as the day it was minted."

"You must have found this in Lochaber or Moidart."

He managed a thin, asymmetrical smile. "Well done! But then, a scholar like you would know where Bonnie Prince Charlie's French gold was hidden."

"I don't know exactly. No one does, which is just the point, isn't it? You've found a clue." Jean beamed on the old man. Oh yes, this promised to be a very exciting story, a historical treasure hunt, no less. "So as a child you played at being the Bonnie Prince on the lam, and as an adult you find a coin that has to have come from his lost hoard. That's karma for you. Fate."

Did he shudder at that? Or did he just droop wearily over his hands knotted atop the walking stick? "Especially when you consider how often I double-timed it through that same area as a youth. Although having bullets whistling past one's ears is hardly favorable to prospecting."

"Now, though, you walk slowly around watching birds, and turn up a needle in a haystack."

"I wasn't searching for the coin," he said, still talking to his own hands, his diction slurred. "You'll excuse me if I don't reveal just where I found it."

The coin glowed like a good deed in murky world. Many a bad deed had been done for just that glow. Was Lovelace worried that bad deeds would follow his discovery? If so, then why not just chuck the coin into his desk drawer? "You've come to the press with this," Jean pointed out.

Abruptly Lovelace sat up straight, as though bracing himself to some unpleasant duty. His gaze was so direct she almost expected him to start barking orders like a drill sergeant. In spite of herself, she shrank against the back of her chair. *Was it something I said?*

"I've come to you, Jean, because I'd like you to help me have the coin declared treasure trove. I'm a widower, so have only myself to support on my pension, but a bit of the ready wouldn't go amiss— the taxes nowadays, some inheritance for the grandchildren."

She managed to lean into his fixed look, like swimming against a current, and said, "I'm not up on the laws of treasure trove, but I know a curator at the new Museum who is. I'll set up an appointment for you."

"Thank you, but no. I'd much prefer you take the coin there yourself."

"Oh." Jean didn't exactly frown, but her eyebrows tightened. "Well yes, I can do that. There's really no need, though; they're very discreet."

"I would greatly appreciate your seeing to the matter." Funny how he was no longer discursive, but as direct as though he'd rehearsed his spiel before he got here.

He must be embarrassed to admit that he needed money. "I'll have to tell the Museum people your name, but they won't pass it on. I won't either, but still I'd like to do something for *Great Scot* about the coin, maybe work it into an article about the lost hoard."

"Yes, yes, that goes without saying. You must make your efforts worthwhile and all. But please leave the particulars unclear. Don't want to cause a gold rush; we have quite enough people beating about the area as it is, leaving gates open, littering, frightening the sheep…." His voice ran down. So did he, bowing over his walking stick again.

Growing more intrigued by the moment, Jean asked, "Are you planning to look for more coins?"

"Oh, no, no, not at all."

Why not? she wondered. More coins, more money.

"This coin," he mumbled, "is worth much more as a historical artifact than as its component gold, I expect. I should hate to see it destroyed."

Now he was evading the issue as deliberately as he was evading her eyes—hot-cold, hot-cold. She tried reassuring him. "The Museum's bottom line is historical value, yes. They won't destroy it. They'll probably want to buy it."

"Right. This is where you can reach me, then." Lovelace reached inside his jacket, pulled out a metal case, and extracted the small white rectangle of a business card.

Jean took it. His hand was trembling. Did he need some sort of special treatment beyond that provided by the National Health Service? Was that why he needed money?

This time she did frown, hiding her expression by looking down at the card. It was engraved with, "George Albert Lovelace," followed by his address and phone number. "Corpach, by Fort William. That's a beautiful area. What's the name of the American millionaire who bought the old mansion out there? Surely you've heard of him."

When Lovelace didn't answer, Jean looked back up. All she

could see was the top of his head, the gray hair meticulously parted and pomaded. "Ah yes, I've heard of the man. We've all heard of the man. One of the local celebrities. We get quite a few celebrities in the area, film stars and the like. I remember Mel Gibson." He sat up abruptly, eyes hard and somehow hurt.

Yeah, well, Jean was not a fan of Gibson's *Braveheart,* but she had a feeling that wasn't the problem.

"If you'd be so good as to give me a receipt for the coin," Lovelace said to the wall behind her, "I'll leave the matter in your capable hands."

"Sure." Might as well play along, Jean told herself. She swiveled around to her computer, tapped out, "Received from George Lovelace one Louis d'Or in excellent condition," printed the message on the magazine's letterhead, signed, and dated it.

He took the paper and folded it into his pocket. "Thank you. Now if you'll excuse me, it's almost time for my train. I didn't drive; my automobile is a bit of an old banger and the traffic in the city is…"

"A circus," Jean concluded when he didn't.

Lovelace levered himself to his feet and for a moment stood supporting himself heavily on his stick. Then he drew himself to attention. Mission accomplished. Nodding gravely at Jean, even while avoiding her eyes, he started toward the door.

Climbing back out from behind her desk, she walked Lovelace through the hallway and past the reception alcove. "I'll be in touch," she told him, and opened the door.

He stepped out onto the stair landing, then spun back around, focused, intent. "Miss Fairbairn, Jean, I think you should know…."

That was one sentence she couldn't finish for him. "What?"

Again he blinked rapidly, bent over his stick, and turned away. "Ah no, I beg your pardon, I shouldn't speak out of turn. Good day."

What the… But he had started down the stone spiral of the medieval turnpike stair. Jean stood, arms crossed, monitoring his progress down the steps by the receding pad of his shoes and the tap of his stick. She was afraid if she shouted after him, asking for explanations, she'd hear the sound of a falling body. After centuries of use, the narrow triangular treads were hollowed and lopsided, and even at her tender age, comparatively speaking, she had been known to catch her heel or stumble.

But no. The slam of the outside door echoed up the stairwell, punctuating Lovelace's departure like an exclamation mark after a shout.

TWO

JEAN HADN'T QUITE reached the level of a frustrated shout. A sigh, though, one that split the difference between bafflement and irritation, that seemed appropriate. With the uneasy feeling that a cloud had just coasted across her sun, she walked back into the reception area.

So what was all that about? Lovelace had been chatty, pouring out numerous petty details of his life, none of which concerned her. Then, as soon as he produced the coin, which did concern her, he'd turned—coy, perhaps. Secretive.

Jean knew only too well that her curious nature had developed a tendency to suspicion. Still, Lovelace had as much as admitted he was hiding something from her. Whether it was anything as straightforward as a medical condition he didn't want to reveal, or something more—sinister, if that wasn't too strong a word—she had no way of knowing. Yet.

For just a moment she wondered, *why me?* Then she ordered herself to can the paranoia. Lovelace's simply was not the let-it-all-hang-out generation. He was being careful of his sensibilities. She'd have to be, too. Like a priest or a lawyer, she was now in possession of privileged information.

Miranda lay in wait in the door of her office, her blond crest of hair tilted forward eagerly. "What was he on about?"

"He found a gold coin from Bonnie Prince Charlie's Lochaber hoard, and since I wrote that article on Charlie last month, he wants me to do the treasure trove legwork for him. At least, that's his story."

"Bonnie Prince Charlie? Gold hoard?" Klieg lights shone in

Miranda's eyes. She grasped Jean's arm, pulling her into the room. "His story?"

"What he told me of it, not exactly chapter and verse."

"Of course he's not telling you the entire story. He's not after giving away the location of thousands of gold coins."

"It's not that he wouldn't tell me where he found the coin, it was more his body language and that he said…." Jean told her own sensibilities to calm down, already. Lovelace had an ulterior motive. She didn't know what it was. Period. "I can write a good article without knowing the intimate details, let alone naming names."

"There you are, then." Miranda inspected her overstuffed bookshelf. She always found what she was looking for, Jean thought admiringly, even though her office looked like an archaeological dig. Magic, probably.

Miranda pulled out an atlas. "The barrels of coins were hidden where? Lochaber?"

"The western Highlands north and west of Fort William, anywhere from Loch Arkaig to Loch Linnhe to the sea. Rough country, even today."

"Bonnie Prince Charlie country. The prince in the heather and his buried treasure. There's a brilliant marketing hook for you. You can make a start with an article, then do up a book—loads of photographs, interviews, and the like. Ghost stories as well. You're always turning up the ghosts; they come to you like bees to honey."

"Not on command they don't," Jean pointed out. Miranda was one of the very few people who knew of what she called her paranormal allergy, although it was more curse than joke.

"We'll post an excerpt on the website, with a click-and-order for the book. And a tour, do you think…."

"Whoa!" Lovelace might ramble, but talking to Miranda could be like careening through Mr. Toad's Wild Ride. "Let me get the coin authenticated first. Not that I think Lovelace made it in his basement. Whatever he's up to is more subtle than that."

Miranda's manicured fingertips drummed on a map. "Western Highlands. Lochaber. The Road to the Isles. Loch Arkaig. Well then, here's a bit of luck. Glendessary House is just there, along the loch. An interview would go down a treat."

"An interview with a house?"

"With the new owner. A dot-com billionaire keen on owning a bit of the Auld Sod. He's taken Glendessary House, the hunting lodge on the north side of the loch, and done it up something posh. I met him last autumn during the Season. He's a bit cracked, I'm thinking."

"Or," Jean suggested, "since he's filthy rich, eccentric."

"Eccentric. He is that, aye. Most Yanks buy themselves a title and ponce about in society circles, Lord-this, Lady-that, but not him. MacLyon keeps to himself with a small circle of friends, I hear. Very exclusive."

"I know who you're talking about, sort of, but I couldn't remember his name. When I asked Lovelace about him, he said something about everyone in the area knowing the man, that he was one of the local celebrities. I got the feeling he wasn't thrilled by the proximity…. Oh my."

"Aye?" Miranda asked.

"What if Lovelace found the coin on MacLyon's property? Maybe that's why he was being so cautious. It sounds like he needs the money and MacLyon doesn't. I don't want to betray the old guy's confidence or get him into trouble—but I'm sure not going to cover anything up."

"Mind you," Miranda counseled in turn, "the coin wants authentication first."

Once again Jean tamped down her questions, an activity equivalent to herding cats. "Then I'll take it over to the Museum right now. I'm not going to find out anything more about it—or about Lovelace—until I do."

"Away you go, then. I'll have the lad organize a hire car and book you a room in Fort William tomorrow night. No need to hang about." Miranda closed the atlas with a decisive thump. "This looks to be a grand story and no mistake. We'll plot strategy the morn, eh? Half-past eight."

Tomorrow, Jean thought. Fort William. A secretive old man. A historic coin. An eccentric billionaire. This was getting away from her. She wasn't in *Jekyll and Hyde,* she was in *Treasure Island.* At least Lovelace didn't have one leg and a parrot on his shoulder.

Shaking her head, she offered her friend a backhanded British salute, said "Aye, aye, Captain," and headed down the hall.

If Miranda's office had once been a drawing room, Jean's was what had once been called a closet. The desk and two chairs filled the few square feet of floor space, leaving space only for narrow shelves crammed with books, magazines, maps, leaflets, and manuscripts. And the window. But she didn't begrudge Miranda the larger office and the responsibility that came with it. Being the silent partner in *Great Scot*, Ltd.—the sleeping partner, in Britspeak—suited her just fine. She was, after all, only a mild-mannered academic. Most of the time.

It was Miranda who'd turned her journalism degree into a trans-Atlantic career. On the way, she'd gathered the skills, the contacts, and the cash to rescue a moribund magazine, expand it into a mini-publishing empire, and plant it firmly in the twenty-first century. Jean expected that soon she'd find the Capaldi coat of arms, which Miranda had duly ordered and paid for, installed above the Castle drawbridge in the same fashion as the Nokia Sugar Bowl or 3Com Stadium. The Capaldi Castle. It had a ring to it.

So far, though, Miranda sponsored only this four-hundred year old building. Jean was just now getting used to floors that creaked and plumbing that groaned and the occasional silken whisper in the hall, which at first she'd thought was the swish of ghostly hoop skirts but which had turned out to be a draft rustling the racks of newspapers. If any spirits lingered here, they murmured so faintly behind the wainscoting that her sixth sense couldn't hear them.

Which was just as well. The occasional ghost that she could sense was quite enough to make her see herself as—hypersensitive. Eccentric, even. But not cracked. At times she felt almost too sane.

Supposedly artifacts could be haunted, but that sensation was not one Jean had ever experienced. Still, she spent a long moment contemplating the gold coin in its box on her desk. She imagined the French ship sailing silently into Loch nan Uamh in May of seventeen forty-six, barely a fortnight after Charles Stuart's cause had come to a grisly end on the battlefield of Culloden. She saw sweating men and pack animals trundling the barrels of gold up into the hills, even as their prince himself wandered destitute through the country whose crown he'd claimed but failed to win.

She saw Charles at last meeting another French ship and making his escape. Until the end of his life, forty years later, he'd believed Scotland was ready to rise again in his family's name. He'd been wrong. But then, being right hadn't exactly been Bonnie Prince Charlie's strong point.

Reality was never all it was cracked up to be. Knowing that, Jean told herself, was both a drawback and an advantage to working in the history business.

She put the lid on the coin box and the box into her small backpack. A dash of lipstick, a tug of her comb through her short, naturally surly hair, and she was ready to go. In her younger days she'd been so afraid of being the type of girl who "had a good personality" she'd fussed over her hair and her clothes. Now she hadn't so much let herself go as met herself halfway, letting her comfort zone find its own level. Occasionally she felt like the sale rack next to Miranda's window display, but then, Miranda liked to shop and Jean didn't, so that was that.

On her way out, Jean stopped by the reception desk. Gavin looked fifteen in spite of claiming to twenty. His very proper suit and tie had obviously been handed down from an older and larger relative. Contemplating an Internet listing of car rental agencies, he asked, "Any particular sort of car you're wanting, then?"

"Something larger than a tin can and smaller than a tank."

He looked up at her, eyes dancing. "Well that narrows the field a bit."

"Mid-size, two-door, decent gas mileage," Jean told him. "Gas stations can be few and far between in the Highlands."

"Gas, is it then? Are you not wanting one that runs on petrol?"

She resisted the impulse to ruffle his hair, said, "Thank you, Gavin," and headed toward the turnpike stair.

Halfway down, she met the postman coming up. She turned sideways and balanced on the narrower side of the treads as he passed by, greeting him with a breezy, "Hi! How's it going?" His return mumble seemed a bit forced. It wasn't until Jean reached the bottom of the steps that she remembered that passing someone on a spiral staircase was considered bad luck.

Don't, she ordered herself, *go looking for omens*. This was going to be a grand story, and no mistake.

THREE

JEAN EMERGED from the cool, slightly musty building and turned her face to the warmth of the sun. Now there was a new habit. After two decades in Texas, she'd gotten used to either hiding from the sun or trudging along in dumb misery as her skin fried and her eyeballs frizzled. But not here, no. Here sunshine was a blessing.

To Jean's right the buildings on either side of the street dwindled to a slit packed with a slice of the Castle. To her left the Royal Mile snaked downhill, two banks of storefronts, historical façades, and sidewalk cafes channeling a roaring stream of traffic. Beside her, a plump middle-aged couple draped in L.L. Bean safari gear—they might just as well have been wearing placards reading *American!*—hesitated outside the tartan-draped doorway of a shop. A tartan-clad clerk pounced. "I'll have a look, just see if we've got your family tartan, shall I?"

The couple could be named anything from Alvarez to Zimmerman, and the shop would carry their family tartan. Jean would say that merchant and tourist alike were participating in a role-playing game that went cheerfully on, over, around, and through real life, except searching for your identity, whether on a personal or a national level, was real life.

She darted across the street and around the corner onto the George IV Bridge, which, from this perspective, looked like just another building-lined street rather than a viaduct crossing a ravine. Ahead rose the new Museum of Scotland. The sleek curves and angles of its walls, part ancient castle and part futuristic bunker, made a stark contrast to the intricacies of the eighteenth- and nineteenth-century buildings surrounding it. So did its stone, shades of amber as yet unstained by the smokes of the city.

Jean paused at the front desk and asked the guard to call up to Michael Campbell-Reid's office. Then she genuflected before the words of the Declaration of Arbroath painted in foot-high letters in the entrance hall: "It is not for glory or riches or honours that we fight, but only for liberty, which no good man will consent to lose but with his life."

Or any good woman. Not that the Scots, men and women both, hadn't through bad luck or bad choices lost their liberty repeatedly. The struggle for freedom was as eternal as that for identity, and as likely to include illusion. But then, playing illusion off reality was as much the Scottish national pastime as nursing old wounds and rehearsing old glories. Jean found the Scots' edgy self-awareness to be as stimulating as it was annoying, both grandly romantic and chip-on-the-shoulder petty. It all depended on the perspective.

She made her way past the familiar displays to a door leading to the rear echelon and found Michael waiting for her. "Jean! Hello!"

"How's it going?"

"Overworked and underpaid as ever," he replied with a grin and a firm handshake. He inserted his key card, pushed the door open, and waved her through a nondescript hallway into an elevator.

At any other time in her life Jean would have found Michael's dashing good looks as compelling as chocolate. But even if she had been in the market for eligible males, Michael wouldn't have qualified. He was as married a man as Jean had ever met. "How's the family?" she asked.

"Waiting to say hello," Michael said. "Rebecca's just come from Holyrood, brought in a ring needs cleaning…."

The elevator doors opened. Michael's wife was reading the notices on the bulletin board just outside.

"…it being a bonny day for a dauner with the bairn and all," he concluded.

"She's not a bairn yet," retorted Rebecca. "The word means 'born,' I'm thinking. Hey, Jean, how are you?"

"Great. Enjoying the pretty day myself."

"Have we seen you since we decided on the baby's name?"

"No. What's it going to be? Mary, after your favorite sixteenth-century queen?"

"Linda, after my favorite twenty-first-century aunt."

"That's brilliant." Jean made a face. After four months in Edinburgh, she had to make a conscious effort to speak in her own American accent.

Rebecca had been here three years. No surprise she spoke with a bit of a lilt and a burr. Whether her bright eyes and rosy cheeks could be attributed to the Scottish air, pregnancy, or her Midwestern American upbringing Jean had no way of knowing. What she did know was that Rebecca's insightful smile complemented Michael's eager intelligence.

And his sense of humor. Thumping on her rounded abdomen, he pronounced, "Not quite ripe. We'd best be giving the wee one two more months."

"Is that an imperial or an editorial 'we,' Michael?" Rebecca waddled through a light, spacious area filled with tables and chairs to Michael's book-lined office, where she lowered herself into the desk chair. "And how are you enjoying life in Scotland, Jean?"

"Very much, now that I've survived the winter."

"Oh aye," Michael said. "Scotland's not for the squeamish."

"Neither are the Scots," added Rebecca with a glance at her husband.

He drew himself up, exuding dignity. "And what's bringing you in the day, Jean? A new article for the magazine?"

"More or less, yes. I have something that needs to be authenticated." She pulled the white box from her backpack.

"It's a box, right enough," Michael said.

Jean opened it with a flourish. "And inside is a gold Louis d'Or of seventeen twenty."

"Well, well, well." Michael took the box and angled it so Rebecca could see the coin.

"Who turned it up?" she asked.

"An elderly English gentleman named George Lovelace. Not that he wants his name spread around, you understand. He found it in Lochaber, not at all surprisingly."

"You're on the trail of Bonnie Prince Charlie, are you?" Michael set the box on a counter that ran the length of the small room, between a computer and a rack holding exhibition leaflets. Folding his long limbs onto a stool and pulling on a pair of cotton gloves, he hefted the coin, turned it over and around, and peered at it through a magnifying glass. "Your auld Sassenach was clever enough not to wash it. We've got bits of dirt—peat, most likely— fluff, a wee thread of some sort, several minor scratches. Did you pack it away in the box or did he do?"

"He brought it in the box. Looks like a jewelry box, actually."

"He's carried the coin about in his pocket for a time."

"When he first found it," suggested Rebecca.

"I expect so." Michael's forehead creased in thought. "Lovelace, George. That name sounds familiar. Lives in Lochaber, you said?"

"I didn't say, but yes, he lives in Corpach."

"Corpach." Michael waggled the mouse of his computer, waded through a couple of screens, typed in a password. "Oh aye. Just there."

Rebecca was craning forward. "What?"

Over Michael's shoulder, Jean could see the words, in plain pixilated English, "George Lovelace, 5 Beaton Terrace, Corpach." *What the…?*

"He brought in a Norse brooch last year," explained Michael. "Said he turned it up on Skye. Not my department, mind, but I remember the announcement. The brooch was declared *bona vacantia,* ownerless goods, and of significant historical interest. I dinna ken how much we paid for it, but I'm guessing it was no small sum. No surprise Lovelace was motivated to look out more items."

Jean's perspective screeched, ran up the curb, and landed on its side. "He brought you a…. He knows the laws of treasure trove better than I do!"

"Maybe he thinks this way he won't have to tell us where he found it," Rebecca offered.

"But if he's already dealt with you, he knows that eventually he'll have to come out with the location." Jean shook her head. "I knew he was hiding where he found the coin—and probably more than that—but this is weird."

"That it is, not sensible at all." Brows knit, Michael put the coin back in its box and replaced the lid, quenching the beguiling glimmer of gold.

"Maybe he found several coins," Rebecca offered, "or at least knows more are there, and he wants to hand them over one at a time so as not to flood the market and bring down the price."

"Or perhaps he found the coin on a protected site," added Michael. "Did he say he turned it up on public land?"

"He said—no, all he did was give me the impression—that he found the coin while he was bird-watching. I did wonder if he found it on private property." Lovelace hadn't actually told her very much at all, had he? About his discovery, at least. As for what he had told her.... "I'd like to think Lovelace is just being a public-spirited citizen and trying to protect the site, but he doesn't need me for that. If anything, his coming to me has made me very suspicious."

"So ask him what he's on about," Rebecca told her.

"You bet." With her entire hand, not just one finger, Jean gestured toward Lovelace's name gleaming in the cold blue light of the computer. "No more Ms. Nice Guy. Tomorrow I am having a very serious conversation with George Lovelace, Leicester University, retired."

"In the meantime I'll report the coin to the Advisory Panel and send it for analysis." Michael took off his gloves and started filling out a label.

What else was going to happen, Jean wondered. "I don't suppose the French government will try to claim it the way Spain's been trying to claim the stuff hauled up from shipwrecks off Florida."

"Louis the Fifteenth gave Charlie the money to begin with," said Rebecca, "but Charlie doesn't have any descendants to claim it."

"Might as well let the Crown claim the coin and pay for it, make an ironic historical footnote out of it." Michael stuck the label to the box. "The Crown's ancestors would have confiscated every last coin and most of Charlie's body parts if they'd ever caught him up."

"Brutality as public policy. A time-honored tradition." Jean leaned back against the door, her arms folded.

Through the windows across the room she could see several rooftops, their slates laced with green lichen. Beyond them rose the gable end of Greyfriars Church. In the sunlight, the old building seemed greeting-card peaceful. One dark, damp evening in March, though, Jean had taken a tour of the graveyard with its rows of broken, moss-covered stones. The guide had stopped beside a walled-off area lined with rotting tombs that had once served as a prison for religious dissenters. Jean had needed neither his lurid stories nor the wind moaning in the naked tree branches to convince her that ghosts lurked there. She could sense their presence, like seeing a whisper or feeling a shadow. But then, Scotland's history was dark and bloody enough to produce armies of uneasy spirits, enough to sneak up even on people who, unlike Jean, had spent their lives blithely oblivious to the presence of the past.

But then, the country provided comic relief as well. "Speaking of private property, Miranda's also setting me up an appointment to interview Rick MacLyon. The rich American who bought Glendessary House."

Michael and Rebecca exchanged a glance of amusement edged by caution. "Oh aye. Rick MacLyon, esquire. Born Richard Douglas in Ro-a-noke Vir-gi-nee-yah." Michael drawled the names.

"Douglas is a good Scottish name," said Jean. "Why the theatrical, not to mention artificial, 'MacLyon'? Do you know?"

"Only that he's gone over the top playing the laird of the castle." Rebecca nodded toward an engraved wine glass sitting at one end of the counter. "The amen glass there, that's his. Or will be."

Michael flicked the glass with his fingernail, producing a clear chime. "A dealer gave me it last week to authenticate, with an eye to MacLyon buying it. And it's authentic, right enough. The provenance is in apple-pie order as well, been in the same family two hundred years. You'd know the name: ancient title, ancient house needing repairs, no money—the usual story. They'll make a packet off the glass, though."

"No need quite yet to marry a son to an American heiress?" Jean looked more closely at the solitary wine glass standing atop a small turntable. An air-twisted stem spread into a trumpet-shaped bowl, which was engraved with several lines of elegant eighteenth-century script and an intricate cipher. "A crown, 'JR', and '8'. Jacobus Rex, James Stuart, Prince Charlie's dad, the Old Pretender, who would have been James the Eighth of Scotland and the Third of England, if Charlie had won. What's the rest say?"

"'God save the King, Send him victorious,'" Michael read. "Sound familiar?"

"That's the British national anthem. Is that where it came from, an old Jacobite hymn? Talk about irony."

"This part of the world is lousy with irony," Rebecca commented.

"I've noticed," returned Jean. "Works for me."

"MacLyon is right keen on Charlie and the Forty-five and all," Michael went on. "He'd fancy this coin especially."

"Unless it was found on his land to begin with, in which case he'd claim it." Second verse, same as the first, Jean added to herself. "So how do I approach MacLyon—with a shaker full of salt?"

"He's reality-challenged, no doubt about it," said Rebecca.

"Living a fantasy," Michael said.

Jean smiled wryly. "Aren't we all."

"But then," Rebecca went on with a laugh of agreement, "Popcorn Technologies is known as much for games as for software. Or was, before MacLyon sold out to Microsoft for God only knows how many million. Talk about timing; he got out of the dot-com business five minutes before the walls came tumbling down."

"*Claymore's* a grand game." Michael joined his hands on an imaginary hilt and made a sweeping motion, lopping off an imaginary English head. "I've seen more historical accuracy on cereal boxes, mind you, but it's a grand game."

"Myth can make a lot better story than the truth," said Jean. "After a while it becomes the truth. If it didn't, I'd be out of work."

"So would we." Rebecca's motion included the Museum and the city surrounding it. "Would you like a cup of tea, Jean? We can actually sit out on the balcony for a change."

"Thanks, but I've got to get home and collect my wits, such as they are. You know how it is, Miranda proposes and I dispose."

"Have a safe trip then," said Michael. "Give us a shout if we can help out."

"Don't worry, I will."

"And let us know what Lovelace's story is," Rebecca added.

"I'll do that, too. Take care." Jean wended her way back to the elevator, allowing herself to remember her one all-too-brief pregnancy, years ago when she and Brad were emotionally as well as legally married. But that water was so far under the bridge it had already evaporated and come back to earth as rain. National past glories were the stuff of legends. Personal might-have-beens were the stuff of neuroses.

She took the door leading from the new building into the vast Victorian atrium of the old Royal Museum next door. The odor of coffee from the snack bar almost tempted her off her course, but no, it was too late in the afternoon for caffeine, the excellent British tradition of teatime to the contrary.

Instead, she pitched a penny into the koi pond. Several other coins shimmered beneath the water the way the gold Louis d'Or had shimmered beneath her desk lamp. On a distant balcony a clock chimed, counting off the minutes, the hours, the years that coin had lain—somewhere.

Gold, Jean thought, was incorruptible. A shame she couldn't say the same about people.

FOUR

BY THE TIME Jean reached the Lawnmarket and the building occupied by the *Great Scot* offices, she'd turned her conversation with Lovelace over and around and peered at it through a magnifying glass, like Michael inspecting the coin.

Her indulgent attitude toward the old man had curdled into resentment blunted only by bewilderment. He could have been trying to hide the site where he found the coin, but what a ham-handed way of doing it! Maybe his real motive was the opposite, to publicize his find and make himself a celebrity. All his protestations could have been intended to pique her interest. And yet, again, what a clumsy way of going about it. Surely she didn't come across in her articles as a reporter who'd rush out and reveal off-the-record details the instant she heard them.

So she didn't have privileged information. What she did have was two options. She could believe Lovelace was a nut case. Or she could give him the benefit of the doubt. She didn't know what was going on in his life. She didn't know what pressures had driven him to—no, he hadn't lied to her, not in so many words. But he'd sure as hell meant to use her. What he'd accomplished was to give her curiosity an edge of urgency.

Two open-topped buses edged by each other in the street, the tourists with their headphones listening to some version or another of national myth. Music leaked out of an open shop door, a lushly-orchestrated easy-listening arrangement of the otherwise fiery "Scotland the Brave."

Now that, Jean thought, was sacrilege. Scottish music was

passion in sound. To buff off its jagged edges, to pour sweet oil
on its turbulence—to take away its challenge—betrayed its beating
heart. But then, she understood only too well the craving for safety.

She walked on by the office and headed up Castle Hill, picking
her way through the tourists crowding the sidewalks and spilling out
into the street, then veered right into Ramsay Lane. In the distance,
a siren wailed. The late afternoon air was thickened by a mingled scent
of musty age and cooking food that was distinctly Edinburgh, where
the dead and the living occupied the same space if not the same time.

Shortening her steps on the steep downhill grade, Jean turned
left into Ramsay Garden, strolled across the courtyard, and arrived
at her own front door.

The Garden was a cluster of buildings tucked in between the
Castle and the University's School of Divinity. Despite having
been built in the heavy-handed Victorian era, the buildings with
their cupolas, towers, and chimneys had a whimsical air, like the
illustration to a fairy tale wedged into a book of sermons. The site
not only suited Jean's taste for incongruity, it was so close to the
office she didn't need to keep a car. Plus her apartment had just
been renovated. The new appliances and colorful Arts and Crafts
wallpaper had not only exorcised any temperamental plumbing,
but also any lingering traces of earlier residents, leaving Jean to
fill the four small rooms with her favorite books, prints, movies,
and music, claiming them as her own.

She opened the door, collected a couple of letters from the
basket attached to the mail slot, and pitched them onto the desk.
In the bedroom she found her roommate dozing on what had been
her neatly-smoothed bedspread, a ball of yarn shredded beside
him. At least it wasn't the yarn from her current knitting project.
Jean pointed to the basket-and-cushion combo beside the coal-
effect fireplace in the living room. "You have a bed."

The small gray cat looked up with a yawn. Jean didn't need
to speak feline to interpret that remark. "Fine," she said. "Have
it your way."

Dougie had had it his way since a week after Jean moved in.
She'd opened the front door one afternoon to find the cat lying on
the stone step, basking in a rare moment of sunshine. He might
just as well have announced, "Lucy, I'm home." The next thing

Jean knew, she had two bowls on the kitchen floor, a litter box in the bathroom, and a warm furry beast to sit purring on her lap when rain, fog, and regret blurred her view.

Today, though, the view through the bow windows was crystal clear, over Princes Street Gardens and past the tidy Age-of-Reason squares of the New Town to the Firth of Forth, a shining strip of silver, and the blue hills of Fife beyond. Today the clear evening lingered like a man with a slow hand....

Jean laughed. Spring must mean the rising of her sap. But even if she could imagine the physical side of sex again, the emotional side, the intimacy—the passion, to use a loaded word—was still beyond her. By initiating an academic scandal, she'd burned the safe bridges of her job and her marriage. Now she was not only reinventing her exterior life, she was rediscovering her emotions. That was quite enough to deal with now, thank you.

She changed into her comfortable old jeans and a sweatshirt and tucked her knitting bag away in a cabinet. Dougie—not the "Duggie" of American dialect but Scotspoken "Doogie"—was waiting expectantly in the kitchen door. Jean triaged the leftovers in her refrigerator, trying to decide which to eat tonight and which to throw out. She'd be gone two nights, probably. Which reminded her....

A strain of music filtered through the wall, one of the more energetic Wolfstone pieces, accompanied by a live fiddle. The band wasn't the first to realize that bagpipes made a splendid rock 'n roll instrument, but it was among the best. Tapping her toe, she poured kitty kibble into a bowl and pitched in a bit of leftover moo shu pork. Dougie's crunches repeated the rhythmic reverberation of the drums.

Jean slipped out of her front door and down the steps to her neighbor's. She knocked. Inside the flat the music came to an abrupt halt. The door opened a crack and Hugh Munro's sharp blue eyes glared through the slit. "Ah, it's you, is it? Thought I was having another visit from the music Gestapo. Come through, I've got a grand new single malt." He opened the door and stepped back, shouldering his fiddle like a rifle.

Hugh's bald head with its fringe of white hair, his crisp gray beard, and his stomach bulging coyly between his suspenders made him look like Santa Claus. But Hugh's sleigh had two left runners. He'd earned his place in Edinburgh's traditional-music scene with social protest folk-rock, skillfully balancing his diatribes about the evils of capitalism with its benefits there in Ramsay Garden, in a flat bequeathed to him by an admirer with a sense of humor to equal his own.

"Thanks, but I can't come in," Jean told him. "I just wanted to tell you I'm leaving town for a couple of days, and ask if you'd mind feeding the cat and cleaning out his box."

Hugh beamed. "No problem at all. Off on another historical quest, are you?"

"I'm doing an article on Bonnie Prince Charlie's French gold and another one on Rick MacLyon and Glendessary House, more or less at the same time. You were telling me about him, weren't you? MacLyon, although you've certainly told me enough about Charlie."

"Oh aye. MacLyon hired the lads and me for a Hogmanay concert. Brought in the New Year right and proper we did, with all the old customs and a few new ones we invented for the occasion. All the same to him."

"It must have been one heck of party," Jean said.

"Brilliant." Hugh licked his lips reminiscently. "Not so many guests but lashings of food and drink even so, all best quality. And his staff and us tucking in with the rest. No sending the working class away with second best."

"Was anybody famous there? Besides you, that is."

He shrugged that away. "A couple of film people, aye. And MacLyon himself done up like a tartan nightmare, dirk, plaid, and all. But mostly there were businesspeople muttering about stock prices and some po-faced sorts I took to be toadies. Several locals were there as well—at least MacLyon's not playing the absentee landlord, exploit and run. The only sour note was some regional functionary quarreling with a retired military chap."

Her ears perked forward like the cat's. "A retired military chap?"

"Pleasant enough old fellow, except for his tendency to blether on and on about his childhood in Orpington."

Orpington. Feeling as though fate was dealing from the bottom of the deck, Jean asked, "His name wasn't George Lovelace, was it?"

"Could have been, didn't really notice. You know him?"

"We've met. He was arguing with a local official? What about?"

"Haven't a clue, just heard them getting up each other's noses. MacLyon's wife Vanessa dressed them down, told them to boil their heads or whatever it is you Americans say. She's just a slip of a girl but she's right—assertive—even so."

Nothing wrong with assertive, Jean thought. Within the bounds of courtesy, at least. She was feeling rather assertive herself at the moment. "I can hardly wait to get out there and start digging around! Not literally, my chances of actually finding gold aren't too good. I'll settle for some explanations and a good story."

"The cast of characters looks to be right dramatic," Hugh said with a twinkle that had a sharply-honed edge to it. "Put the spare key through the letter box then, I'll see to the moggie."

"Thanks, I appreciate it. If you need me, you have my cell phone number."

"Have a safe trip now." The door shut. A moment later the music started up again.

It's got a great beat, thought Jean, and if you don't dance to it, you haven't got a nerve in your body. With a shimmy and a pirouette she regained her own flat.

Dougie, who was named after rock 'n' reel piper Dougie Pincock, was sitting on the window sill washing his face. His ears rotated like radar dishes when Jean walked into the sitting room, but he didn't actually look around. "Already taking me for granted?" she asked. He smoothed his whiskers, concealing what was no doubt a smug smile. Funny, she hated smug in men, but found it appealing in cats.

Lovelace hadn't acted smug. If she had any consolation at all, it was that he hadn't seemed to be enjoying himself while he scammed her.

Sitting down, Jean booted up her laptop and started making notes. While she could come up with any number of scenarios explaining Lovelace's actions, she couldn't prove a thing without more evidence. The nugget that Hugh had given her, that Lovelace knew MacLyon well enough to rate an invitation to a party, could well be irrelevant. Still, there was a chance that Lovelace's relationship with MacLyon or the stuffed-shirt official might have something to do with his true motive.

No, he hadn't told her everything she needed, let alone wanted, to know. Whether he would come clean about his—scheme, scam, whatever—when she confronted him was another matter. Even if he did tell her or the Museum where he'd found the coin, though, that didn't mean archaeologists could uncover the entire stash. The odds were that the barrels of coins had been hidden in different places. Some of the money had been paid out in 1746. The rest could have been stolen either en masse or in bits and pieces down the years....

Just as Jean reached for a reference book, the phone emitted its double blat.

She picked it up and switched it on. Miranda, with another inspiration? "Hello?"

"Is that Jean Fairbairn?" The voice was female.

Jean didn't recognize it. "Yes."

"Stay clear of George Lovelace. He's trouble."

"What? Who is this?"

"Whatever he's asking of you, leave it...." The voice stopped abruptly. Was that another voice, a man's, faint in the background?

Dead air filled Jean's ear. Punching the Talk switch produced only a high-pitched dial tone. She tried bouncing the call back, but the phone rang and rang without anyone answering. It was probably in a public call box, a glass cubicle on a busy street or lonely red-painted booth on a back road.

Frowning, she switched off the phone and put it down. While the mysterious voice had an American accent, the syntax was British. Miranda could do a devastating American accent, even though her normal speech patterns were Brit frothed with Scots, but the voice on the phone hadn't been hers. It hadn't been Rebecca Campbell-Reid's, either. And even though Jean was beginning to feel like the victim of a practical joke, neither Miranda nor Rebecca was inclined to play them.

The voice belonged to a stranger. A stranger who knew a lot more about Jean's work than she should have. Maybe it was a friend of Lovelace's playing a joke on him. Or maybe it was his—enemy was a strong word, rival, maybe?—either warning Jean to keep her out of trouble or warning her off, to keep her from causing trouble. Of the two Jean voted for the latter, on the grounds that anonymous phone calls usually had the welfare of the caller in mind, not the recipient.

"What am I getting myself into here?" she asked Dougie. "What is George Lovelace getting me into? And, for heaven's sakes, why?"

Dougie stretched, strolled back into the bedroom, hopped up on the bed, and curled himself into a snug ball, leaving Jean to her notes and a long list of questions she had every intention of getting answered. Because unlike many imponderables of life, the universe, and everything, these questions did have answers.

FIVE

JEAN LOOKED UP at the three bronze commandos. They looked out over the Western Highlands, stoically square-jawed. The stone panel below their boots was inscribed: *United We Conquer. In memory of the officers and men of the commandos who died in the Second World War 1939-1945. This country was their training ground.* Wreaths of red paper poppies stacked against the base of the memorial rustled in the wind.

A beautiful if harsh training ground it was, Jean thought. To the southwest the dark snow-streaked hump of Ben Nevis resembled a huge terrestrial whale breaching the surface of the land, earth rolling away in waves from its flanks. All around rose smaller mountains, shaggy below, craggy above. Clouds sailed through an achingly blue sky, dragging shadows across the hills. A rosy glow in the sunlight hinted of summer, but the frosty wind felt like a slap across her face. *Thanks, I needed that.*

The landscape lacked only a soundtrack, an emotional Celtic folk-rock piece or a movie score by John Williams or Howard Shore, something that would complement the sensation Jean felt in her chest. Either her heart was expanding with a desire she wasn't prepared to analyze, or her lungs were expanding with oxygen. It was about time she escaped the noise, litter, and jostling crowds of the city, all the bits and pieces of input she'd trained herself to let roll off her nervous system even as she worried she was missing something.

A cloud blotted the sunlight. Above the monument an eagle tipped his wings, dived, and a moment later flew up from the bracken gripping a small, wriggling creature in his talons. Telling herself yet again not to read omens from happenstance, Jean walked past an area set aside for memorials to individual commandos and climbed into her rental car.

This morning Miranda had reacted predictably to Jean's update from the Museum and her account of the cryptic phone call. "Oooh, nothing like a bit of gold to bring out the villains! Hard to credit Mr. Lovelace might be up to something, though, him being such a nice old gentleman and all."

Jean's enthusiasm was tempered with caution—it was her body that wasn't wanted on the scene, not Miranda's. Lovelace *was* up to something, nice old gentlemen being as likely as anyone else to have a secret agenda.

She pulled her cell phone out of her bag and hit redial. She'd tried Lovelace's number from Callander, where the gentle green hills of the Lowlands gave way to the stony mountains of the Highlands. She'd tried again from Fort William, the town tucked between the beetling brow of Ben Nevis and the deep waters of Loch Linnhe. This call didn't produce an answer—or an answering machine—either. So much for contacting Lovelace before she talked with Rick MacLyon. She'd just have to go on out to Glendessary House and try again afterwards.

Dodging a behemoth of a tour bus, Jean turned her car away from the main road and toward Loch Arkaig. The road was a scruffy ribbon of tarmac draped around hills, through patches of trees, and over the Caledonian Canal. Every hundred yards or so it expanded into a passing place and then narrowed again to one lane. Jean expected it to eventually tie itself into a knot, but no, she arrived at Achnacarry, a scattering of houses and shops outside the gates of Achnacarry Castle, without passing herself along the way.

A sign pointed to the Clan Cameron Museum. In 1745 the Lochiel, the chief of the clan, had gone to warn Bonnie Prince Charlie off and ended up fighting for him, both goaded and charmed by the silver-tongued Prince. Lochiel had died in exile, his castle burned and his people brutalized. The newer castle had served as commando headquarters during the war. Lovelace no doubt knew it well.

Jean drove on across a bridge, slowing to look at the shining blue-gray waters of Loch Lochy rippling away to the northeastern horizon. Then, just past the white-painted houses that were Bunarkaig and Clunes, the road turned abruptly left and plunged into the Dark Mile. Ancient gnarled beeches, black of trunk and loden green of leaf, rose from a tangled undergrowth of bushes and bracken, casting the road into darkness as sinister as that of a narrow Edinburgh alley called a wynd.

Jean imagined one of Tolkien's tree-creatures striding along through the forest, or one of his Ringwraiths on its black horse galloping along the road, hoof beats echoing like iron striking an anvil. What she saw in the speck of light at the end of the tree-lined tunnel was no mythical creature, but another car coming straight at her. Fast.

She dived into a semi-circle of gravel wedged unforgivingly against a stone wall, overgrown but hardly padded with yellowish moss. Something small, low to the ground, and glittering with chrome blew by without pausing. A wave of muddy water splatted against the car window. "Thank you very much," she said to the shape dwindling in the rear view mirror. Her tires whispered through shoals of damp, dead leaves as she started up again.

Emerging from the depth of the shadow, the road crossed a stone bridge over the foam-flecked tumble and splash of a waterfall. Then the trees parted and Loch Arkaig stretched away to the west, its water glimmering blue, then silver, then gray, then blue again as wind and sun teased its surface. The rocky hills above were cut with ravines and stubbled with midnight green heather and gorse that from this distance looked deceptively smooth, like brushed velvet. Somewhere in those rugged green and brown hills, George Lovelace had turned up the Louis d'Or. Not that he'd been searching for the coin—or so he claimed. Whatever, Jean knew better than to underestimate the power of luck.

The road wandered over humps and around boulders, at times nestled in trees, at others strung precariously above the loch. The occasional house sat back from the road, where the steep slopes begrudged enough flat space to fit something larger than a bread box. A concrete pier ran out into the water, a sleek little powerboat tied to its side. The boulders beside the road gave way to a brand-new stone wall and a set of wrought-iron gates. A polished brass plaque on one pillar read *Glendessary House.*

The driveway beyond the open gates angled away so acutely Jean drove on by. She'd turn around and come back, very slowly.... The next passing-place was occupied by an old, well-used Ford. Still, the road actually had a gravel shoulder, not just a gully camouflaged by weeds.

She backed and filled, at one point coming so close to the other car she was afraid she was going to knock off its side mirror. No owner came rushing up from the loch, though, fishing pole on his shoulder, to glare accusingly at her. Assuming the owner of an old banger would be overly protective anyway....

A bit of an old banger. Jean stopped, staring down at the Ford's rear bumper. Through the odd splotch of mud she could make out two stickers, one for the RSPB, the Royal Society for the Protection of Birds, the other for the British Legion, the veteran's association. This wasn't Lovelace's car, was it?

She inched forward far enough to get a good look at a small faded sticker in the corner of the windshield. It was a parking permit for the University of Leicester. On the front seat lay a pair of binoculars and a copy of *Great Scot*'s current issue. It was Lovelace's car, then. But if he was visiting Glendessary House, why park out here? If he was watching birds, why leave his binoculars on the seat?

The man was a conundrum wrapped within an enigma, all right. She drove on, trying without success to convince herself that finding his car here was just an innocent little coincidence.

The post on each side of the iron gates was crowned with a sculpted bear holding a shield, an oddly familiar design that played keep-away with Jean's memory. The asphalt drive led into another alley of trees, this time limber young ones. The road hairpinned left, then right, working its way up the slope. Jean drove into a paved courtyard and braked, her jaw dropping in something between awe and a guffaw.

When Miranda said Glendessary House was an old hunting lodge, Jean had known better than to picture a shack. To the wealthy Victorians who turned the Highlands into their own private preserves, a hunting lodge meant a mansion. And this was a mansion, sired by money out of pretension.

A row of tall, arched windows overlooked a columned veranda. Above a second row of smaller square windows rose a frenzy of dormers, crenellations, gables, Tudor-twist chimneys, and round towers like the rooks of a chess set. Except for the antennas tucked in beside several vertical elements, the structure looked very much as it must have when it was first built—massive instead of dignified, faintly contemptuous of its rural surroundings, not quite comfortable in its own stone.

Jean knew that the original house had been damaged in a fire during the war. But only by looking closely could she see where fresh new stone had been used to repair and rebuild. MacLyon had the wealth to back up a perfectionist streak, then. Or, Jean thought, his perfectionism had earned the wealth. You didn't make a fortune in software without crossing every t and dotting every com.

She parked the car on the opposite side of the courtyard from a small tourist bus, gathered up her bag and her laptop, and headed for the house. The bus driver, a newspaper spread open before him, didn't return her inquisitive look.

Mmmm, this air smelled not of diesel but of Highland perfume— peat smoke. All the scene lacked was… Jean grinned. The sound of bagpipes echoed down the wind. The front door, a massive wooden affair braced with iron, opened well before she stepped onto the veranda. Of course. The gate, the walls, the trees themselves were probably festooned with video cameras.

A tall woman with fiery red hair and the exquisite bone structure of a model stood in the doorway. "Ah," she said, her voice flat. "It's you, then, is it?"

Tempted as she was to ask, "Have we met?" Jean instead said politely, "Hello, I'm Jean Fairbairn, with *Great Scot* magazine. Miranda Capaldi made an appointment for me with Mr. MacLyon for three. I'm a little early."

"Oh aye, that you are. We're seeing to a private party just now. But come through, we can accommodate you even so. I'm Fiona Robertson, Rick's housekeeper."

"Thanks. Nice to meet you." Jean stepped through the door with a searching sideways and upwards glance.

Gone were the days when the housekeeper was identifiable by her apron, sensible shoes, hair net—and middle-age. With her stylish tartan skirt and ruffled blouse, the thirty-something Fiona could have been the mistress of the house, except her accent was about as American as haggis. And despite that moment of what seemed like wary recognition, her hazel eyes were now aloof.... Oh. A black band ran from the black circle of the pupil in Fiona's left eye, stopping where hazel gave way to white. One narrow segment of her iris was missing, making it look as though her pupil was bleeding.

Gone, too, were the days when such an anomaly would have branded Fiona a witch. Or was it an anomaly? Could she have been injured? If her eyesight were poor, that would explain why she'd greeted Jean so familiarly. She'd mistaken her for a friend.

Fiona strode off across the tiled entrance hall, her soft-soled shoes making no more noise than Dougie's paws. Jean lagged behind. The massive wooden staircase was a handsomely executed copy, she decided. The rifles and shotguns ranged up the paneled walls were by law inoperable reproductions. The huge rack of antlers was probably only too genuine.

A grandfather clock whirred and struck twice. Outside the piper played on, the music supplemented by the murmur of voices inside the house. The private party, no doubt. Maybe that's where Lovelace was. Jean's mouth watered at the tantalizing odor of baking scones.

"Wait here, please." Fiona waved her through a door and into a sitting room furnished with leather chairs and couches that were contemporary but not blatantly anachronistic. "Would you care for tea?"

"Yes, I'd enjoy some tea, thank you."

Fiona shut the door without saying whether she was actually offering tea or just taking a survey. Shrugging, Jean looked around.

With its paneling and multi-colored tartan carpet—in the MacLyon pattern or sett, probably, bought and paid for like the Capaldi crest—the room was conventionally masculine. Was she really smelling a subtle tobacco and whiskey scent, absorbed into the stone of the building during long Victorian evenings, or simply imagining something that ought to be there?

A full length oil portrait hung over the fireplace. It depicted a man dressed in the full glorious excess of kilt, plaid, brooch, velvet jacket, fur sporran, belt buckle, knee socks, and high-laced leather shoes, posed with his shoulders thrown back and his hand grasping a silver-trimmed dirk. His slight build and anemic complexion were so smothered in folds of cloth and bits of polished metal Jean had to look twice to make out his face. It was MacLyon. She recognized him from the photo on the Popcom Technologies website. His highly-developed frontal lobes made him resemble a Star Trek alien.

Next to the huge painting hung two smaller ones, copies of portraits of Bonnie Prince Charlie in full flush of youth and charisma. There was no copy of the portrait of Charlie in old age, bloated and sagging, his eyes haunted by what-might-have-beens that alcohol and rage had never eradicated.

Were those footsteps in the hall? Jean glanced toward the door. It was as blank-faced as Fiona. Outside the house the pipes played, their music blending with the wind in the chimney to create a lament that made the fine hairs on the back of her neck stand up and sway.

Sternly quelling her shiver, Jean turned to an etching that hung all alone in an expanse of paneling. It was a copy of the famous illustration of Jenny Cameron, who had led her clansmen to Charlie's aid the day he raised his flag at Glenfinnan. Or was this the original? The carved and gilded frame was new, but Jean could see that the ink was faded to sepia and the paper was yellowed and slightly foxed. In other words, old.

She saw no portrait of Flora MacDonald, whose daring escape with Charlie had spawned a romantic virus that had yet to be cured. Her traditional female role had made her a heroine even in London, while Jenny's fifteen minutes of military glory had led to her being accused of both unwomanliness and promiscuity, almost a contradiction in terms. But then, eighteenth-century propagandists hadn't had the benefit of feminist revisionism.

Another shiver started at the nape of Jean's neck. This time she couldn't stop it, and it rippled down her body. The room was icy, the air itself oddly heavy. Wrapping her arms around her chest, she glanced at the electric fire—the space heater—on the hearth, tempted to turn it on. She'd left her coat in the car…. She knew she wasn't sensing the temperature. Her doom had come upon her.

The sounds of the bagpipes stopped abruptly, leaving a reverberation in the air. Then, an instant later, they started up again with a quickly suppressed squawk and grew louder. Title or no title, with his own piper MacLyon was living in ducal style. Jean pulled aside the brocade drapes at the window. Ah, sunlight. And the piper himself, done up in a relatively modest jacket, kilt, and dark socks, pacing past the front of the house. Of course he was playing outside—a piper playing inside anything smaller than an aircraft hanger would implode your eardrums.

With a last glance at the alluring swing and sway of the man's kilt, Jean turned warily back into the room. Her limbs bristled with pins and needles, teased with icy fairy fingernails, and yet the gooseflesh was less on her limbs than in her senses. *By the pricking of my thumbs, something wicked....* She was only sensing a ghost. Ghosts weren't wicked. Most of them were only images, and couldn't interact with the living.

She supposed if you bought an old castle, the household spook would come with it. What had happened here, to leave scraps of leftover emotion floating around like milkweed? While Scotland swarmed with stories of paranormal drummers and pipers who presaged death and disaster, Glendessary's piper seemed quite corporeal. This ghost was something—someone—else.

If it were strong enough, it would appear to her. If it were strong enough, it would appear to anyone, but that was unusual. Most of the time even Jean only sensed ghosts rather than saw them. Not that she'd cultivated her sixth sense any more than she'd cultivated her height or her brown eyes. It was just there.

The ghost, though, was not. Its presence in Jean's nerves faded and then went out like a candle snuffed, leaving a whiff of psychic smoke. She exhaled loudly. Good. It was gone. No matter how many ghosts she'd sensed in her life, she'd never get used to them. Material reality could be disconcerting enough.

Jean stretched her cramped shoulders, thought longingly of that nice hot cup of tea, then reminded herself that if it had been a while since she'd eaten lunch, it had also been a while since she'd used a rest room. She opened the door and looked out into the corridor. Not a soul was in sight. In the distance a man was speaking, by his cadences American, by his tone exhorting his team to win one for the Gipper. What? Did MacLyon stage corporate retreats?

Leaving her laptop perched on a coffee table, signaling her immediate return, she headed down the hall away from the entrance. The kitchen would be in the back of the house, and where there was plumbing there might be a bathroom. A toilet, as the Brits candidly said.

All the doors were closed. With a grimace of embarrassment, Jean walked along, turning the handles. She found the dining room, its long table set with sparkling crystal and china. The kitchen, an electric kettle steaming gently next to a tea tray. A drying room, wooden racks draped with coats, boots lined up beneath. No bathroom. No Fiona to ask.

Now the piper was playing "The Flowers o' the Forest." The tune alone of that old lament would bring tears to a stone. When you factored in the words, all about brave men going off to battle and never coming back, that song was to funerals here what "Amazing Grace" was back home. The chill that coursed down her back this time stemmed from her own emotional imagination.

Around a corner, the hallway ended in three more doors. The center one was a sturdy wooden number—an exit, probably. To its left Jean found what would once have been a gun room but was now a small office. File cabinets, fishing tackle, and tennis rackets shared space with shelves piled with electronic paraphernalia.

She turned the frosty knob on the last door. It opened smoothly and silently into a large room almost as dark as a cave, floored in stark cement. Louvered windows admitted a dank draft but little light. Hooks the size of dinner plates hung from the rafters, attached to ropes and pulleys anchored along the walls. Two sets of antlers bristled on a bench next to the door. The faint smell of decay made Jean wrinkle her nose. This was the game larder, where the laird kept his freshly-killed grouse and venison…. In the far corner, something swung gently in the draft, rope creaking.

This wasn't hunting season, Jean told herself. And the shape in the shadows wasn't that of a deer.

The faraway voices were all chattering brightly now. The sound faded in and out as though she turned a volume knob up and down. The pipes skreeled, but nowhere near as loudly as her brain. Her stomach clenched. The shape was an optical illusion. Please let it be an optical illusion.

She already knew, though, that it was no such thing. Groping alongside the door, she found a light switch and pushed at it blindly. The dangling man's head was tilted to one side, as though delicately averting his gaze. But there was nothing delicate about his face, slightly swollen and ash-pink, his tongue a purplish bulge between blue lips, his eyes slits showing flat, ghastly whites. He wore a no-nonsense tweed suit. An ivory-handled walking stick lay on the cement several feet away. So did a pair of glasses.

George Lovelace. Unrecognizable. Perfectly recognizable.

An electric charge shot from the crown of Jean's head to the tips of her toes, scalding her nerves, drawing sweat to the surface of her skin. For one long, paralyzed, moment all she could think of was a line from a Wolfstone album... *like dead soldiers make no sound.*

Then she turned and ran.

SIX

OHGODOHGODOHGOD.... Jean hurtled down the corridor and almost collided with Fiona, who was walking toward the kitchen.

"I'm sorry...." Jean asked herself why the hell was she apologizing? For being the bearer of bad news? "I was looking for the rest room. The bathroom. The loo. And I found someone— someone dead."

"Well then," said Fiona. She went on into the kitchen and emerged a moment later carrying the tea tray. Without clattering a single dish, she took into the sitting room and set it down on the coffee table.

Ohgod.... Jean remembered she had a cell phone. Swinging her bag around and unzipping it, she said, "I'll call an ambulance." The police, her mind corrected, it was too late for an ambulance.

Fiona's uncanny eyes were focused far beyond Jean's face. "I'll tell Rick, shall I?"

Jean glanced down at her hand holding her phone, noting with an odd detachment that it was trembling. Lovelace couldn't be helped by speed. Or by a debate over manorial protocol. He was dead. Very dead. "Yeah, you do that."

The housekeeper was already pacing deliberately away. Jean jammed the phone back into her bag and followed, only to find herself standing alone in the entry while Fiona disappeared down another corridor. *Ohgodohgodohgod....*

She spun around in a circle, looking for an escape route, maybe. Maybe for coherence. She saw the weapons. The trophies. The clock. A couple of landscape prints. A large striped cat looking through the balusters of the staircase—no, it was gone, not leaving even a smile behind.

Inhale. Exhale. Her entire body was trembling. Her brain was transmitting bursts of static. The pipes segued into "Lord Lovat's Lament," each note slicing Jean's nerves like a razor blade. The chattering voices stopped abruptly. George Lovelace was hanging from a meat hook. *Oh. My. God.*

A door in an alcove off the entry was marked with a brass plaque reading, "Toilet." There, something she could do. Jean hurried toward it.

By the time she'd flushed and washed and splashed cold water on a bloodless face with wide eyes that didn't seem to be her own, she was hearing footsteps and voices. She emerged to see Rick MacLyon ushering maybe twenty men and women decked with bits of tartanalia out the front door. "Thank you so much for coming. Sorry, important business, can't be put off...." Two of the women curtsied to him and a man bowed over his hand instead of shaking it. He really was playing the laird of the castle, wasn't he?

With a solid thud MacLyon shut the door and turned to Jean. He was wearing the equivalent of a business suit—a kilt, a plain leather sporran, a tweed jacket, a blue tie. In person his hair was as pale as his complexion, its fine mousy strands slicked back from his high forehead. His large, square glasses reflected the light, making Jean feel as though she was staring at twin monitors waiting for a download.

The police are going to want to talk to all those people, her mind said, and added, *Please tell me someone has called the police.* She heard her voice saying thinly but politely, "I'm Jean Fairbairn from *Great Scot.*"

"Oh yeah. The interview. You got here early. So what's this about someone dead in the game larder?"

To Jean's Scot-adapted ears, MacLyon's American accent sounded like the whine of a chain saw. Her own seemed even flatter. "Just that. There's a man hanging from a hook in the game larder. Dead."

"I'll take a look. You go sit down." MacLyon walked off down the hall.

Jean stared after him. Had she said anything to Fiona about the game larder? She couldn't remember. She knew darn well she hadn't mentioned it to Rick. Game larder. Hook. Nice old gentleman.

She plodded back into the sitting room. The air was cold and heavy, like the proverbial wet blanket draped around her shoulders. She would almost have welcomed pins and needles. But all she felt was the chill of the leather couch when she sat down on its edge. She poured herself a cup of tea, doctored it with milk and sugar, and managed to get it to her mouth by holding it in both hands. Her stomach shimmied at the first sip, then steadied. Ah, yes. Milky sweetness to wash away the smell of decay. Warmth to ease the horror. Caffeine to—well, she was already wired. *Oh God.*

Outside the bus started up, and with a rumble and a clash of gears drove away. The pipes stopped on a startled squeal. George Lovelace was hanging from a hook like a slab of meat. Her anonymous phone caller had gotten it backwards—pursuing Lovelace's story hadn't made trouble for Jean but for Lovelace himself.… She jerked upright, tea splashing onto her skirt. No. Oh no. Her following his story didn't have anything to do with his—suicide. Surely it was suicide, not.… *Murder.*

Yes, rumors of treasure produced villains. But if Lovelace knew where the coins were hidden, why kill him? Why hang him? Why?

The word beat in Jean's mind like her pulse hammered in her throat. At least the tea was warming her up. She poured herself another cup and forced down a gingersnap from the assortment of cookies on the tray. The clock in the front hall struck three.

Before the last vibration of the chimes had quite died away, Jean heard footsteps coming from far down the corridor, slow, heavy steps that reminded her of Lovelace's steps on the turnpike stair. They drew closer and closer and stopped just outside. The door was hung in British fashion, opening into the room instead of against the wall, hiding the corridor from her cautious gaze.

If Glendessary House hadn't already had a ghost, it might well have one now. Violent deaths left shock waves in space and time, waves that people cursed with a sixth sense might intercept. And yet she was no longer shivering, no longer prickling. The room was cool and the air oppressive, but she could account for the squirming sensation in her stomach and the pucker at the back of her neck without resorting to the paranormal.

When Rick MacLyon burst into the room, Jean wasn't at all startled. He threw himself into an armchair, his kilt billowing upward and giving her a glimpse of thin white thighs. He'd paused outside the door to collect himself, to put back on his captain of industry face. That was all.

He looked up at his own portrait, then at the etching of Jenny Cameron on one side and the paintings of Charlie on the other. "Fairbairn," he said.

For a moment Jean didn't recognize the word. "What? Oh—ah—yes, that's my name."

"Maiden or married?"

"Maiden."

MacLyon's head swiveled toward her. Behind his glasses, his eyes were a muddy brown, opaque as the peat-stained waters of Loch Ness, which never give up their dead. "Fairbairn is one of the septs of Clan Armstrong."

"Being Borderers, the Armstrongs weren't exactly a clan."

"Are you related to Nick Fairbairn of Fordel?"

"Not that I know of."

"When did your family emigrate to the U.S.?"

"At the turn of the last century." She wanted to ask, *Who's doing the interview here, anyway?* Not to mention, *Who cares about an interview, under the circumstances?* And she answered herself. *I do.* The first thing you do after a mysterious death is hold interviews.

"My wife is a MacDonald. Descended from the Lords of the Isles. The MacDonalds were first on the scene at Glenfinnan, when the Bonnie Prince raised the flag of his Cause. MacDonalds helped him escape. The name MacDonald means courage, poetry, tragedy, betrayal."

Jean bit her tongue before she added, *and hamburgers.* She picked up her laptop and flipped open the lid. "I take it the police are on their way?" she asked while the machine booted up.

"Yeah, sure," said MacLyon. "Fiona took care of it. No problem."

Well yes, he did have a problem, but there was no need to rub it in. Jean was trying to think of a lead-off question that was not some variation on: *Do you have many murders out here?* when she heard a muffled electronic trill, the first seven notes of "Scotland the Brave".

MacLyon groped in his sporran and produced a cell phone. "Yeah? Yeah, Vanessa. Yeah, he is. Okay. I'm on my way." With an impatient snort, he switched off the phone, leaped up, and left the room.

Jean blinked. Vanessa was Rick's wife. She'd just heard the bad news. Was she in the house or had someone called her and told her?

MacLyon's footsteps receded up the staircase. Vanessa was at home, then. How many more people were tucked away in various nooks and pantries? A place this size would need a staff, at least some of whom probably lived in. But the house was quiet as a— go ahead, Jean told herself—quiet as a tomb.

No, a male voice was speaking in the distance. Even though she couldn't hear the words she could tell by their rhythm that this man was Scottish. Fiona's cool voice replied. A telephone chirped. A door shut. Jean saw the shape in the shadows, twisting in the chill draft. Hung out to dry. *Why?*

With a long, shuddering inhalation that was almost a sob, she thumped the laptop onto the coffee table, walked over to the window, and peered out into the courtyard. The sun shone. Leaves danced. A gull squawked. It wasn't right that the universe was moving imperturbably on while George Lovelace was not only dead but stripped of dignity and purpose.

A low silver car roared up the drive and screeched to a halt. That looked like the sports car that had almost blown her off the road in the Dark Mile, not that she'd seen much more of it than a metallic blur.

A tall man in an impeccably tailored suit, all knees and elbows and belligerent moustache, scrambled from the car and strode toward the house. The front door opened and Fiona's voice said something unintelligible. "What's all this in aid of? Dead? Who's dead?" demanded a man's voice in one of those Anglo-

Scots accents that sounded like it originated not in the vocal cords but at the front teeth.

Fiona murmured something else. Steps came down the staircase. MacLyon's monotone spoke. The new voice returned. "Lovelace? That doddering old fool?"

"Cool it," MacLyon snapped. Out of respect for the deceased or because a witness was lurking in the sitting room?

Fiona, MacLyon, and the stranger walked past the door and down the hall. Somewhere in the distance the young Scots voice spoke. After no more than two minutes, the blended steps came back up the hall and faded into the distant reaches of the house.

All right then. Jean sat down and pulled out her own cell phone.

"Miranda Capaldi," said her partner's throaty voice.

"Hi. It's Jean. I'm at Glendessary House."

"Are you then? Have you met the MacLyon of that ilk yet?"

Any other time Jean would have laughed. Now she said, "Rick MacLyon's pretensions aren't even remotely the issue. I found George Lovelace. Dead. And not by accident, either. Suicide or even murder."

The air between Lochaber and Edinburgh rang hollowly. Then Miranda exclaimed, "Oh my God! How dreadful! What—who—why...."

Even though she had the grace to emphasize her shock, still Jean could hear the *oooh!* undertone. If Miranda's grand story turned into a murder mystery, she'd be as gratified as she was horrified, even though contemporary murders, at least, were outside *Great Scot*'s history-and-tourism territory.

"I have no idea what happened," Jean said. "It's going to take a while for even the local cop to get here, let alone any crime investigation people. They're going to want to interview me, not vice versa. You're just going to have to sit tight."

"I could be ringing Ian at *The Scotsman*...."

"Miranda, please, just let the news percolate out on its own. This is no time to get the scoop and lose your reputation. Or mine, especially."

"Oh aye. You're right, as always. But I'll be putting together Lovelace's biographical facts, even so. Keep your pecker up," Miranda finished, which made Jean smile, if wanly.

Just as she switched off the phone, she heard another car drive into the courtyard. In an instant, she was back at the window. The car's blue Celtic-interlace logo and the legend "Northern Constabulary" glowed inspiringly. From it climbed a constable, who settled his cap on his head and marched toward the front door, which again opened without a knock or a ring.

At last…. Well, it only seemed like half an Ice Age since she'd found the body. Jean looked out of the sitting room door in time to see Fiona hand the constable off to MacLyon and the man from the sports car, who bellowed, "MacSorley, Kieran MacSorley, by way of being the local judge. Frightful business, simply frightful. This way, step lively now." He hustled the officer down the hall.

MacLyon looked at Fiona. "Great timing," he said.

"Couldn't be helped," she returned. They followed the two men around the corner.

No one took notice of Jean. She was starting to feel like Typhoid Mary. She should yell down the hall, "It's not my fault," except she was anything but sure that it wasn't. And what had MacLyon meant about timing, anyway? Like any time was good for a murder?

Jean was still standing in the doorway when Fiona came back around the corner. Without so much as blinking the woman said, "The tea and biscuits were all right for you, then?"

"Yes, thank you." Fiona had no nerves, that's all there was to it. She was already so fair—not anemic, fair—it was hard to tell if she'd even gone pale. Jean wished there were some way she could trade bodies with her, however briefly, like taking a weekend vacation. "The constable's from the closest station, Spean Bridge, right?"

"Aye, that he is." Fiona walked on by.

Jean slunk back into the sitting room but didn't close the door. Footsteps walked down the hall. One set went up the staircase, another went out the front door. From her post at the window she saw the constable get in his car and hold a long, serious conversation with someone invisible—headquarters, probably. She didn't need to read his lips to know that he was saying, "Fort William, we have a problem. Send back-up."

While Jean's outer adult was dutifully standing and waiting, her inner child was squirming and whimpering. Movement, that's what she needed, although running up and down beating her breast was not an option.

The entry hall was deserted. So was the staircase, and so was a corridor running in the opposite direction from the one leading to the game larder. This corridor was longer and wider, lined with bits of furniture and prints in gilded frames. Each rectangle of glass glinted in the light shining through the one open doorway.

Jean peered past double doors into a huge drawing room, decorated in eighteenth-century style. French windows opened onto a formal garden. Empty cups and crumpled napkins lay on tables. The wall was lined with portraits continuing the 1745 theme: Donald Cameron, the Lochiel. Lord George Murray. Flora MacDonald.

The originals of those portraits were thoroughly accounted for. These, then, were well-done copies, oils polished with the brassy implication of age. The largest painting, though, the one over the marble mantelpiece, Jean didn't recognize. It combined one of the famous portraits of Charlie with a colorized version of Jenny Cameron's etching, so that the two of them appeared side by side, looking superciliously out at the viewer.

This was where MacLyon had been haranguing the tourist group. Where they'd been singing, although rather solemnly, for a pep rally. Maybe the meeting had been a memorial service for someone. Had the people come from a clan society? It could hardly have been clan MacLyon, since there had been no such animal before Rick Douglas invented it.

Pondering the tendency of people to go overboard with their enthusiasms—identity as a state of mind—Jean walked back to the entry hall past several closed doors, none of which tempted her in the least.

From the foot of the staircase she could hear muffled voices interspersed by the clink of dishes. Only MacSorley's sarcasm came through clearly, in tone, not in words, overriding MacLyon's whine. Jean thought she detected Fiona's voice, a calm undercurrent beneath the men's. She was certainly hearing a second woman, one with an upward inflection at the end of each short, sharp sentence that made her sound petulant but was probably only a California accent. Vanessa.

What were they doing, synchronizing watches and getting their stories straight? Like Jean, they had to be making it up as they went along. A dead body in the house was pretty darn awkward—especially if it turned out to have been murdered. Who could possibly have anything against poor old Lovelace, coin scam or.... Wait a minute. Hugh said Lovelace had been arguing with some local functionary. MacSorley had not only called Lovelace a doddering old fool, he'd announced himself as a judge. Not, Jean informed herself, that an argument on New Year's Eve meant anything in May.

Walking past the sitting room, she peered around the angle of the hallway. The constable was standing in the shadows at its far end, in front of the larder door. He shuffled his feet and glanced at his watch. Yeah, Jean thought, I know what you mean; let's get a move on here... .

"Oh, hello," said a velvet voice behind her.

She spun around with a gasp. Barely an arm's length away stood a tall young man wearing the same kilt and jacket outfit as MacLyon, minus a brass button or two. He might have popped out of a bottle—which he was carrying with him, a liter of some obscure and therefore expensive single malt—although his having popped out of the kitchen was more likely.

"Sorry," he said, "didn't mean to give you a fright."

Jean goggled. The man reminded her a bit of Michael Campbell-Reid, although from the way he was looking back at her looking at him he was considerably less married. She managed to say, "I'm a little jumpy. Go figure. Jean Fairbairn from *Great Scot*."

"Neil MacSorley, piper, chauffeur, gardener, general dogsbody." He switched the bottle to his other hand, pumped hers up and down, and dropped it tingling back at her side.

Another MacSorley. "So you're the piper. I saw you playing when I got here."

"Oh aye, I play the twee old songs, 'Over the Sea to Skye' and the like. Rubbish, I'm thinking, but Rick's the boss." Neil shook back his mane of auburn hair and started to smile, then, his eyes darting down the hallway, frowned instead.

The afterglow of that almost-smile stayed imprinted on Jean's retina. The first smile she'd seen since she'd arrived here, it was worth waiting for, a dazzling arc of white teeth cutting crescents between his chiseled cheekbones and chiseled jaw... .

Suddenly and annoyingly she was aware of what his bright blue eyes were seeing—a woman easing into middle-age as though into a cold swimming pool, who even at her best had a nonchalant attitude toward fripperies like make-up and coordinated outfits. And she was hardly at her best now. Her lip gloss was chewed, her brown hair was inside-out, her glasses rode schoolmarmishly down her nose, and the large dark eyes she thought were her best feature were slightly crossed and as intelligent as cabbage.

Like her physical appearance mattered now. Still, Jean drew herself up, trying to claim as much space as possible with her five feet three inches. "I came here to interview Rick—Mr. MacLyon—but he'll have other things on his mind now. I'll set up another appointment."

"Oh aye, Fiona will be seeing to that, she's playing the personal assistant just now." He held up the bottle. "Fancy a wee dram? Nothing like the best of the barley to put the roses back in your cheeks."

She had the uneasy feeling that the roses were blossoming in her cheeks just fine. "No, thank you."

"Then I'll be getting on." He tipped her a salute with the whiskey bottle and headed up the hall.

Jean stood watching the pleats of the kilt dancing above Neil's fully-packed calves until he'd disappeared up the staircase. Then, deflating, she walked back into the sitting room. Of all Glendessary House's special effects, the handsome young piper was the most striking.

Not that she cared. She wanted to get away, into the fresh air and open landscape. She wanted to travel back in time to yesterday afternoon in her office—*No, Mr. Lovelace, I'm sorry, I can't help you...*. Or would that have made a difference? Would anything she did now make a difference?

All she could do was wait, and wonder, and nurse the ache in her gut that was the memory of a nice old man who'd wanted her help badly enough that he'd lied to get it.

Jean sat down on the couch, leaned her head against its back, crossed her arms protectively, and closed her eyes. If she couldn't have what she wanted, then she could at least possess herself in patience until she could have what was available.

SEVEN

By the time a fusillade of slamming car doors roused Jean from something between nightmare and coma, the light filtering through the draperies had taken on a faint bronze sheen.

The cavalry was here at last. The camp followers of the media would be close behind. Jean exchanged a wary glance with Jenny Cameron's black-and-sepia eyes. She identified with Jenny, and not just because the woman was also known as Jean.

Footsteps beat up and down the hall. Voices spoke in varying tones of authority and deference. The clock struck six. A moment later, a sharp rap, between a polite knock and a battering ram, pushed the door of the sitting room further open. Jean stood up.

In stepped a compactly-built man. He wore a neat dark suit, buttoned, and a striped tie, knotted, the same way the police officers wore their uniforms, as identification rather than fashion statement. Behind him came a younger man in a similar suit. With his fresh face and notebook he looked like a student on his way to a class.

The first man strode forward, extended his hand, and announced, "Detective Chief Inspector Alasdair Cameron, Northern Constabulary."

"Jean Fairbairn." She offered her own hand.

He grasped it and let it go. His fingers were cool, and so firm she felt as though he'd taken her prints as well as shaken her hand. "Miss or Mrs.?"

"If you're being technical, I'm a Dr, a PhD. But I'll answer to Miss or Ms., whichever."

"Right," he said, underwhelmed by the essay in nomenclature. "I'm told you discovered the deceased, Miss Fairbairn."

"I found him, yes," she returned, with an emphasis on "him."

"This is Detective Constable Gunn. If you'd be so good as to give us a statement, he'll take it down."

Cameron was telling, not asking. "Yes, of course. Hello, D.C. Gunn."

With a polite nod, Gunn faded discreetly into a chair out of Jean's line of sight.

It was Cameron who was in her face. He might be forty, as she was, or he might be a lived-in thirty-five. The furrow between his eyebrows implied a tendency to frown, and the creases bracketing his mouth suggested a frequently clenched jaw. His dark blond hair was cut short, and would have made an amber waves of grain effect except for its gray sheen, like that of an approaching storm. The same sheen was reflected in the slate-blue eyes that gazed at her with consideration edging into suspicion.

She drew herself up with an irritating rush of self-consciousness, again seeing what the man looking at her was seeing. But Alasdair Cameron was assessing a different potential. The uniformed constable who stepped into the room and took up a position beside the door made that very clear. Maybe instead of calling Miranda she should have called a lawyer.... She doubted if Cameron would appreciate a joke about Miranda rights.

"Sit down, please," he said, quiet, measured, matter-of-fact.

With no ceremony to stand on—without much of a leg to stand on, either—Jean sat down and folded her hands in her lap.

Unbuttoning his coat, Cameron chose the same chair MacLyon had. He started from almost the same point. "Who are you? Why are you here?"

I'm trying to figure that out myself. "I'm part-owner of and writer for *Great Scot* magazine. I had an appointment to interview Rick MacLyon at three o'clock this afternoon. I got here an hour early."

"Why?"

"I'd hoped to stop and talk to George Lovelace on the way, although I probably hadn't allowed enough time for much of a conversation. He didn't answer his phone when I called, so I came on out here. The housekeeper asked me to wait."

"Why, then, were you having a wander round the house?"

She'd probably get past all this only to discover she'd developed a psychosomatic bladder disorder. "I was looking for the toilet. No one was around to ask, so I just walked down the hall, opening doors until I got to the end. And there he was. George Lovelace."

"You recognized the body as Lovelace?"

"Oh yes." She forced herself to loosen the knot that was her intertwined fingers.

"How well did you know him?"

"Hardly at all. We only met yesterday, at my office in Edinburgh."

"Why was he there?"

"He brought me a gold coin he'd found around here. He wouldn't say exactly where."

"A gold coin," Cameron repeated.

"He and I both figured that the coin came from Bonnie Prince Charlie's missing hoard."

"Oh aye? A bit of a treasure, is it?"

"The hoard might be more than a bit, if it's still there after all these years. A historical treasure as well as a monetary one."

"Why did he bring you the coin?"

"He said he wanted me to help him have it declared treasure trove so he could sell it. He said he needed the money. He said I could do an article for the magazine as long as I didn't name names or places. He said he didn't want to set off a gold rush. I saw his point. I still do."

If Cameron caught her meaning—that full disclosure wouldn't necessarily serve the public—he showed no sign of it. He asked his question again, this time with a different inflection. "Why did he come to *you?*"

"Because he liked my articles in *Great Scot,* especially the one in this month's issue about Bonnie Prince Charlie."

"You took him on because he flattered you, is that it?"

Jean tightened her teeth and loosened them again. She'd done nothing wrong. "In a way, yes. And I was very curious about the coin."

"Who else knows about it?"

"So far as I know, only the experts at the Museum of Scotland. I took it over to them yesterday afternoon."

"It's genuine, then?"

"Yes. That's not the problem. The problem is that the people at the Museum told me Lovelace had brought them another artifact last year. He knew all about the laws of treasure trove. He didn't need me to intervene."

Cameron blinked. She swore that was the first time he'd blinked since he walked in the room. "Why was he after lying to you, then?"

"That's exactly what I was going to ask him today."

"And?" Cameron prodded, as if he'd sensed with some sort of police ESP that there was an "and."

"Someone, a woman, called my flat last night and told me to stay away from Lovelace, that he was trouble. I have no idea who it was, but then, I'm not hard to find. I called the number back again. No one answered."

"You haven't got caller ID?"

"I thought an answering machine would cover everything. I was wrong."

Cameron didn't comment on her negligence. "What else was Lovelace on about?"

"He reminisced about his days training as a commando in this area and how he watches birds, that sort of thing. I was sure there was more going on with the coin than he was telling me. In fact, he told me there was something I should know but then cut himself off, saying he shouldn't tell tales out of school or words to that effect. I figured he was just embarrassed to need money, at least until I found out he was scamming me."

The detective's eyes released Jean's—she slumped slightly, then caught herself—and turned to the portrait of MacLyon in full panoply of kilt, plaid, and silver-trimmed Prince Charlie coatee. The outfit was gaudy, yes, but much more attractive than a tuxedo for a formal occasion.

If Cameron had been from New York, he'd probably have said something about chutzpah. "Cheek," he said instead. "Another victim of charlieoverthewaterism, I reckon."

"That's a pretty mild disease," Jean said, suppressing her appreciative but inappropriate smile. "There's as much a market for Scotland's heritage as for Scotland's oil, and at least most of the income from the heritage stays here."

Cameron looked back at her, his stony face not even remotely appreciative. "When you've been stripped of everything else, reduced to selling your own past, a bit of honesty wouldn't go amiss. There's heritage, and then there's tripe."

"Heritage is often more opinion than fact," Jean told him, and told herself, I don't need to debate definitions of honesty with this guy.

"From America, are you?" he went on.

"The United States, yes."

"Why come here?"

"I've spent so much time here over the last twenty years I thought it would be cheaper just to move."

"You're a citizen, then."

"No. Not yet, anyway. Just a resident alien."

"No need to get carried away with one's enthusiasms, is there?" he returned. Jean couldn't tell whether he was being sarcastic or not. Odd, how he'd echoed her opinion of MacLyon's trappings.

The constable at the door suddenly stepped aside, letting another man into the room. This one looked like a Viking gone to seed, broad shoulders and heavy chest slumping downward beneath a freshly pressed suit that had been cut for the body of ten years ago. His face was encircled by blond hair, top and bottom, combed back from his broad forehead and trimmed around a jaw like an anvil. "Chief Inspector," he said, in a bass rumble of a voice.

"Miss Fairbairn, Detective Sergeant Sawyer," said Cameron.

"Hello," Jean said, and bit her tongue before she made some remark about no fair piling on, there was only one of her.

Sawyer handed a clear plastic bag to Cameron. Cameron held it up in front of her face. It contained the receipt she'd given Lovelace for the coin. "This was in Lovelace's pocket. Do you recognize it?"

"Yes, I do. I gave it to him yesterday."

"And this?" He turned the bag so she could see the back of the paper. On it was written, in a fine calligraphic hand, "Two p.m. Tuesday."

Jean shook her head. "Lovelace must have written that."

"When you made an appointment with him?" demanded Sawyer.

"I didn't make any appointments with him. He put that receipt in his pocket, I told him I'd get back to him, and he left to catch his train. If he wrote on that paper, he did it after he left my office."

Cameron contemplated the evidence. "How are you getting on?"

Jean almost answered, "How do you think I'm getting on?" before she realized he was talking to his sergeant. Again she flexed her fingers and, while she was it, her jaw.

"We've made the photos and the video. The lads are lowering the body down now, the locals having had enough sense to leave it as it was." Sawyer shot a narrow glance at Jean, probably wondering whether she was going to have the vapors if he expanded on any physical details.

But even when she found the body, the physical details in and of themselves hadn't upset her. They were more sad than anything else. Here was a polite old man who had been stripped of his dignity. It was little consolation that he was beyond the humiliation at the color photos and the video and the black and white, not to mention what was going to happen to him on a medical examiner's table.

"Rigor's just now setting in," Sawyer went on. "Body's cooling, but then, that's a cool room. Meant to be, isn't it? You found him at two-thirty, then, Miss Fairbairn?"

"Maybe a little before. I'm not sure."

"He might've died at just on two. Even later."

"I got here at two," said Jean. "At least, the clock was striking…."

"So then," Sawyer said with some relish, "he died at the exact time he wrote on the back of your receipt."

She'd known she was a suspect all along. She had to be one, it was standard procedure. But only now did she really feel the suspicion, like the tickle of cold steel between her shoulder blades. Taking a deep but not exactly calming breath, she tried a neutral, "I thought time of death was always uncertain."

"So it is," Cameron agreed, probably more to get the facts straight than to reassure Jean.

"Even so, we've got a right small window this time round." Sawyer took the bag back from Cameron but he was still looking at Jean, his sandy eyebrows set in something between distaste and distrust.

"You already knew Lovelace gave me the coin. Were you making sure I told you about it?"

"Inconsistencies can be very helpful when investigating a suspicious death," Cameron said.

"A probable murder," added Sawyer.

"Murder," Jean repeated, smoothing her hackles. This interrogation was like a root canal. The more she cooperated, the faster it would be over. "Yes, he was murdered. It wasn't an accident, that's for sure, and it wasn't suicide. He couldn't have hauled himself up on one of those—those meat hooks, and there wasn't a stool or bench or anything for him to have kicked over."

"Very observant," Sawyer said, unimpressed.

Cameron asked, "Were you thinking it was a suicide, then?"

"Not really. I just didn't want to think I was stuck in a remote house with a murderer."

"A murderer might have legged it into the hills before you arrived."

"Or he could have driven away. I passed a sports car going hell-for-leather a few minutes before I got here."

"Oh?" One of Cameron's brows twitched but didn't actually rise.

"I thought it might be Kieran MacSorley, assuming I heard his name right. And yes, I was eavesdropping, I defy anyone not to, in these circumstances. But I couldn't swear it was his car, let alone him. If he'd—committed a crime—why turn around and come right back to the scene?"

"Because as a judge he'd have been concerned with a suspicious death."

"Oh." That made sense, Jean thought, although precious little else did.

"MacSorley identified Lovelace, but then, MacLyon did do as well. I gather he was a kenspeckle figure in these airts."

"Conspicuous? Yeah, I can see that. A friend of mine, a musician who played at MacLyon's Hogmanay party, told me someone fitting Lovelace's description was here that night. Someone who got into an argument with a man who, again, might have been MacSorley. MacSorley senior, assuming the—the piper, Neil, is his son."

She'd almost said *the dishy Neil.* But there was an adjective she'd save for a friendly chat, which this emphatically was not. Jean went on, "When Kieran MacSorley got here a little while ago, I heard him say, 'Lovelace, that doddering old fool.' Then MacLyon shut him up."

"Who was telling you about the argument at Hogmanay?" asked Cameron.

"My neighbor in Edinburgh, Hugh Munro. Maybe you've heard of him."

"Aye, I've heard of him, right enough." His tone didn't offer an opinion on either Hugh's music or his politics. Over his shoulder he said, "Interview him about the Hogmanay party here, the row Lovelace had. Which ended...."

Jean picked up on her prompt. "Hugh said Vanessa MacLyon broke it up."

Sawyer pulled out a notebook and pen and either jotted down his instructions or worked up a couple more insults.

"Who's your partner at *Great Scot?*" Cameron asked.

"Miranda Capaldi. The coin's with Michael Campbell-Reid at the Museum of Scotland on Chambers Street." Jean reached for her bag and pulled a couple of business cards from the side pocket. "Here, as long as you're checking my bona fides."

Cameron took one card and handed the other back to Sawyer without looking at either. The sergeant looked at his, though, long and hard, as though trying to read between the lines. "A PhD, eh?" He couldn't have said *a leper, eh?* in surlier tones.

"Carry on, Sawyer," Cameron told him.

The sergeant turned and walked out the door. For a moment Jean imagined herself walking out of the door, too, and then on into the night and away, free and clear.... But no. She wasn't going anywhere.

EIGHT

CAMERON SCANNED the room, taking in the portraits, the paneling, and probably counting the nail holes. Then his x-ray eyes swung back to Jean. He leaned forward, resting his elbows on his thighs, looking as though he was about to catapult from the chair.

His steady voice and steadier blue-gray eyes were getting to her—exactly as he intended, no doubt. Pretty soon she'd find herself confessing to something, anything, a parking ticket, maybe. But that would hardly deflect his attention. He'd only go on to other prey if she were innocent and/or no longer useful as a witness. And that would be his decision, not hers.

She tried leaning back into the cool embrace of the leather couch, putting a few more inches of space between her and her inquisitor. "Where are you from, Chief Inspector?"

"Sorry?"

"I'm trying to place your accent. It's not Glasgow." A Glasgow accent sounded like a cat hacking up something between a hairball and a glottal stop. Cameron's voice was strewn with thistles, not hairballs.

"I was born and raised in Fort William."

"Is that why they assigned you to this case, because you know the area? Or did you just come here as part of the—they call it a cascade, don't they, when everyone's mobilized to investigate a suspicious death?"

"I'm asking the questions, Miss Fairbairn."

Her emotional antennae might have detected an edge of hostility, although not nearly as much as she'd detected from Sawyer. She couldn't allow herself to get punch-drunk. "Sorry. Go on."

"Trace your steps for me. You came away from Edinburgh this morning?"

"Yes. I stopped in Callander for lunch. Then I stopped in Fort William and tried to call Lovelace. I stopped at the commando memorial and tried again. It was too late to go see him then, but I thought I could set something up for later. No one answered the phone then, either, so I came on out here."

"You hadn't told him you'd be phoning him today? You didn't plan on seeing him?"

Jean ignored the implication, the reminder of the cryptic "Two p.m. Tuesday" on the back of the receipt. "No. When Lovelace left my office yesterday I knew he was telling me only part of the story, but I didn't know yet that he was using me."

"And?"

"It wasn't until my partner suggested I interview Rick MacLyon while I was in the area that I wondered whether Lovelace found the coin on MacLyon's property. Although how he thought sending me off to the Museum would protect him from the legal implications of that, I have no idea."

"Did the woman on the telephone mention the coin at all?"

"No. She just said I shouldn't do whatever Lovelace wanted me to do."

"Was her voice distinctive at all? Did you hear anything in the background?"

"I thought I heard a man's voice in the background, very briefly.

As for the woman, she had an American accent but spoke in British syntax, saying 'leave it,' for example, instead of 'let it alone.'"

"Why didn't you leave it, then?" Cameron asked.

"Because, Chief Inspector, all it takes to make me very curious is to tell me not to ask questions."

He actually did smile at that, a quick crinkle passing from one corner of his mouth along his lips and vanishing off the other corner so quickly she almost missed it. Whether he was smiling with her or at her she was fast ceasing to care.

"You passed a sports car on the road? Where?" he went on.

"Along the Dark Mile, beneath the trees. It went by awfully fast, but I thought it was a light-colored sports car. Then, when Kieran MacSorley turned up in a silver sports car a little while ago I—well, I didn't actually put two and two together. I made an assumption."

"Who else was in the house when you arrived?"

"I have no way of knowing. The housekeeper, Fiona Robertson, opened the door...." For just an instant Cameron's eyes widened and went out of focus. He'd recognized the name. "I take it Fiona didn't answer the door when you got here?"

With an infinitesimal shake of the head Cameron threw away the distracting thought. "MacLyon's security guard, Toby Walsh, saw us inside."

"I didn't know MacLyon had a security guard. I'm not surprised, though. Is he Scottish?"

"That he is. Why?"

"I thought one of the voices I heard was Neil's, but it could have been Toby Walsh's. No big deal."

The set of Cameron's shoulders indicated his thought: *Let me be the judge of that.* "Who did you actually see, then?"

"Fiona answered the door, showed me in here, and asked if I wanted some tea. I waited a little while, then went looking for the loo. I found Lovelace. I ran back along the hall toward the entrance. Fiona was coming this way with a tea tray. I told her and she went to tell MacLyon. He was entertaining a private party—I saw their bus in the parking lot. He gave them the bum's rush, more or less...."

"Sorry?"

"He sent them away in a hurry."

"Do you know who they were?"

"No. But the way they were fawning over MacLyon and wearing tartan bits and pieces I put them down as tourists rather than local people. I thought maybe they were having a memorial service, I heard them singing what sounded like a hymn. It could have been anything from 'Will Ye No Come Back Again' to 'God Save the Queen,' actually, but that was right when I found the— when I found Lovelace, so I didn't really notice. Especially with the piper playing, too."

Cameron watched her, waiting.

She was trying to help, darn it. "The bus—the coach—was one of those purple ones with the heather design on the side. Highland Holidays."

"We'll find them. A pity MacLyon saw them off so quickly."

"Yes, I thought so, too."

"Did you, now?"

"I can't help thinking over the situation, Chief Inspector."

She expected him to ask, *Just as you can't help eavesdropping?* but he said only, "Did you talk to MacLyon at all?"

"He came in here and talked about genealogy for a couple of minutes. Then his cell phone rang. It was his wife, I gathered, she'd just heard about Lovelace. So he left."

"She was away, was she?"

"No, I think she was upstairs. At least, a little while later I heard an American woman's voice upstairs."

"The one who phoned you and told you to cry off?"

"It could have been. I don't know."

"If Lovelace died at two, he was killed just as you arrived. An hour early. Unexpectedly. But you didn't see or hear a thing." His voice was edged with either disappointment or criticism.

Well, she'd sensed a ghost. But Cameron was already skeptical without her telling him that. Jean clenched her hands in her lap. "I came close to walking in on a murder in progress, yes. But I didn't. I didn't even see anyone in the back hall. Maybe I heard footsteps, although that doesn't prove anything."

"No, it doesn't. Did you take notice of anything else?"

"Well, the first thing MacLyon said to me when he got everybody out the door was, 'What's this about a body in the game larder?' even though I don't think I said anything to Fiona about the game larder."

Cameron's eyes flicked away, then flicked back again. She'd thought that was an important point but he seemed to dismiss it. "And you've been sitting here 'til now?"

"I walked across the entry hall and glanced into the drawing room. That's when I overheard the woman's voice upstairs. And I ran into Neil MacSorley in the back hall. I didn't see the guard, Toby, at all. I've been in here the rest of the time, yes."

"Right," said Cameron.

Jean concluded, "I don't know why anyone would kill Lovelace."

"Gold, there's a motive for you. One of the best."

"It sure is." She leaned forward. "So just how prime a suspect am I, Chief Inspector?"

"If you'd killed the man yourself you'd hardly have called attention to it, would you? On the other hand...." Ducking her gaze, he looked down at his hands clasped between his knees, hands that looked just as capable of laying bricks as writing up reports. "...well, we'll be making further inquiries."

"While you're checking up on me, ask yourself why I'd kill Lovelace before I'd talked to him. Before he told me anything more about the gold coin. Before I could find out why he was jerking me around."

"Who said you hadn't yet talked to him?" Cameron asked, very mildly, but there was no mistaking the menace in his voice. Before Jean could respond with an emphatic *I did!* he looked back up at her. The look was a slap across the face, like a duelist issuing a challenge. But all he said was, "Where are you stopping for the night?"

Getting her feelings hurt would just make things worse. She didn't feel as though she were entitled to feelings, not under either the circumstances or Cameron's eyes. "I have a room booked in Fort William, at the Mountain View Hotel."

"Good. Then you'll be calling in at the police station tomorrow for another interview. Two o'clock."

Again, he wasn't asking. "Two o'clock. I'll be there."

"Gunn?"

Oh yeah, Gunn. Jean had forgotten he was sitting behind her, playing court reporter.

Appearing in her peripheral vision, he flipped back a few pages in his notebook and in a mild tenor voice started reading off what she'd said. If it wasn't word for word, it was darn close. She was impressed. "Yeah, that's just about the size of it."

"Sign this, please." He offered her the notebook and a pen.

Judging by the indecipherable handwriting that filled the last page, he'd developed his own method of shorthand. She'd always heard that most of a policeman's job was paperwork, but then, she'd never had intimate contact with a policeman before. She couldn't say she was enjoying the experience.

Jean signed her name and turned to Cameron, "If you're—if we're finished here…."

Again the constable at the door stepped aside, this time admitting Rick MacLyon. Cameron rose to his feet. "Mr. MacLyon…."

"Your guy Sawyer, he says your name is Cameron."

"Detective Chief Inspector Alasdair Cameron." He extended his hand.

MacLyon shook it heartily, with both of his. His voice ranged upward an octave. "Camerons are always welcome here at Glendessary House. Are you descended from the Lochiel, do you know? From his brother, the martyr Dr Archie? From Jenny's first marriage?"

Jean could almost hear Cameron's mind skidding. He extracted his hand from MacLyon's eager paws. "Sorry?"

"Vanessa!" MacLyon called over his shoulder. "In here!"

The constable reeled back. Into the room stepped a woman who might just as well have been making her entrance onto a Hollywood sound stage. Her platinum-blond hair was meticulously arranged to give the impression she'd just rolled out of bed. Her green eyes—contacts, no doubt—matched the green blocks of her tartan skirt. While Jean had interpreted MacLyon's and Neil's kilts as business attire, Vanessa's tartan skirt and the velvet jacket framing the bulge of her breasts were very much a costume. She wore it well, shoulders thrown back, one black pump thrust forward.

"May I present my wife, Vanessa MacLyon, nee MacDonald." Her husband made a sweeping *ta-da!* gesture.

"Welcome to Glendessary House," Vanessa said to Cameron, Gunn, and Jean. "I'm sorry we had to meet under such difficult circumstances."

"Mrs. MacLyon," said Cameron, stone-faced.

Jean forced a pinched smile. "Nice to meet you."

Gunn stared.

"I assume your people will want to interview the staff?" Yes, Vanessa's was the voice Jean had heard upstairs, now pitched low and polished for polite company. Whether it was the voice she'd heard on the telephone last night she couldn't say.

"Oh aye," Cameron said. "Everyone who's been in the house today needs interviewing."

"I'll have Fiona send everyone in here in turn. Would you care for tea? Sandwiches? The cook is off today, but Fiona does nicely."

"Thank you, Mrs. MacLyon. Tea would be lovely."

Vanessa turned and swept out of the room, all but pulling her skirts aside as she passed the constable. Jean felt as though she should applaud. Miranda could put on enough airs to inflate a balloon and still be her endearing self, but what Vanessa was putting on was an act. Maybe because airs came naturally to Miranda but Vanessa had to learn them?

When push came to shove, Jean told herself, *I don't care.* Her curiosity had taken a hit. She felt disconnected from what passed for time and space and her usual mental processes, and wanted nothing more than to crawl into a hole. "May I go now?" she asked Cameron.

His head turned toward her. She could get frostbite from those eyes. No, she hadn't given him a single answer that he'd wanted. And she wasn't going to. But that was his problem, not hers.

"Oh aye, away you go. Don't forget, two o'clock tomorrow afternoon. The station's on the High Street."

"I'll be there." Jean gathered up her bag and her laptop and told MacLyon, "I'll make another appointment for that interview."

"Check with Fiona on the way out," he said, and sat down in the chair, every bit laird of the castle and CEO. "Now, Inspector. As far as I can tell Lovelace sneaked into the house right before two this afternoon."

"He did, did he?" asked Cameron. Gunn flipped to a new page in his notebook and flexed his writing hand.

"My security guard saw him walking up the driveway about ten 'til," MacLyon went on, "but no one admits to having let him into the house."

He sneaked into the house? At ten before two? Sawyer was right, they did have a very small window for the murder. But why, but who…. Reminding herself that her curiosity was down for the count, Jean headed for the door. Where she shot one last glance back that intersected Cameron's curious glance at her, one that asked, *are you for real?*

I think so, she thought, more weary than resentful, and walked headlong into something rubbery that reeked of aftershave. Kieran MacSorley. "Excuse me," she said.

He nodded brusquely. "My fault, Madame." His beady black eyes and bristling moustache said otherwise.

Jean wasn't about to challenge him, especially after what she'd said earlier about eavesdropping. She walked quickly off down the hall. Behind her Cameron's calm but forceful voice asked, "Been talking about the matter with your staff, have you, Mr. MacLyon?"

Fiona was standing guard beside the intricately-carved newel post at the foot of the staircase. "You're away, then?"

"Yes. I need to set up another appointment with Rick. With Mr. MacLyon."

"Would half-past one the Thursday work for you?"

"Day after tomorrow. Fine. And this time I won't show up early."

"No, I shouldn't think so." Any amusement drowned in the spilled pupil of Fiona's left eye. "I'll pencil you in, then."

Jean turned toward the door just as it opened. Almost the entire frame was filled by the Scottish version of the Incredible Hulk. The security guard, she assumed, wearing a kilt in the green and blue crossed with yellow and red of the MacLyon tartan. His arms and shoulders strained against the cloth of shirt and jacket. His crew-cut head looked like a bowling ball, his eyes and little rosebud mouth the finger holes.

"Miss Fairbairn, this is Toby Walsh," Fiona said. "Toby, Miss Fairbairn will come back again the Thursday, at half-past one."

"Right pleased to meet you," said Toby somberly. Her coat dangled from his huge hands as though it were a dishtowel. "Here, you'll be wanting this, it's a bit nippy outside."

"Oh, yes, thank you." She was too tired to object to Toby's digging around in her car. She'd left it unlocked, after all.

And here came Neil MacSorley from the back of the house.

Fiona took Jean's laptop and Toby her bag. Neil, exuding an aromatic aura of whiskey, held her coat. Jean promised herself a wee dram of the best single malt in Fort William as soon as she'd parked the car. "Thanks," she said, and slipped her arms into the chilly sleeves. Reclaiming her laptop and bag, she let Neil's light touch in the small of her back guide her out the door, past the lighted colonnade, and around the collection of police cars—among them an ominous black van—and MacSorley's sporty number. The outside air was cold. Cold and fresh.

The sun had sunk behind the mountains to the west but still the sky blushed like firelight on pewter. The small rental car seemed wonderfully ordinary. Neil opened its door. "Those coppers, Cameron and Sawyer, they looked to be getting out the thumbscrews."

"Just doing their jobs, trying to find out what happened." Jean ducked into the cold interior of the car and groped in her bag for the keys.

"No joy, eh?"

"No, I couldn't tell them a thing. See no evil, hear no evil, speak no evil." There were the keys. Some sort of Murphy's physics always sent them to the very bottom of the bag. She inserted the right one into the ignition and looked up.

Neil stood silhouetted against the sky, the icy wind waving his hair. "Have a care. The road's narrow, a bit dicey after dark."

"At least it's not raining." She started the engine.

"Cheers." Neil slammed the door and stepped back.

Good try, Jean thought as she piloted her car around the other vehicles, but the cheer was pretty thin tonight. She glanced in her rear view mirror to see Neil walking back to the house, his kilt fluttering fetchingly, his arms crossed as though warming himself. As though once he'd consoled her, he had little comfort left for himself.

Then she was in the dense shadow of the trees, her headlights picking out the individual trunks but showing nothing behind them. She wouldn't have been surprised to see a phantom hitch-hiker step out onto the drive, a commando, perhaps, or one of Charlie's last broken followers, or even Fionn MacCumhaill, from the myth that illuminated the rim of reality.

A glow beyond the trees resolved itself into the iron gates and their heraldic pillars, illuminated by floodlights.... Oh. The gates looked familiar because they were copies of the gates of Traquair House, an old mansion in the Borders. Gates that were closed after the departure of Bonnie Prince Charlie, so the legend went, not to be reopened until the Stuarts returned to sit on the throne of Scotland.

These gates were already open. Charles Stuart was gone. So was the throne of Scotland. And George Lovelace wasn't going to come back, either.

NINE

JEAN WOKE UP feeling like the result of a scientific experiment gone horribly wrong. Her body parts didn't quite seem to fit together. Washing and brushing and dressing in clean clothes helped restore physical humanity, but her mind was still disfigured by memory.

In spite of her dram of whiskey, supplemented by a sandwich, she'd lain awake for hours, caught in a loop of nightmare: George Lovelace had been murdered. He'd been murdered a few paces away from her. Instead of sensing anything useful, like a call for help, she'd sensed a ghost, which might not even have been his. She'd never felt so helpless, so useless, so....

Hungry. Jean hurried down the main stairs of the hotel and squeaked through the doors of the dining room just as a waiter was closing them. "Can I still get breakfast, please?"

Receiving an affirmative answer, she sat down by the window and looked out over Loch Linnhe to the mountains opposite, their golden-green flanks glowing in pale sunlight. By the whitecaps on the water, she deduced that the wind was blowing briskly. By the passing pedestrians muffled in coats and hats, she deduced that the wind was cold. By the dark clouds seeping into a gray-tinted sky, she deduced that rain was on its way.

So far so good. Her faculties were still functioning, albeit at the level of the lowest common mental denominator.

The teenaged waiter in his starched white shirt and black bow tie arranged a pot of tea, a rack of toast, a bowl of corn flakes, and a plate of bacon and eggs on the table. Jean hoped she wasn't diminishing Lovelace's ugly death by having a good appetite—that ghastly moment of discovery would be a permanent scar. But she knew she couldn't do anyone any good having sinking spells. Of course, she told herself as she slathered her toast with butter and marmalade, whether she could do anyone any good with a full stomach was another question.

A television set in the back of the room was tuned to the morning news. Hearing a familiar voice, Jean turned around, fork poised. Yes, the screen displayed an image of Alasdair Cameron, coolly and correctly telling the gathered reporters, "Several people are helping us with our inquiries." By the way spotlights etched the slightly sagging angles of his face, Jean guessed the media had arrived at Glendessary House in force, and jumped him on his way out last night.

She wasn't going to get her back up about Cameron. The Northern Constabulary was paying him to find criminals, not practice diplomacy.

No one was paying her to find criminals, but, damn it, she could hardly help thinking about the case. Surely the murder had been a random one. Lovelace had discovered a burglar in the back hall.... No, your average burglar was more likely to run away from than kill a witness. If he did feel moved to kill, he'd bash his victim with a handy *objet d'art*, not haul him up on a meat hook. Just as your average burglar would be more likely to wait until no one was home before he set out to burgle.

So what if the murderer was neither a burglar nor average? Most scenarios involving, say, Mafia hit men out to get Rick, depended on someone being able to sneak into the house. But Lovelace hadn't gotten in without being seen, either by surveillance system or by eyeball.

Unless what Toby saw in the driveway wasn't Lovelace at all, Jean thought, but a crisis apparition the old man's ghost emitted—or however ghosts were created—at the moment of his death. He could have been dead well before she ever got there.

Yeah, she told herself, just try going to Chief Inspector Cameron with *that* notion, comforting as it was to her personally.

Maybe the murderer was from the tourist party. Someone could have slipped away from the group and met Lovelace in the back hall. Jean liked that idea. She hadn't spent hours alone with the people from the bus, as she had with Glendessary House's cast of characters and list of suspects.

Rick MacLyon. Vanessa MacLyon. Fiona Robertson. Neil Mac-Sorley. Toby Walsh. Kieran MacSorley. Who'd all been cozily drinking and—no, not necessarily conspiring, just talking over the situation. If that made you a criminal, thought Jean, she'd better turn herself in now.

She poured herself another cup of tea. Funny, she'd never drunk hot tea with milk and sugar in her former life. Now she craved it. She was going native. Swallowing the reviving brew, she considered the prime suspects.

Fiona, housekeeper and personal assistant, the quiet stiff-upper-lip sort. Who was better placed to have her finger on the pulse of the house? And if Cameron's reaction to her name was any indication, she was known to the police.

Rick MacLyon, presiding genius. He'd known Lovelace was in the game larder without Jean having told him. Vanessa MacLyon, nee MacDonald, trophy wife…. Well, even though she couldn't be past her late twenties, and Rick, according to his biography, was forty-three, still theirs could have been a love match, not a business arrangement.

Neil MacSorley, piper and resident hunk. He got credit for being attractive, but a debit for knowing it. Kieran MacSorley, local judge, who was known to Jean, at least, as no friend of Lovelace's. Toby Walsh, gentle giant. Not that body shape was any more indicative of disposition than cosmetic use was of intelligence.

As for who had had the opportunity to kill, Jean couldn't say, other than that the MacSorleys were otherwise engaged at the moment of death, and Rick or Fiona would have had to hustle to commit a murder while tending to the private party, as well as to Jean's tea. Where Toby and Vanessa had been at the time she had no idea.

The means now, the way the murder was done—that had to be significant. Even a civilian like Jean knew that murder by hanging was considerably less common than murder by poison or gunshot or knife. And such a silent murder, too. Just as she had narrowly missed seeing Lovelace in the driveway, she had narrowly missed seeing his murderer in the back hall. Missed seeing his murder, for that matter, and for that she was profoundly grateful. And yet she hadn't heard any raised voices or sounds of violence.

As for motive.... She stood up. Motive. Any murder was the means to an end. So what was the purpose of this one? To get revenge? To keep a secret? To eliminate a rival? She heard Cameron's voice saying, *Gold, there's a motive for you, one of the best.*

Jean paced up the stairs to her room. She sorted her clothes in the wardrobe by color. She arranged her potions and lotions on the glass shelf above the sink, first by size, then alphabetically.

Lovelace, she told herself, had survived bullets whizzing by his head, bird-watching along slippery precipices, the uneven steps of a turnpike stairs—traffic, pollution, all the hazards of modern life—only to die within twenty-four hours of meeting her. Of asking her for help, whether legitimately or not. She'd done what he asked, and he'd been murdered. The two events might be totally unrelated. They might be cause and effect.

Part of her mind said, *Don't get involved.* But the rest of her mind, her spirit, her soul, had to know whether her relationship, however brief, with George Lovelace had brought about his death. She had to have answers, no matter how disturbing they were, and that was that.

Jean opened her bag and pulled out Lovelace's card: *5 Beaton Terrace, Corpach.* All right then.

She went down the staircase considerably faster than she'd gone up. The air outside was cold, scented with that partly salt-fresh, partly seaweed-and-fish, odor of the sea. A seagull squawked overheard. She rescued her car from the parking lot and headed first north up the Great Glen, then west along the road to Mallaig, the Road to the Isles of song, story, and tourist brochure.

Past the uninspired box-buildings of Lochaber High School and over the Caledonian Canal at Banavie, and she was in the village of Corpach. She stopped at a shop to ask directions, and within minutes found herself on Beaton Terrace. Number 5, identified as Corncrake Cottage by a wooden plaque beside the front door, turned out to be half of a white-stuccoed duplex. A picture window looked out at Ben Nevis. A straggly herbaceous border spilled over a low stone fence, branches whipping in the wind.

Jean parked next to the gate and got out of the car. She'd

expected to see a constable standing on the front porch or blue and white police tape surrounding the house. But this house wasn't the crime scene, MacLyon's was. Not that it mattered. What she wanted was less Lovelace's house than Lovelace's neighbors. If she went back to the original "why"—why had Lovelace come to her with the coin—that might lead on to the larger whys. It wasn't as though she was going to interfere with the police investigation. She would simply parallel it.

The garden in front of the other half of the semi-detached house, as they called it here, was set out in apple-pie order. Every group of plants stood to attention and presented leaves and petals. The grassy areas, separated from the flower beds by furrows as straight as rulers, looked like billiard tables. The owner must manicure it with nail scissors…. Speaking of whom, a large shape was unsuccessfully concealed behind a rose bush. Jean called, "Hello?"

A man wearing a floppy hat and a windcheater jacket stood up, pruning shears in hand. He was about Lovelace's age, but rounder and softer, more at ease with gravity. Jean wasn't sure whether his plump cheeks and bulbous nose were red from the wind and the sun or from embarrassment—the former, probably, as he greeted her without a trace of shame. "Hullo yourself," he said in an avast-me-hearties voice. "Come to see poor George's place, have you? Not a reporter, I hope; had to see off a couple of those late last night. Like locusts, don't you know?"

Jean smiled back. "I'm Jean Fairbairn. And I am with *Great Scot* magazine, but Mr. Lovelace came to see me in Edinburgh two days ago…."

"Aye, that he did. 'Miss Fairbairn,' he said, 'she'll know about the—' You know. Thing." He tapped the side of his nose with his free hand, acknowledging the mutual secret. "Ronald Ogilvy here, George's neighbor and landlord. You heard, then. The bad news. Poor old sod."

"Ah—yes, I heard. I was at Glendessary House when the police arrived. I was supposed to interview Rick MacLyon. But mostly I came out here, to Fort William, to see Mr. Lovelace about the—er—thing. You knew about it?"

"He told me last week he'd made up his mind what to do with it. Then he told me Monday night he'd done it. No more than that.

George believed in keeping his business to himself, not like these modern tabloid tarts."

I noticed, Jean said to herself. Still, she was disappointed.

Ogilvy came about on another tack. "Bloody shame, fine chap like George getting himself mixed up with American nutters like MacLyon…. Ah, you're American yourself, are you?"

"Yes. But I agree with you about Rick MacLyon."

"The man's not shy of a bob or two, no doubt about it. Used to come and go in a helicopter 'til the machine went down in the loch—minor accident, everyone cold and wet is all—and he decided he'd best keep to the road. Well, if he wants to support the local economy, more power to him. George, though, I advised George to steer clear. MacLyon, what sort of name is that, I asked him? How can you trust a chap with a frivolous made-up name?"

Jean did not disagree. "Have you ever met him?"

"Once. MacLyon took on about my name, strange to say, something about a historical society. But George was the historian. I've quite enough to do here and now without spending time in the past."

A historical society, Jean repeated silently. The private party? And MacLyon did have a thing about names.

"Every so often I'd ask George," Ogilvy went on, "why he danced attendance on a nutter like MacLyon. All he'd say is that the man was his cross to bear, or one mustn't complain when it came to doing one's duty, or that fate worked in strange ways."

Fate. He'd shied when she'd used that word about his finding the coin. "Mr. Lovelace went out to Glendessary House often?"

"Oh aye. He was putting together a proper scholar's library for MacLyon. Spent a fair amount of time at Glendessary and in Inverness as well, looking out old books, letters, and the like. I reckon he was a wee bit uncomfortable taking a commission for his work, it being a labor of love and all that, but it's only proper, isn't it, to be paid for your work?"

"Yes, it is," Jean said, filing away that nugget of information to be appraised later.

"And George needed something to occupy his time after Annie died, I'll grant you that. Could only spend so much time plowtering about the hills watching birds, could he?"

"How long did Mr. Lovelace live here?"

"Fourteen years. Every night he'd sit at his desk in front of the window. Upstairs, on the right, that was his study—Mildred and I, we'd see the lamp shining. Like a lighthouse on a rocky coast it was, a beacon to the weary traveler and all." Ogilvy's face sagged, his shoulders slumped, and his lips quivered. He was probably thinking for the hundredth time that George Lovelace's beacon was now permanently extinguished.

Jean imagined the two elderly men having a wee dram and reminiscing about old times, Orpington, and a child who loved legends. Diplomatically she looked away, from the small upstairs window to the large picture window below. It reflected the houses opposite and the mountain now half-concealed by clouds.... Her eye darted upward again.

A shape moved in the smaller window. Was it a reflection of an airplane flying down the glen? She turned, looked, neither saw nor heard a plane, looked back. The window was a dark square reflecting nothing, inert. "Is someone in Mr. Lovelace's house?"

Ogilvy peered from beneath the brim of his hat like a badger. "Eh?"

"I thought I saw someone inside. Surely the police have...."

"Oh aye, a couple of constables and a detective named Sawyer—bit of a Saxon if you ask me, not half-chuffed with himself—came by late last night with George's keys. I asked for their identification; not going to stand by and let just anyone into the house, am I?" His red face darkened to purple and he threw down the shears. "A burglar, that's it, some yob heard that poor old George bought it and thought he'd help himself to his things. Wait here, I'll fetch the key, we'll see them off."

Jean opened and then shut her mouth. She wasn't sure she'd actually seen anyone. Even if she had, confronting burglars was hardly her specialty. At least she was reasonably sure she hadn't seen Lovelace's ghost. Ghosts were as likely to hang around places where they'd been happy in life as places where they'd been traumatized, but she hadn't felt a ghost, not here and now.

Ogilvy came bustling back, plunged through the shrubbery and over the fence, and bounded up the front steps. He stabbed a key into the lock and threw the door open. "Aha! Caught you, you filthy beggar!"

Jean heard a distant thud. Another door slamming? "He went out the back. You go through this way, I'll run around the side."

Without waiting to get Ogilvy's opinion, let alone have second thoughts, Jean sprinted around the house, through a gate, and past a metal shed into a garden surrounded by a six-foot-tall woven wood fence. The area was partly paved and partly planted, provided with two bird feeders and a fruit tree. No one was there except Ogilvy bursting out of the back door....

A trellis set against the fence was falling in silent slow motion, trailing morning glory tendrils. It had made a dandy ladder for an escaping burglar, but his—her?—weight had knocked it over.

Jean dragged a wooden bench over to the fence and clambered up on it. She could see only a dozen yards up the hillside, past a tumble of bracken to a wall first of rhododendron and then trees Their leaves were waving as though someone had just pushed through them. Or else they were simply waving in the wind.

She looked left, past the other houses on Beaton Terrace. Nothing. She looked right, to where a perpendicular street dead-ended on the other side of Ogilvy's house. A couple of boys stood there, preparing some feat of derring-do with a skateboard.

"One of them, I reckon," Ogilvy wheezed as he hoisted himself up beside her. "Hello there, my lads! What do you think you're playing at?"

Jean winced at the decibels. But he'd gotten the boys' attention. One of them made his way closer. Before Ogilvy could make any accusations Jean asked, "Did you see anyone climb over the fence here and run away?"

The boy shrugged. "Always people out and about, didn't see anyone in particular. You been done over?"

"We don't know yet. Thanks." Jean got down from the bench, offered her hand to Ogilvy, then quickly snatched it back before he took the offer of help as an insult.

He regained terra firma without tumbling onto his face. "Good idea, treat the lads with honey instead of vinegar, eh? Maybe one of them will grass up the villain."

"If it was one of them." An ordinary burglar or hooligan could have been taking advantage of an empty house. Still, if someone had been sufficiently motivated to kill Lovelace, breaking into his house wouldn't be much of a stretch. The question, again, was why?

"I'll be keeping a weather eye out in the future, no doubt about it." Ogilvy led the way to the back door. "Look here, the pane of glass closest to the handle was bashed in. Simplicity itself."

"Unfortunately, yes. Would you be able to tell if anything was stolen?"

"Depends, doesn't it? The telly, yes. Small items, no. Let's have a recce." Ogilvy walked into the house, his feet crunching over broken glass.

If opportunity knocks, Jean told herself, answer. She followed Ogilvy into a small kitchen scented with sausage and laundry detergent. A few dirty dishes were stacked in the sink and a newspaper lay open on the table, but the room was tidy. Except that every drawer and cabinet door gaped open.

Muttering words that men of his generation didn't say in front of a woman, Ogilvy led the way through the rest of the house. Every cabinet, every closet, every drawer had been opened. And yet a silver tea service gleamed atop the sideboard in the dining room and several ordinary British coins lay on a table by the front door.

Hard to believe Lovelace would have left all the doors and drawers open. "Did the police leave everything like this?" Jean asked from the doorway of the study.

Ogilvy shook his head. "No. They left it all ship-shape and Bristol fashion, I made sure of that before I let them go, even though they wouldn't have me in the house as they searched."

"Were they looking for anything in particular?"

"Clues, I expect."

"Well, yeah," Jean conceded. "Did they take anything away with them?"

"Not that I saw. I'd have asked for a receipt."

"You should call them now, Mr. Ogilvy, tell them about the break-in."

"So I shall. Half a sec." He bustled away down the stairs.

A card-carrying biblioholic, Jean wasn't about to leave without inspecting the shelves lining the study. Her academic credentials gave her an excuse to poke around, didn't they? Even if they didn't, this was no time to be shy.

The shelves were filled with history books focusing on the eighteenth century, plus genealogy tracts and classic novels—no surprise there. The open doors of a cabinet revealed more books, a variety of office supplies, several photo albums, and a stack of blank paper. Beside that sat a shoe box, the lid askew. Jean peeked inside.

A muddy green beret, perfumed with the leather odor of the box, was squashed into one end. Lovelace's commando beret? Below that five medals were jumbled loosely together, their bright-colored ribbons faded. Her father, Jean remembered, had mounted his three Korean War service medals in a frame and displayed them proudly in the living room. Historian or not, Lovelace had been less than enthralled with his own past.

She put the lid back on the box the way she'd found it and inspected the photos arranged on the walls. Among them hung a faded studio shot of a woman in the poufed and rolled hair of the forties. The same woman appeared in several other pictures, some with a similarly aging George, some alone.

Through another set of photos Jean traced the life of a younger woman, from infancy through her wedding to family groups including two children, who were in their teens in the photo that stood on Lovelace's desk. Its frame was Mackintosh-design silver—something else the intruder didn't steal.

The intruder might have been here for hours, with no need to do anything so gauche as throw everything into a pile on the floor. Even so, Jean and Ogilvy might have driven him away before he'd found what he was looking for. Assuming he was looking for anything in particular, that the entire search hadn't been a fishing expedition—although, Jean told herself, a fisherman expected to turn up fish.

She glanced into the desk drawers, but didn't see anything out of the ordinary. Her own weren't much tidier, filled with pens, pencils, file folders, receipts—all the odds and ends that clung to her like lint despite her new life.

The well-thumbed booklet of a metal detector lay on the window sill, beneath a shortbread tin emblazoned with a portrait of a supercilious Bonnie Prince Charlie. So Lovelace deliberately searched for artifacts, then. Nothing wrong with that, he knew the rules. He knew the rules very well indeed—that was part of the problem. It was probably part of the solution, but darned if she could see how.

Did he keep his prizes in the tin? Jean didn't expect to find a box full of gold Louis d'Ors, but still she lifted the lid. Nope, just metal odds and ends, some rusted, some cleaned: buttons, an old key, what looked like bits of a bridle, an ornamental hinge.

She replaced the lid thinking that the room was exactly what she'd expect from a retired professor who valued paper as highly as gold. Nothing was labeled *clue*. Tempting as it was to open up every folder and box looking for, say, a treasure map, Jean recognized wishful thinking and kept her hands to herself.

She glanced again at the photos. The daughter was now an orphan. The children had lost a grandfather. And they had to cope not just with Lovelace's death, but with its shocking manner. Would pinning the crime on its perpetrator bring any comfort to them? In Jean's opinion, the pop concept of closure was much too cheap and easy.

She went back downstairs to find Ogilvy hanging up the phone. "P.C. Walker's on his way. He's a level-headed chap, was here last night with the Saxon. Couldn't get a word in edgeways, though."

Jean pointed up the stairs. "The directions to a metal detector are lying on the window sill. Is that how Mr. Lovelace found the coin?"

"I have no idea. He showed me bits and pieces of things he turned up, but never that. He wasn't all that keen a detectorist, if you ask me, just kept the machine in the boot of his car in the event the birds weren't putting on a proper show."

"His car. I saw it parked in a layby just past the gates of Glendessary House."

"The Saxon said they'd found it there, aye."

The car's being there was no more a coincidence than her being there, Jean thought. She walked into the living room. The paneled walls surrounding the picture window were decorated with Audubon prints and landscape photos. Two china dogs sat on the mantelpiece. A television occupied a corner in front of some bookshelves, which held more history books, several years' worth of digest-sized *Great Scot*'s, and an assortment of guidebooks and maps.

An elderly photo album lay on the coffee table. Jean opened it. Ah, photos from World War II, beginning with a group of soldiers lined up in front of—yes, that was Glendessary House, looking like the "before" photo in a home improvement ad. It had been in fairly bad shape even before the fire.

The next page of the album held more black and white photos, this time of soldiers and tanks and Greco-Roman ruins. There was Lovelace, his face fresh and clean with the years pared away, looking about sixteen. Looking alive…. Jean stifled the image that rose into her mind. "He served in the Italian campaign?"

"Aye, that he did. Decorated for bravery, I understand, but he almost never talked about the war. Some chaps down at the British Legion will go on as though they've had no life since, but not George. A tragic time, was all he'd say. Too many losses. If he talked about the past at all, he talked about his childhood; very nostalgic about that, he was."

No kidding. "Did you and Mr. Lovelace meet during the war?"

"Oh no, no, we didn't meet until he let this house. Fourteen years," Ogilvy said sadly. "Happy days, happy days. I just wish…."

Jean completed his thought, since it was so similar to her own. "You wish you could help find his killer? I'd like to help, too."

"I told the police what I know, but that's precious little. Saw George drive away about one. Then a silver MG pulled up to the curb, oh, it was just past two, I'm thinking. I've seen it there before, belongs to that MacSorley chap who sold Glendessary House to MacLyon to begin with—have to answer for that, won't he?" Ogilvy tried to chuckle, but the sound came out as more of a *tsk, tsk*.

"Kieran MacSorley owned Glendessary House?"

"The ruins of it, yes, been in the family for donkey's years, or so he says."

"And Kieran was here yesterday afternoon just past two?"

"No, it was Charlotte, his wife, who chapped at George's door and then went away looking like she was sucking sour plums."

"I see," Jean said, although all she saw was another name being added to the cast of characters. Charlotte MacSorley must be the driver who'd almost run Jean off the road in her hurry to get here…. Well no, she might always drive like a bat out of hell. She must have handed the car over to Kieran right after she left Corpach, apparently in some disgust at Lovelace's absence. Why?

That word was starting to resemble one of those little yapping dogs, *why yi yi yi*. She asked cautiously, "Was Mr. Lovelace a friend of the MacSorleys?"

"Said once he was in the army with Kieran's dad is all. Don't think they were friends, no, not so much as they simply had something in common."

"Was it MacSorley who introduced him to MacLyon?"

"That was the way of it, aye. Have to answer to that as well."

Jean closed the photo album thoughtfully. In her childhood she'd thought World War II was fought in black and white. To commandos like Lovelace crawling through the heather in a darkness as much metaphor as real, the world really had been sketched in shades of gray. But then, all wars were fought in shades of gray, Charlie's war, World War II, that Technicolor disaster of Jean's older siblings' generation, Vietnam. The question was—wait for it—why? If Lovelace didn't want to dwell on the war, why did he keep the album out on the coffee table?

Feeling as though her brain were being pummeled, Jean glanced out the window and saw a police car pull up in front of the house. By the time Ogilvy ushered her through the tiny vestibule and onto the front step, a constable was coming up the walk. He nodded to Ogilvy and turned an inquisitive look on Jean. "Jean Fairbairn," Ogilvy explained. "She's a friend of George's, was working with him on an article for her magazine. Miss Fairbairn, P.C. Walker."

"Good to meet you," said the young man. "What's all this, a burglar, you say, Mr. Ogilvy?"

Jean glanced at her watch. She had just enough time to check with base camp in Edinburgh before her interview at the police station. "I need to be going," she told Ogilvy. "May I come back and talk to you again sometime?"

"Please," Ogilvy said. "Come for tea, no one makes a finer Dundee cake than Mildred."

"Thank you." Jean went out to her car, and with a last searching glance at the open but uncommunicative door of the house, drove away.

So someone, presumably the murderer, wanted something Lovelace had. The coin? Some other symbolic loaded gun? Had they found it? Jean looked toward the humped peak of Ben Nevis, now concealed by charcoal-colored cloud. The same cloud was thickening overhead, blotting out the sunlight and the colors of the landscape.

Yeah, she thought, the plot is thickening. She could feel it coagulating in her stomach right along with the bacon fat from her breakfast. But she wasn't going to be making jokes, no matter how mordant, to D.C.I. Cameron.

TEN

JEAN LIKED Fort William's unpretentious, down-home main drag, the shops and restaurants lining its pedestrian mall intended as much for locals in search of laundry detergent as tourists looking for hiking and climbing gear. And souvenirs. One shop window displayed throbbing-tenor versions of Neil's twee old songs alongside contemporary-traditional fusion music like Hugh's. Another was stacked with candy, cakes, and shortbread in red tartan tins like the one on Lovelace's window sill.

Some of the tins were decorated with the famous Victorian painting of Charlie bowing over a simpering Flora MacDonald's hand, good myth making good business. There were no tins with pictures of Jenny Cameron, neither her truth nor her myth as appealing as Flora's traditional female role—although, like Jean herself, Rick MacLyon was obviously a fan.

She scurried into the hotel, up the stairs, and into her room. Telling herself that Hugh should be up and about by this time, she plumped down on the bed and punched his number into her phone. Surely today she wouldn't be the first off the mark with the bad news.

"Hello!"

"Hugh, it's Jean. Have you heard what happened out here?"

"Oh aye, that I have, the poor old man done to death in the American billionaire's castle."

"That poor old man is the military man from Orpington, George Lovelace. The one I mentioned the other night. He came to my office Monday. Yesterday I found his body."

Hugh made a sound that was both sickened and sympathetic. "Well now, that's a turn-up. Is that why I've got a message from the police on my machine?"

"Yeah, I'm afraid they're checking up on me. And what you told me about the Hogmanay party and Lovelace arguing with Mac-Sorley and all of that. At least I'm assuming Lovelace was arguing with a guy named Kieran MacSorley."

"Looks like he's wearing a fake plastic nose and moustache, does he? Scornful voice, sharp elbows?"

"That's him. Did you hear what he and Lovelace were saying?"

"No, they were hissing like snakes, not wanting anyone to overhear but not willing to concede the point, either. All I heard was the military chap saying, 'That's not the way of it at all.' Then the MacLyon lassie, Vanessa, got between them. Right keen on hushing them up, she was, like she was scairt they'd say something they shouldn't."

"Did you hear anything *she* said?"

"Oh aye, that I did. She couldn't be bothered to lower her voice, but then, there'd been drink a-plenty, and she wasn't half pissed."

"Pissed drunk, like you'd say, or pissed angry, like we'd say?"

"Both. She was saying, 'It's bad enough out here in the boonies without you two butting heads all the time,' when that red-haired housekeeper cut her off short. Lovelace walked away like a kicked dog, head hanging. MacSorley, though, he ponced off as though the stramach was all Lovelace's fault."

"Hmmm. So Mrs. MacLyon has issues with her location." Jean filed that away.

"Is MacSorley a suspect in the murder, then?"

"No, he wasn't at the house when Lovelace was killed. A group of people was, though. They were all done up in kilts and plaids and—now that I think about it, some of them were wearing Prince Charlie's white ribbon rose. The white cockade of the Jacobites."

"Ah, the Bonnie Prince," said Hugh. "We've got some fine music from the Forty-five, but music doesn't justify suffering. Charlie was just one more aristocrat never realizing that respect is what you earn, not what you're owed. Tells you something about the Scottish psyche that we'd make a hero out of a git like Charles Edward Stuart."

Jean smiled. This wasn't the first time she'd heard Hugh fulminating about what Cameron called charlieoverthewaterism. "If he'd won you'd be—excuse the pun—singing a different tune."

Ignoring Hugh's groan, she went on, "You said there was a group of serious-faced people at the Hogmanay party."

"Oh aye, a dozen or so all kitted out in one version or another of Highland dress. Same group, you're thinking?"

"I hear MacLyon runs a historical society."

"Looks to be an admiration and bootlicking society," said Hugh. "Mind you, he was showing them a good time in return."

"MacLyon's piper was playing for the group yesterday. He's MacSorley too—did you meet him at Hogmanay?"

"No, no one was piping other than our Billy."

"Maybe Neil was too intimidated to get up in front of y'all, although I thought he sounded pretty good. Who else was at the party? The housekeeper?"

"A bit of class she was, too, tall, red hair, odd look to her eye. Robinson? Is that her name?"

"Robertson," said Jean.

"And the personal assistant, sweet young thing but a bit scatter-brained, the sort that goes about leaving a trail of scarves and hair-clips and, come to that, broken hearts."

"A personal assistant? No one mentioned her. Fiona Robertson's doing that job now. You remember the girl's name?"

"Meg-something?" Hugh asked, and with a chuckle went on, "Jean, it's not you needing to ask all these questions. It's a police matter, although I suppose it's no good telling you so."

"No, it's not, not when George Lovelace was murdered within twenty-four hours of asking me to help him out." Jean couldn't keep the edge out of the voice, but then, with Hugh she didn't need to.

He made another sympathetic noise. "Good luck to you, then. Oh, and wee Dougie's getting on well, not to worry."

"Thank you, Hugh. Dougie's welfare is the only thing I'm *not* worried about. If you can think of anything else, please let me know. Well, the police and me."

"That I'll do. Cheers."

Hugh's "Cheers" was more reassuring than Neil's. Not that Neil had sounded particularly cheerful. The word had been a default mechanism. Jean got her notebook from her bag—sometimes plain old pencil and paper worked just fine—and jotted down what

Hugh had said about the commemorative group and Meg-somebody. She was gathering evidence, right? She wasn't just creating busywork to soothe both her conscience and her curiosity.

She punched in *Great Scot*'s number and found Miranda her usual chipper self. "So you've not been chucked into pokey, then. Should I be phoning our lawyer?"

"Not yet. If they arrest me, yeah, you can phone the lawyer, but I really can't see things going that far. I was even on the side of the good guys this morning, almost caught a burglar at Lovelace's house. Which gave me a chance to look around inside."

"And?"

"No enemies' list lying out on his desk, sad to say. Unless that's what the burglar was after. What have you found out about Lovelace?"

Papers rustled. "The usual: name, rank, serial number. Distinguished military record. Tenure at the University of Leicester. Wife died almost two years ago. There's a daughter lives in Derby with her family."

"Not much there."

"Nothing he told you about himself was a lie, if that's any comfort."

Jean emitted a hollow laugh. "It's what he didn't tell me about himself that's got me going. That's the key to his murder. He had a metal detector, so he may not have found the coin accidentally, but does that matter? He didn't tell me he was working for MacLyon, but why should he? The only inconsistency is him already knowing about treasure trove. If I could find any other ones...." Cameron's cool voice said in the back of her mind, *Inconsistencies can be very helpful when investigating a suspicious death.*

"A fine, braw lad he was," Miranda said, meaning Lovelace, not Cameron, "to survive commando training. That was no piece of cake. Forty-five men killed by friendly fire. There's an oxymoron for you."

Some ill omen must be attached to the number forty-five. "He told me they used live rounds. What a horror story for the folks at home, your guy getting shot down by his own side. And poor old Lovelace survives all of that only to be murdered."

"Not fair, not a bit of it. But then, what is?"

"Oh, every now and then the wheels of fate churn out a grain of poetic justice, since the regular kind is so hard to come by." And if I don't really believe that, Jean told herself, then I should. "What about Lovelace's time at Leicester?"

"A second-rank figure, I gather, but respected within his own field, quite the expert on eighteenth-century books and the like."

"That's what he was doing for MacLyon, putting together a library—of eighteenth-century books, I assume, MacLyon being nuts over Charlie."

"Now you're wanting me to suss out the facts on MacLyon himself, is that it?" Miranda asked.

I never have to explain to Miranda, Jean thought. *She can be trusted.* "You got it. Rick and Vanessa MacLyon, and a guy named Kieran MacSorley, a local judge and the man who sold Glendessary house to MacLyon to begin with, and his wife Charlotte."

"MacSorley. Rings a bell. I'm seeing one of those old landowning dinosaurs. Looks like one as well, does he?"

"Like a velociraptor," agreed Jean. "Snout, beady eyes, the works."

"The wife's the sort goes about with her nostrils dilated, as though she's smelling something a bit off. There's a son, I'm thinking…."

"Neil. Looks like a movie star."

"A treat for your weary eyes, then."

Jean wasn't going to touch that one. "Also, MacLyon's got some hired muscle named Toby Walsh."

"Walsh. Doesn't sound the sort I'll be finding in the society pages, not like the others. I'll have Gavin do a public records search."

"And MacLyon had a personal assistant at New Year's, Meg something."

"Ah, that one is by way of the society pages. Meg Parkinson-Fraser, daughter of the Parkinson-Frasers of Morningside and Ibiza. A P. G. Wodehouse heroine with a trendy, serrated edge. Vanessa hired her, fancied having another debutante about, I'm thinking, but no go."

"What happened?"

"She sold a story to *The Sunburn.* Squire MacLyon sacked her so fast she didn't hit the ground 'til she reached Inverness."

"That's what I get for not reading the tabloids," said Jean. "Find the article for me, will you?"

"No article, sorry. MacLyon must have paid good baksheesh to have it killed. I'll ring Derek at *The Sunburn,* see what he knows about it."

"So what would MacLyon want killed…." Jean heard what she was saying. Maybe the days a wealthy man could have someone killed weren't as far in the past as they should be, although she had no evidence Rick was guilty of parking illegally, let alone ordering a murder. "Vanessa was a debutante?"

"Oh aye, and old money to boot. At least, as old as it gets in the U S of A: railroads, drugs, something solid, not like MacLyon's dot-com money. She's a graduate of some posh girl's school in New England—it's never Wembley… ."

"Wellesley, I'll bet." Jean jotted that down. "And do you know about some historical society of MacLyon's, people going around draped with tartan and paying court to him?"

Miranda stage-whispered, "Ah well, that would be the Jacobite Lodge. All very exclusive, not to mention hush-hush. Makes the Queen's Garden Party look to be an open house." She added in her usual voice, "We already knew MacLyon was a bit of a nutter; he can play at secret societies if he wants."

"The Jacobite Lodge?" Jean repeated. "Why am I not surprised?"

"I hear tell you can't join up unless you've got a name dating back to the Forty-five, which lets me out, certainly. Not that I'm keen on joining; they sit about debating battle tactics and tartan patterns, I expect."

"Sounds like our DAR. Daughters of the American Revolution, where you have to prove you have an ancestor who fought in the war. Like you're responsible for your ancestors. I've always wondered whether the DAR would take someone descended from Burgoyne or Howe or Cornwallis—the bad guys, from our point of view."

"Ah, but the DAR's not after keeping itself a secret."

"MacLyon's Lodge can't be all that secret a society if you know… ." Jean interrupted herself. "I take that back. You know everything."

Miranda didn't argue. "We had a police detective this morning," she went on, making it sound like taking a pill. "I gave you a good enough reference to be going on with."

"You want me to go on? You're not going to warn me about interfering with the police?"

"You're not interfering. You're a journalist, serving the public's right to know. You've a legitimate interest in the case."

"Oh yes," Jean told her gratefully. "See what you can do with that list of names, would you?"

"All the dirt, served up on a silver salver," said Miranda. "And Jean, have a care."

That might be a tall order, considering how she'd just chased after a burglar. But the devil drives when needs must, or however the saying went. Jean said simply, "Yes, ma'am. Thanks." Switching off her phone, she scribbled a few more notes and wondered if Cameron, with all the might of the constabulary at his back, had such good sources.

Raindrops spattered against the window. Yep, she thought, rain. That's what it did in Scotland, it rained. And when it stopped raining, its beauty alone would break your heart—never mind love, death, and nostalgia.

She was picking up her phone again when she heard steps coming down the corridor. Nothing strange in that. She was in a hotel. But these steps were uncertain, stopping, starting again, and this time stopping just outside her door. She braced herself. A police escort? A particularly enterprising reporter?

No one knocked. The footsteps walked away again, heavily but also quickly. Jean catapulted off the bed, ran across to the door, and opened it a crack. She caught a glimpse of a man rounding the corner at the end of the hall. A very large man, dressed in army boots, canvas pants, and a waterproof jacket. Toby? What had he wanted with her? And, equally important, why had he changed his mind and walked on?

Telling herself that this was interesting, not intimidating, she made sure her door was locked and placed her third and last call.

"Michael Campbell-Reid."

"Hey, Michael, it's Jean Fairbairn."

"Well now, should I be owning up to knowing you? We've had the police."

"Yeah, it's going around, like the measles. They were checking up on me and the coin, right?"

"Got it in one. Bad luck about Lovelace. And about you finding him, as well."

"Never underestimate the power of luck, both bad and good," Jean said with feeling. "Where's the coin now?"

"Under analysis. With the police interested and the murder and all, it's gone to the head of the queue."

"No surprise there."

"Ah, but there is a surprise. Our pollen expert had a go first thing, says so far she's found heather, birch—the sorts of pollen you'd expect. Thing is...." Michael paused for effect, "...she also turned up a grain of *citrus limon* and two of *olea europaea*. Known when they're at home as lemon and olive. Not exactly important products of Scotland."

"What?" Jean felt like she'd just taken a swift uppercut to the brain. "On the Louis d'Or?"

"Oh aye, just there."

Her brain, still reeling, seized on an explanation. "Lemon and olive. Lovelace was in Sicily and Italy during the war. There's an old shoe box in his house holding his commando beret. Maybe he put the coin in there and it picked up some pollen. Would that work? Or how about that little white box?"

"The beret's a possibility, aye. So's the box."

Jean considered hitting herself in the head with the phone, but that wouldn't cancel out all the assumptions she'd made about Lovelace's story. He hadn't actually told her he'd found the coin in the Western Highlands, although he'd come damn close with his manifesto about gold rushes and frightened sheep. He hadn't told her *when* he'd found it, either. He could have picked it up during his commando training and carried it with him as a good luck token. He could even have bought it in Italy. Charlie spent most of his misspent life in Italy. What if the coin had nothing to do with Charlie at all? But no, he was there, no matter how faintly, like the ghost in Glendessary House's sitting room.

That problem would have to go on a long list labeled, "Not enough evidence yet." And the "yet" was optimistic. She wasn't even sure she'd just come up with another inconsistency. "One more question, Michael."

"Questions are my specialty. Answers are another matter."

"Right now you have more answers than I do," Jean returned. "Rick MacLyon has what looks like the original of that from-life drawing of Jenny Cameron."

"The only from-life drawing extant? The one made in Edinburgh whilst Charles was holding court at Holyrood?"

"Yes, that one. What's its provenance? Is Rick's the original?"

"Aye, that it is. The drawing belonged to some Jacobite family 'til the late eighteen hundreds, when they gave it to Aberdeen University. MacLyon bought it off them last year. Or rather, he endowed a scholarship at Aberdeen and the University gave him the picture in gratitude."

"In other words, he bought it," said Jean. "He does have a thing for Jenny Cameron. For Clan Cameron, I guess, judging by his reaction to Detective Chief Inspector Cameron, Northern Constabulary."

"Oh aye, the officer in charge. Heard his name once already, was told to phone him if I learned anything important to the investigation. Assuming I'd recognize something important to the investigation."

"I can tell you didn't talk to Cameron yourself; he'd have told you to tell him everything, up to and including olive and lemon pollen, and let him decide whether it was important. You'd better keep in touch with both of us…." That made it sound as though she and Cameron were a team. Jean made a face. She was a free agent, thank you very much. "I appreciate it, Michael."

"No problem," he returned. "Have a care."

Funny…. No, it wasn't funny how everyone was telling her to be careful. No matter how much she felt like the victim of a practical joke, this was not a comedy.

The display on her phone, to say nothing of the bedside clock, showed time moving inexorably toward her appointment with the police. With Alasdair Cameron. For a long moment she sat slumped, feeling too heavy to move. This shouldn't be happening….

It was happening. Time to get up and deal with it.

ELEVEN

JEAN'S SKIRT billowed in the raw wind that blustered off the loch and up the street, the sort of wind that blew ships either across finish lines or onto rocks. Fortunately the rain squall had passed. If she opened her umbrella she'd do a Mary Poppins imitation, not that she'd ever identified with Mary Poppins. She preferred taking her medicine straight.

Seagulls looked like bits of white confetti against the deep blue-gray of the clouds. Their harsh cries echoed among the chimneys. Very few people were out and about, except for the cluster of bodies outside the police station. Even from Cameron Square, several blocks away, Jean counted two mini-cams and three microphones. Speaking of medicine... .

"Jean!"

She spun around. Neil MacSorley was walking toward her, hair blowing photogenically. Today he was dressed in civilian clothes: jeans, sweater, and coat. Instead of bagpipes, he carried a furled umbrella beneath his arm.

Well, well, Jean thought, we don't have Venus rising from the waves of Loch Linnhe, we have Adonis. She stepped out of the wind, closer to the weathered red stone wall of the West Highland Museum, and called, "Hi! Doing some shopping?"

Neil stopped just inside her personal space, less than an arm's length away. "I'm needing a roll of tape for my pipes—electrical tape, works a treat—so aye, I'm at the shops. But mostly I'm here being grilled by the police. You as well, eh?"

"My appointment's at two."

"Well then, I've been and gone already and lived to tell the tale. Not that I had a tale to tell. There I was playing the moldy oldies, as per Rick's orders, and Toby steps out and says, you'd better close it down, we've got a dead man in the house. At first I thought he meant one of the visitors had fallen over into his tea, but no." Neil's face went slightly lopsided, a grimace fighting with a smile. "You've nothing better to tell the police, I'm thinking."

"Not a thing," Jean answered, and wondered if all MacLyon's employees called him by his first name. Nothing like democracy in action.

"But you're feeling better the day? Not so peelie-wally as last night?"

I looked sickly? No kidding. "Better, yes. Cured, no. Not until all this is—is worked out."

Neil nodded sagely. "Knew George well, did you?"

"I didn't know him at all. He came by my office Monday…" Jean wondered whether Neil knew about the coin, and decided to err on the side of discretion. "…to say he enjoyed the article I wrote about Bonnie Prince Charlie."

"A long way to go to pay a compliment."

"He said something about the new Museum, too. I wrote an article about it when I first got here in January." Now she was misleading Neil the way Lovelace had misled her, by inference. That was the problem with half-truths, they spread faster than outright lies, like a plague. But unlike outright lies, they were hard to disprove.

"You didn't come out to Glendessary to meet up with George, then?"

"Oh no. My editor sent me to interview Rick. I was shocked and horrified to find George—there," she concluded lamely, and looked down at the water stains on the toes of her sensible shoes.

Neil touched her shoulder, drawing her gaze up to his face, not that that was an unpleasant place for it to rest. "What a scunner, catching yourself up in your own story. A reporter's worst nightmare, eh?"

"I'm not a reporter like that mob in front of the police station. I do history and human-interest stuff, not headline news."

"George gave me your article about Hugh Munro, him being a fellow musician and all. Although comparing me to Hugh's comparing dog food to steak."

"Not necessarily. The pipes are just about the one instrument Hugh doesn't play."

"But he has Billy Skelton, hasn't he? And Dougie Pincock's played with him as well, though I'll never make as fine a piper as Dougie."

"A piper's reach needs to exceed his grasp." Jean realized she was straining upward, shoulders back, chin up, watching Neil's lips and tongue shape each word like a starving man might watch someone eating. She eased back down, hoping he'd think she simply had good posture. "Do you play with a band?"

"I play with Gallowglass from time to time."

"They're good," Jean temporized, having at least heard of the group.

"I missed out Hugh at Rick's Hogmanay Party, more's the pity. I was playing with Gallowglass in Dundee the night. I played with them at the Edinburgh Festival Fringe last year as well, a bit of piping, a bit of tech work behind the scenes. They were after asking me to join up, but one of the older chaps was jealous, talked them out of it."

Neil took a step closer, his height sheltering her from the chill eddies of the wind. Today he didn't smell of whiskey but of a thankfully mild aftershave. His smile wasn't the broad, dazzling smile of yesterday but a more subtle, intimate version, implying he didn't waste this particular smile on just anyone....

Oh. Mentally Jean slapped her forehead. He was responding to her hormone rush, coming on to her. Wasn't he? Was she so out of practice she was mistaking friendliness for romantic—okay, sexual—interest? With her skirt fluttering in the wind she'd probably evoked the famous image of Marilyn Monroe standing on the subway grating. She knew she had good legs. As Ben Franklin said, a woman's decay started at the top and worked its way down.... *Decay?* she asked herself. *Get a grip.*

Maybe Neil wanted her to introduce him to Hugh. If so, he was up-front about it, mentioning the article that George Lovelace, her fan, had showed him. She had to applaud his honesty. And she wasn't going to boo his flirting. She remembered flirting, generating a little superficial friction with an attractive man. Nothing wrong with it, even now.

Especially now, said the cynical part of her mind, when this attractive man was a member of the MacLyon household.

Drawing herself up again, even as she dropped her lashes—flirting was like riding a bicycle, a body-memory—Jean formulated a question about the same household dynamics she been too numb to care about yesterday. And was cut off by a female voice like a police siren. "There you are!"

Neil took an abrupt step back. "It's my mum. Don't let on you're a reporter. Hates the species, she does."

Contracting, Jean looked around to see the Queen bearing down on them.... No, the woman in the coat and scarf was taller and lankier than petite Elizabeth. Her face was similar, though, every curve and sag congealed by propriety. What Jean could see of her hair was swept into a permed and sprayed helmet.

"Charlotte MacSorley," the woman announced. "Mrs. Kieran MacSorley. Bonnie Brae Cottage, Bunarkaig."

"Jean Fairbairn. I work with Miranda Capaldi at *Great Scot* magazine in Edinburgh."

Charlotte thawed abruptly. "Ah, Miranda! Lovely girl, lovely. Good friend of ours."

So social class trumped shady profession. Jean hid her smile. Funny though, how their good friend Miranda had barely heard of the MacSorleys.

"This is all so dreadfully tiresome," Charlotte went on. "Having to talk to the police as though we were common criminals. And those reporters! Like a pack of wolves waiting to rend one limb from limb on the doorstep."

"It's difficult," said Jean neutrally.

Neil added, "A bit harder on George than on us, Mum."

Amen, Jean thought, and glanced gratefully up at the young man's sober face.

"Well now, George worked for Rick, didn't he?" asked Charlotte. "Not that he wasn't a perfectly pleasant old gentleman, for an English academic."

The *he was a credit to his race* was implicit in Charlotte's tone. Her accent was the same as Kieran's, the "proper English" pronunciation drilled into hinterlanders of their generation, so that they sounded as though they had toffee stuck to the roofs of their mouths.

Neil's accent was thicker, but then, he was at the age that avoided conformity at all costs. "Jean's on her way to the police station as well."

"Oh, bad luck," said Charlotte. "That common little fellow, Sawyer, trying to contradict one's every word. Asked me again and again where I was when poor old George died, as though I couldn't be trusted when I told him I'd been going about my errands and had barely walked in the door of my own house when Fiona rang with the dreadful news."

Jean wondered if Charlotte had told Sawyer about stopping by Lovelace's house in Corpach, and if she had, what her story was.

"Kieran went up to Glendessary House straightaway, barely had time for a wash and a brush-up. Mind you, Rick depends on Kieran. He needed his level head to sort the matter, especially with all the visitors. Bad timing, that, but there you are, we can't arrange things to suit ourselves, can we?"

She was not talking about arranging murders, Jean assumed.

"Mind you, it's Rick's house. He can entertain as he wishes. Naturally he's wanting his wife to serve as hostess, but…." Charlotte let the implication flutter away.

"She'll learn," said Neil, a grin permeating his sobriety.

"Rick and Vanessa mean well, of course. One can hardly choose one's parents. If one is raised in an inferior culture, one that sets an excessive value on blunt speech, well then. One can only try to assist, even if one's efforts aren't always appreciated." Charlotte's lips shriveled into a slit.

So what had happened to send Charlotte off down the road as though the hounds of hell were barking up her tailpipe? Had she been "helping" Vanessa set up for the party until Vanessa reminded her which of them was the actual mistress of the house? Why would that mean an urgent visit to Lovelace's house? "Perhaps we passed on the r…" Jean began.

But Neil was already speaking. "We'd better be away, Mum, I'm needing the tape for my pipes, and Toby will have your car serviced by now."

Ah, so Toby was in town!

"It's marvelously fulfilling to have a talented child," Charlotte confided to Jean. "Neil makes a good fist of everything he turns his hand to, don't you, dear? He's overcome so many obstacles. Does his mummy proud."

Neil looked up the street with an expression of long-suffering patience. This time it was Jean who hid a grin, wondering if his flirting was a way of emphasizing his manhood.

"It's been a pleasure to meet you, Miss Fairbairn," Charlotte went on. "Would you care to stop by Bonnie Brae Cottage for tea tomorrow afternoon? Half-past three, shall we say?"

"Oh. Ah, thank you, I'd enjoy that," said Jean. Far be it from her to turn down a chance to interview another witness. Or listen to one, as the case may be.

"I'm sure we have many mutual friends in Edinburgh," Charlotte said, stopping just short of concluding, of the better sort.

"Thank you. I'll see you tomorrow, then. Neil…."

"Oh aye, see you soon," he returned, with a flicker of one set of long lashes that might have been a wink.

Neil and Charlotte walked away past the Tourist Information Office. Her coat fluttered, exposing the pattern of her tartan skirt—more MacLyon. His attitude toward her was just solicitous enough to be mocking. The dynamics of Glendessary House, Jean thought, would have been fascinating even without the sub-text of murder and madness.

Gritting her teeth and lowering her head, she plunged on down the street and through the reporters corralled in the parking lot in front of the police station: "Excuse me, sorry, beg your pardon…." At least one of them called her by name. *Great.*

Unlike Jenny Cameron, she wasn't known by only one pen and ink drawing. Her scandal hadn't been invented as propaganda. How much longer before the reporters got hold of it?

TWELVE

JEAN AT LAST escaped the police station, only to find that the wind had slackened and rain was pouring down. The reporters had probably gone to ground in the coffee bar down the street. She scurried past its plate glass window, hiding behind her umbrella.

Now she had another statement on file with the police: signed, sealed, and this time recorded. She'd steeled herself to face Cameron, but he hadn't appeared. It was Sawyer who'd goaded her through yesterday's events. While Cameron had at least covered his hostility with courtesy, Sawyer seemed determined to find cracks in her testimony even if it was his hammering that put them there. Every third sentence he'd broken in with a caustic remark that, if not quite accusing her of murder, found her guilty of stupidity. By the time D.C. Gunn had at last taken her fingerprints, Jean would gladly have offered Sawyer her entire middle finger.

When she told him what she'd learned, from burglars to pollen, he'd said brusquely, "We're quite capable of doing our own research. You, you keep well out of it." Which sounded a lot like the warning from the mysterious female voice on the phone. But now that Jean actually saw a good reason to stay out of it, she was in it up to her neck—an expression that had taken on a whole new meaning.

She sped around the corner into Cameron Square and halted beside the wall of the Museum. There she caught her breath, rotated her shoulders, and stroked her nerves, which were bristling like the fur on an upset Dougie's spine.

Like the psalmist searching for help, Jean lifted her eyes to the hills. To the northeast, the vee between the mountains that was the Great Glen was clotted with mist, leaving only the lowest slopes exposed. Ditto to the southwest, where the Glen opened out toward the sea. There, the mist and clouds were thinning out, their individual shapes teased from the mass by a hint of sun, gray on gray like designs in smoked glass.

She lowered her eyes to the town. Fort William had once been An Ghearasdan, a military garrison. Now the old fort was only a few cropped stone walls between the loch and the massed parking lots of the Safeway, the McDonalds, and the train station. The original houses had huddled close beside the loch. Now the newer streets looped freely up the steep slopes behind, white houses strung like Christmas lights against the green.

Inhaling the tang of peat smoke that hung on the air like incense in a cathedral, Jean thought, yes, a little perspective helped. Eventually today's headlines would become yesterday's cautionary tale. Neither railing at fate nor cussing out the constabulary would make it happen any faster. Keeping on would.

Rainwater gurgled through the gutters of the Museum, one of the oldest buildings in town. Its outer door stood invitingly open, the lights inside shedding a soft glow into the gloom. Yesterday's cautionary tales weren't exactly safe and soothing—especially not here, where the myth warriors fought many a pitched battle—but still she ducked inside.

She paid her admission to the elderly lady at the front desk, handed over her umbrella, and plunged into the recesses of the building. For one precious half-hour she lost herself in contemplation of arrowheads, broken pots, stuffed birds, farming implements, medals, and *memento mori* from too many wars. The sonorous tick of an old clock provided as much allegory as background noise.

Finally, lured up the stairs by portraits of Charlie's feckless relatives, Jean came to the room dedicated to Jacobite memorabilia. After a long look out the window into the square—still raining—she turned to the display case holding the famous secret portrait of Charlie. To the unenlightened eye it appeared to be a smear of colored paint on a wooden tray. You had to look into a shiny silver cylinder, placed at just the right point on the tray, to see a reflection of Charlie's smug features.

Everything was a matter of perspective. Relationships. Murder investigations…. A second reflection moved in the gleaming surface of the cylinder. The wooden floor creaked. Jean's shoulder blades tingled. She turned around to see D.C.I. Cameron standing several paces away, his blue eyes cold and hard as ice. He said, with about as much warmth, "Good afternoon. I was walking past the Museum and saw you looking out the window."

Damn! She should have known better than to break cover when predators were on the prowl. What were they doing, tag-teaming her? Just when she did not want to be jerked back to reality—no pun on the word "jerk" intended. But there was no help for it. Jean managed a civil if strained, "Hello."

"Clever picture," said Cameron. "Art by way of optical illusion. The cylinder distorts the already distorted picture and reverts it to normal. A double negative making a positive. Two wrongs making a right."

Well, she was always up for a discussion of history. "This one's less art than political statement. After the Forty-five, it was illegal for any household to display a portrait of Charles Edward Stuart. Just like it was illegal to play the pipes or wear the kilt. Some of the milder aspects of the English ethnic cleansing policy."

"Charlie was no Scot. His mother was a Polish princess named

Sobieski. His grandmother was Italian. His great-grandmother was French. He'd never set foot in Scotland, but still had the bloody cheek to say 'I am come home.'"

"Maybe home is where the heart is."

"Charlie's only contribution is to the tourist industry, tripe selling better than truth."

"And your business is truth?"

He considered the secret portrait. "Making a search for the truth."

Yes, the man was historically literate. But then, Jean knew a lot of hard-assed historians. They'd come down to drink at the faculty club watering hole, and if you were spry enough you could get off the odd pot shot from the shelter of the academic grove. "So you have to prove you haven't been taken in by a legend, is that it?"

"By nostalgia for a world that's never existed. William Wallace, Rob Roy, Charlie's great-great-grandmother Mary—they're none of them what Hollywood and the Tourist Board make them out to be."

"Mary, Queen of Scots, was Charlie's great-great-great grandmother."

He didn't so much as blink.

"If your point," Jean went on, "is that history, like truth, is filtered through people's emotions, I agree."

"You writing your papers and your articles, then, you should be admitting the truth when you hear it. That life in these airts was no tartan fantasy but was nasty, brutish, and short. That regiments of Scots fought for the English against Charlie. That Scots have a long, bloody history of committing atrocities themselves."

He knew she'd both published and perished because he'd checked up on her, the same way she'd been checking up on Lovelace and MacLyon and the MacSorleys. *Check.* "The sentimental old stories don't excuse atrocities any more than they diminish heroism. They don't hurt anything."

"They dilute the truth into pap. Legends. Romance. Fantasy."

She expected him to add, *bah, humbug.* What, he'd been dragged into this Museum so many times as a child he'd developed an allergy? Or did his frigid disposition find sentiment offensive? It would be easier just to agree with him, but taking the easy way out seemed like cheating. "Fantasy is the revenge for reality. It's not a disease, it's an antidote."

"Is it now?" He lowered his head but didn't start pawing the floor.

"Some true believers are like alcoholics, yes. But most of us don't have to believe a fantasy to find meaning in it. Most of us don't use myth to justify terrorism. A good story helps us transcend our own lives." Realizing Cameron hadn't raised his voice one decibel, Jean moderated her tone. "Do you think MacLyon's case of charlieoverthewaterism has something to do with the murder?"

"I'm after seeing the entire picture."

"That's what I'm after, too."

"We're needing to have a blether, then, you and me."

"Listen, I just put in two long, weary hours at the police station with D.S. Sawyer treating me like something between a clown and a criminal."

Cameron's mouth twitched, but she couldn't tell if he was smiling or grimacing at Sawyer's behavior. "Not at the station, nothing formal."

"Okay." Jean told him. "Fine. I have nothing to hide. I haven't done anything wrong."

"Who's saying you have done?"

As much as she wanted to retort, *You have, you and your pal Sawyer,* she held her tongue and headed toward the stairs. Two more anamorphic paintings in another case displayed naked women with rolls of creamy flesh that today wouldn't be pornography but studies in body image. Perspective, yes.

She clumped down the staircase and retrieved her umbrella. A policeman was trained to be mistrustful. Free-floating cynicism was an occupational hazard. Even so, she had to ask Cameron as he expressionlessly held the door for her, "Why keep after me?"

"Maybe I'm needing someone with a bit of historical expertise to help me move that cylinder about."

Like historians weren't a dime a dozen, or a penny a pound, whatever. If all he wanted was expertise in charlieoverthewaterism, one of the Museum people would do just fine. But Lovelace hadn't come to any of them for help. And none of them had found his dead body. Cameron was smart, no doubt about it. Whether he had a wider perspective than his sergeant remained to be seen.

Jean stepped outside, umbrella at the ready. The rain had slowed to a mizzle—part mist, part drizzle. Two paces behind, she followed Cameron across the square into a steamy cafe. Its garish plastic tables and chairs blurred as her glasses fogged up. Before she could dive into her bag for a tissue, a handkerchief appeared in her peripheral vision, offered by Cameron's sturdy hand. It wasn't exactly Raleigh's doublet spread across a puddle, but she accepted the gesture as she assumed it was intended, with a thank-you and a mop at her lenses.

At the counter he ordered a cup of coffee. So did she. He paid for his, she paid for hers. Without stopping to doctor the coffee with sugar or cream—maybe he regarded them as affectations—he strolled to a table in the corner farthest from the door, took off the bulky jacket he wore over his suit, and sat down with his back to the wall.

Jean emptied a plastic pot of artificial cream into her paper cup and took a chair on the opposite side of the table. The odors wafting from the kitchen implied fried fish and chips. Fried sausage and chips. Fried haggis and chips. A sign advertised American hamburgers, and bags of spongy white buns stacked on the counter backed up the claim. None of it did anything for Jean's appetite. Besides, eating in front of Cameron would be like having lunch with the head of the tenure committee—she needed her full attention to keep her balance.

The detective gazed around the restaurant, evaluating the decor and the diners both. He took a healthy swig from his cup. Only then did his arctic eyes meet hers.

Let's get this over with. "This morning I went out to George Lovelace's house in Corpach...."

Cameron listened. Every now and then he'd blink, slowly, or nod, even slower. If he already knew what she'd found out about the Jacobite Lodge or the Hogmanay party, he offered not a clue. By the time she finished with the suspicious incident of Toby Walsh in the hotel and the amazing episode of the pollen, she was beginning to wonder if he was the scientific experiment, a new variety of robo-cop.

"I told Sawyer all of this," she concluded, "and he said he was capable of doing his own research."

"Andy Sawyer's a wee bit ambitious," Cameron said, as though ambition were a handicap.

Jean agreed with that, too, but her opinion of Sawyer was worth as much as he was paying for it. She went on, "Lovelace could have bought the coin from a dealer, but he wouldn't get any more for it than he spent on it. It all boils down to why he deliberately misled me."

"If he misled you about being known to the Museum, how else was he misleading you?"

"About where and when he found the coin, but I can't see why."

"Could be the coin was only the means to an end. You."

"You mean the whole charade was to get him in to see me? To get me to write about—if not the coin, what? Charlie?"

"Lovelace was working for MacLyon, mind."

"If MacLyon wanted to suggest an article, he could have picked up the phone and called me, he didn't have to send Lovelace with a line of bull."

"Oh aye." Cameron said softly. He turned to look at the windows at the front of the cafe, which lightened in a gleam of sun and then darkened again. Several drenched and bedraggled backpackers walked in the door, teasing each other in German.

Jean sipped at her coffee—it had the muddy flavor and watery aroma of instant—and considered Cameron's profile. His features weren't distinctive: not handsome, not ugly, just symmetrical and proportional. His skin was fair, but not pasty. His ears lay flat to his head, reserved. His appearance wasn't ascetic so much as it was pared to a monastic minimum—except for the elegant ogee curve of his lips, like the tracery in a Gothic window. A stone window. Maybe his own face had become as much protective coloring as his suit. Maybe he was curious over and beyond conscientious. Maybe still waters ran deep.

She should have learned from his rebuff yesterday not to get curious about his private persona. Assuming he had one. For all she knew, he lived in a locker at Northern Constabulary headquarters. Retracting her antennae, she asked, "Has the postmortem been done on Lovelace yet?"

Cameron's head swiveled toward her. "Aye, the report's come in."

"Tell me about it. I promise not to get the vapors."

His right eyebrow actually rose a millimeter, as though he really were amused with her, but his voice was hard and matter-of-fact. "Lovelace was garroted, then hanged."

Oh. The facts of the matter not being at all amusing, Jean tried to copy his detachment. "I'd thought that it would be hard to hang someone who was conscious and fighting back. How can you tell he was garroted first?"

"Clear ligature marks in the creases of the skin—bruising and swelling—on front and both sides of the throat. Horizontally. The marks from the hanging, a v-shape up the back of his head, are much fainter."

"The killer sneaked up on him from behind and twisted a cord or rope around his neck."

"A length of twine. Good-sized spool of it in the garden shed. The murderer looped the twine round Lovelace's neck, inserted a stick into the back of the noose and rotated. Quicker than some forms of strangulation, for what that's worth. An old guerilla trick. Takes a bit of strength, but with the surprise, not so much as you'd expect. Lovelace wasn't a young man."

"He wouldn't have put up much of a fight, no."

"He was hauled up on the hook either just before or just after death."

"How can… ." Jean began.

"After death, the blood coagulates in the lowest part of the body. In Lovelace it was in his legs and feet, meaning he was pulled upright straightaway. That's no trouble at all, just lower the hook, catch up the cord, and haul away with the block-and-tackle rig."

"So any reasonably fit person could have killed him." *Including Fiona or Vanessa. Or me.* But Cameron didn't have to make that point.

The police knew how Lovelace had been killed. An old guerilla trick. An old commando trick. A trick used on an old commando. But how wasn't why. How was only a means to why. She looked up at Cameron. He was watching her like Dougie watching a mouse hole. To him, she was only a means to why. "Go on," she told him.

"The medical examiner sent a number of items to be analyzed. The contents of Lovelace's stomach. Bits of plants and threads clinging to his clothing. A stick lying on the floor, probably the one used in the garrote. We're analyzing the fingerprints in the room as well."

"Mine are on the doorknob. I never said I wasn't there."

"No, you've not," said Cameron mildly, menace scaled back to caution.

"So unless you think I'm capable of some sort of fake-out-the-cops scenario, I'm not your number-one suspect."

He didn't react.

"I did almost interrupt the murderer in the act. If nothing else, they probably intended to have a lot longer time before Lovelace was found."

"You might have upset someone's plans, right enough."

Jean hadn't really wanted to consider that, not least because she sure didn't want police protection. But she couldn't hope for a broad perspective in others and refuse to use one herself. "What about Toby Walsh? He was hanging around my hotel room a little while ago."

"Walsh said he saw Lovelace sneaking into the house."

"With some sort of video surveillance system?"

"No. From the upstairs window. The CCTV's not been installed yet."

"Oh. Okay," Jean said. "Is Toby telling the truth, though? If he killed Lovelace, he might be trying to fudge the time."

"The coach driver saw Lovelace as well. Time of death is not in doubt."

Well no, it wasn't. Ogilvy had seen Lovelace leave Corpach and the bus driver had seen him arrive at Glendessary House. Walsh's sighting hadn't been a crisis apparition. You didn't go for paranormal explanations until all the natural ones were exhausted, and that could take a long time—especially with Cameron on the case. No matter how she looked at it, she'd come within a gnat's eyelash of interrupting a murder in progress. Her hand tightened around her paper cup and the vile coffee brew surged up toward the rim.

"Walsh has previous track," said Cameron.

Jean released the cup. "A criminal record?"

"He was sent down for breaking and entering several years ago."

"Lovelace's house was broken and entered this morning. Toby was in the area, and with the MacSorleys' car, too."

"We'll be looking into that."

"Any one else with criminal records?" Jean asked, hoping he'd explain his odd reaction to Fiona's name.

"Rick MacLyon was done twice for drink-driving in the States."

"That's downright conservative behavior these days." Jean frowned, trying to remember the exact sequence of events at Glendessary House. It would help if at certain moments whistles had blown and bells rung—pay attention, this is going to be important! "I assume the people from the bus are MacLyon's Jacobite playmates. Their meeting or pep rally or whatever was going on at two, with Neil's musical accompaniment outside, although I don't know whether MacLyon himself was there then. Or Vanessa."

"They'd both arrived by half-past two, we're told."

"I heard Rick's voice while I was wandering around the back hall. Fiona, though, I only saw her for a few seconds when I came in…."

Cameron made a quick, sharp gesture, like shooing away a fly. *Have it your way,* Jean thought. "I assume you're tracking down the Lodge members."

"The coach company was very helpful."

"Has anyone contradicted anyone else?"

"No. No one's agreed too closely with anyone else either. They've not sat down together and planned out their stories."

Jean had had that same thought, at the foot of the staircase yesterday afternoon. Great minds, and so forth. "Several people had the means and the opportunity."

"True, but at the end of the day it's the motive that matters, or so I'm thinking."

"I'm thinking that too. And while I was upset that Lovelace was jerking me around with the coin, that's hardly a motive to kill him."

"Motives can be right slippy," Cameron said, noncommittal. Again he turned toward the window, this time with his arm propped on the back of the plastic chair. His posture indicated he'd much prefer being somewhere else—pushing a pencil, maybe, or climbing a mountain.

His suit coat fell open. A copy of *Great Scot* was tucked into its inside pocket. It was the issue with her article on Bonnie Prince Charlie, the one that had attracted Lovelace's attention. Jean pointed. "Checking all my angles?"

"I've looked out your academic work and your magazine stories, aye. The former is history, straight. The latter run to

legends, second sight, ghost tales. True ghost tales, you're saying."
Turning, he leaned across the table and focused on her face.

Even without trying she could sense an energy field emanating
from the man, like a tickle in her follicles. What if it was positive
curiosity, like her own, rather than negative hostility? Ordering
herself not to shrink away, she said, "Ghosts are supposedly trans-
mitted emotion. Some people can pick up paranormal transmis-
sions, some can't. Some can only pick up certain ones. I happen
to…" She checked herself in mid-phrase—she only owed
Lovelace a certain amount of self-revelation—and finished,
"…think that ghost stories can be true."

A crease appeared between his eyebrows. Ghosts, he was going
to say. Hearsay. Irrationality. Emotions. Sissy stuff, like romance.
Personally, Jean felt that romance was only for the strong of stomach.

"Aren't Scotland's ghosts getting a wee bit tired by now?" he
asked.

Whoa, a mild response. Keeping her balance with him was
harder than she'd expected. "Not necessarily. It depends on
whether they've got what they want. Acknowledgment. Not so different from what most living people want. And, speaking of dead
people…" Time for a preemptive strike. "I'm not going to give up
on Lovelace's story, the treasure hunt and Charlie and everything.
Of course it's gotten way the hell away from me, but…"

"…it's a murder mystery now. Proper tabloid material."

"You'll have noticed that *Great Scot* is no tabloid." She leaned
across the table herself, into that elusive energy field, so close she
could count the creases at the corners of his eyes. "Don't tell me
this story, this case, is none of my business. It is my business.
Lovelace came to me for help, even if he wasn't honest about his
motives. I need to know whether I had anything to do with his
death, and, if possible, I'd like to help catch his killer."

For a long moment Cameron returned her steady gaze. He might
be trying to intimidate her, or assessing her own motives, or he
might simply be counting the rods and cones in her eyes. At last he
said, "I'm thinking that if I tell you to stop asking questions you'll
only become more curious. Or so you were telling me yesterday."

"Call it a matter of ethics. A search for the truth. If you checked
up on my history back in the U.S., you know that I value the truth."

"You reported a PhD candidate for plagiarizing. Put the boot right in, didn't you?" Cameron leaned back. Even though his eyes didn't waver, she had the feeling that he was finally allowing her a few inches of wiggle room.

"Yes, it would have been a lot safer to keep my mouth shut. He started a propaganda campaign, claiming we'd had an affair and I was trying to punish him for jilting me. The university fired me without checking out his story. But you know that, too."

"You had your position back when you won your wrongful termination lawsuit. Then you resigned, divorced your husband, moved house."

"It was time to move on. I may be a historian, but I'd also be the first to admit that if you dig yourself too deeply into the past…"

"…you've got no future." Cameron's eyes lost their focus and looked past her. The crease between his eyebrows deepened, plowed by memory.

Odd, that a cop would understand what she meant when many of her academic colleagues did not. What was in Cameron's past? His left hand wrapped around his empty cup displayed no wedding ring…. Don't waste your time and energy psychoanalyzing the man, she told herself. "My name used to be Jean Inglis. Scots for 'English.' I'd say something about irony but there's no need to hammer it home."

With the merest trace of a shrug he focused back on her face. "Jean Inglis. Jean Fairbairn. All the same to me."

It hadn't been all the same to Brad. Not by a long shot. But gender politics wasn't the issue.

"Ask your questions, then," Cameron went on. "Just mind how you go. Don't overstep yourself. And keep in touch."

She almost said, *Sure, if you'll keep in touch with me,* but decided she should quit while she was at least neck-and-neck. "Is that it? Can I go now?"

"Oh aye, that's it. For the present."

Was Cameron hoping that if he played out the line she'd eventually snag herself even more securely on the hook? Suppressing a sigh of aggravation—he didn't deserve that—Jean gathered up her bag and her umbrella and held the door so it wouldn't slam in his face.

She hadn't felt claustrophobic until she stepped outside. Blue sky glinted between swags of cloud. Sunlight flowed across the distant hills, across the loch, up the street, and then vanished on the mountainside like the beam of a lighthouse sweeping across the landscape. What had Ogilvy said about Lovelace's desk lamp, that it shone every night like a lighthouse?

The pedestrian mall teemed with shoppers and tourists and, Jean supposed, reporters. The seagulls were making their rusty screen door cries. The wind keened through the chimneys and telephone wires like the sound of bagpipes.... No, she really was hearing the sound of bagpipes, issuing from the tartan tchotchke shop down the street. From the pub next door came the thump-thump of a rock band. Combine the two and you had rock 'n' reel, the sound the blood made going though your heart.

Cameron probably preferred light jazz, something she found annoying as water torture. She glanced over at him, but he was already walking away, head down, cutting through the crowd without so much as a "Good-bye," let alone a "Cheers."

He'd drawn her in by challenging her assumptions, hadn't he, then fed her just enough information about the case to draw her out. Offering no reaction was an old interviewer's trick. Feeling uncomfortable with the long silences, the subject spills her guts. Jean almost had. Cameron was playing good cop to Sawyer's bad cop, keeping his friends close and his enemies closer.

But she wasn't his enemy. They were on the same side—or should be. Sawyer to the contrary, all she'd done was be in the wrong place at the wrong time. And according to Cameron's analysis of the secret portrait, that produced a right.

Are you for real? Jean called silently after him. And answered herself, oh yeah, he was for real, even if he did keep his personality locked away, safe from any awkward emotion. She didn't know what to think of him. Not that she needed to think anything of him; he was simply part of the municipal facilities, after all.

Jean jammed her fists in the pockets of her coat. *Great.* She still had Cameron's handkerchief. She took two steps after him, then stopped.

Fiona Robertson was standing on the doorstep of a clothing store. Dressed in a shapeless coat and scarf, she was as incognito as a beautiful woman could ever get, less animated than the sweater-clad mannequins in the window behind her. But when

Cameron materialized beside her, her head jerked toward his. He stepped into her personal space the way Neil had stepped into Jean's. They spoke in words but not in the least bit of body language, like Princess Grace exchanging statistics with Mr. Spock. Then Cameron did his disappearing act again, leaving Fiona to walk briskly in the opposite direction.

So, Jean thought, as her eyebrows drifted back down from her hairline. Fiona wasn't known to the police in general, but only to one policeman, personally. Coincidence? Or conspiracy? There was one more question for her ever-lengthening list. Because Fiona wasn't part of the municipal facilities. Fiona was a suspect.

THIRTEEN

JEAN STOPPED her car in a passing place and indulged in a moment of appreciation. Below her Loch Lochy glowed enough shades of blue—aquamarine, azure, sapphire—to beggar a thesaurus. The light of the afternoon sun made etchings of the ridges beyond, the western sides glowing green, the eastern sides shadowed into olive-drab. Billows of white cloud seemed substantial enough to pick up in handfuls, like clotted cream. Hard to believe they were only water vapor that would vanish in a breath.

Life was like that, Jean told herself. Illusion. Ephemeral illusion at that, just to make a double cognitive whammy.

Two days ago she'd come driving along this road, if not without a care in the world, at least without the albatross of survivor's guilt that now hung around her neck. But then, as Neil had aptly pointed out to Charlotte, the situation was a lot harder on George Lovelace.

Jean pulled back out onto the road. Today she could reasonably expect not to run into Charlotte MacSorley trying out for the NASCAR circuit, since Charlotte was dusting off the welcome mat for her arrival. When it came to Fiona Robertson, though, Jean had no idea what to expect, although some conspiracy with Cameron didn't seem at all reasonable. Coincidence, now—coincidence happened all the time.

Fiona had called this morning, changing Jean's one-thirty appointment with MacLyon into a dinner invitation. "And perhaps," Fiona went on, "you'd fancy staying through the weekend as well?"

Jean had accepted the invitation with both alacrity and gratitude. Maybe MacLyon had decided if he had to tangle with the media, better a mild-mannered journalist from *Great Scot*. Whatever his motive, Jean wasn't about to turn down an exclusive, either for the magazine or for herself. That an exclusive meant putting herself back into the house with a killer was a trade-off between caution and conscience. But just because Cameron thought she'd gotten in the killer's way didn't mean she had. No one had proved that the killer was not a member of the Lodge or some other outsider. No one had proved that he or she was, either.

Bunarkaig consisted of several houses wedged between the road and the hillside. Slowing, Jean spotted a plaque proclaiming "Bonnie Brae Cottage" attached to stone wall. She turned through a narrow opening into a gravel parking area beside two stories of stucco so white it looked bleached.

Swathes of flowers stretched down to the road and banked up against the inside of the wall. On pristine patches of grass stood a freshly-painted set of lawn furniture and a sundial. The short summers in this part of the world tended to produce fanatical gardeners. Jean's lawn back in Texas had usually been wildscaped by default, the plants she set out in March becoming weedy wonders by November, when, if she was lucky, a freeze would at last end the watering and trimming season.

Jean pushed the doorbell. Before the chime had quite died away, the door opened. Every wave of Charlotte's sienna-brown hair—a shade too dark for her complexion—was lacquered into submission. Her flowered dress was accessorized with a string of pearls. In her jacket and twill pants Jean felt underdressed.

"Here you are," Charlotte trilled. "Come through, come through."

Jean stepped inside. "You have a beautiful garden."

"One does what one can, Miss Fairbairn. My son Neil and that layabout Toby Walsh help out when Rick can spare them. Which is very seldom, mind. In the old days a great house like Glendessary would have had an army of servants, but young people nowadays would rather stand about on street corners in the city than take up respectable work in the country." Charlotte led the way down a hallway lined with half a dozen trophy heads. The five deer and a mouflon were lined up like criminals in an identity parade, their dark glass eyes hurt, as though they'd been wrongly convicted.

The sitting room resembled a *House Beautiful* photo, every piece of furniture and every ornament posed self-consciously. The scent of potpourri didn't quite mask that of cigarette smoke. "Neil seems to enjoy working for the MacLyons," Jean said, her nose wrinkling.

"He's absolutely indispensable to them. I don't know how they'll get on when he leaves for university this autumn."

"Is he going to study music?"

"Oh no, no. He's a brilliant musician, true. He's always receiving offers of professional employment. But he's decided to pursue a proper career, business or law. He has his family name to uphold, after all. The MacSorleys are Camerons, did you know that? Related to the Lochiel himself."

"Yes, I...."

"Neil attended the best public schools, we made certain of that. Shocking how so many of the other boys were jealous of his talents and family name. Little boys can be beastly, can't they? But we made it very clear to the authorities at each school we wouldn't tolerate any harassment. Sit down, I'll fetch the tea." Charlotte disappeared through a swinging door.

Jean knew only too well that trying to keep boys—or men, for that matter—from teasing was like spitting into the wind. Not that Charlotte had asked her opinion. She might not have asked Neil's opinion of the "proper career," either. But of all the things that were none of Jean's business, Neil's relationship with his mother topped the list.

Instead of sitting down Jean looked around, into a cabinet filled with Venetian glass and another stocked with alcoholic beverages, then through the contents of a small bookshelf. She noted biographies of eminent figures such as Churchill, some Italian guidebooks, and a gilded, leather-bound set of Walter Scott novels.

Several photos in polished frames were ranged along the top shelf. They were mostly of a handsome little boy who morphed into the adult but equally handsome Neil, although one showed Kieran and Charlotte, grinning fatuously, beside a bemused Prince Charles. The present Prince Charles, who was no doubt more intellectual than his predecessor, but who would never be called "bonnie." A tiny photo of a fresh young couple who had to be Charlotte and Kieran on their wedding day only pointed up how they had soured over the years, by now well past their sell-by date.

The last two photos were old ones. Jean looked closer. Yes, the first was the same shot of the commando school as the one she'd seen in George Lovelace's album. The second was a close-up of a young man with Kieran's beak of a nose, wearing a commando uniform. Neil had certainly won the genetics sweepstakes when it came to noses—his was patrician but not beaky.

Charlotte swept back into the room and set a tray on the coffee table. Jean sat down on a couch so soft she had to peer out past her knees.

"This is our exclusive blend of China tea," Charlotte explained as she poured. "Chinese is ever so much more refined than Indian."

Making a noncommittal noise, Jean grasped the tiny, convoluted handle of the cup between thumb and forefinger, curled her pinkie under, and sipped. The tea was winy and bright. She hoped her questions would be as palatable. "Is that a picture of Glendessary House during the war, when some of the commando trainees were billeted there?"

"That it is," said Charlotte. "Kieran's family owned the house, mind you. His father Archie is in the front row. He was a decorated war hero, died for king and country."

"I'm sorry to hear that," Jean returned, although she suspected she could just as well have said she was happy to hear about the medals. "Did he train here the same time George Lovelace did?"

"Oh yes, yes, showed young George the ropes, didn't he? His father, Kieran's grandfather, being the local landowner and all. George was very fortunate to have encountered Archie. Very grateful he was, always sent a nice little card at Christmas even though he was—well, it was hardly his fault he was in straitened circumstances, was it? Really, there should be a Home Office inquiry into inadequate pensions."

Jean dangled some bait. "I understand he enjoyed using his metal detector. Maybe he got a little extra income that way."

"I believe he found a Viking brooch once, but nothing else of note, only odds and ends. Or so he was telling Kieran."

Did that mean Lovelace found the coin sixty years ago, that he hadn't told Kieran about finding it recently, or that Charlotte simply wasn't talking? "You must have been pleased when Mr. Lovelace moved to Corpach, then, to have him close by."

"We weren't particularly close, just thrown together, you might say. Still though, it was a dreadful shock to hear he was, er, dead. Appalling business. Murdering an ineffectual and useless old man right there in Glendessary House!" Charlotte shook her head. "Have a biscuit, they're Fortnum and Mason's best. I have them delivered specially, Kieran does like a good biscuit with his tea."

Jean chose a cookie and did not ask why being murdered in a mansion was worse than being murdered anywhere else. There was nothing suspicious in Charlotte's not wanting to talk about it—most people would be squeamish about the details. As for why she was so eager to diminish Lovelace's status, the easy psychological answer was that she was insecure in her own. "A shame the old house was gutted by fire during the war."

"It was a frightful old pile, actually. There was some talk of selling up long before the war. We're well rid of it."

"How did the fire start?"

"No one knows. Good job we had quite a few old family photographs and the like to guide the workmen during the restoration."

"They did a great job. I expected to see Queen Victoria come walking out through the portico." Or an actress playing Victoria, Jean amended.

"She visited here, did you know that? And Prince Charles has done, as well. Did you see that photograph?"

"Yes I did. I assume he was interested in the restoration work."

"Very much so, questioned Kieran and myself quite closely. Of course he was perfectly gracious when we introduced Rick and Vanessa. They did their best. Well hello there, come on in, have yourself a good look around!" Charlotte said in a contrived American accent. "Royalty has to deal with all sorts, part of the job description, isn't it?"

Oh yeah, Jean told herself. Same with magazine writers. And cops.

Two lines ran from Charlotte's ever-distended nostrils past the corners of her red slit of a mouth and disappeared into the slack flesh of her jaw line. They were the equivalent of the crescents framing Neil's dazzling smile, Jean supposed, but they made Charlotte look like a marionette, chin moving up and down as she spoke. Her voice was part plummy BBC accent and part helium screech that set Jean's teeth on edge. But the fact that she could do an American accent was very interesting. Ordering herself not to show any irritation, Jean asked, "Did you and the MacLyons meet when he was looking for property in this area?"

"In a way, yes. Rick was making historical inquiries of the West Highland Museum. Have you visited there? Fine collection, very nicely maintained, but then, Kieran and I are always available to offer advice. We answered Rick's letter and, well, here we are!"

Yes, indeed. Here they all were.

"Really," Charlotte added parenthetically, "a man of his position calling himself Rick, not Richard. A child's name. Americans have such a maddening fondness for nicknames, don't they?"

And what about the legions of British cabinet ministers and bankers called by their schoolboy names of Blotto or Squeaky? Jean said, "Well, you don't call Bill Gates William, do you?".

"No, no," said Charlotte, brightening at that association. "So then, you're going to write Rick up for *Great Scot*. And quite right, too, he's contributed ever so much to the area. At the end of the day, breeding will tell. He's from Virginia, the principal British colony. And Vanessa attended one of the Seven Sisters. Of course she's very young, isn't she?"

"Yes." Jean remembered her cookie and bit into it. The buttery sweet crumbs complemented the slightly astringent taste of the tea.

"Do you suppose Miranda might run a series of articles? There's so much to tell about the restorations and all. Kieran and I have been at Rick's side every step of the way; who better to assist you with your work?"

So Charlotte hadn't asked her over because of her sparkling personality. Jean was hardly staggered by the news. On the other hand, there was nothing like getting an engraved invitation to be nosy. Washing down the rest of the cookie, she said, "Well then, we'll have to set up a formal interview, when I have my laptop and everything, and when your husband can be here, too. Maybe just a few preliminary questions now?"

"Of course." Charlotte sat back, radiating gentility, like a child hoping Santa Claus will notice her good behavior.

"Rick must value his privacy, to settle in such an isolated spot. You said he had trouble finding people to work out here?"

"That's why he depends on us. Poor Toby, the less said about him the better. We must all do our duty to the lower classes, I suppose...." She let her sentence evaporate into rarified air. "Just between you and me and the gatepost, Fiona does well enough, but fancies herself a little grand for her position. Norman's a brilliant chef, prepares lovely, posh cuisine. We found him in Inverness and recommended him to Vanessa."

That's right, there was a cook. But Tuesday was his day off, which was why Vanessa offered to have Fiona make sandwiches for Cameron and crew. Odd, to entertain a group of people on the cook's day off.

Charlotte went on, "Vanessa's taste in cuisine is acceptable, if a bit unformed, but Rick doesn't much care what he eats. Maybe he's missing his American cheeseburgers and hot dogs." She emphasized the "r's" in "burger" and made "dog" come out "dawg".

"Doesn't Rick have a personal assistant?" Jean asked.

"He did have, yes. I was so looking forward to her arrival. She attended Roedean, very exclusive. She was such a disappointment though, turned out to be a frightful little creature with no manners and positively vulgar clothing. But then, her family money's from industry, isn't it? I'll never understand why these young girls have to go about with their stomachs exposed. It makes them look no better than cheap tarts. Of course, most of them are tarts, aren't they? Libertines." With a sniff, Charlotte drained the teapot into Jean's cup.

Since a girl had a stomach worth exposing for only a few short years, Jean figured she should go for it. As for manners and morals—well, the pendulum swung back and forth between promiscuity and Puritanism and never seemed to stop at a golden mean. "I thought Vanessa looked very nice in her kilt skirt and velvet jacket the other day, but I assume she doesn't wear that outfit all the time, only for company. Like the people who were there when Mr. Lovelace died. The Jacobite Lodge, isn't that who they were?"

"Oh." Geniality punctured, Charlotte set the teapot down with a thud that jangled the cream pitcher and sugar bowl. Something small and furtive moved in her colorless eyes, something that seemed almost like fear. "Oh, well, Miranda told you about that, did she?"

"Yes, she did," Jean returned, happy to be able to tell the truth.

"I—I…" Charlotte folded her hands in her lap, twisting her fingers together, and said to them, "I'm not really at liberty to talk about that, Miss Fairbairn. It's Rick's doing; mind, you should be asking him about it. When the time comes, of course, well then we'll all…."

The front door of the house opened with a crash and footsteps strode down the hall. Charlotte shut her mouth so fast Jean could hear her teeth click together. *We'll all what?* she wanted to demand. *When what time comes?* But it was too late, dammit.

Kieran burst into the room like a bull coming out of a rodeo chute. He was red in the face, dressed in limp, sweaty shorts and T-shirt, and wore running shoes that looked more like an abstract sculpture in manmade materials than footwear. "The car in the drive, who… Oh, it's you, Miss Fairbairn."

"Hello, Mr. MacSorley," Jean said, since she couldn't say, *Go away, I'm pumping your wife for information.*

Without preamble, he returned, "You were up at Glendessary day before yesterday. You found the body."

"Yes, I'm afraid I had the bad luck to find Mr. Lovelace."

Kieran's voice oozed sarcasm like his scrawny limbs exuded the odor of sweat. "There's a reporter for you, poking and prying into business that's not your own. Nasty suspicious minds, reporters have."

It wasn't as though she'd been going around looking for murder victims. Jean tried evoking the magic name. "I work with Miranda Capaldi at *Great Scot*. She asked me to interview Rick MacLyon. Mrs. MacSorley has been telling me how much you've helped him."

"Oh she has, has she?" Kieran turned on his wife.

Charlotte's lips turned down like a horseshoe with the luck running out. "You remember Miranda Capaldi. Skibo Castle, the National Trust conference. Very posh. Here we are such close associates of Rick and Vanessa, it's only fair our contribution be recognized…."

"We don't deal with the press," stated Kieran.

"Rick's invited her for the weekend. I didn't think…."

"That's just the problem, isn't it? You don't think."

Losing ground fast, Jean groped for her bag and stood up.

Kieran did look like a velociraptor. His head was thrust forward from his shoulders, his black eyes were reptilian beads, his hair receded from a sloping forehead. If that hair had ever been the golden-red of Neil's, his liberal application of something like bear grease had permanently darkened it. And the moustache—his huge nose and its attendant broom really did look like plastic fakes.

The nose and the moustache swept toward her, all too real. "I'll see you out, Miss Fairbairn."

"I can find my own way, thank you." Jean wondered for a split second if she should hang around, just to make sure Kieran didn't punch Charlotte out. But from the petrified rage on Charlotte's face, Jean figured she was no doormat. "Mrs. MacSorley, the tea was excellent. I'll have to recommend those biscuits to Miranda."

"Please do," said Charlotte. Her lips smiled but her teeth were set.

Ominous silence followed Jean as she hurried down the hall and out the door. Well, well, she thought, Kieran was acting as though he feared Charlotte was going to spill the beans about something. The same way Vanessa had acted when she stopped Kieran and Lovelace from arguing on New Year's Eve. Charlotte had gone from self-importance to anxiety very quickly there.

Jean collapsed into the car, seething with new questions. So what was the big secret about the Lodge? Was that the story the ex-secretary tried to sell *The Sunburn,* before Rick paid to have it killed? If Kieran and Charlotte were members of Rick's Lodge, why hadn't they been at the meeting Tuesday? Surely Charlotte's craving for social advancement would have overridden Vanessa's territorial imperative.

Jean pulled out her paper notebook and starting jotting down notes, quickly. That shape in the front window of the house, lighting a cigarette, was Kieran watching her prove his point about reporters. Not that she didn't appreciate how much damage a media mill could cause. Ironic, that she was a variety of reporter herself now....

Cigarette or no cigarette, Kieran was a jogger. Charlotte said yesterday he'd rushed off to Glendessary House when Fiona called about Lovelace so quickly he hardly had time to wash. Had he been out jogging when Lovelace was killed? If so, where? And how did Charlotte know Jean was spending the weekend, anyway?

Okay, so she had a nasty suspicious mind. That was *her* cross to bear. Jean pitched her notebook into the other seat, started the car, and headed for the epicenter of it all, Glendessary House.

FOURTEEN

JEAN EDGED CAUTIOUSLY out of the MacSorleys' driveway— between the stone wall and a curve in the road, she could see maybe ten yards in either direction—and turned toward Glendessary House. It was about three miles away, she estimated, making a mental note of the number on her odometer.

A conditioned runner could run three miles in what? Fifteen minutes? Less? And Kieran was a conditioned runner, you could tell that from his lean, wiry body. Not that he was a young man. If his father died during the war, he had to be pushing sixty, hard. And despite her touching faith in hair coloring, Charlotte couldn't be much younger.

Neil was an only child who had come along later rather than sooner in his parents' reproductive lives. He'd been a bit over-indulged, it seemed. That would explain his sublime self-assurance.... Jean told herself she didn't need to waste time and energy psychoanalyzing Neil, either, beauty being its own excuse for being and all that.

Media vans choked the area around Glendessary House's gates. Jean's hands tightened on the steering wheel. She knew the drill. When she stopped, she lowered her window just far enough to announce to the officer in attendance who she was and that she was expected. Then she sat staring at her odometer, not meeting the eyes of any of the reporters who surged forward, mini-cams and microphones pressing up against the windows. She felt like a fish in a barrel, the kind that was easy to shoot.

Impassively the cop outside the gate called up to the house, received confirmation, and opened the wrought-iron portal. Her ankle spasmed, but Jean kept herself from flooring the gas pedal. Once in the shadow of the trees, around the first bend in the drive, she registered what the odometer was reading. She'd come just over three miles from MacSorley Mansion.

So much for Kieran's alibi. He had had the opportunity to kill Lovelace. Whether he had a motive…. Well, as Cameron said, motives could be slippery. But someone had one. You didn't garrote and hang a man by accident.

The row of tall, arched windows above the toothy grin of Glendessary House's colonnade made Jean think of the sunglasses on a movie star, shiny and impenetrable. Today the garage doors stood open, revealing an SUV and a red sports car. A BMW sat shining like new pound coin on the threshold of the third doorway, the gravel around it wet and slightly sudsy. She doubted if any of those cars belonged to Toby or Neil. Or Fiona, for that matter.

Several police vehicles clogged the courtyard. Fitting her rental car into a narrow space beneath the eaves of the trees, Jean plucked her suitcase from the back seat and this time remembered to lock the doors. As she turned toward the portico, two husky uniformed officers and D.C. Gunn's boyish form walked around the end of the house.

The two uniforms collected piles of electronic equipment from a van and went merrily on their way back around the corner. Gunn lagged behind, carrying a computer monitor so large his knees wobbled perceptibly.

"Oh, hello," he said to Jean. His eyes peering over the top of the casing were crinkled pleasantly.

She returned his smile. "Hello. It looks like you're setting up the incident room here."

"Oh aye, that we are, overmuch media attention in Spean Bridge and Fort William. But we're obliged to bring in all the IT equipment." He turned to follow the others. The cord that had been coiled neatly on top of the monitor slithered off the edge and flopped down around his feet.

"Stop right there," Jean called, "you're going to trip yourself up. Here, rest your chin on it." She picked up the end of the cord, cold and smooth as a snake, and wedged the plug beneath his jaw.

"Thank you kindly," he said between his teeth, and staggered away.

All right! She wasn't going to be out here alone with a killer after all. She'd have Cameron and Sawyer and crew, underfoot, yes, but maybe she could think of them as chemotherapy. You just hoped you survived the treatment long enough to survive the disease.

Speaking of political rather than physical survival, she had kind of sort of made a deal, hadn't she? And she had something she needed to return. Pulling her suitcase around the puddles from yesterday's rain, she followed Gunn through an open door and into the house, finding herself in the hallway opposite the one leading to the game larder.

The first door opened into a billiards room. The table in its center was covered with plywood and loaded with computers, scanners, faxes—all the technology of twenty-first-century business, be it manufacturing widgets or solving crime. Wires were gathered together in bundles and plugged into power strips along the walls. The hum of processors and fans hung in the air.

Shaded lights hung low over the table, hiding the faces of the people behind it, although Jean recognized Sawyer's barrel chest. She parked her suitcase and picked her way past a wet bar holding a hot plate and kettle on the boil. There was Gunn, waggling his arms in relief. When a uniform headed her off, Gunn intervened. "Can we help you, Miss Fairbairn?"

"I'd like to see D.C.I. Cameron. Is he here?"

"Oh aye, just there." Gunn pointed toward a second door.

"Thank you." Jean walked into what must have been the original smoking room. The gentleman's hangout, in other words, where they could smoke, drink, curse, and utter implications about the ladies that wouldn't warm the shell-pink ear of a grandmother nowadays. Unlike the sitting room, with its aroma of cigar smoke and whiskey, this room smelled of contemporary stale beer, popcorn, and WD-40.

Cameron sat at a small desk, wearing wire-rimmed glasses and inspecting the receipt she'd given Lovelace. Behind him an antique gun rack was filled with paintball guns and related equipment. The mantel of a handsome stone fireplace held a stack of paperback science fiction novels. Old hunting photos ranged along the walls…. No, not all those photos were Victorian-era. Several were of Kieran MacSorley and his cronies, posing with dead grouse and dead deer and probably dead ducks as well, their faces fixed with self-satisfied smirks.

"Miss Fairbairn." Cameron took off his glasses and came out from behind the barricade of the desk, polite if cool.

Funny, she hadn't noticed that he was only five or six inches taller than she was, not quite five-nine. Nothing like a commanding presence. Drawing herself up, she launched into her recital. "Charlotte MacSorley asked me to tea this afternoon, but when Kieran came in, he threw me out. He'd been out jogging. I'm wondering if he was out jogging Tuesday afternoon. We're only three miles from the MacSorleys' house. Kieran could have killed Lovelace and been back home by the time Fiona called with the news."

"Aye?" Cameron may well have known all about it, but damned if she could read his expression. If he wasn't a poker player, he ought to be.

"When Kieran got here on Tuesday I heard him say, 'Lovelace, that doddering old fool.' With the Hogmanay argument, I'd say there was no love lost between them."

"We've got no evidence MacSorley was here at the time Lovelace was killed," Cameron told her, and conceded, "but then, we've got no evidence he wasn't."

"Well, unless Charlotte's figured out some means of teleportation, she didn't kill Lovelace. As for why she rushed out to his house at the very time someone else was, your guess is as good as mine."

"I prefer not making guesses, Miss Fairbairn."

"So do I, Chief Inspector Cameron. But I'm not able to question all these people and review the evidence, like you are."

That quick sine wave of a smile passed along Cameron's lips and vanished into the ether, as though it occurred to him that most deals ran two ways. "Well then, what are you wanting to know? Mrs. MacSorley's excuse for visiting Corpach Tuesday? Rick MacLyon sent her to fetch a book."

"She almost ran me off the road because of that? Well, she did make some snide remark yesterday about Vanessa rejecting her help, maybe she was driving that fast because she was mad. Angry," amended Jean, reserving "mad" meaning "crazy" until she needed it.

"None of the MacSorleys is known for discreet driving."

Or for modesty, she suspected. "Have you learned anything about the break-in at Lovelace's house?"

"Loads of fingerprints, but you'd expect that. Like as not the burglar was wearing gloves."

"What about the forensic reports on the murder?"

"Some threads and plant particles look to be significant."

"Fingerprint results?"

"Nothing conclusive, no."

"What about my receipt there?"

"Your prints and Lovelace's."

"And the 'Two p.m. Tuesday' on the back is in his handwriting?"

"That it is."

Jean had had more luck getting something edible out of a hard-shell pecan. But Cameron was probably being as forthcoming as he could. "Lovelace must have written on the receipt because it was handy when he made an appointment with someone. Probably someone from the house or from the Jacobite Lodge—their meeting was here then."

"Did Mrs. MacSorley tell you anything about the Lodge?" Cameron asked, his left eyebrow registering interest in the new topic.

"She clammed up real fast when I asked her about it, only said something about 'when the time comes,' like there's going to be a launch party. That's when Kieran came in and said they don't talk to reporters."

"Mr. and Mrs. MacLyon aren't so keen on telling us about the Lodge, either. They're insisting it's not relevant to the murder."

"Which makes you think that it is."

"Oh aye," he stated. "Do you know anyone who's a member?"

"I just heard about the Lodge myself yesterday, from Miranda. She says that it's open only to people whose names are the same as Charlie's supporters in the Forty-five, although whether you have to actually be descended from one of those people I don't know."

"I'd not be a viable candidate for membership, name or no name."

"Well no." Inspiration buzzed in Jean's brain like a mosquito in her ear. "What if you got someone else to sign up and report back to you? Don't look at me, they've already got my number around here. Literally, with that anonymous phone call. But Lovelace's next door neighbor is a retired naval officer named

Ogilvy. A Lord and Lady Ogilvy raised the Forfarshire regiment for Charlie. Maybe he could join up. MacLyon asked him to, once, and he said he'd like to help solve Lovelace's murder."

"I see," said Cameron, with a slow nod that made Jean think he did see, every last shade and sign, including the yellow triangle warning of danger ahead. "Easier—and safer—simply to have a word with the man, ask what Lovelace told him about the Lodge."

"Yes," Jean conceded in turn.

"I'll have Sawyer interview the neighbor again."

"No, not Sawyer, he and Ogilvy didn't exactly hit it off. Send Gunn, he's a nice…" Jean cut herself off. He'd given her an inch and she'd taken a mile.

This time Cameron smiled, in a flare of slightly uneven white teeth like the quick burst of a flashbulb. She hadn't intended to be the comic relief today…. Suddenly she wondered again if he were being appreciative rather than critical.

"All right then," he said, "I'll have Gunn see to it. But you didn't come all the way out here to hound me with questions and tell me my own business, did you now?"

"You asked me to let you know if I learned anything. Besides, I have an interview with Rick MacLyon—which is why I was here Tuesday, you may remember. I've even been asked to stay the weekend."

He didn't come back with *no accounting for tastes* but with, "The MacLyons have a use for you after all, do they?"

"I figure MacLyon wants to do some promotion for his games. And do some damage control, too, a murder being a little inconvenient."

"You'll be telling me what you hear, then. And overhear, come to that. They'll be talking more freely to you than to me, I reckon."

"You expect me to spy for you? No way…."

"Spying's all right for this Ogilvy chap but not for you, is that it?"

"You want to protect Ogilvy from danger but not me, is that it?"

"You're the one with all the questions," he retorted without the least hint of a smile. "Here I was thinking we were on the same side."

"Touché." Jean was beginning to think Cameron had ESP, the way he could pick up on her thoughts and use them to bend her to his will. Not that his will was exactly opposed to her own. "All right, I'll see what I can do for you. Within reason."

"No one's expecting you to be unreasonable, Miss Fairbairn."

"I don't know what anyone expects of me, Chief Inspector Cameron. Oh. Here." She pulled his handkerchief out of her bag and held it out.

"Thank you." He took the cloth from her hand.

While he avoided actually touching her, still his energy field sent pins and needles up her arm. That was supposedly what people felt like just before they were struck by lightning—a frisson of fear, or disgust, or maybe awe. She stepped quickly back and collided with the chill stone of the fireplace.

"Good stone, that, old masonry, probably original to the house," Cameron commented blandly, and folded the handkerchief into his pocket.

"Yeah." She could go on about the restoration, or MacLyon's games, or anything, but there was no need to keep up a conversation. The meeting had been concluded, and the chairman was no longer entertaining motions from the floor.

A stir in the doorway was a female constable, very pert in her epaulets and dark stockings. "Sir?"

"Later, then, Miss Fairbairn." He dismissed her with a curt nod.

"Later," Jean returned with foreboding, but Cameron was already following the constable into the other room.

Jean followed in turn, stopping while they went on toward a group of police people ranged in front of a chart propped on an easel. Across the chart were printed several words of which she could make out "Time" and "Place." Down its left-hand side ran a column of names. The cast of characters, starting with "Jean Fairbairn" and running through the two MacLyons and the three MacSorleys, Walsh, and Robertson. Jean glanced at Cameron, but his expression was impenetrable. She must have imagined that grin.

Below Fiona's name was written Ronald Ogilvy's. Cameron had to have recognized it. The list continued on with Meg Parkinson-Fraser and Norman Hawley—oh, the cook—and a block of names grouped after "Angus Lockhart, driver." Murray, Mackintosh, Nairn, three Stewarts…the Lodge members.

Hugh, Miranda, Michael, and Rebecca's names anchored the chart. Jean was rather surprised Cameron hadn't included little

Linda Campbell-Reid, although even he couldn't get answers from an unborn child.

"Uncle Tom Cobleigh and all," Sawyer proclaimed. He stood to attention beside the chart, his thick forefinger bludgeoning each name. "Every last one's been interviewed. Some want a second go-round. Some want bringing in. Co-ordinate times, who was here, there, everywhere. Cleaners come on the Monday, landscape service on the Wednesday...."

Jean edged away, thinking what Charlotte had said about the army of servants. Having a cleaning service and professional gardeners to do the heavy lifting made sense. But what about other services? No names that could be a valet, a maid, or a butler were listed. Since Neil had given himself several job descriptions, Jean assumed that the MacLyons had a casual attitude toward the social graces, the Lodge members notwithstanding.

On one end of the billiard table sat a computer monitor glowing with another list. Jean glanced at it, recognizing an inventory of garments, each attached to a name: Kilts, shirts, jackets, kilt-skirts. The words "wool, MacLyon tartan" occurred over and over.

Some threads look to be significant, Cameron had said. Had they found threads of MacLyon tartan on Lovelace's body? Great, that eliminated nobody except Kieran, unless he'd been out jogging in a kilt or plaid.

Sawyer's serrated voice made her jump. "Do you mind, Miss Fairbairn?"

She looked around to see a sneer escape his beard. Every other face was turned toward her except Cameron's. "Not at all, Detective Sergeant Sawyer," she called.

Stepping over the wires, Jean made her way to the door and retrieved her suitcase. She didn't outrun the hectoring voice until she'd walked out the door, around the corner of the house, and into the chill breeze of the courtyard. There she was confronted with the scenic vista of Neil waxing the BMW.

His right arm was braced on a fender. His left hand made meticulous circles with a soft cloth. The posture and the motion set off his T-shirt- and jeans-clad body to perfection. His face and body were sculpted by youth: clean, lean, and flexible.

While he might have his lean body from his father, Kieran's

face seemed to be the product of an acid attack. Of his own bile, Jean supposed. And Neil might have his blue eyes from his mother, although Charlotte's were pale and watery, exhausted by her vigil over propriety.

By the time you slogged into middle-age, you pretty much had the face and form you'd earned. Look at Sawyer, pulled down by the weight of his own self-importance. Or Rick, his muscles sucked away by the energy it took to feed his brain. Or Cameron, cloaked by a deliberate minimalism. As for Jean's own body, its not-terribly-ample curves were a compromise between her appetite for food and her appetite for movement. Her antsiness, Brad had called it. She could have made a recording of his exasperated voice: *Can't you sit still!*

Neil turned around, sensing he wasn't alone. Probably, for that matter, sensing that he was being admired. "Jean! Here for your interview, are you?"

"Yes, I am. And I've been invited to stay the weekend."

"Oh aye, I had a word in Vanessa's ear, told her a friendly journalist is all to the good, eh?"

So Charlotte knew from Neil that Jean was booked for the weekend. There was one minor mystery solved. "I had tea with your mother on my way here."

"Sorry to hear that." Neil left the cloth on the fender and walked toward Jean, wiping his hands on his denim-clad flanks.

With an effort she kept her eyes on his face. "I hear you're off to university soon. Which one? Glasgow? Edinburgh? Further afield?"

"Mum's at it again, is she? I looked over the University of London in March, aye, but I'm not away to university just yet. Some day, I reckon, but life's too short to spend it swotting up old books."

"Those old books have their moments."

"Aye, that they do. Especially to Rick." Again Neil advanced to just within her comfort zone. Again he unleashed his smile, knowing exactly what its effect was, admitting it, making no apologies for it.

Oh the heck with it, Jean thought, and leaned toward him, into an aura warm and intimate as a caressing hand.

"I'm not after keeping you from your work," Neil went on, "but some time when Rick's busy with his books and his computers we could take his car here for a wee ride, eh?"

"Joy riding?" Jean teased.

"Rick lets me take out the cars whenever I like. I play the tour guide to his clients. And Vanessa won't drive herself, being nervy about heading up the wrong side of the road, as she says it."

Jean barely heard him. His eyes were the dark blue of the sea with its unexplored depths. He exuded a slightly musky young-animal smell. She'd thought her pheromone receptors had burned out long ago, but no, there they were, jumping up and down like teenagers at a rock concert. She might have had a maternal moment with D.C. Gunn, but she didn't feel the least twitch of maternal now. With Neil she was on estrogen overload.

Not that there was anything wrong with that. During the lawsuit she'd had to cloak herself as strictly as Cameron—contents under pressure. But now…. Well, some day she might figure out how to let go again, but now she told herself that anyone as attractive as Neil had to have a girlfriend. She stepped back. Recess over. Back to work. "Tell me, Neil. Are you a member of Rick's Lodge?"

The word didn't spook him. If anything, he looked a bit embarrassed. "In a way. Sort of swept along with the group. Harmless loonies, if you ask me. And you are asking me, eh?"

Harmless loonies. She'd take Neil's word for that, although someone who was manifestly not harmless had murdered Lovelace. "So what…."

The front door slammed open. "…signed on to cook," shouted a man's gruff voice, "not to be handed this sort of aggro."

As one, Neil and Jean turned to look. Fiona stood in the doorway, Toby hovering behind her, at least so far as a man his size could hover. Spurting through the portico came a much smaller man carrying a suitcase. His face looked as though it had been pressed in a vise, top to bottom, so that his chin curled up to meet his brow ridge and his lips jutted petulantly. With the addition of his round stomach and short legs, he reminded Jean of a garden gnome. An irate garden gnome.

"Norman," said Fiona in dulcet tones, "Mr. Hawley, could you at least stop over the weekend? We've got guests to feed…."

"You've got a house full of police, lassie, that's what you and your Yank friends are having."

"Could we discuss a rise in wages? I'm sure Rick...."

Norman—the cook, Jean realized—kept right on walking. "A man returns from his day out and finds a poor old sod hanging from a hook in the back room. You can't pay me that much I'd hang about with murderers."

"They'd already carried him away before you came back," observed Neil as Norman stumped by.

"And now they've turned over my room as well, haven't they?"

"The police are searching the entire house," said Fiona, the voice of reason. Toby's head pivoted worriedly from face to face.

"Murders, secret societies, Yanks poncing about like royalty, no thank you, I don't think so, I don't think so at all. I'm away, back to the restaurant in Inverness; manager's a right prat but we've got only the odd drunk, no murderers." Norman opened the door of a battered car parked on the far side of the courtyard, threw his suitcase inside, climbed after it, and drove away in a spray of gravel.

Neil made a warding movement in front of Jean, but the bits of stone pattered down harmlessly. She waited to hear the sound of rending metal from the end of the drive—did everyone drive like a maniac here?—but didn't.

With a heartfelt sigh Neil picked up his cloth. "A wee bit on the nervy side, our Norman, but he knows his way round a cooker. Venison collops in raspberry wine sauce. Smoked haddock over lemon caper linguini. Ginger crème brulée with soft fruit. We'll be eating mushy peas now, mark my words."

The words Jean remembered were George Lovelace's, describing a modern meal as *a few stunted vegetables in a pool of muck*. Yes, Norman's sort of cuisine was intended more for the eye and the tongue than the stomach, but it wasn't Lovelace who'd paid his salary.

Fiona stepped back from the door. "Toby, Norman's cooked the dinner already, all that needs doing is the final touches. I'll lend a hand once I show Miss Fairbairn to her room." She swept Toby into the recesses of the house and beckoned Jean inside.

"See you later," Jean said to Neil and received The Smile, Variation C, wistfully lopsided, in return.

She dragged her suitcase across the portico, asking herself just what it was she was doing here, hanging about with murderers.

FIFTEEN

FIONA LED THE WAY past the grandfather clock and up the stairs. Jean spared a glance for Toby, ambling dejectedly toward the kitchen, and hitched her bag up the steps behind Fiona's trim pants and blouse outfit. "I must apologize for subjecting you to such a scene," the housekeeper commented, eyes front.

Jean didn't reply, *No problem, it's all grist for my mill.* She said, "I hear great cooks are temperamental sorts. Nervy, as you'd say around here."

"Jumpy, as you'd say in the States. I'm afraid so, aye."

"Anyone would be jumpy after what happened Tuesday. But Hawley—that's his name, right?—he wasn't here then. Even though y'all were entertaining the Lodge."

Fiona glanced back over her shoulder, but if any expression crossed her face Jean didn't catch it. The woman's emotions were as closed-off as Alasdair Cameron's. Maybe they were long-lost brother and sister, like Princess Leia and Luke Skywalker. Except Fiona hadn't yet turned out to be one of the good guys. She could have told Rick that Lovelace's body was in the game larder, but Jean hadn't told her. She hadn't even seemed surprised by what Jean did tell her. And why did Fiona seem to recognize Jean at the front door? There was nothing wrong with her eyesight.

"Rick finds Norman Hawley's name to be a bit awkward," said Fiona, as though sensing that any explanation would be better than none. "He told him to have his day out the Tuesday instead of the Wednesday. Toby and I fixed the scones and sandwiches."

"Fixed" the scones? That was an Americanism, too. "His name.... Oh, I get it. General Hangman Hawley, one of Butcher Cumberland's right-hand men, who left a trail of death, destruction, and degradation across the Highlands in the aftermath of the Forty-five."

"That's it in one."

"Hawley doesn't seem too fond of Americans. Or the police. Although Cameron would make Mother Teresa feel guilty."

Did Fiona chuckle at that? Or was she just breathing hard after the long flight of stairs? Whatever, she ignored Jean's bait and led the way past closed double doors into an open area lined by tall windows and furnished with couches and tables.

What Jean took to be a striped bolster laid across a love seat opened clear golden eyes. Oh, it was the cat she'd seen looking through the balusters. She was relieved to see it again, not being ready to add ghost animals to her paranormal vocabulary. The cat sniffed at her extended hand, then yawned. "I know tabbies run large," Jean told Fiona, "but she's a real Amazon. Like something out of a Popcorn game."

"She's mine, actually. Rick and Vanessa have been kind enough to take her in as well." Fiona scratched the cat behind the ears. "She's part Scottish wild cat. In a moment of sentimentality I named her Clarinda. I suppose I should be apologizing to her for that."

"Nothing wrong with a little sentiment," Jean stated. What she saw was the plain gold band on Fiona's left hand, glinting against Clarinda's soft fur. She was married, then. Or had been. Burns' poem about Clarinda was about love and loss, after all.

Fiona headed off down the hall, Jean hurrying along behind. "You've picked up some American expressions from the Mac—from Rick and Vanessa."

"I've studied in the U.S."

"Really? Where? What's your field?"

"University of Pennsylvania, library science."

"Ah." Housekeeping, Jean supposed, segued more naturally from library science than from, say, microbiology. Was part of her job description, then, working with Lovelace in MacLyon's library?

Fiona opened the door of a room labeled "MacPherson." "Here you are. This all right for you?"

Jean had seen five-star hotel rooms less well appointed than this bedroom with its paneling, plaster, and fabric embroidered in Jacobean designs. "It's lovely. Thanks."

"As Rick prefers eating his dinner early, usually it's served up at half-past six. Today, though, we'll be serving up at seven. No need to dress." Fiona turned back toward the door.

Jean accidentally-on-purpose blocked her way with the suitcase. "Are you feeding the police dinner, too? Was that one of Norman's complaints?"

"No," replied Fiona. "To both questions. Although I daresay Norman might have fancied the opportunity to rant about Philistines who don't appreciate good cooking."

"Philistines like George Lovelace? Or maybe D.C.I. Cameron?"

Fiona's face went from impassive to a studied blankness. She said quietly, "Policemen aren't necessarily Philistines. Nor are old men. George might have been a bit old-fashioned, but then, he was going on for eighty years old."

She hadn't taken the bait with either name. Jean tried again. "Were you helping George put together Rick's library?"

"In a way, aye."

"I only met him briefly, but even so I'd say George had his own rants, about contemporary manners and morals."

"He was an honorable man. Too much so for his own good, I'm afraid. If you'll…." Fiona feinted toward the door.

Jean stood her ground. "Years of studying the eighteenth century, not to mention living through World War Two, can affect your perception of antique notions such as honor."

"Someone once said the past is another country."

"Yes, but we've all lived there."

"Oh aye," agreed Fiona, her words trailing off into a sigh.

"So why was George too honorable for his own good?"

"Sometimes it's better to let…." The corners of her mouth tucked themselves in protectively.

"…sleeping dogs lie?" suggested Jean.

"To let well alone."

"You mean he shouldn't have come to see me in Edinburgh?"

Fiona ducked that question by dropping her gaze to the floor and crossing her arms across her rib cage.

Jean was beginning to interpret her blankness as stubborn refusal to acknowledge the issues, let alone talk about them. She persisted. "Do you know why he came to see me?"

"Miss Fairbairn," Fiona said to her shoes, "the dinner needs seeing to. If you'll…."

"Did someone kill George because he came to see me? Coincidences happen, yes. So does cause and effect."

"There's no avoiding one's fate." Fiona looked up, meeting

Jean's curious gaze. Her uncanny eyes were calm, collected, closed. Not hostile, not even stubborn, simply closed and locked.

Did she think murder was fate? Was she entirely passive? Or…Jean tried a stab not in the dark but in the twilight. "Did you call my flat, trying to warn me off by telling me George was trouble? Is that why you acted as though you recognized me?"

"You had an appointment. You arrived early." Fiona's gaze didn't waver.

Jean couldn't remember whether a steady gaze or rapid blinking was a sign of a liar. She tried another question. "Was George trouble enough that someone murdered him? Why?"

"Maybe he was killed because he asked too many questions, Miss Fairbairn. I suggest you save yours 'til your interview with Rick. Now I must be getting myself to the kitchen." Fiona pushed gently but firmly past Jean and paced off down the hall.

Jean stared after her, trying to read the set of her shoulders or the rhythm of her walk, but found herself suddenly illiterate. Fiona's last statement, though, hadn't sounded like a threat, just a statement of fact. Maybe Fiona did see herself as life's spectator, not participant. Fatalistic. Or maybe she had a sluggish nervous system or a thyroid problem, some condition that was the flip side of Jean's hyper-alertness.

The only time Fiona had bristled, almost imperceptibly, was when Jean asked what George's mission to Edinburgh had been. Not when she asked about the telephone call. Although once she'd asked the former question, the latter wasn't a surprising follow-up—assuming Fiona was the anonymous caller.

Maybe Fiona was hiding what she knew because she was frightened of her employer—Rick fired Meg for talking to the press. However, it seemed more likely that Fiona was keeping quiet out of loyalty to her employer. In the end, Jean told herself, the question was not why Fiona wouldn't talk to her, but whether she would talk to the police, especially to Cameron. Her friend, relation, adversary—something.

Before shutting the door Jean made sure it had a functioning lock with a nice, heavy, old-fashioned key. *Jumpy?* she asked herself as she swung her suitcase up onto a rack. *You bet.* Fiona wasn't the first person to think Jean never left well enough alone, either. But she'd much rather regret something she'd done than something she hadn't done.

She checked that the massive wardrobe didn't have a false back. Ditto the headboard of the canopied bed. She inspected the basket of soaps and lotions in the bathroom. She examined the tray holding a china tea set, tea bags, and cookies. She poked through the vase of roses on the table in the window. She looked inside the lamps and behind the brocade curtains and beneath the top of the toilet tank.

No secret passages, no microphones, no poison darts, nothing that didn't belong in a luxurious bedroom. Still Jean felt like a character in something between an Agatha Christie mystery and a P. G. Wodehouse farce.

Miranda had called Meg, the ex-secretary, a character out of Wodehouse. Charlotte, on the other hand, had called her a libertine. Why? Because Meg, who presumably had as much estrogen as Jean but perhaps less skepticism, had gone beyond flirting with Neil? You'd think Charlotte would be glad to see Neil involved with a young lady of hyphenated name, but she was probably aiming higher, for Princess Beatrice, at least.

As for Neil, he probably couldn't resist flirting with every woman in sight any more than a dog could resist watering a fire hydrant. And for much the same reason, to mark his territory.... Sometimes Jean wished that either the cynicism or the romanticism would win their tug of war in her psyche.

Again she pulled out her notebook and made notes. She'd have to transfer everything to her laptop when she turned it on for Rick's long-delayed and much-anticipated interview. Now she had some good snooping time before dinner.

Jean locked the door of her room, stowed the key in her jacket pocket, and walked back into the sitting area at the head of the stairs. From somewhere came a listless easy-listening version of "Wild Mountain Thyme." Humming, she zeroed in on the cat.

One of the set of doors at the top of the staircase opened a crack. A female hand with long shimmering purple nails wrapped around its edge and a flat American voice, pitched low and urgent, leaked through the aperture. "You can't stick to the original timetable. You've got to go public now, while you can still put the right spin on it. Before that mob at the gates and the police figure it all out and we lose control."

A masculine mumble came from further inside the room.

"I set you up with this woman, Rick. If you don't take advantage of having her here, I will. I mean it."

The door opened further, then stopped as the male voice spoke again.

Jean backpedaled, hustling toward the far end of the hall. Well, well, well. Her—and Cameron's—nasty suspicious natures had it right. Two days ago her interview would have been about the restoration of the house, but now Vanessa, at least, wanted to use Jean's media connections to…what? Not confess to a murder, that was for sure. Announce a new game, one that would provide a grand unified theory of physics and cure cancer all at once? *Wait and see,* she ordered herself.

Affixed to each door she passed was a tartan-backed plaque bearing the name of a clan that was "out" in 1745. Not that all the clan members responded unanimously to their prince's call. Some men were forced out by threats. Others informed Charlie that his sense of entitlement was not universally applauded. Those men and women who followed Charlie did so with their hearts, not their heads. And all too soon hearts as well as heads were rolling. Whether they belonged to rebels or refuseniks didn't matter to people like the original Hawley.

While Jean understood Rick's shudder at Norman's name, she couldn't help but think there had to be a better reason for ejecting the cook on Tuesday.

A second, more modest staircase was fitted into an alcove at the far end of the hall. Unless the place had been re-designed by M. C. Escher, this staircase would come out next to the billiards room. Yes, Sawyer's blustering voice drifted up from below, accompanied with a whiff of either coffee or brass polish.

The staircase also led upward, to what in American dialect would be the third floor but in Britspeak was the second. Servant's quarters? More guest rooms? Belfries for the MacLyon family bats?

"Yo, Jean! Hi there!"

Jean spun around. Vanessa MacLyon, another prime suspect, was walking briskly down the hall toward her.

SIXTEEN

JEAN HARDLY RECOGNIZED Vanessa. She was wearing wide-legged denims, clunky sandals, and a snug jersey blouse that barely contained her breasts. She resembled two olives on toothpicks, stylishly and painfully thin except for the protuberances on top. A navel ring winked between the hem of the blouse and the waistband of the pants. She was wearing a light sweater, but still Jean could count the goose bumps.

"Hello," Jean said, and, since she could hardly pretend otherwise, "I was just looking around. Great restoration."

"Yeah, Rick's really good with detail, comes from designing all those games. Would you like the nickel tour?"

"Yes, please. I appreciate y'all agreeing to an interview after—well, after everything that's happened."

Vanessa's green eyes flicked quickly toward Jean's and just as quickly flicked away again. "To be honest, Rick only agreed to talk to you originally because of Miranda. And then after poor old George died, I expected Rick to dig a moat, install a drawbridge, and pull it up, but moats and drawbridges aren't the right period, are they? Neil says you're okay, though, not like the jackals who only want the sensational stuff."

"I'm after the historical and architectural story," Jean assured her, giving a lick and a promise to the truth. "It was nice of Neil to speak up for me."

"It was George who got him to reading *Great Scot*. Poor old George, what a way to go." Making a face, Vanessa fluttered her purple fingertips toward the back staircase. "Up there, that's where Fiona and all of them sleep."

"All of them" meaning everyone except Rick and Vanessa, Jean supposed. At night, with everyone asleep, the house must be very quiet, nothing stirring except mice and shadows.... She'd be finding out what the house was like after dark very soon now. No need to borrow dread. "Are the police staying here?"

"Some of them. It's not like we're short of space or anything." Vanessa turned toward the main staircase. "All these rooms and there's hardly ever anybody here. And Rick knows loads of celebrities, too."

"My next-door neighbor, Hugh Munro, he was here for your Hogmanay party. I guess that was the exception that proves the rule?"

"Oh yeah. Rick wanted to make some social points with that, but everybody else who comes out here is deadly dull."

Jean didn't expect Vanessa to say *present company excepted,* and sure enough she didn't.

"And he picks dull employees. Except for Meg, his personal assistant. She was fun but she turned out to be a Benedict Arnold, you know?"

"Oh?" Jean murmured, adding to herself, from the British perspective Arnold was a patriot.

"At least Neil's here. He's brilliant."

"He's definitely easy on the eyes."

"You think so?" Vanessa raked Jean with a shrewd glance. "I saw in the newsp… But it's not true, is it, about you having sex with a student and getting him expelled and everything?"

Jean winced. She should have anticipated that one. Through her teeth she answered, "He got himself expelled by plagiarizing a published work. The sexual harassment angle was a lie."

"That's what I figured," Vanessa returned, with a shrug that pretty much said, *You must be almost his mother's age.*

Like Rick wasn't old enough to be Vanessa's father? But Jean hadn't come here to debate gender politics. "Thanks for giving me the benefit of the doubt," she said, and followed Vanessa back up the hall. "Fiona's wearing a wedding ring. Is her husband in the area?"

"No, she's a widow. It was sad and everything, you can't really blame her for doing the ice princess bit, but geez, she can be a little hard to take. Not real friendly. Kind of judgmental, even."

A widow? Tragic would be a better word than sad, then. That might explain Fiona's reserve—she wasn't hiding something, she was chilled to the bone, numb. Jean understood emotional survival mode, although, not, thank God, to that extent. "What happened to…"

"Fiona helped with the decorating," Vanessa said at the same time, and went on, "she's got a great eye for fabric and knows her antiques, even though she's way too conservative when it comes to putting it all together. But Rick wanted, like, classic stuff, and he pays the bills."

Vanessa was certainly being chatty. Since Jean could hardly run back into her bedroom and get her notebook and pen, she commanded her short-term memory to pay attention and her brain to adjust to Vanessa's mosquito-whine California accent. *Fiona's husband's death. Ask Miranda.*

"And poor old George—I know he's gone, I don't mean to knock him—but George was dead boring. We owe Toby to him, thank you very much. Not that there's any harm in helping with his rehabilitation, it's just that he's a couple of sandwiches shy of a picnic, you know?"

No, Jean didn't know, but Miranda was already on that case.

They walked through the sitting area at the head of the main staircase. The cat opened an eye and shut it again. "Hey, Clarinda, good kitty-cat. I eat breakfast here; in the winter the sun shines in. When the sun shines at all."

"There ought to be a way to base Scotland's gross national product on clouds," agreed Jean. The large windows overlooked the courtyard and the driveway, barred with the long shadows of evening. Was it from here Toby saw Lovelace walking up the drive? And if so, so what?

Vanessa was halfway down the opposite hall. Jean caught up with her, asking, "Do you help Rick with his work?"

"Absolutely. I act out story lines for him, and I interface with the accountants and lawyers. Rick's freelancing now, though you'd never notice it the way he's glued to a keyboard or a phone all the time. He's wired, connected."

"And what about you? Do you ever get away?"

"I'd go nuts if it wasn't for the Internet. Sometimes I'll get to Edinburgh or Glasgow, do some shopping and clubbing, you know, remember that this is the twenty-first century. A couple of months ago I spent a long weekend in London."

"A place where they actually have sidewalks, let alone a place where they never roll them up."

"What? Oh, rolling up the sidewalks. I get it. Here's our bedroom." Vanessa threw open the door at the end of the hall.

Jean glimpsed a king-sized bed with a canopy, decorated by feathers and streamers like a Regency nightmare. Not the aborted regency of Bonnie Prince Charlie, for a change, but that of George IV, whose visit to Edinburgh in 1822 had spurred a tartan frenzy.

Vanessa shut the door, leaving Jean staring at its plaque. It didn't read "MacLyon" but "Cameron." Odd, she thought. Rick seemed eager enough to plaster his name and his tartan over everything else, not that clan tartans were any more authentic than his name. While tartan was genuinely historic, the clan tartan business was created during that same Regency frenzy by Walter Scott and the Sobieski-Stuart brothers, amiable charlatans who claimed to be Charlie's grandsons.

Vanessa started back down the hall. "Dinner's going to be late, Norman bailed out this morning. That's gratitude for you. I mean, Rick hired him even with the mediocre references. Of course he was all Kieran's idea."

"Kieran MacSorley?" Jean asked, scurrying along behind, although she knew exactly who Vanessa meant.

"Yeah, Norman worked at Kieran and Charlotte's favorite place in Inverness. I figured they got tired of driving up there so they got Rick to hire Norman. They're always here for dinner anyway."

"Maybe the MacSorleys won't want to come now that Norman's gone and the police and all the reporters are here."

Vanessa brightened at that. "You think?"

"Why did Norman have mediocre references? I thought he was a good cook."

"He is. He does a salmon mousse to die for. It's just that he's so negative, thinks everyone's out to get him. Like anyone would even notice a weasel like him. He made poor old George look like an elder statesman or something. But hey, we've got to eat."

The choice being between a cook and starvation, Jean deduced.

The saccharine murmur of music was broken suddenly by the slam of doors and the roar of engines. Below the windows of the sitting area, several uniforms, Gunn, Sawyer, and Cameron were swarming into cars and racing off. Apprehension trickled through Jean's body. She didn't need twitching thumbs to tell her that this fresh cascade did not bode good news. "They look like they're on their way to a fire. Now what?"

"We'll be finding out soon enough," groaned Vanessa.

The last car vanished down the drive, leaving not so much as a dust mote behind. Jean hoped the cops were off to happy hour at the pub, or at least nothing worse than a fender bender on the highway…. Vanessa was right. They'd find out soon enough. No need to borrow dread there, either.

With an air of resignation and her finger to her lips, Vanessa opened one of the doors at the top of the stairs and revealed a room that, except for the wood and tartan trim, might have been Mission Control. Before the screens and the keyboards sat Rick, hardly noticeable in his ergonomic chair. An electronic sound track thweeped and bumped in time to the swirling colors and shapes on the screens, clashing with the tinkly version of "Flower of Scotland" Jean could hear in the background. Rick must have set up an intercom sound system and was playing his own program of elevator music.

Vanessa led the way behind Rick's back to a wrought-iron spiral staircase that wound its way down into a stunning library. Jean stopped at its foot to breathe in the scent of books: paper with an afterglow of mildew, a headier perfume than that of the roses in her room. Only here, now, was she jealous of Rick's wealth.

Tall windows looked out over gardens and tennis courts. Between each window stood cabinets and shelves. Some were filled with books, others held a collection of Jacobite memorabilia, professionally displayed and spotlighted: rings, brooches, miniature paintings, a sword, a pistol, even a small round shield called a targe. Every item gleamed, reminding Jean of the gold coin.

Overstuffed chairs hinted of long afternoons, a good book, a glass of Scotch, a fire in the fireplace, a purring cat, the music of Vaughan Williams or Debussy instead of that homogenized Greatest Scottish Hits soundtrack. Although silence would be good, too, broken only by the whisper of rain and the turn of pages…. Firmly turning her back on the seductive murmur of the shelves, Jean asked, "Did Kieran suggest George Lovelace to Rick, too?"

Vanessa stood with her hands on her hips, looking critically around the room. "Yeah, Kieran strong-armed Rick into taking him. Rick figured he could get by with just Fiona, you know, doing double duty. But she's not an eighteenth-century expert, said so herself."

"Kieran had worked with George before?"

"No. They weren't even friends, not that I could tell, constantly giving each other static over—well, the equivalent of angels dancing on pins, if you ask me. Like the divine right of kings. Big deal."

It had once been a big deal, an issue people died for. "Did Kieran doubt George's competence?"

"Oh, no. No way. It's just that Kieran gets up your nose. So does Charlotte, la-de-dah, the fish forks have to be arranged just right or it's the end of civilization as we know it, know what I mean?"

"Yes I do," Jean said with a grin.

"Hard to believe Neil is Kieran's son," Vanessa went on, "he's a sweetheart but his dad's, like, a total manipulator."

Jean expressed no more opinions about Neil. "Won't George's death put a crimp in Rick's plans?"

"No, not really. George was pretty much done with the collection. He was just saying last week how glad he was he didn't have to go back to Inverness again; he spent days on end in the Highland Archives at the Public Library in Farraline Park, researching books of the period." Vanessa angled a bit of bric-a-brac an inch to the right.

"Fiona must have been grateful for the help; it would be hard for her to spend days in Inverness and run the house, too."

"Well, she and poor old George got a territorial thing going a time or two. Though since Fiona's into everything else around here, you think she'd be glad to share the burden. But they got along all right most of the time."

Was there a note of acid in that? *Fiona's into everything else around here.* Like what, exactly? Fiona had implied it was George who was exceeding his commission. Jean tried, "I'm sure George's expertise paid off."

"Oh yeah, it paid off." Vanessa laughed, not a giggle but a deep-throated guffaw. "Some of this stuff cost Rick a fortune and a half. I mean, he's got a fortune and a half, and rare books are really collectible right now, especially a themed collection with the artifacts. But Rick's just a little gullible at times—big surprise, right, he wouldn't be filthy rich if it wasn't for his imagination."

"You think Rick paid too much for some things?"

"Hard to say," said Vanessa with an easy-come, easy-go grimace. "It all depends on what the market will bear. He did have George look over all the books and papers, and the other stuff he sent to the National Museum in Edinburgh."

He had George.... Suddenly Jean wondered if Lovelace had been, well, embezzling. He'd said he needed money. She essayed, "George came to me about an artifact he'd found."

"The gold coin," Vanessa returned, with no more emphasis than if she'd said *the Pez dispenser*. "Yeah, he said he was going to take it to you to do the treasure trove thing with."

So Vanessa knew about the coin, not to mention George's visit to Edinburgh. "I'm surprised Rick didn't buy the coin from him."

"He wanted to, but George wouldn't sell up to him. It was funny, Rick's eyes all bugged out, checkbook ready, and George saying it was his civic duty to sell it to the National Museum. I think George really enjoyed asserting himself with Rick right then. He was as cheerful as I ever saw him, usually he was sort of apologetic, you know."

"He seemed very polite," Jean said. "He was keeping the coin in what looked like a jewelry box."

"Oh yeah, that. I was throwing it out and he asked if he could have it. Said it wasn't proper to keep a historical artifact in an old sock."

No, an old sock wouldn't make as good an impression on a gullible journalist. "Do you know when and where he found the coin?"

"Around here somewhere. I got the impression he'd had it awhile." Vanessa ran her fingertip along the edge of the mantel like a drill sergeant inspecting for dust.

Jean's eye followed her motion, then stopped. How about that? The expanse of chimney above the fireplace was startlingly unadorned. Rick had missed his chance to post another portrait or even the MacLyon arms there. Surely he hadn't neglected to order a set of MacLyon arms.

Vanessa was still talking about Lovelace. "It was hard to tell what was going on in his head, he was so old-fashioned. Kind of like Charlotte and her everlasting etiquette, you know, though George would deliver sermonettes about honor and courage and famous warriors, dead boring, and here's Rick swallowing every word."

"Rick got along well with George?" asked Jean.

"As well as Rick gets along with anybody. Still, he was sort of spooky—George, I mean. You'd be talking to someone or doing something and you'd look around and there he was—like, how long have you been standing there?"

"He eavesdropped?"

"I don't think so. It's just that he blended into the background, you know?" Vanessa opened the door to the entrance hall. "And before you ask, no, I don't know why anyone would want to kill him. He could get on your nerves but that's hardly a killing offense, is it?"

"No, it's not, and a very good thing that is, too. Just what is a killing offense, do you think?"

Vanessa opened the door to the entrance hall and walked through, either not hearing Jean's question or not wanting to answer it.

So, thought Jean, whether the coin had been found on MacLyon land wasn't the issue. The coin itself wasn't the issue, as Cameron had pointed out, darn him anyway. What if Lovelace overheard something he shouldn't have.... That's what she got for asking questions. Too many answers.

Vanessa was waiting. With one last yearning glance back at the books, Jean stepped out onto the tiled floor of the entrance hall. "How did you and Rick meet?"

"I was in a play, a historical thing about Charlie and Flora, and Rick was one of the backers. The show sucked, opened and closed before it even made it to off-Broadway, but Rick said I did a good job as Flora, being a MacDonald and all. I thought it was because I was a good actress, myself." Vanessa curtsied, eyes downcast, hands spreading a make-believe skirt, chin set and back straight. Jean's eyes widened. For just a moment Vanessa was the pliable and yet intrepid Flora, to the life. Then Flora vanished and Vanessa went striding off in her thick-soled shoes.

"You majored in theater arts in college?" Jean asked.

"No, accounting and business, in case the acting stuff didn't pan out. I guess it did, though." Vanessa waved her hands, taking in the hallway, the house, and, presumably, Rick upstairs.

Maybe their relationship was a commercial arrangement. Maybe it was part of Rick's fantasy life. Maybe it was none of her business, Jean told herself, but without conviction. George's death made it her business, however indirectly.

She had expected to find Vanessa annoying. In reality she found her take-no-prisoners attitude refreshing. The young woman combined the self-absorption of an actress with the calculation of a corporate CEO. She was bored, yes. The question was whether she was actually spilling her guts to a stranger, and a reporter at that. Maybe this tour, with its spate of gossip and commentary, was a disinformation campaign designed either to soften Jean up for Rick's interview and/or conceal a murder.

If nothing else, Vanessa mixed bits of British dialect with her contemporary American syntax. Jean asked, "Did you meet the MacSorleys when Rick was looking for property in the area?"

"No, it was the MacSorleys who recommended the place. Rick knew them before he knew me, met Kieran through some genealogy seminar ages ago."

"Oh." That wasn't Charlotte's version, but the inconsistency could be a simple mistake. Not that anything else was simple around here, Jean thought as she heard the faint wail of a siren in the distance.

Vanessa headed down the hall that ended in the billiards room and waved at two doors, one open, one shut. "Media center. And that's my office."

Jean glimpsed several easy chairs, a big screen TV, and an impressive collection of speakers layered incongruously onto a room with the same wood-paneled ambience as the sitting room.

"Now," announced Vanessa, "it's happy hour." She darted across the hall, into the drawing room Jean had seen Tuesday. Its eighteenth-century blue walls, white dado, reefed draperies, and gilded picture frames didn't clash as badly with the predominantly blue colors of the MacLyon tartan carpet as they would have with a period Turkey rug.

Vanessa made a beeline for a mahogany cabinet. "I'll say one thing for Fiona, she fixes a good martini, and on schedule, too."

"Should we wait for Rick?" Jean asked.

"Naw, he's having his upstairs. I'm sure the happy house-keeper's already taken it up." Producing a silver shaker misted with condensation and a long-stemmed glass, she poured and offered the drink to Jean.

"Ah, no, thank you." Alcohol tended to make her flirtatious and giggly. "I see some Perrier...."

"Sure. It's okay. Some people have this thing about booze, you know?" Skillfully Vanessa assembled ice, lime, and water. "Here you go."

"Thanks." Jean sipped, the bubbles tickling her nose. She looked up at the portrait of Charlie and Jenny Cameron that hung center-stage, then noticed a painting of Clementina Walkinshaw hanging next to the one of Flora MacDonald. Both Flora and Clementina were painted in similar styles, typical of the times—level gaze, high forehead, a sadness around the lips. "Charlie had a way of leaving women sad," she commented.

"I hear he beat up his wife, what's her name?" Vanessa said. She fluffed her hair in the mirror mounted above the cabinet.

"Louise of Stolberg. I'd like to think the abuse was propaganda, but I'm afraid it wasn't. He was brutal to Clementina there, too, even after she left Britain and joined him in France. Even after she bore his only child."

"Rick says he had a bunch of kids."

"In legend, yes. I suppose Clementina Sobieska Douglas, a.k.a. the Finsthwaite princess, might've been legit—that is, actually another daughter by Miss Walkinshaw, not legitimate. Charlie used to call himself Douglas, after all, when he wanted to go around incognito."

"You really are up on all this stuff, aren't you?"

Vanessa's tone was respectful, not sarcastic. Jean took the plunge. "The Forty-five is a fascinating subject. Miranda was telling me about your Jacobite Lodge. Do you think I could join? I'd love to swap war stories with some other enthusiasts."

Vanessa's green eyes narrowed, suddenly wary. "Ask Rick about that," she said, and turned toward the French doors.

Jean eyed her back. All this ducking and weaving was making her more and more curious about the Lodge. It was like hearing a siren in the distance, a sure sign that something was up.

"One of these days it has to warm up," Vanessa said. "I'm going to throw a garden party. We've got the lights and the electronics all ready to go, we just need something for the midges. Flamethrowers, maybe. Look, there's Neil."

He was standing in front of a tall yew hedge, next to a row of bushes that were probably roses, still dressed in jeans and T-shirt—his kilt had been confiscated by the police, more's the pity. He lifted his bagpipes, set the mouthpiece between his lips, and with a wheeze and a wail began to play "The Flowers o' the Forest." That was the last sound George Lovelace had ever heard. Jean shuddered. Someone she knew was a murderer. Maybe even the personable young woman standing beside her.

"Again with the depressing stuff," Vanessa groaned, then, "Oh, here we go! Yes!"

One lingering note leaped suddenly upward in a smooth change of tempo. Neil's fingers danced on the chanter and the first notes of "Andy Renwick's Ferret" made Jean smile in spite of herself. Yes, indeed!

He began to pace back and forth. For several minutes both women stood and enjoyed the show, music that stirred the heart and the feet and a man who stirred the areas between. Then Jean glanced over at Vanessa. Surely her own face didn't look like that, lips parted and moist, eyes blank and dreamy....

Oh boy. Vanessa had gone to London a couple of months ago. Neil had looked over London University in March—a couple of months ago. If he chauffeured her around, what better opportunity for cozy chats? What better opportunity to find a bit of privacy, for that matter? They were certainly on excellent terms, close to the same age and of similar disposition.

Jean informed herself that if leaping to conclusions were an Olympic sport, she'd be up for the gold medal. If she hadn't been suspicious of the entire household to begin with, she'd never be assuming anything more than a flirtation—which seemed to be Neil's specialty. However...

Vanessa turned toward the door. "That's the tour. The cops are in the billiards room, no need to stick our noses in there."

"No," Jean stated, with absolute certainty for once.

The grandfather clock showed five to seven as Vanessa, martini glass at point, guided Jean into the opposite hall. The air was redolent of subtle spices and warm carbs "You saw the sitting room on Tuesday. Toby's office and the game larder are at the end of the hall, but you know that, too. It's time to turn the game larder into an exercise room, like I wanted all along, never mind what Kieran says."

Jean was about to ask just what Kieran was saying when Vanessa raked her with another shrewd look. She leaned in so closely Jean smelled the gin on her breath. "Before we go in to eat, I have a confession to make."

No way was it going to be the confession Jean wanted to hear. "Yes?"

"It's one of the reasons I wanted you to spend the weekend. I was afraid I was losing it, you know? Going nuts."

She hardly felt qualified to analyze anyone's sanity. "Yes?"

"George. He's still here."

He's still.... Good Lord, had the paranormal allergens in the sitting room been strong enough that Vanessa had sneezed? "He's what?" Jean asked, committing herself to nothing.

"The last couple of days I've heard footsteps here, in the hallway, when there was nobody there. Things move around in the sitting room, but the staff knows better than to move things around. Poor old George was murdered just down the hall. I figure he's unhappy. He wants revenge."

Maybe so, maybe not. Jean managed to keep her voice neutral. "That is a motive for haunting."

"You write ghost stories. Can you make him go away?"

"I'm a historian, not an exorcist. Still, please tell me...."

The clock struck seven. The dining room door swung open. Fiona stood in the opening. "The dinner is ready. I'll fetch Rick, shall I?"

Vanessa plunged into the dining room. Jean followed, but not without a long look at Fiona's face. *How long have you been standing there?* But Fiona walked on down the hall, impassive as ever.

SEVENTEEN

JEAN ENJOYED "The Antiques Road Show" more for the historical anecdotes and human interest stories than for the furniture. Even so, she recognized a Chippendale table and ditto sideboard in the dining room, both polished into mirrors. Real or reproductions?

The walls were lined with copies of historical tableaux such as Bonnie Prince Charlie's entrance into Edinburgh. A copy of the omnipresent painting of him bowing over Flora MacDonald's hand hung above the sideboard.... Wait a minute. In this version the woman under the green velvet bonnet looked like Jenny Cameron. Except Jenny had been twenty years older than the prince, which gave the lie to this woman's minuscule waist and simpering pose.

Well, playing fast and loose with history was part of Rick's job description. And if he wanted to tartanize his house into a stage-set for his own private production of *Brigadoon,* that was his business. The house had more personality than many more pedantic restorations.

Jean eyed the door leading into the hallway, envisioning each room beyond consumed by shadow; each artifact, each architectural detail, each antique, whether faux or genuine, fading into the darkness and yet still there, like memory. Like a ghost.

Had Vanessa heard George Lovelace's ghost? Was the ghost in the sitting room his? Vanessa seemed to be a practical, unimaginative person, not the spooky sort like Jean herself. But a sudden death, like a murder, could leave strong emotional resonances that could sneak up on the unsuspecting passerby. Jean had to wonder, though, if the ghost story was a gimmick like Lovelace's "help me with the coin," calculated to snare the interest of a helpful journalist.

Now Vanessa stood by the window drinking her martini, watching Neil pace through the lengthening shadows outside, and offering no more clues, legitimate or otherwise. Seizing her chance to tackle someone else, Jean pushed through the kitchen door.

Good! Toby was alone, standing over the stove and stirring a pot with the same partly panicked, partly deliberate air as a paramedic who finds himself delivering a baby. He looked around. His eyes widened. He said, "Oh, hullo Miss Fairbairn," and turned abruptly back to his task.

"That smells wonderful, Toby."

"It's Norman's sweet potato and lemon grass soup. A right mixtie-maxtie of odd things, hardly worth the eating."

"You're not a big fan of Norman's cooking?"

"I'd just as soon have a fish supper, meself."

There was as much to be said for fish and chips as for George Lovelace's chop and veg. "George would, too, I bet. Did you know he came to Edinburgh on Monday to see me?"

"The police told me so, aye." Toby bent even closer to the pot.

She hated to make him uncomfortable, even as she wondered whether his discomfort signaled anything more than grief. "Did George get you your job here?"

"That he did; he and me granddad was old army pals."

"You must miss him."

"That I do."

Gritting her teeth—she was far from comfortable herself— Jean asked, "Didn't I see you in the hallway at the Mountain View Hotel on Wednesday, Toby?"

The spoon banged against the pot like a clash of cymbals. "I— erm—Mrs. MacSorley told me to sit with her car at the garage, make sure the mechanics didn't scratch it or nothing, but there they were, finished, and no sign of Mrs. MacSorley, so I had meself a dauner up the High Street."

"And you saw me going into the hotel?"

"Aye, that I did."

"I'd just come from George's house in Corpach. Someone broke in."

"The polis, they was telling me that, too."

"Did you want to talk to me, Toby? Is that why you came to the hotel?"

"Just thought I'd have a blether about your writing," he said to the soup. "George was helping me learn to read and write proper. He had me reading your magazine. But then I thought, no, not polite to follow you when you was away from work, so to speak. George was always helping me with my manners as well. And Fiona."

That was smooth. But then, Toby had had time to come up with an excuse and try it out on Sawyer or Gunn. Or his story could actually be true. Someone around here had to be telling the truth. And in spite of Vanessa's remark about sandwiches and picnics, Toby seemed more uneducated than stupid.

He'd reminded Jean yet again that George had been a fan of hers. That he'd expected her to do—something—for him. Jean was becoming increasingly convinced that that something was not so simple as taking the coin to the Museum. Which made Cameron right yet again, drat the man. "When I get back to Edinburgh, I'll send you some back copies of the magazine."

"Thank you, Miss," Toby said. "Right kind of you."

"Yo, Jean!" called Vanessa from the dining room. The door slammed open, missing her shoulder by a hairsbreadth. "Rick's here."

Jean went back into the dining room to find Fiona herding Rick to the head of the table. He was shambling along with his cell phone pressed to his ear, wearing khakis and a polo shirt. Tuesday, in his kilt and Argyll jacket, he'd seemed taller than the five foot ten of his biography. Now his shoulders were rounded and his head outthrust, as though he'd frozen in the over-the-keyboard hunch that was only too familiar to Jean herself.

"You do that," Rick said into the phone. "Take care of it. Now." He switched it off and set it down next to his fork, just another utensil.

Toby peered around the door. "I'll start serving now, shall I?"

"Go for it." Sitting down at the other end of the table, Vanessa tossed off her martini and handed the glass to Fiona. "Thanks. You can go now."

Wordlessly, expressionlessly, Fiona glided into the kitchen. Neil stopped playing and marched away around the corner of the house. Was that a last echo of the music lingering on the air, or another distant siren? What was going on in the real world, anyway?

Jean took the third place, on the long side of the table. Putting down her Perrier, she considered the wine glass poised at the end of her knife. Maybe just a glassful…. Toby emerged from the kitchen door and plopped an ice bucket and a bottle of chardonnay down in front of Rick, who poured for himself and passed the bottle to Jean. Since chardonnay held all the charm of varnish, she passed it on. Vanessa filled her own glass to the brim.

Toby dealt out a soup tureen, a basket of rolls, and several covered dishes—in his huge hands they looked like a child's tea set—and then disappeared into the kitchen. Vanessa filled bowls and passed them down the table. With his best boarding-house reach, Rick grabbed a roll. He crumbled it into his soup and started ladling the resulting lumps into his mouth. "What about the police?" he asked Vanessa between bites.

"What about them?"

"Did you ask them if they needed any food?"

"We can't feed a dozen people, not without notice. Besides, most of them went charging off up the road a while ago."

"They did? Why?"

"They sure as hell didn't stop to tell me."

Jean dabbled her spoon in her soup, reminding herself that if any more stuff was flying toward the fan, she'd better take nourishment now.

"Norman took off, too," Vanessa added.

Rick's pale eyes blinked. "With the police?"

"No, he just quit is all."

"Did you try offering him more money?"

"What do you think?"

"Shit," said Rick. "Still, some of that stuff he fixed was pretty weird, you've got to admit."

"Innovative. Creative."

Jean wanted to say something about being a slave to trendiness but the soup was good, neither as heavy in texture nor in flavoring as she'd feared.

The door to the hall opened. Vanessa glanced around so quickly Jean winced, feeling sympathetic whiplash. Oh, it was Clarinda, the huge cat, pushing wider a door that hadn't been completely shut. She wore a collar, a tartan band with a gold dangler. In a house this size, what she should be wearing was a GPS unit.

Rick took the lids off the serving dishes, helped himself, and thrust them at Jean. Since she'd been spared any food allergies—divine compensation for her sixth sense, perhaps—she took a bit from each dish. Crab ravioli with artichokes. Lamb pie baked with Guinness. Slightly overcooked baby vegetables and light-as-air potato blini. Very good.

Incongruous, she thought as she chewed, that while the gold-rimmed china was so delicate it chimed like a bell at every stroke of her silver fork, the MacLyons' style was so casual your average barbecue seemed top-heavy with protocol. Charlotte would have had a hissy fit. Maybe Vanessa ran a tighter ship when the Mac-Sorleys were there. Maybe, defiantly, she didn't.

Rick hunkered over his plate, forearm resting on the table. Every now and then he'd straighten into a regal posture, then slowly slump down again. Vanessa slipped a bit of meat to the cat, who was circling the table like a shark around a life raft.

"Fiona says not to feed her," Rick commented to his ravioli.

"This is my house, not Fiona's," retorted Vanessa.

"Yeah, but it's her cat."

Elaborately, Vanessa wiped her hands on the crisp linen napkin. "Shoo, Clarinda. Go find Mummy."

With the feline equivalent of a shrug, the cat trotted back to the doorway and squeezed through.

In the silence Jean could hear Neil's voice in the kitchen, along with a subtle jangle of dishes and pots. Vanessa sat cutting her food into tiny bites, but not, apparently, eating them. Was she anorexic or embarrassed? Jean should open a Ghosts Anonymous chapter, like Alcoholics Anonymous, where people could get understanding, not ridicule.

Or was Vanessa intimidated by Rick? Jean had talked to everyone except him, the presiding genius, the head eccentric, the central figure of Glendessary House mythology. It was time to yank his chain. "Rick," she said.

He looked up from beneath his brow ridge as though surprised to see her at the table. "Oh. Yeah. The interview."

"I'd prefer to just visit rather than do anything formal. Have a blether, they'd say here. But however you want to handle it." Jean felt Vanessa's gaze on the side of her face like the glare of a heat lamp.

Rick edged his eyes toward his wife and then back to Jean. "Fairbairn. That would be your father's name. And his father's."

Again with the genealogy. Cameron wasn't the only person playing cat and mouse with her. Concealing her impatience, Jean explained, "My great-grandfather Fairbairn came from Stow, in the Borders. My great-grandmother was a MacKay from Sutherland, at the opposite end of the country. They met on an immigrant ship. My mother's maiden name was Graves, which is English, but her mother was a Thompson, which I understand also counts as MacTavish."

Rick nodded, his jaw still working.

Jean did not conclude by asking, *Do I pass the test?* "I'd like to write an article about the history of Glendessary House, its restoration, your collection of Jacobite memorabilia—that sort of thing. Like the Louis d'Or George Lovelace brought to my office on Monday."

Rick swallowed. "I offered to buy it. He said it should go to the Museum of Scotland."

"Did you ask him where he found it?"

"Yeah, but he was pretty vague about that."

Vanessa said, "He was pretty vague, period."

"He knew his business," said Rick. "He was a nice old guy, too."

Yes, he was, Jean conceded silently. "Have you thought about looking for more coins? The barrels were buried in this area. But then, that might attract more attention than you'd like. George was concerned about that."

Rick tore another roll in half and mopped it around his plate. "Attracting attention isn't the problem, Jean."

"Not now, anyway," said Vanessa.

So whatever it was Rick was supposed to tell her, to go public with, would attract attention. No surprise there. But Jean wasn't supposed to know that he was going to—announce, reveal, come clean with—something. "Tell me about the house," she prompted.

Vanessa sighed. "Here we go. Potted history one-oh-one."

"Glendessary House," said Rick. "The house that was here in seventeen forty-six probably belonged to Donald Cameron, the Gentle Lochiel. Who laid down his honor for Prince Charles. Or the house might have belonged to Jenny Cameron's family. They were all related. One of the noblest clans of the Highlands."

Jean didn't point out that often the local people would take on the name of the chief as a survival tactic. A clan wasn't necessarily a family.

"That house was burned by Butcher Cumberland's troops in seventeen forty-six. The Cameron properties were confiscated.

Not returned until the eighteen hundreds, when the English government at last recognized the heroism of the Jacobite chiefs."

And after the formerly Jacobite chiefs sent their men to fight Britain's battles in America and India. To say nothing of first beggaring and then selling out their tenants, to buy themselves social positions in London.

"In the eighteen thirties, one of the Lochiel's relatives built a small hunting lodge here. Lots of money to be made off hunting rights."

Jean thought of the trophy heads at the MacSorley's house and the photos in the smoking room. "Do you hunt, Rick?"

"No point to it. You want meat, order it. You want to shoot things, play paintball." He shoved his plate away and leaned back in his chair, looking up at the pictures. Outside the windows day faded into night. The chandelier above the table emitted a warm glow, pushing back the darkness. "The house was expanded in the eighteen eighties by an industrialist Cameron," Rick went on. "He was a recluse. Lived here all year around. Then the house passed to a cousin. Guy named MacSorley who lived in Fort William. He'd rent the place out, only have his buddies in during hunting season."

Hunting ran in the MacSorley family, then. "The house was damaged in a fire during World War Two," Jean prodded.

"Glendessary House was taken over by the government. Part of the commando school based at Achnacarry. This was the infirmary. One night the place caught on fire. Badly damaged and pretty much abandoned after that."

"You'd never know, looking at it today."

"I hope not," said Vanessa. "Even with Kieran finding architectural elements recycled from other houses, Rick dropped a fortune rebuilding the old place."

"And you rebuilt the game larder, though you don't hunt," Jean said.

"The place was a hunting lodge," said Rick, that explaining everything.

Vanessa added, "This end of the house wasn't badly damaged. There was a west wind the night of the fire, and it was the end with the billiards room that was gutted. I did some rearranging down there—the stairs are a bit different, for one thing."

The door to the kitchen swayed gently back and forth. Toby or Neil or even Fiona could be listening, Jean supposed, but then, it wasn't as though Rick was saying anything they didn't already know. He'd probably given each of them a prospectus with bullet points when they signed on. "How did you hear about Glendessary House to begin with?"

"Kieran MacSorley offered it to me," answered Rick, committing himself to neither Charlotte's nor Vanessa's version of events. "That was a deal I couldn't refuse. The Camerons were indispensable members of Prince Charles' team. He didn't have a workable rebellion until the Lochiel brought the Camerons out to Glenfinnan to meet him. Set an example for everyone else."

Jean reserved judgment on the wisdom of following examples.

"And Jenny Cameron at the head of her troops! Courage and beauty. A true heroine! The Prince lost his heart on the spot."

Did he? Rick was within spitting distance of the version published by the English propagandists. Jean leaned forward, feeling as though she was finally getting a glimpse into Rick's thought processes.

"The Camerons took Edinburgh for the Prince. They were at his side at Culloden. Saved his life. The Lochiel called all the chiefs together here at Loch Arkaig. That's when they buried the coins. He never surrendered. Went off to France with Charlie. Died planning a new rebellion."

Would Lochiel's or even Charlie's surrender have convinced the English the Scots were no longer a threat and prevented the ethnic cleansing campaign? Probably not. Frightened people had little appetite for mercy.

"Fear God and Honor the King. That's the motto of Clan Cameron."

Jean followed Rick's gaze to the painting of Charles in Edinburgh—men cheering, women fainting, banners flying. The Bonnie Prince had held court in Holyrood Palace like his ancestors. He could have had the crown of Scotland, but no, he'd wanted that of Britain, and invaded England. He should have quit while he was ahead. Left well enough alone…. She shifted uneasily.

Charlie and his dynasty had had courage without common sense, charm without compassion, hot tempers, a taste for hedonism, and centuries of bad luck. Their failures had become tragedies for their followers. Yes, it was all a good story, but Rick wasn't seeing it as a cautionary tale.

The door to the kitchen opened. Toby stepped into the room holding a large serving tray like a shield. He collected the dishes, Vanessa flinching at every ding of plate and dong of cutlery, and pushed back through the door. Jean glimpsed Neil leaning against the counter holding a bowl and a spoon, and beyond him Fiona sitting at the long worktable reading a newspaper, the cat washing its face at her feet.

Toby reappeared with dishes of apple-bread pudding, drowned in crème fraîche and exuding the odor of cinnamon, then brought out a carafe of coffee. Just before the door swung shut, Neil presented his spoon to the dining room like a gladiator his sword: *We who are about to dine salute you.*

Jean smiled at him, then from the corner of her eye saw Vanessa, too, smiling. Okay, so which one of them was Neil saluting? Did it matter?

She accepted a cup of coffee mostly to inhale its aroma. The pudding was delicious, melting on her tongue. "Miranda lets me write restaurant reviews every now and then. What's the name of Norman's restaurant in Inverness?"

"La Brasserie," said Vanessa.

Rick smashed his pudding and crème fraîche into a cow pat. "The Scots were the leaders, the true patriots, during the American Revolution, you know."

Except for those who were patriots for the Crown. Like Flora MacDonald and her husband, immigrants to North Carolina.

"It was a Revolution against the English mentality," Rick went on. "Religious prejudice, class distinctions. Everything the Stuart kings fought against."

Jean almost swallowed the wrong way. Clearing her throat, she stared up at his thin, intense face. The same Stuart dynasty that had murdered thousands of people in the name of class and religion? Not that the other religious persuasion didn't commit its own excesses, but still, there was a reason many Scots hadn't supported Charlie. No matter whether the name was spelled in the Scottish fashion, Stewart, or in the French fashion, Stuart, or even in the Gaelic, Stiubhart, they hadn't wanted him and his kind back again.

"Goes to show you the enormous popularity of the Stuarts, how hard the Hanoverian usurpers had to work to suppress their followers. Years later you have Robert Burns mourning their loss. Burns was an aristocrat himself, a cousin of the Dukes of Hamilton. Blood will tell."

This was the same Burns who'd written "A man's a man for a' that" and prided himself on working as a farmer? Yes, Jean thought, blood will tell, but only to a scientist splitting DNA.

Rick's sallow complexion glowed in the soft light of the chandelier. "Did you know Prince Charles was offered the Crown of America? He turned it down, though. Supported democracy."

Yeah, right. Jean smothered her guffaw in a bit of caramelized apple and shot a glance toward Vanessa. She was poking holes in the mound of food in her bowl, her chin propped on her elbow. This was nothing new. No big deal.

It was a deal to Jean, though. Rick's eccentricity ran deeper than she'd suspected, from charmingly off-base to way the heck out in left field. How could she write an article about him without it sounding like a joke? It wasn't Cameron who wasn't for real, it was Rick. He was starting to look more like some sort of alien tartan-bearing creature every moment.

Maybe all it had taken to get Norman sent on his way during the Lodge meeting was his name. Rick had only hired a man named Hawley because Kieran had pressed him. On the other hand, Rick might have taken on a dubious character named Walsh because Charlie had had a disreputable follower named Walsh. There had been a Robertson somewhere in Charlie's retinue as well—although Jean had no idea just how Fiona had ended up here, in an asylum run by its owner-inmate.

Then there was Ogilvy. Rick had invited him to join the Lodge on five minutes' acquaintance. And he'd greeted D.C.I. Cameron like a long-lost relative. No wonder she'd been put through her own genealogical quiz. Fortunately Fairbairn was an innocuous enough name.

Why, she wondered, had this particular bee built a hive in Rick MacLyon's bonnet? Had he grown up sitting around campfires with a group of Civil War re-enactors, singing, "Save your Confederate money boys, the South will rise again"? The Old South owed more than a little to Walter Scott and the Celtic twilight….

The door to the hall opened so wide it thumped against the wall. Vanessa leaped an inch off the seat of her chair. Rick turned to the doorway. Jean put her last spoonful of cream-bedewed pudding back into the bowl. Think of the devil and he appears. *Here we go.*

Alasdair Cameron stood in the doorway. The only color in his face was the crisp, unyielding blue of his eyes. The knot of his tie dangled halfway down the front of his shirt. The sleeves of his coat were wet and muddy. He opened his mouth, inhaled….

"Sit down, Sandy," Rick said brightly. "How about some coffee?"

Cameron stared, mouth still open.

"Alasdair is a version of Alexander, right? In England that'd be Alex but here in Scotland that'd be Sandy."

Cameron shook his head dismissively, a movement that was almost a shudder. "Mr. MacLyon, Mrs. MacLyon, Miss Fairbairn. There's been an accident. Norman Hawley came away from Glendessary House at half-past five, clocked out of the gate by one of my constables. A few minutes later, as he was passing through Bunarkaig, he veered to avoid a car driven by Charlotte MacSorley, who was just leaving her drive. Hawley's car ran off the road, down the hillside, and into the loch."

Jean covered her mouth with her hand. She knew what was coming next.

"Mr. MacSorley phoned emergency services. They alerted us straightaway. We discovered Hawley in the water. He never escaped from his car."

"He drowned," said Rick, flat, his glow extinguished. "He's dead."

"Aye," Cameron said, even flatter.

Norman left in such a hurry, thought Jean, because he didn't want to stay in a house with a murderer. He would have been safer here…. His death was an accident. Accidents could happen any time, anywhere.

"That's such a narrow twisty road. I never drive it, I always…." Vanessa turned toward the kitchen door, raising her voice. "Neil?"

The door opened the rest of the way, revealing the unlikely triumvirate of Fiona, Toby, and Neil jammed together in the opening. Neil was looking a little green around the gills. "My mum?"

"She's not been injured," Cameron told him. "The police surgeon gave her a sedative, and W.P.C. Grant is sitting with her. Your father's just arrived here, if you'd like to have a word."

"Oh aye," said Neil faintly, and vanished.

Cameron walked two heavy steps toward the kitchen. Taking his place in the dining room door was Sawyer, looking like a troll with a goat stuck in his craw. "Toby Walsh," said Cameron.

Toby's round face puckered. "Aye?"

"Mr. MacSorley tells me you had their car in to be serviced yesterday."

"Oh aye, so I did, they let me drive it and all."

Sawyer shouldered his way past Cameron. "Come with me."

"What?" asked Vanessa.

They think Toby and the car had something to do with the.... Jean interrupted her own thought. Maybe it wasn't an accident.

Toby, with a despairing glance back at Fiona, went quietly. Fiona shut the kitchen door. Vanessa looked from Jean to Cameron and back as though pleading for help. Then she threw down her napkin and fled.

Rick opened his mouth, shut it, finally managed to ask, "You want a glass of port, Sandy?"

Cameron was already turned toward the door, and Jean could only see a three-quarters view of his face. Even so, she could swear that he glanced toward her, as though he, too, expected some response. "No. Thank you." The door shut softly but emphatically behind him.

Jean pushed back her chair. Interview. That's right, the interview. "Rick, we need to sit down tomorrow and continue our conversation. I'm very interested in your take on Scottish history." And that was no lie.

"Sure. Tomorrow morning. Ten o'clock. The library. You'll get a real exclusive. It'll be worth your while."

It had better be. With a wan smile Jean broke free into the corridor, leaving the warm but suddenly stifling light of the dining room behind.

EIGHTEEN

WALL SCONCES shaped like candles looked good but shed little light into the darkness of the hall. Hunching her shoulders, Jean strode off toward the entrance, harboring some vague idea of talking to Cameron. She'd accumulated more than a few bits and pieces of information over the last few hours. Whether any of it or none of it helped the investigation was for him to decide, as he would no doubt remind her.

Vanessa, Fiona, and Charlotte were all capable of doing a composite British-American accent. In the anonymous phone call sweepstakes, though, Fiona was in the lead. The caller's accent had been impeccably American, not Charlotte's mocking exaggeration. And of all three women Fiona was the only one to express caution about George's activities. Charlotte dismissed him out of hand. Vanessa saw him as a benign annoyance.

One problem with that theory, though, was that of the three, Fiona seemed the least likely to make waves. The other was that Cameron, otherwise an intelligent person, refused to consider Fiona a suspect.

Jean's stride slowed into a mosey, which stopped at the foot of the staircase. Cameron wouldn't appreciate her butting in right now, not when he was dealing with another death. Instead of talking to him, she could—yeah, she could collect some more information. Not fooling herself one bit, Jean doubled back down the hall and pushed through the kitchen door.

The room was lit only by the small light above the stove. Fiona sat alone at the table, silhouetted against the window, Clarinda tucked up on her lap. Or at least part of the cat was on Fiona's lap. Her tail and a couple of legs didn't quite fit and hung down on either side. The two faces turned toward the door. "May I help you, Miss Fairbairn?" asked Fiona.

"I thought I could help you wash the dishes or something." Jean knew very well how confidences could be exchanged over a dishtowel.

"We've got an automatic dishwasher, thank you." Fiona's profile turned back to the window. Clarinda laid her head down again.

Jean remembered the hours she'd spent cuddling Dougie and staring out her window, lost in memory and regret. So what was Fiona remembering and regretting? Being driven to murder? Or something personal, like a good marriage lost or a bad marriage never abandoned?

Fiona's silence was so profound Jean felt like an intruder. Deciding she could wait awhile before turning over any more emotional rocks, she made an about-face and went back out into the hall. Now what? She glanced warily from the corner of her eye toward the game larder.... Behind her the dining room door slammed open. She jerked back against the wall, hands raised defensively.

Rick walked out of the room, his cell phone pressed to his ear. "Kieran. Where are you? Well, when you get rid of the cops come up to the office. We need to make plans." With a beep he switched off the phone and disappeared up the staircase.

A well-developed startle reflex was nothing to apologize for. Jean peeled herself off the wall and ducked into the familiar but less than reassuring cube of the sitting room. Rick wanted to make plans for what? Her interview tomorrow? Or how to handle the cops? By the dim light leaking through the door she located and turned on a table lamp. The glow reflected off the paneling and from the array of portraits: Charlie, Rick, Jenny Cameron.

Taking deep breaths through her own very average nose, Jean considered Jenny's Roman nose, arched eyebrows, and stubborn round chin. Even in this idealized sketch, Jenny hadn't been candy-box pretty. Whether helping Charlie had been the smart, let alone the right, thing to do had been open to debate even before Jenny discovered she had sacrificed her reputation for him. Her supporters claimed that no man of twenty-five would have an affair with a woman twenty years older, which was a backhanded defense, especially at a time when elderly men married sweet young things as a matter of course.

But the concept of the double standard had been two centuries in the future. Even now it was honored more in the breach than in the observance. Of all the wounding aspects of the lawsuit, the one that had hurt the most was the assumption of many people, from hidebound university pundit to reporter to Vanessa MacLyon, that a female professor who slept with a male student was subverting the natural order.

Stop it, Jean told herself. It was over. It was finished. If nothing else, the considerable sum she'd won from the university had bought her freedom, to say nothing of part-ownership in *Great Scot*. Although at this moment, in this house, she wasn't sure that partly owning *Great Scot* was the smart, let alone the right, thing to do. But how many Lovelaces, how many MacLyons, could she attract, for God's sake!

The sound system came on again, thankfully playing one of Hugh's genuinely emotional fiddle compositions rather than more of the synthesizer pieces that only simulated emotion. Jean looked up at Rick's grandiose portrait. What he lacked, she decided, was not emotion but a sense of humor, some perspective…. Footsteps echoed in the hall. Vanessa said she'd heard ghostly footsteps. But Jean's sixth sense was snoring gently in the vicinity of her well-filled stomach, exuding nothing more than the faint taste of cinnamon. Those steps belonged to someone perfectly corporeal.

The door opened, revealing Neil, in the flesh indeed. "Ah, here you are then. I chapped at the door of your room but you weren't to home."

"I was looking at the pictures," Jean explained, that sounding better than *I was hiding out.*

He held up two crystal liqueur glasses and a plump-bellied bottle. "Bramble and whiskey cordial. Blackberry and Scotch, in American. Good for what ails you in any language."

Jean wasn't so sure about that. Neither was she sure that Neil was good for what ailed her. She'd never know without trying a sip, though. One sip, on a full stomach, that wouldn't hurt. "Thank you."

Shutting the door with his foot, Neil poured, set the bottle down on the coffee table, and handed over a glass brimming with a shimmering crimson liquid. "Slainte, Jean."

"Slainte." Jean drank. Oh now, that was good, a rush of sweet-tart berry and then the lingering astringent heat of the whiskey, blending incongruity with flavor.

Neil sat down and patted the couch cushion beside him. "Have a rest. Things haven't happened as you expected, have they now?"

"No." Jean sat down, leaving half a cushion's width between them, and gestured toward the ceiling where she assumed the speakers were hidden. "Hugh's new album. That's good music."

"Oh aye, I thought you'd enjoy hearing from Hugh."

"How's your mother?"

"Away with the fairies, Dad says. Only thing unusual in that is that this time she's had a medical sedative instead of an alcoholic one."

Oh. But Neil was holding up his glass, catching the light on its ruby-backed facets, his expression more thoughtful than distressed. Children accepted their family situation as normal, didn't they? Not that Neil was even remotely a child. He was a consenting adult, just like her. He lifted the glass to his lips again.

The heat kindling in Jean's gut didn't come entirely from the liqueur. "Do they know what happened yet? The accident, I mean."

"Mum drives too fast, says so herself, says that's the only way to avoid the motion sickness. I've been thinking it was only a matter of time 'til she ran some poor sod off the road. Pity it was Norman."

"Why did Sawyer want to talk to Toby? Something about the car?"

"Oh aye." Leaning back, Neil propped one arm on the back of the couch. His long, dark, eloquent brows tightened, crinkling his smooth forehead beneath its thatch of auburn hair. "The brakes packed up, that's why Mum couldn't stop quick enough to keep Norman from diving into the loch. D.C.I. Dour Cameron said himself the brake line's been interfered with."

"Why would Toby do that?"

"Dad says he was trying to kill one or the other of them; he had no way of knowing who'd next be driving the car." Neil shook his head. "What a scunner, a chap you've worked with and come to like, having a go at your family. But then, there's no getting away from your life history, Toby being raised in the worst part of Glasgow and all."

"Some people can rise above their early programming," Jean pointed out. "Does Cameron think Toby killed George?"

"He's not exactly the talkative sort, is he now?"

"No." She looked past the light playing along the facets of Neil's handsome face to the two painted faces of Bonnie Prince Charlie on the far wall. "Why would Toby kill George? George was helping him out."

"Aye, but there was George with that gold coin and Toby hasn't a bean." Neil intercepted Jean's gaze, his smoky blue eyes contrasting with the glitter of crystal and crimson that he held to his lips. "No need being bashful about the coin, by the by. I didn't know George was bringing it to you, but I knew he had it. Picked it up a long time past, maybe even when he was in commando training here."

"But Toby wouldn't have had to kill George to rob his house. Assuming it was robbed."

"Maybe Toby wanted to, well, convince George to tell him where he found the coin so he could turn up the rest. Rick's gone on about Charlie's treasure often enough. Toby's a bit lacking in the head, mind. Doesn't always think things through, like whether the old man could remember where he found it." Neil left his implication dangling just as George had dangled from a meat hook.

It was much too easy to explain away motive with a shrug and a suggestion of mental incapacity. Jean couldn't see Toby torturing an old man to death, especially with a crowd of people in the house, whether he was lacking in the head or not. She tried, "Why would Toby go after your parents?"

"Ah, my dad pretty well runs things round here, Rick having other things on his mind. So does Vanessa, come to that. And chaps like Toby resent people in a position like ours."

For just a second Jean heard Charlotte's voice coming from her son's lips. Then she told herself, again, that children accept their families as the norm. Which was close to Neil's thesis about Toby, although he'd hardly intended to point out what they had in common. "So what is on Rick's mind?" Jean asked. "The Lodge?"

"Jean," said Neil, "it would be as much as my job is worth to put the boot in there. Although it is almost time for me to move on, I'm thinking."

"Move on?"

"I'll be putting together my own band, no need to let Gallowglass and their resentments stand in my way. I'm after playing in London; that's where you go if you have something to contribute. And I have something to contribute." He set his empty glass on the table. As he sat back he closed the half-cushion gap and his denim-clad thigh pressed up against hers.

There went her pheromone receptors again, responding to that elusive but undeniable male scent, something between steak and sandalwood. If Charlie's followers thought with their hearts and not their heads, Jean was thinking with her gonads. Not that her gonads had had any workouts recently. Exercise was beneficial for all the other body systems…. "I've heard some really good Celtic folk-rock bands in the U.S."

"Then maybe I'll go there. I can do better than a rich man's toy boy, don't you think?" His voice was caressing, but something raw moved in his eyes, a small creature begging for approval.

That hint of vulnerability made him all the more appealing. Jean's body told her to lean toward him. Her brain told her to back off. She was poised at equilibrium, between spinning into space and crashing to the ground.

A toy boy. That expression disparaged the man's subordinate position, not its sexual connotation. She thought again how sick she was of double standards, historical or otherwise. A woman was a slut for sleeping around. A man was a stud. She was cheap. He was lucky.

Neil no doubt got lucky on a regular basis. He was a kilt and pipes fantasy. Maybe he was exactly what she needed. After all, they'd been drawn together in adversity. They'd bonded. She was single, she was over twenty-one—an affair might be just the thing, sex with no strings attached….

Neil's right arm slipped around her shoulders. His left hand took away her glass. His warm, vital body pulled her into its gravitational field. Her hands waved in mid-air, looking for a neutral place to land, and settled flat against his chest. No, his chest wasn't neutral. Her palms molded themselves to his Gallowglass T-shirt as his slender musician's fingers played an inspiring reel on her rib cage. Skillfully maneuvering around her glasses, he closed in.

She turned her head so that his lips brushed her cheek. Neil was a toy boy, decorative but immature. Maybe he was two-timing a girlfriend. Maybe he was between engagements, so to speak. It didn't matter. Flirting was mild amusement. Sex was serious business, not cheap and easy entertainment. There were always strings attached.

"Mind you," he murmured against her skin, so that she felt his accent as much as she heard it, "I'm right comfortable with my sexuality."

"I'm not," she admitted, more to herself than to him. "Comfortable with your sexuality, that is."

"We need to be working on that, then." He angled his head the other way and came around for another pass.

Again Jean ducked. "Neil, no." Leaning back far enough to focus on his face broke the suction of his arms.

He cocked his head to the side. "No?" His sigh bathed her in the odor of blackberries.

"This isn't...." Footsteps walked down the hall, the hesitant steps of someone old or ill. The hair on the back of Jean's neck, already standing to attention, quivered in a nonexistent breeze, and the air seemed to thicken. Oh great. *More input.*

"Eh?" Neil asked.

"Did you hear someone walking down the hall?"

"No. No one's out and about. Rick's in his office, Vanessa's watching a film, Fiona's pulling her usual long face in the kitchen. If that's what's put you off," he added with his patented intimate smile, now buoyed with an encouraging lift of the eyebrows, "we can go on up to your room. Or mine, but the guest rooms are the more comfortable."

"No, it's not that—it's just—this isn't right."

His face fell. "Ah Jean, you're the nervy one. We could be turning that to our advantage, now."

Good try, she thought. But no. "I'm going upstairs. Alone." Neil lifted her hands toward his face, but before he could made the romantic gesture of kissing them, she pulled them away. Hoping her smile was more affectionate than acerbic, Jean extracted the rest of her body from his aura and stood up. "Later, Neil."

"I live in hope, Jean." His own wistful smile followed her to the door. When she glanced back she saw him curve into the attitude of The Thinker, as though, once out of the presence of a woman, he could admit to doubt.

Then she was alone in the chill of the hall. As she'd expected, no one was there. But it wasn't until she was on the staircase that the fine hairs on her nape fell back against her skin, with a caress like that of Neil's lips on her cheek.

NINETEEN

THE DENSE AIR seemed icy against Jean's warm face. She scurried up the stairs, trying to outrun her—no, not embarrassment. Not even confusion, not when it came to Neil. Overload of both mind and body. She was trying to outrun the ghost and the darkness, both symbolic and real, of Glendessary House.

The grandfather clocked ticked away, measuring out the irrevocable passages of time. The sound of Hugh's fiddle emanated from the shadows, now playing a lively jig. But even the most cheerful Celtic music was edged with pain. History was much too uncertain to commit yourself to joy.

From the upstairs window Jean saw Sawyer and a constable put Toby in a car and drive away, headlights ripping the twilight's last gleaming. Two figures walked from the parking area around the corner of the house. Their faces were concealed by the darkness, but by their body language, one fawning, the other alert as a stalking cat, she deduced it was Kieran lecturing Cameron. Who was probably giving him lots and lots of rope.

Jean could hardly blame her hosts for abandoning her. In spite of Vanessa's ultimatum, this was a lousy time to be entertaining a journalist. Besides, the journalist was happy to have been abandoned. She desperately needed a few moments alone. And, since it was one of Mother Nature's jokes that the memories you didn't want clung to your brain like Velcro and the ones you did want slid like an omelet off Teflon, those few moments alone had better be spent with her notebook and laptop.

Pulling the massive key out of her pocket, Jean unlocked the door of her room and groped inside for the light switch. Occasionally she had nightmares of running from someone or something in the dark, of flicking light switches only to have nothing happen.... The ceiling light glowed brightly. *Ah, sanctuary.*

She inspected her face in the mirror of the dressing table. It was pink of cheek and bright of eye. The pulse of her blood made her skin resound like the surface of a drum. Or a bodhran, to be Celtic. A good thing Neil hadn't realized just how stimulating his attentions had been, or he might have pressed his case. Not to mention his entire delectable body…. No. Not even then.

Jean reached for her notebook. Her hand froze. Hadn't she left the book lying to the left of her laptop rather than to the right?

Quickly she looked over her belongings. The dresser drawer wasn't quite shut. Her suitcase was turned the other way around, with the zipper facing the wall instead of the wheels. Vanessa had said the ghost moved things around—that was a well-documented ghostly activity. Had she said that in order to cover up a search of Jean's room? Vanessa had no way of knowing that Jean knew the presence was focused only in the sitting room, and, unless she was completely misreading her senses, the corridor.

She touched her laptop. It was warm. So much for that, then— ghosts weren't known for their computing skills. That the material saved in her laptop was protected by passwords didn't matter. All the notes she'd taken in the notebook were utterly damning. So who had searched her room? She hadn't had a single member of the household in her sights the entire time since she locked the door and walked away.

Jean sat down hard in the desk chair. But she was a reporter, she rationalized. Why shouldn't she be taking notes on the events she found herself caught up in? Would—the killer, she forced herself to articulate—hold that against her?

If the killer was someone in this house, someone she now knew, and not a Lodge member or other wild card, sure, they might hold it against her. Blaming her either for finding George's body or for being curious wasn't reasonable, but murder wasn't particularly reasonable.

Oh God. Jean put her hand to her throat, feeling the cord tightening around her neck. Cold fear snuffed the last of the glow in her stomach. A grand story, huh? Up close and personal is what it was, and getting closer and more personal all the time.

And yet her own still-alive-and-kicking person was only a secondary issue. Her hand closed into a fist and thumped the desk. She wasn't going to take the safe way out now, any more than she had the day she'd read the plagiarized dissertation. Short of running into the night—or attaching herself to Cameron or Gunn like a limpet—all she could do was keep on keeping on. Funny, how having the cops downstairs now seemed less like having rats in the wainscoting than like having angels in the rafters.

With an aggravated sigh at both herself and at whoever had violated the refuge of her room, Jean pulled out her cell phone and called her backup. Miranda was an inspiring example of the power of positive thinking.

"Hello," said the voice emanating from the phone, "this is Miranda, I'm engaged just now; leave me a message."

"Hey, Miranda, it's Jean, I'll call back." That's what she got for waiting until she had to call Miranda at home. If Miranda was even at home. She could be holding forth at one of Edinburgh's posh restaurants. Going on to Plan B, Jean dialed Hugh's number.

Bingo! "Hugh Munro, forward into Scotland's past!"

"Hugh, it's Jean. How's it going?"

"Raining like stink here, other than that, no problems. Wee Dougie's come for a visit, he was a bit peaky, I'm thinking."

She'd never been able to convince Hugh that Dougie could survive a day on his own. "Thank you, Hugh. Just don't spoil him too badly. You should see the cat here, she's huge, part wild cat."

"But a right softie still, I reckon," Hugh said indulgently. "I should be asking you how it's going. The papers are making a meal of it, your biography, Chief Inspector Cameron's biography, the lot. Mostly they're on to Rick, though, a wealthy nutter being like catnip to a cat and all."

Cameron's escutcheon probably didn't have a single blotch on it, not like hers. "The papers will be having an even bigger feast tomorrow," Jean said. "Now the cook's died in a car accident rushing away from the scene."

Hugh whistled amazement.

"Also. Well…" Okay, so she was feeling obscurely guilty about Neil, even though she hadn't led him on. Maybe she could still help him out.

"Aye?" Hugh prompted.

"I think I told you about the young guy here who plays the pipes."

"He's good, is he?"

Jean skipped any expressions such as "to die for." "He sounds good to me. And he's quite an admirer of yours."

"Any professional experience?"

"He's played with Gallowglass several times."

"He has? When?"

"At the Edinburgh Festival Fringe last year. And in Dundee over Hogmanay, when you were here."

"Well now," said Hugh, so cautiously Jean's radar blipped. "Not to speak ill of your laddie, but Gallowglass' van ran off the road in a snowstorm outside Aberdeen and knocked the lads about so badly they've not performed in public at all, let alone at the Festival, a year since."

"Oh…." She didn't add the four-letter word.

"They're planning a comeback, laid down some tracks at a couple of recording sessions—could have been over Hogmanay, right enough. Filled in with some studio musicians. Maybe that's what your laddie meant to say."

Neil shrunk from a prince into a frog right before her eyes. *No, my laddie meant to build up his resume.*

"If he'll come to Glasgow in June," Hugh, always kind-hearted, went on, "Billy and I'll be playing at the Kilmarnock Club, I'd be glad to give him a listen."

"Thanks Hugh, that's…" The phone beeped in her ear. Call waiting. "I've got to go. Scratch Dougie's ears for me, please."

"Will do. I'd be telling you to have a care, but this Cameron chap looks to be the dependable sort. You're in good hands."

"Thanks." But the hands she'd been in were Neil's…. She switched channels both mentally and on the phone. "Hello?"

"Jean," said Miranda's whiskey-flavored voice. "You rang?"

"Yes I did. The plot's thickening." Jean told her the story of Norman Hawley, from soup to nuts to what Vanessa had said about his paranoia. "I'm wondering if he had some reason to be wary of the police or whether it's just that general police car in the rear view mirror feeling we all get."

"I'll have a look into Hawley's background. Where did the MacSorleys find him?"

"La Brasserie in Inverness."

"Oh aye, good food and close to the Public Library in Farraline Park. You can feed your belly and your brain in one go."

"It's near the Library?" Jean filed that factoid away for consideration. "Do you have anything for me?"

"Of course I do. First of all, you've probably heard by now that Toby Walsh is a lag. A ticket-of-leave man. A paroled convict. Sent down for breaking and entering."

"Yes, Chief Inspector Cameron did tell me that."

"I hear from Toby's mum that her father was in the commandos with George Lovelace. Killed in action in Sicily. George kept in touch with the family, sent them money when they fell on hard times, then offered to help Toby by finding him work."

"George being conscientious to a fault," Jean said. Honorable, as Fiona said.

"He felt that getting Toby away from his fellow neds would rehabilitate him. He had a point there."

"Toby seems well-meaning enough. Maybe that translates into easily led. But I sure can't see him murdering George. Or messing with the brakes on the MacSorley's car, although if Cameron says they'd been messed with...." When did she start considering Cameron an unimpeachable source? "Toby's lucky to be named 'Walsh;' that gave him an in with Rick."

"Sorry?" Miranda asked.

"Rick and his Jacobite mania."

"Ah. You've not heard anything more about this Lodge of his, I gather."

"Only the odd hint or so. Rick's going to make some announcement tomorrow, though."

"A press conference?"

"Well, if you call one reporter, me, 'press.'"

"Oooh, an exclusive! Well done Jean!"

"Thanks, but it's Rick's idea, not mine."

Murmuring dissent, Miranda went on, "Secondly, I've had a chat with Derek at *The Sunburn*. Miss Meg never gave him anything to go on. He's thinking now she was winding him up and never intended any sort of exposé more interesting than that Rick eats peas with his knife."

"I wouldn't say his table manners were as refined as some," said Jean, "but I'm sure Meg could have come up with something better than that."

"But she was intimidated out of it, I'm thinking."

"I can see Kieran MacSorley sending the girl away in tears."

Jean could tell Miranda was nodding in agreement; she could hear jewelry jangling discreetly, as good-quality jewelry should do. "Speaking of Kieran," Miranda went on, "did you know that his father Archie died in the war?"

"Oh yes. A decorated war hero, Charlotte said."

"He was given some sort of compensation medal posthumously, aye, but he never had the chance for heroics. Remember the forty-five men who were killed at the commando school?"

"Archie was killed here?"

"That he was, during a live-fire exercise in nineteen forty-two. Left the family a ruined mansion and the land but little else, it appears. I'm surprised it took them almost sixty years to sell up to an American billionaire."

"Maybe they didn't have one in their sights until now." Jean drummed her fingers on her notebook. So Vanessa's version of the sale was probably the right one. Kieran had been very clever to troll the Internet genealogy sites for someone who would buy his white elephant of a house and provide him with cash. "Miranda, do you have any idea what the terms of the sale were? Kieran's acting like the foreman of the factory or the overseer of the plantation or something. Is he on a retainer?"

"Good question. I'll see what I can turn up." A brief pause—Jean heard a keyboard clicking. "Thirdly...."

"You have something else?"

"I take my work seriously," said Miranda. "Thirdly, I've sussed out Rick MacLyon's mother's maiden name."

"Does that matter?"

"It's good for the entertainment value. He was born Rick Douglas, mind, and his mother's name is Sobieski."

Jean grinned. "Cool! Same as Bonnie Prince Charlie's mother! And those charming rascals the Sobieski-Stuarts with their book of ancient tartans! I'm beginning to see why the whole name thing is so important to him—he must think he's a relative."

"He wouldn't be the first person to set himself up a posh family tree."

"I bet there's a Cameron branch in there somewhere, too, he's got a real thing about the Camerons.... Genealogy. That's one of the things he must have had George doing for him, digging around in the Highland Archive at the Inverness Public Library. Close to Norman's restaurant."

"We've come full circle," said Miranda.

"I'm certainly dizzy," Jean told her. "One more thing. The

housekeeper, Fiona Robertson. Vanessa says she's a widow, something about a soap opera."

"Is Robertson her married name?"

"Hm. I don't know. Can you find out?"

"Oh aye," Miranda said equably.

"Fiona went to the University of Pennsylvania. Is there any chance she knew either Rick or Vanessa back in the States? You said Vanessa went to Wellesley, but what about Rick?"

"Left school before he was ever granted a degree, if I'm remembering correctly. I'll put Gavin onto it."

Jean wondered whether Gavin had realized what he was getting into when he'd signed on at *Great Scot*. She certainly hadn't. She'd seen herself digging through ancient attics and pottering away among old books, like Lovelace had done before his date with a murderer. "I'm curious how Fiona got her job, too. Whether she's another one of Kieran's bright ideas or an independent force or what."

"We shall see." Miranda laughed. "Jean, Duncan's waiting at the door; he's booked a table at The Witchery."

"Sorry, didn't mean to interfere with your love life."

"No worry, the man's been trained properly. I'll be in touch tomorrow, shall I? Have a good evening."

Jean had already missed her chance for an evening, however good or bad she'd never know. "Thanks. You too." She switched off the phone and stared blankly around.

For a moment she'd been in Miranda's chic top-floor flat with Duncan, a distinguished silver-haired, silver-tongued, and silver-laden lawyer, bringing them glasses of champagne. Jean decided she should model her love life, if she ever got brave enough to go looking for one, on Miranda's. Mutual respect and mutual space. Honesty. No games.

No less-than-distinguished but undeniably charming young rascals. Laughing ruefully, she stood up and stretched. If she could forgive her own momentary temptation with Neil, then she could forgive his lie. His small lie. Inflating the resume ran in the family. At least he was breaking the mold by wanting to be a musician. She'd gotten him an audition with Hugh. Whatever happened after that, the situation was out of her hands. And she was out of Neil's.

Stowing her telephone in her bag, Jean tucked it away with the notebook and computer in a bottom drawer. Locking the barn door well after the horses had become dog food, in other words.

At George Lovelace's house, all the doors and cabinets had been left open, the searcher knowing the owner wouldn't be coming back. Had that searcher been Toby? What he been looking for? Had he found it?

Toby had been convicted of breaking and entering, that was fact. And Jean doubted if he'd come to her hotel room for a literary discussion. Maybe he'd intended to search it, too. Maybe he'd searched her car Tuesday night, when he'd brought her her coat. But for what? Her notes? The coin?

Just because she wanted to give Toby the benefit of doubt just as much as she wanted to give it to Neil, didn't mean Toby wasn't guilty of everything from burgling to murder, as soon-to-be charged.

She had stalled around long enough. It was time to do the info-dump on Chief Inspector Cameron—including her suspicions of Fiona—and get it over with. If he really were the dependable sort, if he really were an unimpeachable source, then he had to listen to her.

TWENTY

JEAN HAD TO STOP HERSELF from sidling crabwise down the corridor, keeping her back to the wall and leaping past every doorway. Even at the best of times she would have found the shadowed nooks and crannies of the house sinister rather than picturesque. Now she thought fond thoughts of searchlights. But then, George had been murdered in broad daylight.

There were times she wished she could switch off her imagina-tion. This was one of them. But no, it was tied into her perceptions.

She tiptoed down the back staircase and stopped at the bottom. Amplified theme music reverberated in the media room to her right. The speakers hidden in the stairwell emanated a female voice singing in Gaelic. From the open door of the billiard room came a haze of cigarette smoke and Kieran's voice, dripping rancid oil. "…wife's in shock. What are you after doing about that?"

"I'm not a doctor, Mr. MacSorley," returned Cameron's measured tones. "It would be unethical for me to either diagnose or treat your wife."

"I do beg your pardon, Inspector, I'm hardly suggesting physical care. I'm asking you how you plan to go about doing your job. My wife was almost killed. She almost took the bullet for me."

"Oh, was there a gun fired?"

Kieran's voice rose. Obviously if he spoke more loudly, Cameron would understand him. "Here, Inspector, I realize you have many things on your mind just now. Allow me to explain. That lag Walsh set the trap for me, not my wife. He had the car in to be serviced yesterday. He bashed one of the brake lines so that the fluid would leak out—there's a bloody great puddle of it in the driveway."

"We're trying to determine how the puncture was made in the brake line. Running over a rock, perhaps. Any number of rocks about."

"I realize you weren't there at the time, Inspector. Let me assure you that the crash was no accident."

"You watched it happen, then." Cameron's voice was so dry Jean expected to see a dust devil whirl out the door of the room. She shook her head in reluctant admiration.

"I heard the squeal of brakes and an almighty splash. I ran to the road, helped my wife from our car, returned to the house, and phoned emergency services straightaway. Ghastly moment, made worse when I found that it was Norman's car in the water. It's been a very difficult day, Inspector, let me tell you. Very difficult. But we have to cope, don't we?"

It was a bit harder on Norman than on you, Jean thought.

"Why, then," asked Cameron, "did emergency services take down your call thirty minutes after my constable saw Hawley leave here?"

Good point. The way Norman was driving he should have made it to the MacSorley's house in five or six minutes, if that long.

"I have no idea, Inspector. Probably the operator who took my call was somewhat—let me put this delicately. Slow. Dense. Many of these people are hired from job centers, after all."

Cameron said nothing.

"Now Inspector," Kieran went on, enunciating very clearly. "Please excuse my saying so, but if the police had pulled their fingers out to begin with—I beg your pardon, that was a bit rude, surely you'll understand how upset I am over the situation—if the police had worked as efficiently as they might have done, this deliberate attack upon myself and my family would never have happened."

"Oh?" Cameron said, still dry, still cool.

"Far be it from me to tell you how to go about your work, Inspector, but this lag Walsh should have set off alarm bells when you first arrived. He was George's idea. The bleeding heart academic giving the poor yob a hand up. It's these liberal politicians—they mean well, I'm sure, but let's face the truth, they're a plague on the land. And on the honest landowner. Why they've made it next to impossible to have a good day out shooting!"

Jean didn't disagree with Kieran about politicians of any hue being a plague, but she wouldn't have cited his example.

"Now look what's happened, Inspector, George is dead, my wife was almost killed, and the cook I chose for Rick—an artist, I tell you—is cut down in his prime. I suppose I have poor Norman to thank that it wasn't my wife or myself gone tumbling into the loch, although, mind, he hardly intended to throw himself in harm's way." Kieran clucked his tongue. "It goes to show who was the better judge of character, eh? George, for all his scholastic virtues, was quite ignorant of the world."

"How did you get on with Mr. Lovelace?" asked Cameron.

"As I've informed that unfortunately ill-mannered sergeant of yours, we got on well enough, for two people of very different social backgrounds who had little in common."

"You have nothing against him, then?"

"I never speak ill of the dead. Let bygones be bygones, I always say."

"What did you have against him when he was alive?"

"The man was a dreadful old pedant, could bore a turnip to tears, but he knew his business. I believe it was your wee schoolboy constable who took that down already, but of course I may be mistaken, being overwrought with my wife's brush with death and all."

"You staffed the house for Mr. MacLyon, did you?"

"I found Norman and George. Fiona, she made her own way here. It's no fault of mine George brought in a yob like Walsh. A dangerous man, I've thought so all along. But I don't make disparaging remarks about anyone."

"How did you meet Rick MacLyon?"

"Through mutual friends, venture capitalists and the like. He was very pleased indeed, let me tell you, to find someone capable of helping with the restoration of this fine mansion."

Cameron didn't offer an opinion on that. Jean could imagine his face, stone still, only the faintest twitch eroding the corners of his mouth. Thinking. Evaluating. Computing. Sensing.

"Well then, Inspector," demanded Kieran, "what are you going to do about this attack on me and my wife?"

"I'm suggesting that you get on about your business and leave us to get on with the investigation."

After a long, ominous moment of silence, Kieran said effusively, "Of course, of course, no rest for hard workers such as ourselves, eh, Inspector? My member of parliament will be hearing from me, how good it is that my tax burden is going to pay the salary of such a fine representative of our law-enforcement services."

"This is the member of parliament who's a plague on the land?" Cameron asked. "Good night, Mr. MacSorley. Oh, and it's Chief Inspector."

"Yes, yes, of course, I do beg your pardon, Chief Inspector it is."

Jean peered around the corner to see Kieran burst out of the billiards room and stand in the corridor scowling, clenching and releasing his fists. Even though Jean had also been worked over by Cameron, whose silences were harsher than any rubber hose, she managed to contain her sympathy. None of the MacSorleys could tell a story straight if you gave them a plumb bob.

Kieran headed not for the door but toward her listening post. Jean bounded up several steps, managed to make a pirouette without tripping herself up, and started back down again. Kieran burst around the corner like a bull on his way to a china shop, any china shop, just as long as it was filled with lots of breakables.

"Hi," she said, butter not melting in her mouth.

With a baleful look he surged on by.

Jean walked on down the stairs. Cameron, minus his jacket and tie, was just opening the outside door. He spun around at the sound of Jean's steps. "Ah. It's you, is it?"

"It's not anyone else," she replied.

The rolled sleeves of his shirt and the stubble shading his granite jaw made him appear a little less formidable. So did the lines engraved even more deeply at the corners of his mouth. His brows were very serious and straight, like soldiers at attention. Jean thought of the commandos lined up before Glendessary House confronting duty, honor, and country. Confronting the self-control that duty, honor, and country demanded.

Cameron gestured her through the open door. *Okay, fine.* She'd steeled herself to talk to him. Maybe he'd steeled himself to talk to her. Stepping into the night, Jean inhaled the fresh-chilled air and walked beyond the floodlighted island of the house into the garden. The darkness was less intimidating when she wasn't alone. From her memory she dredged the prayer of St. Francis: "Lord, make me an instrument of thy peace." But right now peace seemed as elusive as truth or justice.

A hint of mist veiled the sky overhead, making the stars shift and blur like eyes filled with tears. Except for the wind in the leaves and an occasional bird call, only the crunch of two sets of steps on the gravel path broke the silence. The softly illuminated walls of the house gleamed an antique gold, each architectural curve and angle deeply etched by shadow. Two windows to the right—the kitchen—were defined by a pale fluorescent gleam. In the center the tall windows of the library glowed brightly. Above them the windows of Rick's study lightened and darkened as though a small thunderstorm were captive inside. All the computer monitors, no doubt.

Cameron was a shape in the darkness. Jean glanced up at his profile, turned toward the house, unreadable. "I talked to everyone in the house this afternoon. Would you like to hear what they said?"

"Please," he said, without moving, let alone looking around at her.

Jean outlined all her conversations, editing only the more awkward parts of her encounter with Neil, and drawing no conclusions, about Fiona or anyone else. Cameron responded to Fiona's name the way he responded to all the others, silently.

She finished with, "I was standing there in the stairwell listening to Kieran stroke you with one hand and stab you with the other. Has he been going on at you ever since he got here?"

"Not a bit of it. I made a phone call or two, and I let Andy Sawyer butt heads with him whilst I had a word with Toby."

"You mean Kieran and Andy didn't just cancel each other out?" Jean asked—out of turn, she told herself too late.

But Cameron must have felt as tired as he looked. He laughed. It wasn't much of a laugh, more of a scorched snicker, but still it was one more indication the man was harboring a sense of humor.

Well, Jean thought. "Do you think Toby's guilty?"

"Of bashing the brakes on the MacSorley's car? Maybe. Of killing Lovelace? It doesn't seem likely, does it?"

Jean didn't delude herself that he was asking her opinion, even though she agreed with him. "Was Kieran telling you that Toby's motive for damaging the brakes was envy? And that he killed George out of greed, wanting more of his gold coins?"

"Something to that effect, aye."

"But neither scenario really holds up. Toby respected George. And even though Charlotte drives like a bat out of hell on the road, you're blind as a bat coming out of that driveway. Surely she would barely have been idling."

"Quite right. However, Mr. and Mrs. MacSorley had a row, during which Mrs. MacSorley took to drink. She left the house in a rare temper. Neither drink nor temper lending itself to cautious driving."

"That was my fault," Jean said. "Kieran bawled her out for talking to a reporter. Me."

"Don't flatter yourself. There's enough fault to go round."

Thanks. "Did anyone tell you how Norman ran out of here like his tail was on fire?"

"Aye, so I'm hearing. I wonder…" Cameron didn't complete his sentence.

"…whether the car wreck is only a side-show to the real circus," Jean ventured, "with all due respect to Norman's petulant soul?"

The profile turned toward her. "You might could be saying that."

She faced front and center, avoiding his gaze flickering in the corner of her eyes. Turn-about was fair play. "Anything new in forensics? Threads, pollen, that sort of thing?"

"Several bits of garden plants were found on Lovelace's body, also threads in the same tartan pattern, the MacLyon sett."

"Do you think he was killed in the garden?"

"No, there were quite a few people in the drawing room overlooking the garden at the time."

Jean glanced toward the French doors of the drawing room, now dark. "And none of them saw anything?"

"The problem is that they all saw something, but no one's agreeing on what, whether it was Neil with his pipes or Toby cutting a bouquet of flowers, or MacLyon himself preparing to make his entrance. Or one of the women; they were both dressed in tartan skirts."

"I see. Why they didn't see, that is. The rose bushes and the hedge are enough of a screen that you could tell someone was there but not who."

"The killer then went on round the corner of the house to the game larder and met Lovelace. It could have been a chance meeting, but then we'd have to explain the 'Two p.m. Tuesday' note on your receipt."

"You don't think the killer was anyone from the Lodge?"

"No, they're all vouching for each other's whereabouts at the time of the murder. More than one of them could be working together, but as yet we've got no evidence of that."

Lack of evidence, Jean told herself. What else was new? "For what it's worth, Rick's going to announce something to me at ten tomorrow morning. I overheard Vanessa goading him to it. A new game, maybe, although I hope it's something about the Lodge. Everyone's being so damnably coy about that, I'm ready to pinch Rick's fingers in my laptop."

"That's not the most efficient of torture devices."

Jean laughed hollowly. "When I went up to my room—my locked room—after dinner, I noticed that it had been searched. Or at least my notebook and laptop had been moved around. Someone was reading the notes I've been making." Bracing herself, she went eyeball to eyeball with Cameron. "Do you think I'm in danger?"

His slate-blue eyes didn't blink. "It's possible."

"At least you don't seem to think I'm the killer any more."

"I not so sure I ever did do, Miss Fairbairn."

"Oh really?"

"Just doing my job is all." Cameron looked toward the mountains, a looming black mass edging the star-dusted charcoal of the sky.

A sarcastic *Thanks* wouldn't be appropriate, so Jean said nothing. The skin on her arms and legs was breaking out in goose bumps—her tweed jacket was little protection from a chill spring night in Scotland. Not that the temperature was bothering Cameron. He was a native, with veins full of anti-freeze. Or in his case, ice water. Neither of them, she suspected, wanted to be there. Not there in the nighttime garden, not involved in the case at all. But crime-solving was his job, just as asking questions was hers.

Suddenly she asked herself if he were on the verge of burning out. He didn't have the most stress-free of occupations. And she knew only too well that when you feel the candle flickering you focus on it, blow on it, fan it, force it to throw out a brighter light—and burn it out all the faster. If he gave her any clue, she'd offer cautious understanding. But he remained only a shape beside her, impersonal as a marble column. *Don't get curious about his personal life,* she reminded herself.

"I'll tell you what another side-show is," Jean went on. "George's coin. Rick, Vanessa, Neil—they all knew he had it, and they all agree he had it for a long time. With the pollen evidence, he probably found it when he was in commando training here."

With a hiss like a ruptured pipe—oh, it was a sigh, she could see his breath, ghost-like, swirling from his lips—Cameron said, "He came to see you for some reason that led him to lie to you."

"And yet both Vanessa and Fiona talked about George being very honorable and ethical. Look at the way he was helping out Toby's family. Or do you know about that?"

"I know about that."

Of course you do. "Anyway, that makes me doubt George was cooking the books, whether he needed money enough to sell the coin or not."

"A man can convince himself of all manner of things and call it 'honor.' Even so, I'll be having a look at the accounts."

Jean wrapped her arms around her chest. Cameron's wintry aura felt like snowflakes against her upturned face, so cold they were hot. The small light-storm in Rick's study went dark. A vulture-like shape appeared in one of the library windows, a tiny point of fire at its hairy lips.

"MacSorley," said Cameron. "Like a bad penny, he keeps turning up."

"Rick called him on his cell phone right after y'all left the dining room, said for him to come see him as soon he'd 'handled the cops,' that they needed to make plans. For tomorrow's announcement? To hide the truth about George's death? To solve global warming?"

She sensed rather than saw Cameron's subtle curve of a smile. "MacSorley doesn't think MacLyon could get on without him. And he may be right. He hired both Lovelace and Hawley."

"Maybe Norman knew George before he came to work here. Vanessa says George was spending a lot of time at the Inverness Public Library, which is close to the restaurant. Not that George liked that kind of 'let's see what weird ingredients we can mix together' cuisine...."

Cameron turned on her. "That's interesting."

"What?" she blurted. "I finally told you something you don't already know?"

"There might could have been a prior connection between Lovelace and Hawley. And now they're both dead."

"Well yeah, but Norman wasn't murdered."

"That's as may be."

Wheels were turning in Cameron's head. Jean hoped they were grinding more finely than hers. "Vanessa's resentful of Kieran, which isn't surprising. He's encouraging Rick's *Brigadoon* mania, but I get the feeling she's only going along for the bennies."

"Bennies?"

"Benefits. Money, clothes. She's bored, though, and getting impatient. I don't know how killing George would get her a social life, though." Her goose bumps stretched her skin so tight she shivered.

"It's a wee bit nippy the night. We should be going in." Cameron's firm hand in the back of her jacket urged her toward the door.

She slipped on the gravel path. The hand tightened briefly on her waist, then released her the second she'd regained her balance. "Thank you," she said. Cameron's strong, steady grip could have pulled Norman's car out of the loch single-handedly.

He held the door open for Jean and shut it behind them. A few electronic clicks and cheeps filtered into the hall from the billiards room, but if anyone was inside they were working quietly. The air seemed close and still, scented with the odors of cooking food, coffee, various cleaning products, and smoke richer and sweeter than the acrid stench of Kieran's cigarettes. Rick must've broken out the cigars.

What was that in the hallway, a moving shadow, an elusive shape… Oh. It was Clarinda, slipping in true feline fashion, sinuously and soundlessly, down the stairs and away up the corridor. Jean told her nerves to stand down.

Kieran, too, was hanging in there for the bennies. And unlike Vanessa, he was quite happy with the status quo. Or the status quo as it had been before George's death. Jean turned on Cameron. "Maybe George wasn't embezzling. Maybe George knew someone who was embezzling."

"MacSorley. I was wondering if you'd think of that."

She should have known he'd be quick on the uptake. And quick to rub it in. "I've heard three different versions of how Rick and Kieran first got in contact. Maybe Kieran went looking for Rick, maybe it was the other way around. But the bottom line is that Rick is a real cash cow for the MacSorleys. You should see their house: new furniture, Venetian glass, the works. Before Rick came along, though, they'd been having financial problems ever since Archie, Rick's father, was killed in the war. Killed here, in training."

Cameron leaned so close she wondered if he could smell the blackberry and whiskey on her breath. A tiny flame like a pilot light was thawing his eyes. "A peculiar millionaire must have seemed a gift from God."

"Oh yeah. Especially when he's a little gullible—Vanessa said that—and he's spending a fortune and a half—she said that, too—on books and memorabilia and architectural elements for the house."

"MacSorley could well be creaming off a commission from dealers in everything from books to bricks. Though it was George who was actually buying the books."

"Which is how he found out about Kieran's scheme. Being the honorable person he was, he confronted Kieran with his knowledge and gave him the chance to straighten up and fly right. Except

Kieran found another option." The prickle of her skin warned Jean that she was within Cameron's personal space, but this time she didn't back off.

His breath was scented with whiskey, straight. "Another option. Just that."

"Kieran may have been the only person not wearing tartan at the time of the murder, but does that really matter? With all the tartan carpets and everything, George could have picked up any number of threads all by himself."

Cameron returned her gaze, his hands braced on his hips, his mouth set in a tight smile. "And MacSorley's right keen on implicating Toby, isn't he? Just one problem with that."

Over and beyond the fact that Kieran was Neil's father. Jean said, "Would Kieran damage his own brakes?"

Cameron's smile lost any vestige of amusement and defaulted to grim. Yes, the wheels were turning in his head, she could almost see the sparks flying and hear the gears meshing.

What she was hearing was footsteps. Nothing paranormal though, just Fiona's soft-soled shoes climbing the upper stairs to her bedroom. Fiona. Jean hated to burst the not uncomfortable little bubble of mutual respect, but.... But she couldn't respect Cameron fully until he stopped dismissing her questions about Fiona. "Vanessa said something interesting when she was talking about George and Fiona. That, the book collecting aside, Fiona was 'into everything else around here.'"

Cameron said, "Aye?"

"You remember the woman who called me before I left Edinburgh? The one who warned me in an American accent, using British syntax, that George was trouble and I shouldn't do whatever it was he wanted me to do?"

"Aye?" This time the word was much more cautious.

He saw where she was going. She plunged on. "I think it was Fi...."

"It was her, like as not," said Cameron.

Jean deflated so completely she almost sagged against the wall. "What?"

His face was lined with fatigue, his voice so low she could hardly hear it. "I'm thinking I know why she phoned you. She meant no harm."

"So you did know her before you came here. You just didn't know she was here, did you?"

"No. That was a bit of a surprise."

"Fate, she'd probably say."

"Aye, she would do."

He was stonewalling her, damn him. Jean took a step closer into that fiery cold energy field. "She meant no harm? Fiona may have known George was in the game larder without my telling her!"

"Aye, she would do," he repeated, but now his expression was locked down, revealing nothing.

"We may have built a case against Kieran, but some of the arguments we used against him can be used against Fiona—maybe she's the embezzler."

"Trust me, Miss Fairbairn, Fiona had nothing to do with the murder."

Jean hissed, "Don't patronize me, Detective Chief Inspector Cameron. I can make my own decisions about whom to trust!"

"And you, don't get your knickers in a twist...." His growl trailed away. His eyes darted to and fixed on something behind Jean's back.

She spun around. A shadow moved at the bottom of the staircase. Great, someone had been standing there, listening.

But no one was standing on the steps to cast a shadow, and the shadow wasn't on the staircase after all, but beside it, and it wasn't a shadow but a pale man-shape in the gloom of the alcove, ash on black. The cat, Jean told herself, but she knew it wasn't the cat.

The hair rose first on the back of her neck and then all over her body, each follicle tightening not in fear but in recognition. Her cheeks tingled to a feather-stroke of something more tenuous than even a spider's web. She'd always wondered if that's what ectoplasm was, the nerve endings in the skin firing just as the optic nerves in her eyes fired, in response to a stimulus from another dimension.

She sensed Cameron's physical presence just behind her, motionless, steady, cool, just as she sensed the air itself. A large, strong hand closed on her upper arm as though preventing her from going in for the tackle. Good God. He couldn't, he didn't.... Her own voice was a gossamer thread. "Do you see something beside the stairs?"

"Oh aye," said Cameron's husky whisper. "It's a ghost."

Jean blinked, less amazed at the apparition than at his admission. Either she or reality was definitely losing it. She tried, "Vanessa thinks George Lovelace is haunting the house."

"That's never George Lovelace."

Cameron could see it. He really could see—not it, but him. "No. That's Archie MacSorley."

The ghost stood beside the staircase, about six inches to the left of the treads. In mid-air. Jean could see every wrinkle in his uniform, every insignia, every button, sketched with shadow upon darkness. He wasn't wearing a beret on his head but a bandage, which hid nothing of his craggy face with its arched nose. His small dark eyes stared imperiously into the distance, as though he was very put out to find himself dead…. No, his eyes were utterly empty.

The air swirled in a slow eddy past her ears as Cameron inhaled. "Smoke. Not from a cigarette or a cigar. Burning timber."

"Vanessa said this end of the house was the one most damaged in the fire." Distantly Jean heard shouts and cries and the crackle of flames.

The ghost marched up the steps. Or where the steps had been during his life, offset from the contemporary ones. Even when he stood beneath the ceiling light he was perfectly visible, from bandage to belt to boots. And then he was gone, between one heartbeat and the next.

In the sudden silence the clock in the entrance hall struck ten. Jean exhaled, blowing the stink of smoke from her nostrils. Cameron's body stood inches from hers. Before she could jerk away he dropped her arm, so emphatically he almost pushed her aside, and stepped back. She wondered if she'd have a bruise across her biceps from his grasp.

"Archie MacSorley," he repeated. "How did you know that?"

"George had the same photo of the commandos in an album that the MacSorleys have in their living room. They have a close-up of Archie."

"He was killed here, in training?"

"That's what Miranda says. Feel free to look it up for yourself."

"No need."

Jean looked around, not knowing whether to hug him or hit him. "No snappy comebacks? No skepticism? Or have you known all this time you're allergic to ghosts, too?"

"Well then," he said, with a crimp of his mouth that was almost a rueful smile, "I suppose I was wrong about all the ghosts being tired. Not for those with eyes to see and hearts to know." The *like us* hung unspoken in the air.

Suddenly Jean was dog-tired and bone-weary. She didn't want to talk any more. She didn't want to feel any more. She certainly didn't want to explore whether her discomfort at seeing a ghost was equal to her discomfort at sharing something so private, so—intimate—with Alasdair Cameron. "Good night, Chief Inspector."

"Good night, Miss Fairbairn."

She sensed his aloof, almost bleak, eyes on her as she climbed the stairs and walked unscathed through the dark, cold spot where the ghost had vanished, but she didn't look back.

TWENTY-ONE

PARTING THE DAMASK curtains, Jean leaned close to the window. The glass panes radiated cold. Outside the clouds hung low over the mountains, making them look less substantial than Archie MacSorley's ghost. The sun might have risen in the sky, but the earth was swathed in gloom.

A Gothic sort of morning, sketched in shades of gray, suited Jean's hungover mood perfectly. She'd lain awake for hours, brain spinning, senses wheezing. When she'd at last dozed off, she'd jerked awake at every noise, in spite of having locked her door and hooked the desk chair beneath the knob.

Doors opened. Doors shut. Several sets of footsteps walked up the hall, one of them stopping outside her room. The doorknob had turned, then fallen back. That hadn't been a ghost. It sure hadn't been the cat, either.

Now she turned on all the lights in the room, then brewed herself a pot of strong black tea and surveyed the selection of edibles. Crackers, oatmeal raisin cookies, and shortbread. Good, enough for a breakfast. Until it was time to at last get the goods on Rick, she intended to glory in solitude. And, with no music emanating from the sound system, in silence.

Her laptop humming, her notebook open, Jean began organizing her notes and with them, she hoped, her mind. The gold coin. The murder. The car wreck. The telephone call.

Whatever had happened between Cameron and Fiona might not matter. Irritating as the man could be, she had no evidence he couldn't be trusted and a fair amount of evidence that he could. Even so, his allergy to ghosts was just one of those odd congruities of life, not a character reference. Plenty of people could see ghosts, if not on a regular basis. She'd just never shared a sighting with anyone else before, was all…. Well no, it wasn't all. It was too much for her to wrap her mind around right now.

The history of the house. The portraits. The artifacts. Rick's tartan fantasies. Pouring herself another cup of tea, Jean told herself that Rick MacLyon made his fortune writing and producing games. Not just fantasy games like Claymore, but historical campaigns where you could fight Bannockburn, Agincourt, or Waterloo over and over again. Was the Lodge a gaming group testing some beta version of a new Culloden game? If so, she'd expect its members to look, well, funkier.

A knock on the door made her look up. "Who is it?"

"Fiona. Breakfast is served at nine."

"Thanks, Fiona, but I'm skipping breakfast today."

"Very good." The soft steps padded away.

Jean ate the last package of crackers—bland and blah, some salsa would have helped—and read through her notes. Maybe she could get another ghost article out of all this, too.

Had Archie been walking the ruins all these years, or had he returned to the house after its restoration? No surprise that he was walking—sudden, unexpected death could unsettle a man. Still, Jean wondered not only which aspect of Archie's life had been left unfinished, so that he'd stay on in the last place he'd known, but also why his ghost was accompanied by echoes of the fire. Had he been brought to the infirmary wounded and then died in the blaze?

Vanessa was sensing Archie, in a low-resolution sort of way, not George. Did anyone else know he was there, especially his descendants Kieran and Neil? She replayed the scene, the shape in the shadows, the small dark empty eyes, the firm hand on her arm….

Whoa. It was almost ten. Leaping up, Jean applied make-up, dressed in a skirt and sweater, and armed herself with notebook and laptop. *Carpe diem,* she pep-talked herself. Although there were some days that you seized and then dropped again, like a hot potato.

She moved the chair away from the door and stepped out into the hall. A faint miasma of burned sausage made her glad she'd passed on breakfast. Clarinda was stretched out on her love seat in front of the windows, utterly relaxed. Promising herself to get in touch with her inner feline as soon as possible, Jean headed on down the stairs.

The first person she saw was Alasdair Cameron. He stood in front of the clock, holding a coffee mug, his stance anything but relaxed. He looked around with a sober, "Good morning."

"Good morning," Jean returned.

He looked a bit hungover himself, even though he was clean shaven and back in his coat and tie, the former charcoal gray, the latter a lush Book of Kells interlace pattern. His eyes were un-adorned, hard and cold as polished steel. Seeing him warm up a bit last night had been like seeing cracks suddenly appear in the stone beneath Edinburgh Castle.

Cameron pitched his voice only a little above a whisper—for her ears only. "Andy brought Walsh back this morning. The mechanics at the garage agreed he'd been there with the MacSorley's car, right enough, but they said the brakes worked a treat when he left."

"He wouldn't have messed with the brakes right in front of them," Jean whispered back.

"That's as may be, but it gives us nothing to charge him with." Cameron drank thoughtfully from his mug. "Walsh is still saying he went to your hotel to blether about your writing. I'm thinking he's lying."

"If he's not the killer himself, then he's scared of who is."

"Oh aye. And we'll not be fainting in astonishment at that."

Jean allowed herself a thin smile. "You think Kieran's the killer?"

"No. He's right out."

"What?" she demanded, feeling houses of cards tumbling past her ears.

"We've turned up a witness who saw MacSorley jogging past the Clan Cameron Museum at two p.m. Tuesday."

"Great." Jean looked around—fake weapons, antlers, twin corridors—and back at Cameron. If he were disappointed he'd never

show it. She could do that, too. "So it's not him. It's none of the
MacSorleys. You've pretty much eliminated the Lodge members
and won't hear anything against Fiona. Our suspects have boiled
down to Toby, Rick, and Vanessa. If you don't mind my using the
word 'our.'"

"Feel free," Cameron told her.

"I'm only the amateur consultant," she said, and, with a flourish
of her laptop, "I'll report in after I beard the lion in his den. No
pun intended."

"Right." His cup to his lips, Cameron walked away, broad
shoulders not as stiff as a soldier's, but set, even so. No *thank you,*
no *excuse me.* But then, why bother? They'd reached a detente of
sorts last night, unanswered questions or not.

The clock struck ten. Setting her own shoulders, Jean opened
the library door. "Hello?"

No one was there. A fire leaped in the fireplace. Several lamps
and the spotlights over the artifacts sent out cheerful yellow gleams
that made the garden beyond the windows look even murkier.
Taking the fire and the lights as an indication Rick didn't intend
to stand her up, Jean dumped her computer and bag beside an
armchair and headed for the bookshelves.

Oh my. Yes. This was a very fine collection, from modern over-
views to historical novels to document boxes labeled with lists of
letters and pamphlets to antique tomes emitting the scent of damp
attics. She read the authors' names: Lang, Blaikie, MacBean, Tayler,
Seton and Arnot, Chambers—the historians of the Forty-five. But
the book that made Jean look twice was the three-volume nineteenth-century edition of Bishop Forbes' *The Lyon in Mourning.*

That book had been dismissed as propaganda, even though
Forbes compiled his account from eyewitnesses to the atrocities
committed after Culloden…. *The Lyon in Mourning.* Was that
what had inspired Rick's last name? Mac-Lyon, son of the lion.
The red rampant lion, the ancient heraldic symbol of Scotland.

Several of the "bloodline of the holy grail" books, fantasies
clothed as non-fiction, were ranged just beneath the Forbes. Jean
had read several of them. In spite of herself, she had to admire the
bravado with which their authors careened from straightforward
explanations of the origins of the Masons and their Scottish rite

to lunatic fringe baloney about the Stuarts being the descendants of Jesus Christ. A vast multi-national and multi-generational conspiracy concealed this "fact" from the public, of course, as the authors proved by crawling to the far ends of perceptual limbs and there clinging to twigs and fallacy alike.

While Jean ducked and covered the moment the word "conspiracy" was breathlessly uttered, still she found "secret history" fantasy entertaining. As many insights came from free association in history as in literature.... Suddenly she wondered if the Lodge was into some sort of occult rites. The people bowing over Rick's hand had resembled a congregation leaving a church. No wonder no one would talk about it. They were embarrassed.

She eyed a miniature of Charles Edward Louis Philip Casimir Sylvester Maria Stuart, who even as a bewigged child had a self-satisfied smile. A shield-shaped plaque sat between the miniature and a photo of a small, thin, pale boy wearing a kilt—Rick himself, waiting for the bullies to kick sand in his face and accuse him of wearing a dress. Jean angled the plaque toward the light. The name "MacLyon" was engraved below a coat of arms. So Rick had bought himself a coat of arms. Why wasn't it emblazoned over the fireplace?

Because, she realized with a frisson of something between incredulity and horror, this wasn't even as legitimate as a one-size-fits-all coat of arms you could order from an ad in a genealogy magazine. Two of the four quarters of the shield displayed the royal arms of Scotland, the red rampant lion against a gold background surrounded by parallel red lines and fleur de lys. Each of the other two segments showed the leopards of England quartered with the lilies of France. These arms were, more or less, those of the Stuarts.

Yes, heraldry was just one more mutually agreed-upon game, another element in the quest for identity. But still....

Three memories, one verbal, one visual, one musical, slid off the surface of Jean's brain and splashed into her stomach like rocks falling into a well. Norman Hawley had said something about Yanks poncing about like royalty. The feathers and streamers on Rick and Vanessa's bed formed the same design as the crest of the Prince of Wales. The words the Lodge had been singing while George Lovelace hung in the game larder had been not "God Save the Queen" but "God Save the King."

Her knees buckled, dropping her down in a chair. Her stomach gurgled with crackers and that unease she thought of as free-floating anxiety, a sense of the impending enactment of Murphy's Law.

A sudden roll of drums and squeal of pipes goosed Jean's heart into her throat and her body back to its feet. Hidden speakers erupted with "Scotland the Brave." Rick MacLyon, Murphy himself, came stepping down the spiral staircase from his office, dressed to kill in silver-buttoned coat and black tie, kilt and draped plaid, bejeweled brooch and silver-trimmed dirk. She didn't think Cameron had given Rick back the kilt he'd been wearing Tuesday, but a rich man—a rich obsessed man—could afford more than one, to say nothing of the far from inexpensive decorative addenda.

Only now, as perceptual twigs broke off in her hands, did she recognize the pattern of the MacLyon tartan. Its blue and green blocks crossed with red and gold lines had been copied from a fragment of tartan actually worn by the Bonnie Prince. *Oh no,* Jean thought, *he's not going to....*

Rick paraded in to his soundtrack, his drawn, pale cheeks flushed and his glasses glaring like signal mirrors. He extended his hand. For a moment Jean thought he expected her to kneel and kiss it. Then she saw the folder he held, embossed with the same coat of arms. "Here's your press kit. Go on, sit down."

Shutting her mouth with a snap, Jean took the folder and thumped down into the chair.

"We might as well be informal. This is only a preliminary press conference. A dry run." Rick paced toward the fireplace and struck a noble pose on the hearth.

Jean opened the folder carefully, as though it were a can about to spout paper snakes. Inside were several eight-by-ten color glossies of Rick in full regalia, Rick and Vanessa in full regalia, Glendessary House with Neil in full regalia holding his pipes in the portico. The last one was of Rick posing in front of the glass case in Edinburgh Castle holding the Honors of Scotland—the crown, the scepter, the sword, the Stone of Scone. And whose palm had he greased to be allowed to take that shot?

The other side of the folder held thick, creamy sheets of paper imprinted, again, with the coat of arms. A biography. A family tree.

Some sort of register. Copies of letters in eighteenth-century hand-writing. Smothering a groan, Jean set the folder aside and hazarded, "The Lord Lyon, the heraldry authority, wouldn't appreciate you making up your own royal arms. Neither would the Queen, although these days that sort of thing doesn't get you thrown into the Tower of…."

"Elizabeth Battenberg," Rick said, "is the latest in a long line of Hanoverian usurpers. Her family tried to cover that up by taking the name Windsor, but we know better."

Yes, he is going to do it. He wasn't just out in left field, he'd climbed the fence and was haring off down the freeway. Nothing for it but to hoist her laptop and start typing. To play along…. She'd told herself that about Lovelace, and his play had become a tragedy.

"Circumstances have forced my hand," said Rick. "I'd planned to spend more time laying the groundwork. But there's a tide in the affairs of man, or whatever the quote is. Fate brought me someone with the right background and the right connections to help get the word out. The time is right. My people must be prepared. This will come as a shock to them."

No kid…. He was talking about Jean. But she'd come here because of George Lovelace.

"It's time to reveal the true story of the Stuart succession. The Hanoverians usurped the throne in sixteen eighty-eight. They exiled Charles's grandfather James the Second and the Seventh. They hid the truth about Charles' children. They manufactured evidence that he died without an heir. They invented a diverted succession, claiming that the Stuart inheritance is now in the hands of some insignificant family in Bavaria. Hah!" He gestured grandly. "My father was Charles Douglas. My mother was Anne Sobieski. It wasn't until several years ago I realized the significance of those names. Fate had brought my parents together generations after their family lines diverged. Or was it fate?"

Jean looked up, but with little hope he'd launch into some touching story about his parents meeting at a sock hop or a malt shop. *Abandon hope, you are now entering an alternate universe.*

"Their meeting was the fruit of a conspiracy," Rick said.

"You have evidence?" asked Jean, although she knew she was wasting her breath.

"Of course there's no evidence. That goes to show you how thorough and how devious the conspirators are."

Yeah, right. Even Cameron, with his two wrongs making a right, wouldn't buy.... Oh, great. Cameron. Jean looked back at her screen, for a moment seeing instead two cool slate-blue eyes.

"The pro-Jacobite movement opposes the Hanoverians. Its members have moved very carefully over the years, in great danger from the present British government with its 'official' history." His forefingers curved into the quotation marks. "Our goal is to re-establish the true lineage of the kings and queens of Scotland."

"And your parents are members of this movement?"

"Oh no, no. They're very active in Clan Douglas. I grew up going to Scottish Games and Festivals all over the country. But I've only recently told them what the real deal is."

Leaving them to wonder how they'd managed to infect little Ricky with such a virulent tartan virus. "So you're in contact with other Jacobites?"

"A few, yes, but each cell must be kept separate from every other one until the day comes. Fortunately one of my followers, a man with the courage of his convictions, stepped forward. Kieran MacSorley, a relative of Cameron of Lochiel. He's worked long and hard on my behalf."

Jean turned her guffaw into a throat-clearing ahem. MacSorley, who kept turning up like a bad penny.

"He brought me to Glendessary House, close to where my illustrious foremother Jenny Cameron set out on her mission to history."

"Your illustrious..." No, not poor Jenny, not again.

Rick paced back and forth, fabric swirling, hardware jingling, his hand clasping the hilt of his dirk, his face glowing with fervor. "The moment Charles saw Jenny at the head of her troops in August of seventeen forty-five, he fell deeply and passionately in love. How could she resist him? Why would she want to? Jenny came to her prince after the battle of Falkirk in January of seventeen forty-six, and told him she was pregnant. With his first child. His heir. They were married at Stirling. Clementina Walkinshaw was their lady-in-waiting. But to foil the Hanoverian spies, word was given out that Charles was sick and Clementina was nursing him back to health at her home. At Bannockburn, right? Where Charles's ancestor Robert the Bruce won Scotland's independence. How appropriate!"

Was it? Clementina's sister worked in the household of the Prince of Wales. The real Prince of Wales, the one whose father actually sat on the British throne.

"The child, a son, of course…"

"Of course," Jean murmured, starting to feel giddy.

"…was born soon after the tragedy of Culloden. Charles risked life and limb to come here to Loch Arkaig in August of seventeen forty-six, a year after he'd raised his standard. What a year it had been, triumph snatched from his grasp through the betrayal and ineptitude of others! He came here not to see the treasure of his gold Louis d'Or, but the treasure of his son and heir, who was hidden with Jenny among her people. Later, Clementina Walkinshaw brought his son to Charles in France."

Jean added, "And bore him a daughter."

"Who can blame him, in his tragic exile from his home, turning for comfort to the woman who reminded him of his lost wife?"

"Lost? Jenny didn't die until seventeen seventy-two."

Rick turned on her, forefinger raised. "Yes. Exactly. Jenny died in seventeen seventy-two. That's why Charles never married Clementina. He was still married to Jenny. It was only when Jenny died that he agreed to marry that lying little Louise of Stolberg."

"Which proves he was married to Jenny," Jean said wearily. Yes, this was the sort of "proof" she'd expected, the sort of manic algebra employed by conspiracy buffs, where if a equals x then y is blue, Q.E.D. She could ask why Jenny never went to France or Italy herself, but she figured Rick would have some sort of answer. "And you're the multiple great-grandson of this kid of Charlie and Jenny's?"

"Yes I am. Douglas is the name the prince assumed when he went undercover. Sobieski is the prince's mother's name."

"Your name is MacLyon."

"It's a new millennium. There's a new Scottish parliament. Can total separation from tyrannical England be far behind?"

There was another rhetorical question Jean didn't bother to answer.

"When the people of Scotland turn to me to head their new state, I want to offer them a fresh start, a new dynasty with a new name."

She was still tempted to duck and cover, but no, her fingers were moving too fast over the keyboard. While it wasn't the story Rick thought it was, it was still a story. "Are you a British citizen, Rick?"

"I refuse to become a citizen of that awkward combination, plodding Anglo-Saxon tying down the fiery Celt. I'll become a citizen of Scotland when it regains its independence and calls me to be its monarch."

"And the good times will roll," Jean said under her breath. So that's why he hadn't bought a title. He was going for The Big One.

"You're skeptical." Rick smiled indulgently. "That's quite understandable. That's why I included copies of all the important papers in your press kit. The genealogy, the marriage certificate, letters from Charles to Jenny calling her his dearest wife and re-ferring to their child. How fortunate the Hanoverian spies never intercepted any of those letters!"

Yeah, right, she thought again. Like the Stuarts would have committed any of this to paper. "You have a marriage certificate?"

"I have documents proving the true lineage of the house of Stuart, suppressed by centuries of Hanoverian conspiracy. First they worked to surround Charles with incompetents, leading to his defeat. Then they worked to keep the people of Britain in thrall to their elitist policies. Scoundrels!"

"And have these papers been authenticated?" Jean inquired.

"Of course. By the Museum of Scotland. I've got a letter from the curator, some guy named Campbell. Which worried me, Clan Campbell betrayed the Prince and all he stood for, but this guy promised to keep everything quiet until I need him to step forward and testify. Sometimes people do rise above their heritage, don't they?"

Some guy named Campbell? Jean couldn't wait to hear what Michael Campbell-Reid had to say about his name being taken in vain. Assuming she'd be coherent once she got out of this fun house. She'd thought Rick was a bit of a wuss, but now she was seeing fire and brimstone in his pale eyes, even if his tongue couldn't quite decide whether to speak colloquial American or proclamational bombast. "Where did you get these documents?"

"From my loyal follower, Kieran MacSorley. He had George
search them out."

"And Kieran, your loyal follower, took them to the Museum?"

"Yes, yes, of course…." The electronic trill of "Scotland the
Brave" stopped Rick cold. He fumbled in his sporran, pulled out
his phone, and switched it off. "Poor old George, what a shame
he didn't live to see this day! You and Miranda can set up the press
conference in Edinburgh. At Holyrood Palace. We'll need all the
pageantry, of course, the heralds and the Black Watch and the clan
chiefs. It'll be an important day in the history of Scotland. The
Stuart heir announcing that he's back again and ready to take up
his duties."

"And what about Elizabeth Battenberg?" asked Jean,
thinking that the Tower of London was looking more feasible
by the minute.

"She'll be confronted by an accomplished fact, won't she?
She'll just have to settle for England and Wales and Northern
Ireland. I'll let her keep on vacationing at Balmoral, of course.
They get into the swing of things there pretty well, considering."

Jean hit the exclamation point on her keyboard so hard it
dinged. What cheek! What chutzpah! What bloody nerve! For a
moment she wondered if this was, after all, just a publicity ploy
for some sort of game. Maybe Rick was about to whip out the box
holding the disks and say, "April Fool!"

No, he was beaming paternally on her. "Did you notice the gates
of the house when you came in? The copy of the Traquair gates?"

"The gates are standing open because the Stuarts are back. Or
they were, until George Lovelace was murdered." Jean saved
everything and closed the lid of her computer. She had to get those
documents, the original documents, to Michael. "Rick, I appreciate
the press kit with the copies of the papers, but don't you think the
originals would be better off in Edinburgh?"

The light in his face dimmed. "But the Hanoverian conspiracy…."

Forcing a smile, Jean stood up. "Papers so important to the history
of Scotland should be in the Museum of Scotland, with all the other
unique Scottish relics, where your people can appreciate them."

He brightened, probably seeing his documents in the main hall
of the Museum surrounded by security guards.

"You'll need the papers at Holyrood," Jean went on, using the same tone of voice she'd use to cajole a balky niece or a nephew into bed.

Slowly he nodded. "Yes. You're right."

"I'll tell you what," she extemporized. "I bet D.C.I. Cameron would send those papers to Edinburgh with a police escort. Don't you think? I mean, maybe it was fate that sent a man named Cameron here at all. You can't defy fate, can you?"

"No. That's what Fiona says." Rick set his chin. "All right then. Go find Cameron. Send him in here. I'll give him the documents."

Overpowering her urge to say, *Your wish is my command,* Jean gathered up her laptop and her bag and headed for the door. Once in the hall she broke into a trot, heading toward someone sane. Annoying, but very sane.

Rick not only took all the Jacobite myth seriously, he'd built his entire castle in the air, from dungeons to a flagpole flying the rampant lion, on papers that Kieran MacSorley said George Lovelace had searched out. In her ears Jean heard Miranda's gales of laughter. In her heart she felt a stirring of pity for Rick. And somewhere in her back-brain she sensed Cameron's voice saying, *There's a motive for you.*

TWENTY-TWO

DETECTIVE SERGEANT SAWYER was standing just inside the door of the billiards room. Jean brushed by him. "Is Cameron here?"

"Why?" Sawyer demanded.

But Jean had already spotted her quarry. He was weaving his way over the power cords, at the same time pulling his bulky jacket on over his suit. She started toward him. "Chief Ins…"

A meaty hand grabbed her elbow. "Hang on there, lassie."

"Hey!" Jean yanked her arm from Sawyer's grasp.

"Give over, Andy," said Cameron's quiet but intense voice. "Miss Fairbairn? I'm away to Spean Bridge, can it…"

"No, it can't wait. Come here." Jean only realized she'd seized his forearm when she found herself standing several paces down the hall holding a handful of squashy jacket and very solid flesh. "I talked to Rick. Or rather I listened while he talked to me."

"Aye?" Cameron retrieved his arm. The door of the billiards room slammed shut, knocking a nearby picture askew.

No way could she explain it all in twenty-five words or less, but she did her best, ending up, "…so I told him you'd take the documents to Edinburgh with a police escort."

She had to hand it to the man, he only spent five or ten seconds looking as if he'd been smacked in the face by a salmon. "You're not joking, are you?"

"Hell, no. The guy's crazy as a bedbug. About the only thing he didn't say was that he'd been chosen by God."

"Bugger," Cameron said reverently, and started down the hall. "Let's have a look at these documents of His Majesty's, then."

Jean hurried after him, and was at his side when he knocked briskly at the library door. Without waiting for a reply, he pushed it open. "Mr. MacLyon? You wanted a word?"

Rick was posed in front of the fireplace, the firelight reflecting from all his buckles, badges, and buttons. In one hand he held a leather portfolio tooled in a Celtic interlace design similar to Cameron's tie—something he noticed immediately, and approved with a benevolent smile.

Jean commended Cameron's fortuitous choice of accessories.

"I have here documents important to the state of Scotland," Rick announced.

Cameron extended his hand. "I'll see these are cared for properly."

"Great." Bestowing largesse, Rick handed over the portfolio. "Now. I'm having a small dinner party tomorrow night in honor of the occasion. Just my inner circle. Fiona's arranging with the Montrose Inn in Spean Bridge to cater and serve. Jean, she can find you something to wear. Sandy, since your technical people still have my employees' kilts, I've ordered new ones from the hire service in Fort William. Including one for you, too."

Cameron's eyes rolled toward Jean. *Did you know about this?*

She tried a barely perceptible shake of her head at him, and to Rick said, "Thank you. We're honored."

"Oh aye, so we are," Cameron added in a half-strangled voice.

His thin smile indicated that he felt a command performance was a good excuse to keep an eye on the suspects.

With a regal wave, Rick dismissed them. "Off you go. Jean, call ahead and tell the Museum to expect the papers."

"I'll make sure they treat them as they deserve." She managed to get out the door and down the hall before she exploded with a sound that was both guffaw and groan.

Cameron walked up holding the portfolio at arm's length, like a snake. "Fall about laughing, then, but mind we've got two dead men. George's murder, at the least, must be tied up with Mad MacLyon."

"I mind, I mind," Jean said. "It's all so absurd. It's all so pathetic."

"Aye, that it is. And it might could be the break we've been needing." His smile was balanced between grim and rueful. Again the pilot light flickered in his eyes. "Gunn and I are away to Spean Bridge to interview Meg Parkinson-Fraser, she refusing to come here. I'll have him take the papers on to Edinburgh."

"Tell him to give them to Michael Campbell-Reid at the new Museum on Chambers Street. I'll warn Michael to expect them. Rick says Michael authenticated them, but there's no way he even saw them. I bet it's all a scam of MacSorley's."

"That's one bet I'll not be taking." Tucking the portfolio under his arm, Cameron left the building.

Rick's soundtrack continued unabated, pipes blaring and drums thrumming. What, would silence expose his thoughts to creeping rationality? There was merciful fantasy, and then there was fantasy-as-opiate, repudiating the outside world and glutting the world within.

The outside world. Jean hadn't been in Glendessary House for twenty-four hours, but it felt like a month. Despite its size, there was something claustrophobic about the place. She turned toward the staircase to see Vanessa strolling along the hall from the kitchen, dressed in MTV casual. "You want lunch, Jean? Toby fixed some sandwiches."

"No thank you, I'm going to run some errands in Spean Bridge."

"Sure. Take your time. Oh, and Jean," Vanessa stepped closer. "What about the ghost? Have you heard it yet?"

"Yes, I heard it. And…" Like seeing ghosts was going attract comment in this house? "…I saw it. It's not George. It's Archie MacSorley."

"Who?"

"Kieran's father, who died here during the war."

"So what's he doing haunting the place?"

"Ghosts don't reveal their motives," Jean said, and, still a bit giddy, added, "It's like there's some sort of paranormal union with a non-disclosure policy."

"A union… Oh. Funny." Vanessa bared her teeth but didn't exactly smile. "And does this union keep ghosts from hurting you?"

"Pretty much, yes, unless you count being frightened as being hurt. Why? Are you feeling threatened?"

"Not really, it's just that I wasn't thrilled when I thought it was George haunting the place, but I figured he'd be, like, Obi-Wan Kenobi."

"A benign presence."

"Yeah. I just hope Archie's not anything like Kieran." She made a sour face. "You know?"

"I know," Jean assured her. "I wouldn't worry about the ghosts. There are plenty of other things to worry…."

Along the hall came Neil, holding a cracker with a bit of cheese on it. "Have a go at this," he said, and presented it to Vanessa's red lips. His glance at Jean said, *See what you're missing?*

It was Jean's brain that was doing the calisthenics now, not her gonads, thank you anyway. "Y'all know what Rick told me this morning?"

"Mmm-hum," said Vanessa her mouth full.

Neil said, "So Rick put you in the picture at last."

"And?" Jean prodded.

Vanessa fluttered her hands. "It's Rick's baby. I mean, either you get with the program or you're out. I'm with the program. No problem."

"Oh aye," said Neil. "Mind you, I'm only the piper."

"You're more than that," Vanessa told him. He grinned.

They seemed to think Rick's mania was just an innocent hobby. Jean turned up the volume a notch. "George had to know about this, this king stuff."

"Sure. But he was sworn to secrecy with the rest of us." Vanessa grinned back at Neil.

They reminded Jean of students skylarking in the back of the room while she went over the material for the test. "Hello? Rick's talking about a press conference at Holyrood!"

"Sweet." Vanessa's green eyes lit with visions of ball dresses and glass slippers, then faded. She was too smart to think her pumpkin would always be a coach. "Okay, yeah, I know, it's not going to happen like he imagines. Still, he's not hurting anything."

"It's all just a bit of fun," added Neil.

"It wasn't fun for George," Jean said. "Or for Norman, either."

Neil had the grace to look shamefacedly at the floor. Vanessa shook her head and sighed. "Yeah, you're right. But getting up Rick's nose isn't going to help George."

Toby loomed out of the hallway. "The lunch is ready. Last night's soup's not half bad; my mum always says soup's all the better for sitting a day."

"Okay," Vanessa told him. "I'll tell Rick, although he probably won't want to eat anything. He can get really hyper."

"I'll be back in time for dinner," Jean stated, and headed up the stairs, more determined than ever to touch bases with the real world, such as it was. But she had a couple of calls to make first.

She packed her computer and notebook in her carry-on bag, so she could take them with her, then punched Michael's number into her phone.

"Michael Campbell-Reid," said his energetic tenor.

She paced across the room and back, the phone to her ear. "Michael, it's Jean. You'll never believe what I just heard from Rick MacLyon."

He listened, interrupting her again and again with increasingly indignant exclamations. By the end of her recital he was making the same simmering noise as a teapot on the boil. "Well if that isn't… If those papers had come here I'd have heard, and if they've not come here, then they've not been properly authenticated. No matter what MacLyon is saying about a letter with my name on it. You and your detective friends are thinking this has something to do with George Lovelace's murder, are you?"

She let "detective friends" pass without comment. "It has to."

"Well then, I'll be waiting for—what's his name? Gunn?"

"Yes. Detective Constable Gunn. He should be there by three or so, barring any Friday afternoon traffic jams."

"All right then."

Jean left Michael girding his loins for historiographic battle, punched *Great Scot*'s number, and told herself she was going to wear a rut in the carpet. "Gavin, it's Jean, is Miranda there?"

"Ah," said Miranda's voice a moment later, "Jean Fairbairn, girl detective."

"Actually I'm more of the straight woman. Get this." Once again Jean started at the top with the coat of arms and *The Lyon in Mourning* and wended her way down to the leather portfolio, now on its way to meet its destiny in Edinburgh.

Just as Jean had predicted, Miranda erupted into shrieks of laughter. "The man's bloody daft! Hasn't anyone told him he has no clothes? Are they all scared of him?"

Scared? Of Rick? Yes, maybe they were. "Humoring the guy with the money has been part of the toady job description since long before the Bonnie Prince himself. And speaking of toadies, this whole—plot, scheme, whatever—reeks of Kieran MacSorley. Did you find out whether he actually has a paying job with Rick?"

"He earns a small salary as the local justice of the peace, but if he's making anything off Rick legitimately, it's not been reported to Inland Revenue."

"Why am I not surprised?" Neither was Jean surprised that Miranda had sources among the tax collectors just as she had sources in the Vatican. "Can you answer one more question?"

"That I can," said Miranda, not waiting to hear what the question was.

"Archie MacSorley, Kieran's father. Can you find me the exact date of his death? And the date of the fire at Glendessary House?"

"Piece of cake. What are you on about?"

"Maybe no more than another ghost story. I'll let you know. Right now, though, I'm out of here. I'll call you tom…"

"Half a sec, I've another answer for you. You asked about Fiona Robertson."

"Oh. Yeah." Funny, Jean thought, how in spite of everything she'd almost taken Cameron's word that Fiona was an innocent bystander.

"Her husband was Kenneth Robertson, a police detective in Inverness. Three years ago he was caught taking bribes from drug dealers. Tried, convicted, and sent down to prison. Where he killed himself."

"Oh my God. Poor Fiona." Jean stopped dead in the middle of the room, smacking face-first into an invisible wall. Now it was her turn to look down shamefacedly. Fiona was a suspect. A suspect's private life might become the detective's business, but sometimes the detective got her fingers burned.... "Wait a minute. Inverness? Was Alasdair Cameron involved?"

"He was Robertson's partner. Blew the gaff when he realized he'd gone wrong. Testified against him. Earned Cameron a promotion and one more commendation to add to his collection."

Like that mattered to him. She collapsed on the edge of the bed, weighed down first by knowledge, then by sympathy. *Poor Alasdair.* If Fiona had been numbed by tragedy, then he had been eviscerated by it. He wasn't a stone, he was a shell.

"Rumor said he did Robertson over because he was having an affair with Fiona."

"No way!" blurted Jean, and then reminded herself that motives could be slippery.

"I've no way of knowing, right enough, but his own divorce happened round about the same time. The rumormongers made a meal of it."

Jean never thought she would identify with Cameron, but she did now. Except her own exercise in whistle-blowing was starting to sound like a very small toot.

"You're quick enough to defend him," said Miranda. "A good man, is he?"

Jean could answer that, she just wasn't sure she should. Thank goodness the sound system had lapsed into something innocuous.... No, it was Hugh's version of "The Water is Wide." That one would wring tears even from Alasdair Cameron. And she wasn't going to psychoanalyze him. *Right.* "Miranda, I've got to go see if I can track down my wits; they're chasing haggises through the heather right now. I'll call you tomorrow."

"All right then. Cheers."

Jean put her all-too incriminating notebook into her bag and gathered up her computer. She went out into the rain, stowed the laptop in her trunk, and climbed into her car. The chill interior felt soothing, like a cool compress on a fevered brow. She took several deep breaths while her thoughts did a pinball routine, caroming from rampant lions to domestic ghosts to enigmatic police detectives and similarly enigmatic housekeepers. Okay, she told herself firmly. She had misjudged Cameron. That didn't mean her pendulum had to swing so far and so fast the other way.

Not that he was the issue. George Lovelace was the issue. Rick MacLyon was the issue. The congruence between the two of them, aided and abetted by Kieran MacSorley, whether Vanessa or Neil or Toby had any role in it or not, that was the issue. Just because she tended to break into a rash at the word "conspiracy" didn't mean conspiracies didn't happen—if in much simpler patterns than conspiracy buffs liked to believe.

Her breath was leaving a sparkling fog on the windshield. She started the car, switched on the defrost, and headed down the drive. Droplets tambourined onto the roof from the overhanging trees. The bear sculptures atop the gates looked dingy and dismal. Only a couple of media vans were still parked outside, lights gleaming in their windows.

Jean could barely see the loch for the mist and rain, let alone the distant mountains. Her headlights felt their way along the narrow road and through the Dark Mile, which lay in such impenetrable shadow the back of her neck crawled. Bonnie Brae Cottage looked more ashen than white. Across the road, a huge tow truck plunged and struggled in the mud like some antediluvian beast, winching Norman's car from the cold waters of the loch. Jaw clenched, Jean focused on the road.

Achnacarry, Gairloch and the Caledonian Canal, the Commando Memorial, the bronze soldiers still keeping the faith—each materialized from the mist and then disappeared behind her, phantoms from an uneasy dream. At last she came to the white buildings of Spean Bridge and went to ground in the dining room of the Montrose Inn, named after a famous warrior who had fought for both sides and, in time-honored Scottish fashion, gave his life for the losing one.

Spicy mulligatawny soup and toasted cheese sandwiches warmed her stomach, and a gooseberry tart washed down with cappuccino quelled the anxious shrieks of her nervous system. One of these days, Jean told herself, she needed to stop sublimating her overactive senses with food and music. Maybe she should try a formal workout instead of her usual exercise of bouncing off walls and jumping to conclusions.

There, in the hallway running between reception and the dining room, stood Fiona like another figment, this time of Jean's uneasy conscience. That's right, the Montrose Inn was catering Rick's announcement party tomorrow night. Jean was debating whether to stare out the window or wave a greeting when Fiona glanced into the dining room. Her casual pose stiffened into that of a bird dog at point. Jean tried a pleasant nod.

Instead of turning her back, Fiona walked up to Jean's table. "May I sit down?"

"Please." Now what?

Fiona pulled out the second chair. The teenaged waitress wafted in their direction. "Nothing for me, thank you." Gathering up Jean's empty dishes, the waitress wafted away again.

Between the dark day and the discreetly lit restaurant, Fiona's spilled pupil was barely noticeable. Her face was as pale and fine as exquisitely molded but unpainted porcelain. Even the wave of red hair that edged it was drained of color, its fire extinguished. Something immeasurably sad moved in her eyes.

No. Something beyond sadness, immeasurable calm, perhaps, radiated from her eyes, her face, her clasped hands resting on the tablecloth. "Rick told you of his plans, did he?"

"Oh yes. D.C. Gunn's taken his documents to the Museum of Scotland."

"He'll never believe they're anything but divinely inspired."

"No, I don't guess he will." Jean didn't need to add any cheap psychoanalysis about rationality and ego.

"If it were only his own—his own private game—it's not my place to criticize…" Fiona looked out the window. "I don't know why George kept on catering to Rick's fancies. He knew better. But he only brought you the coin? He never mentioned Rick's name?"

"Only when I asked him, and very noncommittally then."

"Right." Fiona turned back to Jean, spreading her hands with their long, fragile fingers flat on the tabletop. The gold wedding band looked like brass. "Aye, it was me who phoned you. Disguised my voice and all. When George told me he was intending to talk to you, I thought for certain he'd made up his mind at last, was after speaking his piece, and I was scared for him."

"You were scared for him? Why?"

"Because I'd seen him hanging in the game larder, seen it so strong I fell sick." Her eyes gazed unblinking into Jean's.

"You saw him…" Vanessa had interpreted Fiona's cool neutrality as disapproval. It wasn't. It was just that Fiona's stillness, like Cameron's, could make you nervous. If she was lying, Jean would never trust her perceptions again…. She suddenly realized just what kind of perception was at work here. "You have ESP. Second Sight. You're clairvoyant. You catch glimpses of the future. It's not quite the same way I—well, I can see ghosts, but the two abilities, skills, curses—they're on the same paranormal continuum, in a way. And neither kind is voluntary."

Fiona nodded, unsurprised. "There's a stream near my grandmother's croft on Mull; she'd never go there at night for fear of seeing the *beann nighe,* a sort of banshee, washing out the clothes of the next person in the village to be dying."

"And what she saw, what you see, can't be changed?"

"No."

"But you have to try," Jean said, putting words in Fiona's mouth. "You have to fight, no matter what."

Fiona clasped her hands again, but not before Jean saw them trembling. "I might have agreed with you, once. I've tried in the past to change fate, and I've failed. I failed this time as well. Trying, fighting, it only hurts you and those around you. The Buddhists have it right. No desire, no pain."

Jean almost retorted, *If there's no desire, what's the point,* or *That's throwing the baby out with the bath water,* but no, the woman had a right to her own feelings.

"I saw you as well, standing on the doorstep. I'd seen your photo in George's magazines, I knew it was you. I knew there was some connection between you and George's death, but I didn't know what it was."

"You thought if you warned me off then he'd be all right. But your warning just made me all the more eager to get out here."

"Aye, it did." Fiona's porcelain face creased in a grimace of pain, quickly smoothed away. "Rick had already told George not to come in the Tuesday. I told him myself, there's no need to be driving all this way, have a day out. Still he crept into the house."

"Why? To meet someone?"

"I don't know. If I did, I might could help."

"We all want to help," Jean said. "I guess if you'd told the police the murder was going to happen you'd either have been laughed at or arrested."

"Not if I'd told Alasdair. But then, what could he have done? Telling him would have been handing him one more burden." Fiona tilted her head to the side. "You know about my husband and Alasdair, do you?"

"Yes," Jean admitted. "Sorry."

"Alasdair agonized over his decision to grass up Kenny, not least because he and I were friends. But he had to do the right thing. I knew he was after doing it. I knew it would be Kenny's death. I'm not blaming him for it."

"He blames himself," Jean stated.

"He does that, aye. For the rumors as well, the scandal about him and me. His marriage was over then, that had nothing to do with me, but the timing was bad." Fiona looked out the window again, as though searching for something in the rain-draped hill-sides but not finding it.

"Cameron didn't know you were working at Glendessary House, did he?"

"No. I wanted a clean break with the past. I was denied a widow's pension, under the circumstances, so I answered an advert in the newspaper and Rick and Vanessa took me in. They've been kind to me. I've encouraged Rick's view of destiny, though, and now he's gone round the bend."

"He's gone way around the bend, but I doubt if anything you said pushed him there. It's probably the cumulative effect of years of brooding and scheming."

"Thank you for that." A dry and distant amusement moved in Fiona's eyes and softened the set of her mouth and chin. "You can't make a clean break with the past. Ever. All you can do is sur-render to it."

"And appreciate its ironies."

"Oh aye." Hitching her handbag over the shoulder of her raincoat, she stood up. "Have a care, Jean."

"You, too."

Jean watched her walk away, thinking that graceful surrender to circumstance was all well and good, and yes, a sense of humor was a much underrated virtue. But Fiona was wrong about one thing. All too often passivity meant leaving ragged ends for other people to sew up. If sewing up her own ends meant not leaving well enough alone, or going out on a limb, or making waves, well, so be it.

TWENTY-THREE

JEAN WAS STANDING on the hotel doorstep, trying to decide whether to while away some time at the Weaving Mill Shop or the Commando Museum, when her cell phone chirped. She unzipped her bag, found her car keys immediately, then excavated the phone from beneath her billfold. "Jean Fairbairn."

"D.C.I. Cameron here." Even filtered through the tiny speaker, his voice was unmistakable.

"How did you—oh, I gave you my business card."

"You're in Spean Bridge, are you?"

"Yes." She looked around the parking lot, at the windows of the surrounding buildings, up the street. Aha! The third or fourth house beyond the hotel displayed a blue sign reading "Police." Sure enough, there was Cameron, standing between a police car and a child's swing set, his hand to his cheek.

Jean waved her phone at him, then put it back to her ear. "I thought you were interviewing Meg."

"She's just now gone away in her posh sports car, trailing clouds of one of those perfumes named Guttersnipe or Rubbish Tip."

Whoa. The man had made a joke. Smiling in something close to gratitude, she said, "Gunn's taken the car to Edinburgh, so you're angling for a ride back to Glendessary House, right?"

"Aye, if it's no trouble."

"No trouble at all," Jean said, then remembered that she hadn't had time to digest what she'd learned about him, let alone decide whether she should pretend she didn't know it or go ahead and admit she did.

Too late now—Cameron was closing in fast. She'd just have to see what circumstance and the man himself demanded. She switched off her phone and stowed it in her bag. Now her car keys lay at the bottom. She was fishing for them when he appeared in her peripheral vision. "I was by way of phoning for a taxi when I saw you."

He'd probably been evaluating the countryside for snipers or something. "I was going back to the house anyway," she told him, without adding, "eventually," and opened the car doors.

He strapped himself in the passenger seat and pulled a tape cassette out of his pocket. "I can pay my fare with the interview."

Good, she wouldn't have to talk to him just yet. She negotiated a tricky right turn across traffic and took off up the road. "Why did Meg refuse to go to the house? Did she see the ghost, too?"

"No, no ghost. Have a listen." Cameron plugged the tape into the dashboard. His recorded voice identified the place, the time, the people present, the interviewee. Then it asked, "Why would you not come out to Glendessary House?"

"After what Rick said to me? I don't think so," said a female voice in the sort of elite screech, all tortured vowels and buckshot consonants, that Jean had thought was a Monty Python joke until she heard it for herself.

"What did he say to you?" asked Cameron's voice, while the actual man contemplated the water-colored greens and browns of the landscape behind the thinning veil of the mist.

"He said I was a traitor, that I ought to be horsewhipped through the town. I thought he was winding me up, but no, he was dead serious. I expected him to take that precious dagger of his and run me through."

"His dirk?"

"The one he wears when he's done up in his kilt, yes."

"Why did he call you a traitor?"

"Because I told my pal Derek at *The Sunburn* I'd write an article, behind the scenes at a millionaire's mansion or some such rubbish."

"What was going on behind the scenes?" asked Cameron's voice.

"Rick's mad for Bonnie Prince Charlie. Dresses up in full Highland rig and all. Jolly good wheeze, I thought, no worse than people I could name dressing up in leather and chains, but Rick didn't think so."

"You were planning to expose his plans for the future?"

"His plans?"

"Involving the Jacobite Lodge."

"Oh. Them. They'd sit about talking about royals dead and gone 'til you ran screaming mad from the room. Don't know what sort of plans he could have made for them, bar burial plans." Meg heehawed.

Jean imagined a stylish young woman so self-centered she generated her own gravity field, a time-honored human trait if ever there was one.

Cameron's voice asked, "What were your duties at Glendessary House?"

"Word processing, filing, writing copy for the games. Ringing up libraries and antiques dealers looking out old books and letters. Naff sort of work, but Vanessa handed me a good reference, an apology for Rick, I expect, and now I have a positively brilliant job with a PR firm in London."

"How did you get the job with MacLyon?"

"My mum met Charlotte at an antiques fair; next thing you know I was on my way to the wilderness." Jean could almost hear her shudder.

"Did you get on well with everyone else in the house?"

"With everyone who wanted to get on with me. Vanessa's fun, though how she lives out in the back of beyond without going crackers I don't know. I hope she has a good strong pre-nup. If it weren't for Neil, the entire episode would have been a bleeding waste of time."

"Neil MacSorley."

"Oh my yes," said Meg. "You know how it is. There he was, there I was, no clubs, no restaurants, no life. So we had sex. A bit of a giggle. But Vanessa, she was jealous. Makes me wonder what's going on behind the scenes with her and the lad o' parts. And oh, they're nice parts."

No, Jean thought with something between a wince and a sigh, sex wasn't anything more than a physical function, a bit of a giggle, no big deal. Or so kids rationalized their taste for instant gratification. And Meg was a kid. So was Neil. Jean, as an adult, consenting or otherwise, told herself not to try and save face by pretending his grapes had been sour, after all.

The taped Cameron said nothing. She imagined him giving Meg his best we-are-not-amused look. The real-time Cameron advised, "Mind the center line, you're drifting."

Jean eased back into the lane. As for Vanessa's jealousy—well, whether Neil was a platonic playmate or a sexual one was only Jean's business if it had something to do with George. Who, with his antique but hardly invalid sense of honor, would have been shocked at any affair, pre- or extra-marital.

There was the Commando Memorial again, the bronze soldiers only marginally more impassive than Cameron. His head turned toward them, watching until they vanished from view, unreadable as always.

"Toby's a big teddy bear," Meg's voice was saying. "Can't say the same for Charlotte and Kieran, though. First Charlotte's chatting me up, who do I know, that sort of thing. Then she found out about the article for *The Sunburn*—listening in on my phone conversations, mind you—and oh, did the shit go flying then! She grassed me up to Rick, I'm sure of it. She's no more than a jumped-up little oik. Hard to believe she could produce Neil."

"And Kieran?" asked Cameron's voice on the tape.

"Unbelievable pillock. Some sort of local judge, it appears, although his actual job is supporting Rick's official line. Didn't half argue with George over historical trivia—between them they almost ruined the one decent party Rick ever gave, at Hogmanay."

"You took George's side, then?"

"I stayed clear of them both, but of the two George gave me the least aggro. He was inclined to lecture, though, about honor and duty. Once he told me he owed the MacSorleys a debt of some sort. Borrowed money, maybe, never really said."

"George owed the MacSorleys a debt?" Jean repeated. "Ogilvy said something about that, too."

Cameron said, "I'm not thinking he meant in coin of the realm."

"Now," said Meg's voice, "I've told you everything I know about the terrible murder at MacLyon Towers, which is to say, sod-all. I'm off, my pal Tarquin's expecting me at his pad, Dowally Castle. Filthy weather—we'll have to ask Jack and Nettie to dry out the tennis courts with their helicopter. No worries, though, Tarquin's champers is top-hole, better than your tea, Constable. No hard feelings?"

A background mumble from the no doubt bemused constable was cut off when Cameron reached up to the dashboard and popped out the tape.

"Now there's a good question," said Jean. "Did Vanessa sign a pre-nuptial agreement?"

"In the event of a divorce she gets a tidy settlement. Financially she's still better off living with the man. Can't say about emotionally."

"So Charlotte's an eavesdropper. Not that I haven't overheard the odd tidbit myself, but I try not to do it deliberately." Jean felt the electrical impulses of Cameron's glance cross her cheek, but he said nothing. "Funny, Rick's secretary never knew his biggest secret."

"I reckon they set her to work with the trivial bits so Vanessa and Fiona could handle the matters vital to the state of Scotland." He emitted his scalded laugh. "Does the man not realize the moment he stands up and delivers himself of Charlie's 'I am come home,' he'll be pelted with tomatoes?"

"Better than cannonballs...." Something loomed through the mist and trees. Jean dived into a passing place. The huge tow truck carrying Norman's mud-smeared car churned past at the pace of a funeral cortege, spewing dirty water from beneath its wheels. Yes, Rick's mania would be either funny or sad if people didn't keep dying. As it was, his mania was dangerous. She pulled back onto the road.

Beside her Cameron turned the tape over and over in his hands as though it were a deck of tarot cards he was just about to deal. "You said charlieism is a minor disease. Doesn't seem so now, does it?"

Again he was reading her mind. "Yes, Rick's gone way overboard. But there's nothing intrinsically wrong with myths of origin and identity, just like there's nothing intrinsically wrong with whiskey."

"Look at Charlie himself, refusing to believe Cumberland would permit his soldiers to pillage and murder, because he refused to believe he himself could have caused so much suffering with his wee ego trip."

"If you're drawing a parallel between Charlie and Rick, fine. Just stop throwing the baby out with the bath water." The way Fiona is doing, she concluded silently. She wasn't ready to mention Fiona, not yet.

Cameron's smile wasn't a bit like Fiona's. She could feel its tautness without seeing it. "Be that as it may, George had to have known the documents are false. No need waiting on the Museum to confirm that."

"No," Jean agreed.

"It could be MacLyon killed him, thinking he'd come to you to blow the gaff."

"There's just one problem with that theory."

"If MacLyon doesn't know—doesn't accept—that the papers are false, he'd not feel threatened by George's disclosure. Aye, I'm seeing that."

"But if he thought George was a traitor to the cause, not with the program, not a member of the team.... Is Rick crazy enough to kill?"

"Most killers of my acquaintance have thought they were acting quite logically to rid themselves of a problem," said Cameron, with chilling sanity. "MacLyon has the motive, the means, and the opportunity, right enough."

"So did Vanessa. Maybe she killed George to try and preserve her investment."

"That's possible as well."

Jean took one hand off the steering wheel and made a frustrated gesture. "Even after all this I don't understand why George came to me with the coin. To lure me out here and to draw my attention to Rick?"

"To force MacLyon's hand?" Cameron slipped the tape into his pocket. "Was MacLyon intending to go public with his delusions or is he simply playing a live-action game?"

"He could have gone on for years with his Lodge, that's true. It was George's death that forced his hand. My showing up was secondary." If she knew what George's expectations had been, she thought glumly, she could at least try to live up to them. But she could only guess, and without enough evidence for that guess to be a particularly educated one.

The road ran alongside a bay in Loch Lochy. Relatively youthful trees screened the view, of misty mountains seen through many a rose-colored memory. The young George wouldn't have known the trees, but he'd have known those dark waves with their sheen of lead running into the pebbly beach, one after the other, inexorably. The commandos used to stage "opposed landings" in this area. Surely at least several of the accidental deaths had occurred then.

But not Archie's. At least, his ghost was somehow connected to the fire in the house. Had it been George who'd accidentally wounded him, leading to his being trapped in the burning house? Now there was a thought.

"We—you—need to talk to George's neighbor, Ronald Ogilvy. He might know what George meant about owing a debt to the MacSorleys. Something about Kieran's father, maybe. George said something to Ogilvy about fate working in strange ways." Fate. There was another reminder of Fiona, as though the woman were riding in the back seat of the car.

"Gunn interviewed the man, but then, he didn't know what to ask, did he? I'll phone, set up another appointment."

Jean sped up a bit as they passed the MacSorleys' cottage, the better to avoid looking at the mud wallow beside the Loch.

Cameron, she saw from the corner of her eye, gazed long and hard at it. "Andy Sawyer talked with the manager of Hawley's restaurant in Inverness. The MacSorleys ate there often, he says, were always sending bits of food back to the kitchen and demanding it be cooked properly this time round."

Jean snorted humorlessly.

"More than once they came in with an elderly man with a gray moustache and an English accent. He always had a carrier bag filled with books and papers."

"George, in other words. That makes sense, the restaurant was close to the Library where he was working. But he wouldn't have wanted to go there, he hated that kind of food. Kieran and Charlotte must have taken him in there to—what? Get him to slip the faked papers in with the real ones.... Oh!" Her eyes ricocheted off Cameron's, like striking sparks from a flint, and returned to the wet strip of tarmac ahead.

"Have we been looking at the accident the wrong way round?" Cameron asked. There was that "we" again. "What if one of the MacSorleys deliberately ran Hawley off the road, then bashed the brake line themselves?"

"They were afraid Norman had overheard them plotting with George at the restaurant."

"Was the job at Glendessary House by way of a bribe?"

"Or simply a way of keeping an eye on him?"

"I hear MacSorley, not MacLyon, gave Hawley his day out the day of the Lodge meeting. A day out just when he'd be expecting to work might could have roused his suspicions. Maybe he went so far as to talk about them to MacSorley. He was the cunning sort, I'm hearing."

"But how would Charlotte or Kieran know Norman was going to be driving by at that exact moment?"

"Could be someone rang them from the house. MacLyon's always going about with his mobile phone."

"At dinner he didn't know Norman had quit."

"So he was saying."

"Yeah, so he was saying," Jean conceded. "If Rick more or less ordered Norman killed, he could have done the same with George. Charlotte and Kieran have alibis for the murder—so does Neil, for that matter—but Vanessa and Toby don't." She left Fiona's name dangling unspoken.

"So we're back to thinking the murder was MacLyon's personal do-it-yourself project."

"I don't know about Toby, though. Is he hired muscle or scapegoat?"

"Both," said Cameron, his voice murky as the day.

The Dark Mile closed over the car, the trees dripping and drooping in the moist gloom. The moss-covered stone walls and thick underbrush that pressed close against the road muffled the noises of the car, the engine, the swish of the tires, the tic-tac of the windshield wipers. Jean tensed and then loosened. Even now, no evil ringwraiths would come galloping along. The evil at Glendessary House was only too human.

Cameron shifted in his seat. "This forest reminds me of Tolkien's Fangorn Wood, where the trees walk and talk. Although, under the circumstances, we'd be more likely to see Black Riders. Ringwraiths. Nazgul."

Naz... Jean almost slammed on the brakes so she could stare at him. He was familiar with Tolkien! She'd thought he disliked fantasy. But then, he wouldn't fear its misuse if he didn't know its power. If he'd never been seduced by fantasy himself. And it wasn't as though Tolkien had claimed his Middle Earth was the definitive version of existence, or used it to justify any less than palatable ends.

She confined herself to a quick glance at the spare angles of Cameron's face, illuminated less by the dashboard lights as by her moment of perspective. That's why his manner was so intense. Like her, he had to concentrate to keep his mind from winging away into forests of unfettered imagination and free association. That sort of alertness, constant input, constant evaluation, made overload and subsequent burn out an ever-present threat. Eyes to see and hearts to know....

Okay. That was the last straw. She had to clear the air, now more than ever. Now that he, however inadvertently, had extended a tendril of personality from his shell. "Meg never mentioned Fiona at all. Do you think she has one of Tolkien's magic rings, so she can make herself invisible?"

His sudden jerk of startlement—of recognition, like seeing a ghost—didn't escape her. "His are rings of power. Fiona's never wanted power."

"No, she doesn't. That's one of Tolkien's themes, how power can consume you." The sudden taste of acid in her mouth wasn't from the cappuccino. *Get on with it.* "I ran into Fiona while I was eating lunch. She told me about her second sight. How she's chosen surrender—no desire, no pain. Everyone to her own choice, of course, but me, I'll stick to believing in free will. To fighting fate."

"I'd never have guessed you were a fighter." A quick edge in his voice, like a blade drawn an inch from its sheath, made Jean look across at him. He was sitting to attention, just as she was, his face turned away from her.

"Did she tell you she 'saw' George hanging in the game larder and me standing on the front porch?"

"Aye, that she did."

"I assume you have no problem with her ESP. Some of your colleagues would, though. I know how you must feel, having to hide an awkward sixth sense."

"Do you know how I feel, then? You make a living off your ghosts."

"And off history, whether fantasy or truth or some weird mixture of the two. I wouldn't be here if I didn't. You wouldn't have asked me to help out with the case if I didn't. Or that's what you said you wanted, anyway."

"That's what I said, aye."

"You're one of a very select company—few people know I can see ghosts. And of them, you're the only one who can do it, too. It's not that I lie about it. I just don't mention it. Maybe that's dishonest. Dishonorable, even. Maybe it's simple self-preservation. I don't know."

He didn't reply.

"It's a shame you never met George. You'd agree with him about honor." A chill was starting to emanate from the passenger seat, and it wasn't one the defrost would ease. But she was in it like quicksand now. "Fiona didn't have to tell me about her husband. I already knew that."

"Aren't you the proper little detective, then? I let you into the case and you've repaid the favor by investigating me."

She could retort, *You were investigating me.* Or, *Your bio's been all over the papers.* But she'd already breached his privacy. She didn't need to insult his intelligence.

The road emerged from the dark tree-lined tunnel. To the right whiskey-colored water plunged down the hillside, leaping and foaming over boulders smooth as bones. Jean guided the car into the parking lot next to the falls, shut off the engine, and sat with her hands braced on the steering wheel. Water, water everywhere. The waterfall. The fog-shrouded mountains. Picnic tables spread with raindrops. A muddy path staggering from rock to rock up the hillside. Puddles of every shape and size.

Cameron faced the window. All she could see of his expression was a thin reflection against the rocky slope. But she knew what he looked like, lips crimped, eyes frosted, each hair rigidly in place. His breath must be cold—it wasn't fogging the glass.

She realized only now how much he'd loosened up, comparatively speaking, since they'd first met. That she cared whether he had loosened up with her was not something she wanted to examine. Neither did she want to examine just why it was important that she be ruthlessly honest with him now. Why she had taken advantage of an opening to drive in a wedge, when she could just as easily have thrown out a line.

He said, "I should have stopped with my first impulse, to see you off as simply another reporter."

"But you decided you could use me."

"No more than you've been using me."

"To get a story? Yes. But there's one hell of a lot more to it than that. I have to know whether I caused George's death." She slapped the steering wheel, as though that would help her find the right words. "And okay, yes, I'm noticing your personal story because it's like mine. I realize the guy I turned in is alive and well, if working in a Burger King because he'll never be able to get a job in academia, thanks to me. He wasn't actually hurting anyone by copying his dissertation. It was the principle of the thing. At least you were serving the community." She wasn't going to get out of her paragraph gracefully, but she blundered on. "He fought back, viciously, which dulled the guilt I felt for starting the whole messy episode. Though it didn't dull one moment of the pain."

"Pain?" said Cameron. "They promoted me. They gave me a commendation."

"Fiona doesn't blame you."

"I know that."

"It would be easier if she did, wouldn't it?"

He said nothing.

Some men would have retorted, *What do you mean by that?* This man knew what she meant. He'd rejected surrender in favor of suppression. His calm, silent surface, like an arctic ice sheet, concealed rip tides beneath. "The scandal didn't cost me my marriage," she went doggedly on, "not directly, at least. It just made me realize it was over. That it was time for me to find myself, if you'll excuse the expression."

He turned on her. No, his eyes weren't frosted at all. They were blazing, hot as a clear August sky. "Marriage. I should just have cut my own throat and had done with it."

Before she could reply—not that she had a reply—he opened the door and reached for the clasp of his seat belt. For a full minute he sat looking out at the rain and the mud. The roar of the waterfall filled the car. That was what the inside of Jean's head sounded like, thoughts plunging and splattering on the boulders of her emotions. *You had an alliance with him. Detente. And you threw it over the edge by getting personal. You just can't leave well enough alone.*

Cameron slammed the door. "Are you driving or not?"

"I'm driving." She started the car and sped up the road as fast as she could without careening into the heather. A dirt road ran off to left and crossed a small bridge. The length of Loch Arkaig's choppy gray water was concealed by mist. What she saw, what she felt, was Cameron silent beside her. So he hadn't stooped to the grand gesture of walking back in the rain. It was obscurely comforting to know he was smart enough not to cut off his nose to spite his face.

The constable at the gate, bright as a canary in his yellow slicker, waved them through. Jean didn't exactly squeal the wheels on the drive's switchbacks, but she didn't go slowly, either. The second she pulled into her usual parking place at the side of the courtyard, Cameron was out the door and away into the house, spine straight, like a duelist advancing onto the field of honor.

Jean now knew, with a certainty like a shot between the eyes from a dueling pistol, why he made her nervous. Unlike Fiona's serenity, rueful and untouchable, Alasdair Cameron's stillness was that of an unexploded bomb.

TWENTY-FOUR

MAKING A FIST, Jean came within an inch of punching the dashboard. Like that would prove anything, she told herself sternly, other than that her own prickly shell had thinned way too much. That she'd rediscovered her emotions with a vengeance. She flexed her fingers and reached for her bag.

What? She'd gotten personal, knowing how Cameron would react, just because she was beginning to realize how much she had in common with him? Because she was afraid she was almost sort of beginning to like the guy and he was almost sort of beginning to like.... *Don't go there. There be dragons.*

She slammed the door of the car so hard the report echoed like a gunshot off the trees and the façade of the house. She'd breached his shell, all right. While her sapping expedition had been motivated by issues of truth and trust, it had also been motivated by fear. By retreating to safety, truth and trust be damned.

The problem with finding herself was that she wasn't exactly comfortable with what she found.

She retrieved her computer from the trunk of the car. Okay. She couldn't go back to Edinburgh and Dougie and Hugh's music filtering through the wall instead of Rick's incessant sound system. She couldn't ignore Cameron. Having a conscience could be very annoying. He probably felt the same way. Not that she cared how he felt.

Finding one more *yeah, right* in her gut, she deployed it in his general direction and trudged through the rain toward the Glendessary house.

Which was looking more mysterious than ever this dark afternoon. Even the windows that glowed with light seemed more secretive than welcoming, as though the acts played out in those rooms wouldn't bear scrutiny by daylight. Jean tried to open the front door. It was locked. She rang the bell. Toby answered, his round face pleated in what he probably intended to be a smile of greeting but which came across as a shell-shocked grimace.

"How's it going?" asked Jean, with her own fixed grin.

"Just grand, Miss," he replied, and locked the door behind her.

"I think I'll find a book in the library and read. If you'd like to join me, I'll tell you about my articles for *Great Scot*."

"That's right obliging of you, Miss, but Vanessa has me washing dishes and dusting and the like. Exclusive dinner party tomorrow night, she says."

"Some other time, then." What she wanted was to pump him for information, but it seemed only fair to contribute to his literacy program in the process. Assuming she wanted to be alone with him, Jean thought as went up the stairs. With any of the suspects. Playing decoy wasn't in her job description. But then, neither was playing detective.

An electronic mutter seeped through the doors of Rick's office. From the hall outside her door, Jean could hear a murmur of voices from the police incident room. Cameron had said he was searching for the truth. Well, he'd gotten it. So had she. The problem was, it was a truth peripheral to the investigation.

She unlocked the door of her room and scanned the area. The bed was made, her tea things washed, and her basket of cookies refilled. So the lock was for decorative purposes only. Gritting her teeth, Jean searched the room—no one there—and sat down with her notebook, laptop, and Rick's press kit.

The hidden speakers were playing a vapid version of "Will Ye No Come Back Again," making the song sound less like a yearning summons than a perfunctory farewell. Even after the Bonnie Prince had been reduced to the bitter dregs of alcoholism, he refused to admit defeat, still thinking he would go back again, that he was entitled to the throne of a country that didn't want him. More. That he'd been cheated out of it.... She yawned, the heavy lunch settling into her limbs like lead.

There was something to be said for Neil's and Meg's careless attitudes. Be merry, for tomorrow you die. Not that there was anything wrong with merriment, but since your time was limited, it was better spent in work and relationships that demanded some effort.... She yawned again, having used up a lot more adrenalin on Cameron than he deserved.

Her marriage to Brad had been worth having, but they'd stayed in it much too long, not so much trying to make it work as refusing to admit defeat and let it go. But neither of them had ever felt as bitter about their marriage as Cameron felt about his. Marriage was like sandpaper. It could smooth and polish or could rub raw.... Jean's eyelids went down for the third time. To hell with it.

Throwing herself down on the bed, she found herself running through smoky dream corridors trying to find her classroom—it was time for class, she was late—there was an exam in tartan weaving, but she couldn't remember the MacLyon sett. Footsteps marched up and down the halls, entire squadrons of soldiers chanting her name.

She jerked awake. Outside the windows the dark day had deteriorated into dark evening. Neil's voice accompanied a brisk cadence of knocks. "Jean?"

She staggered across to the door, opened it, and only then realized how bleary she must look. Well, that was nothing new.

Neil, as always, looked like a figment of an early morning wet dream. He grinned. "Toby's laid on a supper of sorts. At least Fiona's had a hand in, there's hope for us yet."

"Thanks," Jean told him, and watched the view as he turned and walked away. She could still look. Looking was free.

She freshened up and hurried downstairs, turning on lights as she went—darkness was already oozing into the hall. Outside the silvery mist congealed into charcoal fog that pressed against the windows. And she'd felt claustrophobic earlier.

In the dining room Jean served herself leftovers from silver-plated chafing dishes, and ate a few bites while Vanessa chattered about the dinner. Rick, back in civilian clothes, slumped over his plate when he wasn't talking arcane cyber-sentences on his phone. The sound system whined away in the background, like a gnat hovering next to Jean's ear. Like the bland American voices of her hosts.

When they moved to the media room, Jean went along, safety being in numbers and all of that. She hadn't quite ratcheted her paranoia to the point of thinking they had all done it.

Vanessa and Rick, each holding a remote like a pistol, started dueling over which DVD to watch. Rick wanted *Braveheart* or *Rob Roy*. Vanessa wanted a Julia Roberts comedy. They compromised on *Tunes of Glory,* the 1960 classic. Good. Jean wasn't up for either the violence or the historical howlers of the more recent films. She sank into a recliner as the glorious strains of pipe music overwhelmed the cautious bleat from the speakers in the ceiling.

Toby plunked a bowl of popcorn onto the table and himself onto the floor. Neil and Fiona tiptoed in and found chairs of their own. Clarinda clambered from lap to lap like an amiable tiger and finally settled down with Fiona. Jean tried to enjoy the movie—it had always been a favorite. Now, though, her mind bounced around like a grasshopper. Means, motive, Mad MacLyon.

Just as another stirring skirl announced the end credits, two or three cars started up outside and drove away. Must be the end of the shift in the incident room. Which of the cops spent the night here? Someone had to keep an eye on the equipment and the evidence. Jean wondered if anyone was keeping an eye on her.

Neil flipped through the rack of DVDs. "What do you fancy for the second feature, Rick? *Terminator? Matrix?*"

Since no one was offering one of *The Lord of the Rings* films, Jean seized her chance to escape, following Fiona into the corridor. Fiona set Clarinda on the floor and asked, "Everything all right for you then?"

Jean didn't have a chance to answer before Clarinda meowed

softly, a low guttural trill that sounded like Marlene Dietrich clearing her throat. Both women looked around.

The cat looked toward the entrance and crouched, ears back, tail bristling. Slow footsteps walked down the opposite hall. Jean could see nothing. Not the least shape passed through the soft light of the sconces and their mock candles. But her sixth sense, the one sense that wasn't already stretched to its limit, went to red alert.

"What are you hearing?" Fiona asked.

"Footsteps. You can't hear them?"

"No. I sense the future, not the past."

Clarinda leaped for the stairs and scuttled upwards. The footsteps advanced into the entrance hall. Now Jean could see the shape, the commando with his belt and boots. But no beret, because he'd died before he graduated. She beckoned Fiona to the side of the corridor, out of his way, and whispered, "It's Archie MacSorley."

"Not George? Vanessa was thinking the footsteps were George."

The shape became more and more solid. By the time it passed within an arm's length of them it looked like an ordinary human being, except for a lack of definition around the eyes and the mouth, where an ordinary human being would show emotion. Again Jean smelled smoke.

Fiona watched Jean watch Archie climb the stairs by the billiards room, the ones he remembered. "Have you told Alasdair what you're seeing?"

"Oh yeah. He's seen it too."

"Well then," Fiona said, as though that cleared everything up. "Good night." She walked down the hall, toward the bar of light that extended from beneath the door of the billiards-cum-incident room. Someone was still there. Cameron? Maybe Fiona wanted to touch bases with him. Maybe she was simply going up the back stairs to bed.

Jean scuttled up the main staircase as fast as the cat, and made it safely to her own room, where she locked the door and braced the desk chair beneath the knob. She tried rearranging her notes, but no patterns leaped out at her. She wished she'd brought her knitting. The quiet repetitiveness was always soothing. But then, sitting here knitting she'd feel like Madame de Farge beside the guillotine.

When she went to bed, she expected to lie awake listening for more steps, but she didn't. She slept long and hard, and swam up through the mist gathered in the low places of her mind to find thin sunshine gleaming through the curtains. She'd barely finished washing and dressing when her cell phone rang. Eagerly she snatched it up. "Hello?"

"Good morning, Jean," said Michael's voice. "Only you'd have me working on a Saturday."

"You got the papers all right."

"Oh aye. I'd have been in trouble at home for stopping late at work except Rebecca was here as well, having a good look."

"And?" Jean asked.

"Fine examples of the forger's art. Paper's almost right, size, shape, age. Except it's all from Italy. The ink was made up specially, so as to fade properly. The penmanship is spot-on. So is the spelling and word use. The forger even made a good fist of creasing the letters, so they'd look like having been folded for a couple of centuries."

"But they're forgeries?"

"Oh aye. Dead wrong. What's written on that brilliant Italian rag paper is a pack of lies."

She heard Cameron's voice saying, *That's one bet I'll not be taking*. She sat down, her notebook open and her pencil poised. "I know you'll have to make an official report, but what can you tell me now?"

"Enough to be going on with, I reckon. The genealogy charts here, gey detailed, the places and dates and titles all perfectly logical."

"Just not true."

"Oh, real people are grafted on, right enough, but taken out of context in some way or another—married to the wrong person, or died at the wrong time."

"Hi Jean," said Rebecca's voice on another extension. "One of these papers is supposedly a page from the birth register at Bannockburn kirk. Born to Charles Edward Sobieski Douglas and Jean Cameron his wife, a son. Only problem is, the real page for that date is tucked away in the Stirlingshire archives. This one was hand-copied and the relevant line added in."

"So," Jean said, "it would include the magic words 'Sobieski' and 'Douglas,' the names of Rick's parents."

"Is that what brought all this on?" asked Rebecca.

"An ungodly brew of things brought all this on. I hope to be back in Edinburgh telling you about it real soon now." Jean sent a pleading look heavenwards. "What else do you have?"

"Letters from Jenny's friends and relations saying what a fine lad the child is, the very image of his father. Ditto from Charlie's henchmen about the child after he was taken to France."

"If they were trying to hide the kid from Hanoverian spies, they'd have burned letters like that immediately. Or, even better, never written them."

"Oh aye," Michael said. "We've got some later documents as well, bringing us up to the present day: birth and marriage notices, transcripts, ephemera. If there's anything right in all this other than Rick's own birth certificate, I've not noticed."

"What's both funny and irritating," said Rebecca, "is the letter that's supposed to be from Michael himself, testifying that all this is genuine."

Michael harrumphed. "The letterhead and my signature were copied from my letter certifying two amen glasses."

"But," Rebecca added, "this letter has Michael not only saying all the papers are genuine but recognizing Rick as Charlie's legitimate descendent, as though it was all up to him!"

"Some cheek," concluded Michael.

Jean shook her head, not that she was going to turn her other cheek. A lot of work had gone into making Mr. MacLyon look good, too, but he wasn't right, either.

"We've muckle work as yet," Michael went on, "but since the papers are evidence in a case of murder, just now D.C. Gunn's carried them to police headquarters for fingerprint analysis."

Yes, the papers were evidence, but only indirectly. Somebody somewhere down the line might get a good civil suit out of them, whether or not Cameron solved his murder case.

"If you don't mind our taking the rest of the weekend off," said Rebecca with a laugh, "we did have plans."

"Please, go have a nice weekend. Thanks."

"Just doing our bit for truth, justice, and the Scottish way," Michael told her. "It being our civic duty to debunk this sort of rubbish, even if there weren't a murder involved."

"I know a police detective who would agree with you," returned Jean. One who had a way of being right. And solving cases, she bet. She punched Miranda's home number into the phone.

Miranda's voice mail answered. "If that's Jean Fairbairn, hello, I'm away just now. Aye, the date of Archie's death is the same as the date of the fire, if that's what you're wanting to know. If that's anyone else, leave a message. Cheers!"

Yes, that was what Jean was wanting to know. Part of it, anyway. Official army records must list the details of Archie's injury, but government offices would be closed until Monday. She'd have to talk to Ogilvy again, even it meant shoving Cameron out of the way, an image that did not fill her with anticipation.

She wondered where Miranda had gone. Away with Duncan to Paris or Barcelona, probably, on what the Brits called a dirty weekend. She allowed herself a moment of envy. One of these days she was going to have sex again, expanding sensitivity into sensuality, really she was. Just as soon as she figured out how to balance selling her soul and being lonely.

Right now, though, breakfast would have to fill in the empty spaces. She stopped on her way downstairs to appreciate the vista of green and gold and blue framed by the windows in the sitting area. Ragged streamers of cloud spilled over the mountains but overhead the sky was clear. The sun sparkled off every tender green leaf, every pale stone. The sight alone was cheering. So was the dining room, empty except for an array of cereal boxes and racks of cold toast with all the fixings. A pot of coffee sat on an electric ring.

Jean filled a bowl with raisin bran, smeared butter and jelly on two pieces of toast, and sat down. Rattles and clinks in the kitchen next door, not to mention the odor of silver polish, informed her that the dinner campaign was under way. Through the windows Jean could see Neil in the garden, pruning shears, weed digger, and spray bottle—of what? varnish?—in a basket at his side, the sunlight gleaming on his auburn hair.

The door to the corridor opened. "There you are," said D.C.I. Cameron.

Jean pretended she hadn't jumped, and emitted a "Good morning" that was much too strained for her comfort.

Taking no notice, he walked across to the sideboard, dressed a bit of toast, and bit it in half. "You'd better be getting on with your breakfast; we've got an appointment with Ronald Ogilvy at the Clan Cameron Museum."

"What?"

"We've got an appointment—"

"I heard that. You mean you want me to go with you?"

Cameron crunched down the other half of the toast. "He's wanting to see you. And I thought you were wanting in on the case." His face was deadpan as always. Any gleam in his eye was hidden as well as the sun behind storm clouds.

"Well, yes, but...."

"I'll collect you in the car park at half-past nine." He wiped his hands on a napkin, threw it down, and vanished as abruptly as he'd appeared, leaving Jean with her spoon still halfway to her mouth, dribbling milk back into the bowl.

Men! she told herself, and hurried to finish up.

TWENTY-FIVE

JUST REWIND yesterday's—confession, confrontation, whatever— Jean told herself. That's what Cameron was doing. No need to re-establish any boundaries when none had been trespassed. No need to talk about what had happened. It was talking that had made it happen to begin with.

Shells all around, then, like an oyster bed. Or like a weapons dump.

She met him in the parking area at nine-thirty. Without saying a word, she pitched her computer into the back seat of his car and climbed in. Without cracking an expression, Cameron drove away. She waited until he'd maneuvered through the gate to ask, "Have you heard from D.C. Gunn about the documents?"

"Oh aye. Deliberate fraud, I'd say."

"Rick told me he got them from Kieran. He and Charlotte have been to Italy—they could have picked up the paper there. They could have had the forgeries made there, for that matter. Venice is known for its skilled forgers." She looked past Cameron's carved-in-granite profile toward the blue water of the loch. Deep blue, with a slight silvery tint.

Cameron glanced at her, his eyes the same color. "Anything else?"

Jean nodded, then, figuring he couldn't hear her head rattle, said, "Yes. It turns out that Archie MacSorley died the same day as the fire at Glendessary House."

"The military records say he was killed in a live-fire accident. No pun intended."

Of course Cameron had already checked the official records. "If Archie really died in the fire, then the authorities covered up the truth, either to spare the feelings of his family or to cover themselves. The question is why Archie was in the infirmary to begin with."

"I doubt George Lovelace was involved."

"You doubt…oh." Linguistic whiplash. "You suspect he was involved."

"Although if MacSorley had been murdered, Lovelace would have been brought to trial."

"So either it was an accident or George somehow got away with murder. I'd vote for the former, myself."

Cameron abstained. Raindrops spattered across the windshield. The Dark Mile was gloomy and wet, and the MacSorleys' house huddled truculently in its garden. The silver car was poised at the end of the drive, Charlotte leaning forward over the steering wheel to peer up the road. Shooting a wary glance in her direction, Cameron speeded up.

Jean watched in the side mirror as Charlotte turned toward Glendessary House. "Here's a thought. I overhead Vanessa urging Rick to go ahead and come clean about something that turned out to be the Charlie stuff, even though she knows it's a delusion. What if she's just trying to get it all over with?"

"Make the announcement, watch his castles in the air collapse, and get on with her life, either as Mrs. MacLyon or otherwise."

"Maybe she has Neil in mind as the otherwise. Do you think Rick is the jealous type?"

"Hard to say." The car passed back into the sunshine, even

though the mountains to the east were still draped with wispy curtains of gray.

"So when are you going to blow up Rick's castle?" Jean asked. "At the dinner party tonight? You'll have all your suspects together, that would be a great time to announce the name of the killer."

"I don't know the name of the killer. As yet." Cameron slowed the car and turned through the gate into the tree-lined drive leading to Achnacarry Castle and the Museum.

"What about the Lodge members? How many of them are true believers?"

"I've sent the lads round to have another go at them."

The trees parted to reveal a collection of buildings, among them the white-painted Clan Cameron Museum, nestled beneath an escarpment studded with scrubby trees. Jean's particular nemesis of a Cameron turned into the parking area and stopped. At least he was still willing to talk about the case with her, she thought as she stepped out into the cold wind. "Was it Ogilvy's idea or yours to meet here?"

"His. He's donating several artifacts to the Museum."

"And he wants to see me?"

"So he said."

The caretaker, a man in a dark blue sweater, was unlocking the door of the building. "Alasdair! Good morning to you. And this is…."

"Jean Fairbairn," said Jean.

Wispy sideburns framed the man's long face and impish smile. "Welcome, welcome. Any friend of Alasdair's and all. Have a tour on the house."

"Thank you." Leaving Cameron at the front desk, she strolled into the display area. The first glass case held the battered kilt of a Queen's Own Cameron Highlander, the last kilted regiment from World War II. The World War I Germans had called the Scottish soldiers "ladies from hell."

Behind her, the caretaker was chatting with Cameron about various relatives and their activities. *Whoa.* The man had relatives. He hadn't sprung full-blown from the brow of the Chief Constable. And he wasn't as hostile to his own history as he claimed, either, if he'd participated in clan gatherings and commemorations. Although Jean had already noticed he was a deep and complex individual.

She scanned an exhibit of material from the commando school. Beyond it other cases displayed memorabilia from Bonnie Prince Charlie and his long-suffering Cameron supporters, the huge boots of an earlier Cameron, the dress of the Cameron who was a bridesmaid at the wedding of the present Prince Charles, and a set of dishes from the replica *Titanic* built for the movie directed by, yes, a Cameron.

History and culture under glass, Jean thought. Museums put human history into compartments, filed away the rough edges, made it look tidy. Reminded you that this too shall pass.... *Yes!* In the back corner of the back room hung an etching of Jenny. The picture was even more idealized than Rick's drawing, so that what might have been a stubborn chin in the real woman was here innocuously plump. Words were handwritten below the picture:

Miss Jenny Cameron, a genteel handsome woman with pretty eyes and hair as black as jet, of a sprightly genius and very agreeable conversation. So far from accompanying the prince's army, that she went off as soon as she had accomplished leading up the Major's (her brother) men, neither did she ever follow the camp nor ever saw the prince but in public and when he had his court in Edinburgh.

So, Jean thought with a grin, spin doctoring was not a modern phenomenon. Someone had waded in with a nicely balanced defense, supporting Jenny but not criticizing Charlie. The fine calligraphic handwriting and syntax could be eighteenth century or later; without an analysis of the paper and faded sepia ink, she couldn't tell.

Male voices spoke hearty greetings from the other end of the building. Offering Jenny a conspiratorial wink, Jean headed in that direction. Sure enough, Ronald Ogilvy was standing there with Cameron and the caretaker, a plastic carrier bag clutched in his hand. His round rosy cheeks and bulbous nose made him look like a cross between a cherub and a camel.

"Miss Fairbairn!" he called. "Good to see you again."

"You too, Mr. Ogilvy."

"Very good of you both to meet me here, indulge an old man."

"No problem," said Cameron. "Let's sit down outside."

Two leather-jacketed bikers were just coming in the door. Everyone jockeyed around each other, mumbling apologies. Cameron herded his flock to a bench next to a World War I artillery piece, mopped the rainwater up with his handkerchief, seated Ogilvy in its center, and sat down himself on the far end. Jean winced at the chill of the wooden slats, like the spank of reality at birth.

Cameron did Ogilvy the courtesy of not mincing words. "We've released Mr. Lovelace's body to his family."

"Good, glad to hear it. Time the man was laid to rest with all the proper observances. His daughter and her family stopped in at the house Thursday, cleared some things away, tried to make arrangements—you know how it is, with the shock and all."

Jean didn't, thank goodness, know how it was to cope with a murder in the family, but she nodded sympathetically.

The old man reached into his plastic bag. "George's family thought the Commando Museum at Spean Bridge might like to have these. I suggested the display here. George always liked stopping by here on his way home from Glendessary House. Said he enjoyed the peace and the quiet all these years on; goes to show you that time heals, eh?"

"Oh aye," said Cameron, but he didn't sound convinced.

Ogilvy produced the photo album that Jean had last seen on George's coffee table, and the shoe box from his upstairs cabinet. "Here are his beret and his medals, just need a bit of a brush-up is all. He kept the album with them and the gold coin, and showed me them the day before he went to see you, Miss Fairbairn. The album here, he said everything was in it, all the answers or something to that effect. Puzzled me a bit at the time, but—well, maybe I'm understanding a bit better now."

Aren't we all, Jean told herself.

"Mind you, George rarely talked about the war. Too many losses, he'd say. Memories too painful. But your chap Gunn," Ogilvy said to Cameron, "fine lad, make a good detective, he will. Some of the questions he asked made me think about what George did say. And you, when you phoned last night, did I know what George might owe Kieran MacSorley. So maybe I've put two and two together and come close to making four, if you take my meaning." He gazed out over the grassy field across the road, past the delicate green of the trees, to the bank of ash-gray clouds seeping down the far mountainside.

Jean squinted to see ruined walls emerging from the undergrowth, the gravestones of a vanished culture. A young George Lovelace had trained in this rugged, heather-clad landscape, which had changed little between his day and Prince Charlie's. If anything, it was more desolate now, after two centuries of depredations both military and economic.

Cameron, of course, was fixed in the here and now. "Did Mr. Lovelace know Kieran's father Archie?"

Ogilvy brushed the top of the book as though dusting it. "That's what's in the album here, photos of him with a man labeled by that name. George talked once or twice about his 'oppo,' his opposite number. They were assigned to train together and support each other here at the commando school. He never mentioned his name. Must have been Archie, don't you think?"

"Yes, I do think," said Jean. "Archie died here in nineteen forty-two. Do you have any reason to believe that George contributed to his death? Accidentally, of course. No malice aforethought or anything like that."

"I think that's what happened, yes. A thing like that would prey on one's mind, wouldn't it? No wonder George never talked about it."

"Aye," said Cameron, the word a chip of ice.

"That's why George felt he had to work with Kieran," Jean said, not expanding on just what she meant by "work with."

Ogilvy opened the box, peered at the contents as though for inspiration, and closed it again. The medals clattered like a distant machine gun. "George and his oppo were injured abseiling down a cliff. The high one, beyond those houses."

The only cliff Jean could see was the one behind the Museum, and it looked bad enough, a minefield of gravel, loose boulders, and brittle branches.

"They were sent to the infirmary at Glendessary House," Ogilvy went on. "Once past those bare facts I'm forced to—well, triangulate, you might say, from different things George said over the years. He tended to ramble a bit, probably told me the entire story in bits and pieces. If only I'd known, I might could have helped."

If only I'd known. Those words served as the motto beneath the coat of arms of the human race.

"I think what happened was this. Late one night George and Archie and several other soldiers were playing poker by the light of a lantern. One of the men had a bad run, lost all his money, so he laid on the table a gold coin he'd found whilst on maneuvers in Glen Camgarry at the head of the loch."

"One of the places the coins were traditionally hidden," said Jean.

"George described the shine of the coin, the fine etching of the face, and the inscription. Even as a lad he had a taste for history. That's why he wanted the coin, not for its value as gold."

The Louis d'Or had gleamed seductively beneath her desk lamp. She'd thought then that many a bad deed had been done for that glow, whether it was the glow of gold or of a history burnished out of all recognition, with no rough edges, dark blotches, or uncertain provenances.

Ogilvy sighed. "George held the winning hand and won the coin. And the man who found it went for him. Maybe playfully, maybe seriously, I don't know. He never said it was Archie, mind."

Cameron spoke, slow and measured. "The lantern was overturned. The house caught fire. Archie died."

"Yes." Ogilvy's voice stretched like a rubber band, "George shouldn't have kept it all to himself. There's too much of this ego business nowadays, showing your innermost feelings off in public as though they were something to be proud of. Still, keeping every last bit of it tucked away is no good either. Leaves you with rotten spots in your mind, like abscesses."

Jean couldn't stop herself from looking at Cameron, on Ogilvy's other side. He was scanning the horizon, his stiff upper lip firmly in place against its opposite number, displaying no stress fractures. The only thing moving on his body was his short hair rippling in the wind.

"Do you think George had abscesses in his mind?" she asked Ogilvy.

"He insisted on working for this MacLyon chap, didn't he? There was more to that than I thought. I expect MacSorley had a hand in. Here." Ogilvy handed the photo album to Jean. "Have a look at this, use it to write up an article on the commando school. George would like that. It might could ease his mind a bit, even now. You can send the album back here when you've finished."

The book's leather cover was clammy against her fingertips, a hand reaching from the grave. "I'd like to do an article on the commando school. Thank you."

"And you, Chief Inspector." Ogilvy turned to his other side. "You don't yet know who killed George, do you?"

"No," said Cameron, voice tautly at attention. "You yourself saw Charlotte MacSorley at the time of the murder, did you?"

"Yes, afraid so. Always thought the woman was a bit of a witch, but still, she can hardly be in two places at once, can she?"

"Peter, the caretaker here, saw Kieran MacSorley at the same time. Even if MacSorley hid a car amongst the trees, he could hardly have reached Glendessary House before Miss Fairbairn found Mr. Lovelace."

Jean's lips thinned. "And I both saw and heard Neil MacSorley playing his pipes outside the house at the time of the murder. I don't see how he could be involved at all, unless you believe in guilt by association. The sins of the fathers visited upon the sons. Or the grandsons."

With a snort of something that might have been agreement, Cameron stood up and offered Ogilvy his hand. "Thank you very much, sir, for your help."

"The least I could do. I'll hand these other things in to the care-taker, shall I? And tell him to expect the album at some future date. Good morning, Miss Fairbairn. Chief Inspector." Ogilvy walked haltingly away toward the door of the museum, bent beneath the burden of time and memory.

A fine spray of raindrops brushed Jean's face and misted her glasses. She pulled up the hood of her coat. The wind was brisk and bracing, like a scouring pad across the smudged recesses of her mind. Something was starting to gleam down there, but she couldn't quite make it out.

Cameron stood with his hands in his pockets, contemplating whatever plane of existence he was usually contemplating. She held the album toward him, having to actually poke his arm with it to get his attention.

He focused, taking the book from her hands. "Aye?"

"I'm going to walk back to the house. Not by the road, that swings all the way out to Clunes and then back in, makes an acute angle. By that path, there. According to the map inside the museum it runs past the Castle, crosses the bridge, and comes out just past the waterfall."

His head turned in the direction she was pointing. "Oh aye. The hypotenuse. If you run you might catch me up."

"I'm no commando, fifteen miles to Ben Nevis and then up the mountain in a full pack. But I've got to get some exercise, my brain is sluggish." And if her nerves weren't shot, then they were at least standing against a wall, blindfold in place.

"All right then. I'll have this album and your computer in the incident room." He turned toward his car, casting an analytical glance at the two black and chrome motorcycles parked nearby.

Instead of carrying her bag over one shoulder as she usually did, Jean hoisted it onto her back. She stepped out down the road, arms swinging, breathing deeply of the fresh damp air with its scents of mold, mulch, and an elusive tang of the sea. There was Achnacarry Castle, a tidy, square-cut early nineteenth-century mansion with regular ranks of windows and decorative turrets ranged above. It wasn't nearly as pretentious as Glendessary House, even though it was the home of a genuine clan chief, the present Lochiel.

She marched on, avoiding the puddles in the gravel road. The sun came back out with the force of an explosion. Through the tumbling leaves of the trees ahead she caught the glimmer of Loch Arkaig.

The hypotenuse. The straightest way between the corners of the triangle. Maybe the same triangle Ogilvy had used to put together George's story. Like Occam's Razor, stating that the simplest, straightest explanation, no matter how little you want to believe it, is the right one. Sherlock Holmes had said something similar. And yet Holmes, like Cameron, admitted that people's motives were rarely simple.

Jean emerged from turbulent shadow of the trees, crossed the little bridge over the River Arkaig, and turned onto the main road. She didn't see any cars coming, not Charlotte burning rubber nor Cameron driving like he did everything else, in tight focus.

Tight focus. Broad perspective. She looked up the funnel of the loch to the west, to where the mountains made closed ranks of olive drab, khaki, and bronze. Jenny Cameron, born and raised in those mountains, wouldn't have thought of those colors. Maybe she'd have thought of sepia, like the faded writing on her etching at the Museum.

Jean wondered again whether the writing was contemporary with Jenny. Hard to say—anyone with knowledge of the syntax and handwriting styles of the time could have added that notation. They could even have faded the ink, so it would look old. Forgers did that all the time. Like on Rick MacLyon's precious documents, proving a fantasy in a fine calligraphic hand.

A fine calligraphic hand. She'd thought that before. When?

She stopped in the middle of the road, crashing into the barricade of the answer: when she saw the handwriting on the back of the receipt she'd given George Lovelace. When she saw his own hand.

Before her she saw not the magnificent landscape written in water and rock and shadow, but George's study in Corpach. References. Paper. Pens. Probably bottles of ink, if she'd looked for them. He was an expert in eighteenth-century writing, wasn't he? Why should the MacSorleys hire someone in Italy to make their forgeries when they already had an expert, an expert who had spent years with a gold coin rubbing a blister in his mind, a blister that had become an abscess?

Jean breathed a four-letter word. George Lovelace hadn't just helped Kieran with his scam, had he? He was the scam. For a time the honor of paying his debt trumped the honor of being honest with his employer. Until, torn between the two, George figured out a way of doing both.

He'd used her, yes. And he'd paid for it with his life. In a way she had caused his death—an accident, manslaughter, not murder, but still she owed him. Cameron had said something about people interpreting honor in their own ways. He had her number, too, no doubt about it.

She strode out again, as fast as she could go without actually running.

TWENTY-SIX

HEAD DOWN, Jean raced past only three reporters and edged between the gates the moment the constable pushed them open. Once around the first bend of the drive she slowed down, but only a bit.

The other reporters had gone barking off after fresher meat, no doubt. They'd come back again fast enough, as soon as the case was solved. And it would be solved, she had no doubts about that now. All she and Cameron—that was not an editorial "they"— needed was a name.

She emerged into the parking area. A florist's van sat beside a van marked "Montrose Inn." Beside that stood Cameron, the album and her computer beneath his arm, talking to D.C. Gunn.

"…any number of prints," the younger man was saying. "MacLyon, Lovelace, MacSorley, they're all there."

"And you've sent the documents on to the lab in Inverness?" Cameron asked him.

"Oh aye, requested the full…. Oh hello, Miss Fairbairn."

Jean stopped, chest heaving, hair waving, glasses probably gleaming maniacally beneath their water spots. She opened her mouth to speak.

"Why go to Italy for the forgeries?" Cameron asked her. "Lovelace was an expert. He'd already put himself into MacSorley's power, although whether MacSorley knew the full story is hard to say. I reckon Lovelace made the forgeries himself."

Jean's prepared statement dissipated in an exhaled breath. Yeah, they were on the same wavelength, weren't they? This was no more comforting a thought today than it had been yesterday. She said with a thin smile, "I just cannot get ahead of you, can I?"

"We're by way of being on the same side, or so you've been reminding me." His own smile reflected more challenge than humor, but the humor was there.

"George brought me the coin, knowing the story of Charlie's treasure would be like catnip to a cat. And he knew once I started poking around in Lochaber I'd find Rick MacLyon's story, too. Heck, George hadn't even made it back to the train station before

Miranda set up an appointment for me to interview Rick. No problem there—George had already talked me up as a sympathetic journalist."

"He was planning for you to uncover the truth about the forgeries, his forgeries, without him having to break whatever promise he'd made to MacSorley. There's a fine balancing act for you."

"Not a balance of powers. A balance of guilts…." Jean wasn't going to go there. "Whether it was Archie who found the coin to begin with or not, in George's mind it became associated with him."

"He brought you the coin by way of confession, to try and make everything right."

"I'm a historian, not a priest. I don't appreciate him using me. I don't appreciate him putting me in…."

"We're not so sure you've ever been in danger."

"Thank you," she retorted. "Tell me that again after you've got the killer behind bars."

Gunn was looking from Cameron's face to Jean's and back again. "Lovelace did the forgeries himself? He confessed to something?"

There was the light in Cameron's eyes again, not the heat of anger but the warmth of a finely tuned intelligence at work. No wonder he was so cool on the exterior, he needed to keep his brain from overheating. "Lovelace thought of a way to square his sense of honor with what he'd done. Clever. If ultimately fatal."

"He didn't know he was in danger. He was probably prepared to take whatever the legal consequences of the fraud turned out to be. But it just doesn't make sense that Rick would kill to protect his fantasy—he doesn't realize it is a fantasy."

"MacLyon's the killer?" asked Gunn.

"With MacSorley's help, he could have played at his fantasy for years to come," Cameron said.

"I bet Kieran kept finding reasons to put off the 'lo I have come among you at last' announcement, because he knew everything would come tumbling down as soon as Rick went public. It was George who wanted Rick to go public, to reveal the truth. Killing him made it happen sooner."

"Because you were on the trail."

"So in a way I caused George's death." There. She'd said it.

"No." Cameron dismissed her attempt at confession with a

sideways jerk of his chin and a glance sharp as a scalpel. "He came
to you, mind. You did what he expected of you. That's all."

The ache drained from her own abscess. As usual, he was right.
"Yeah. Yeah, that's all."

His not unsympathetic gaze moved on past her, to the distant hills,
and the crease that indicated deep thought appeared between his
brows. "We've followed MacSorley's financial trail. He looks to have
been helping himself to the restoration funds, as you suspected. If
Lovelace knew that—well, money's a good solid motive for murder."

"Funny, isn't it?" murmured Jean, half to herself. "Land used
to be wealth. Then manufactured things became wealth. Now information is wealth. Nothing substantial, just pixels. Just ideas, like
royal ancestry."

"We could be charging MacSorley with embezzlement, with
selling MacLyon forged documents, for mining his fortune with
lies, come to that. But we'd need MacLyon's cooperation, and I'm
not so sure we'd have that."

"So MacSorley's the killer?" asked Gunn with a frown.

"He can't be," Jean said.

"He might could have corrupted someone else into doing his
work for him. Sawyer's saying he's finally making progress with
Toby." Cameron turned toward the house.

He wasn't going to get rid of her now. Besides, he was still
carrying her laptop and George's photo album. Jean matched him
stride for stride through the door at the end of the wing, leaving
Gunn to close it behind them. The music of the moment was a
tinkly version of "The Bluebells of Scotland," which even Hugh's
fiddle couldn't render less than sappy.

There seemed to be fewer people in the billiards room today.
But then, it was Saturday. Maybe some of the Indians got to go on
rotating shifts, leaving the chiefs on watch.

The chart had leafed out with post-it notes. Used cups and
empty fast-food wrappers lined the wet bar. A plastic-draped kilt
and jacket outfit hung from one of the cue racks. A uniformed constable stood by the door to the back room, and another just inside.
Sawyer sat behind the desk, his sleeves rolled up, his tie askew, a
smug smile on his face. Jean expected him to leap up and thump his
chest with his fists. "We've got him dead to rights," he announced,

then waited one beat, two, before peeling himself out of the chair and offering it to his superior.

Ambitious, Jean thought. Oh yes. He wants Cameron's job.

Sending Sawyer a steady glance, Cameron handed the computer and the album backwards without looking around. Jean grabbed both items. They'd been tucked against his side, and warmed her chilly hands.

Toby slumped on a chair by the fireplace. Worriedly Jean scanned the desk top for thumbscrews, but nothing lay there but papers, folders, a couple of notebooks, and a tape recorder. Sawyer must simply have hectored him until he cracked. Confession may or may not be good for the soul, but it could get a persecutor off your back. The witch-hunters knew that.

Spurning the chair, Cameron leaned against the edge of the desk. "Did you search George Lovelace's house at Corpach?" he asked Toby.

"Aye," mumbled Toby. "That I did."

"Why?"

"Was told to."

Sawyer rolled his eyes. "We've already been over...."

"By whom?" asked Cameron, with admirable grammar.

Rick, Jean thought.

Toby said, "Mrs. MacSorley."

"Charlotte MacSorley?" Cameron repeated, without the least trace of surprise. "Why?"

Jean blinked rapidly, so no one would see how her eyes had widened.

"She told me she'd have me sent down again," said Toby, "if I didn't do what she said."

"No one can send you back to prison without cause," Cameron told him.

Sawyer snickered. "We've got cause now."

Toby contracted his massive body, as though by occupying less space he'd escape notice. "She told me to look out some papers. Pages in old-fashioned handwriting. She showed me letters, said they'd look like those."

More documents? Jean wondered. Ones that Lovelace was still working on?

Cameron shot a keen glance at her and then past her, toward the constable standing outside the door. "Bring Mrs. MacSorley here," he ordered, and asked Toby, "Did you find the papers, then?"

"Not those, no. Bags of papers there, right enough, I spent hours in George's study. I'd been there before, mind; he'd set me down to read *Great Scot* or *Harry Potter* whilst he worked at his desk."

"What was he working on?"

"Writing of some sort. With peculiar pens, not biros. Right slow and careful, talking to himself like he was trying out the words."

Sawyer looked at Cameron as though to say, *There you go.*

Cameron didn't take any notice. "You drove the MacSorleys' car out to Corpach, then brought it back to the garage in Fort William?"

"Aye, that I did."

And either Toby had been smart enough to leave the car a couple of blocks away from Lovelace's house, Jean told herself, or Charlotte had told him to. She didn't need the car herself—Neil had already driven to town in one of Rick's cars. Whether he had known what his mother was up to was a good question. "Were you finished searching the house when you looked out George's study window and saw me talking to Mr. Ogilvy from next door?"

"Here," Sawyer began. Now Cameron did look at him, sharply, and Sawyer desisted, but not without curling his lip at Jean.

"All but the attic," Toby answered.

Jean shifted her weight. Something was punching into her hip.... Oh, the key to her bedroom was in her pocket. She'd seen a key in George's house, hadn't she? Was the answer hidden in plain sight? "There was an old key in a box on George's desk. Do you know whether that goes to anything?"

"No, Miss. I was thinking he found it detectoring."

Cameron nodded, taking in the implications. "Why were you hanging about Miss Fairbairn's hotel?"

"I saw her there at George's house. George told he me was going to see her about a problem he was having with those papers he was writing. I thought maybe she knew where they was. I waited 'til she drove away, then followed her into Fort William, saw which hotel she was stopping at."

Good going. She'd never noticed a car on her tail at all, let alone a distinctive one like the MacSorleys'.

"But then," Toby went on, "Mr. and Mrs. MacSorley get right narky when you don't do just exact what they say, and they never said to ask no one else. So I walked on by. Sorry, Miss Fairbairn."

"That's okay." At least her seeing him in the hall had given them one more lead. Sort of.

Sawyer turned on Toby. "This is all well and good, Sunshine. But you've not yet told us why you killed George Lovelace."

Toby's already pale face drained to a faint green. "No, sir, I never; George, he was good to me and me mum, he was."

"Not the first time a yob takes advantage of some do-gooder," Sawyer said to Cameron. "I'm telling you, we've got him dead to rights."

"That remains to be seen."

The constable peered around Jean. "Sir, Mr. and Mrs. Mac-Sorley...."

"Chief Inspector, I must lodge a protest about your sending a uniformed constable to interrupt very important preparations." Pushing Jean aside, Kieran surged into the small room, Charlotte in his wake. Jean found herself pressed against the side of the desk and Cameron's compact body both. Quickly she stepped back into the corner, but not so far she didn't notice that Kieran's gag-a-moose aftershave did not complement the metallic odor of lubricant hanging over the paintball guns.

Cameron stood up very straight, which still left him four inches shorter than Kieran, and looked past him to the door. "D.C. Gunn!"

Gunn materialized just outside. "Sir?"

"Drive Walsh here to Fort William. We'll be holding him overnight."

Did Kieran smirk a bit at that? Jean wondered. Hard to tell. The hostility in his beady lizard eyes canceled out the unctuous upward curve of his lips. And Charlotte's red mouth was set as rigidly as the sculpted waves of her hair.

"D.S. Sawyer, take two lads to Lovelace's house in Corpach, find this key, and look out a lockbox of some sort in the attic." Cameron's eyes edged toward the MacSorleys, seeing what effect that had on them.

None. They stood so stiffly posed Jean had the impression they were trying not to exchange any incriminating glances.

Sawyer's mouth opened, shut, and then emitted a graceless, "All right, then."

He'd probably have preferred prisoner transfer, thought Jean. More chance to bully the already cowed Toby. Sawyer brushed roughly by the MacSorleys, barked like a seal at the people in the outer room, and stamped out the far door. The constables frog-marched Toby from the room.

Housekeeping accomplished, Cameron turned to Charlotte and Kieran. His voice was calm, quiet, and menacing. "Now then. Mrs. MacSorley."

"Yes, Chief Inspector? How may I assist you?"

"By telling me why you threatened Walsh into burgling Lovelace's house."

Charlotte's slit of a mouth flapped wordlessly. Kieran leaned into Cameron's face. "Inspector, I realize you have very demanding duties to discharge, but may I suggest you focus on the convicted felon, not on a lady of good character. Threats. Very strong language. Quite inappropriate."

Jean could see the ice forming on Cameron's brow ridge and cheekbones. "Walsh says Mrs. MacSorley asked him to look out some papers amongst Lovelace's effects. What do you know about that?"

"Not a thing," Kieran blustered. "Why should I?"

"Did you take several documents belonging to Rick MacLyon to the Museum of Scotland?"

"Documents? What documents?" He was about as guileless as a T. Rex.

"May I suggest you start cooperating?"

"It's always my aim to cooperate with the police, Inspec—Chief Inspector, but when you make such ridiculous charges…."

"No one's charging you with anything. Not just yet. Mrs. MacSorley, did you have Walsh search Lovelace's house? Yes or no?"

Charlotte drew herself up. "Of course not. The man is a criminal, I've had as little contact with him as possible."

"And the papers, MacSorley?" Cameron asked. "MacLyon's set of documents proving his claims?"

"Ah, those," said Kieran, with a fly-shooing gesture. "You should simply have said so, Chief Inspector. Those were all George's doing, he found them amongst the archives whilst he was drawing up genealogies. He took them to the Museum of Scotland, he did, then showed round a letter certifying their authenticity. Amazing story. Positively mind-boggling."

"We had our doubts, mind you," Charlotte hedged. "It's quite difficult to reconcile such claims with an American of—well, perfectly solid ancestry, I'm sure. But George was a respected expert; we had a very good look at his credentials before we allowed Rick to hire him."

So they were blaming George for the whole thing, Jean thought. How convenient that the man wasn't here to defend himself.

Judging by the skeptical angle of Cameron's head, to say nothing of the glacier creeping down his jaw line, he agreed. "So you wouldn't be surprised to learn that the documents are not genuine at all?"

Charlotte gasped and put her hand to her mouth. Kieran tut-tutted. "I'm shocked, Chief Inspector. Who'd have thought an erudite old man capable of such a devious lie?"

"I should imagine," said Cameron, "that erudition and intelligence make lying all the easier." .

If either of the MacSorleys caught his meaning, they showed no sign of it. Kieran lifted his arm, ostentatiously pushed back his sleeve, and consulted his watch, a thick, shiny model that probably calculated stock quotes as well as the time. "If you're quite finished, Chief...."

"Your father," said Cameron, "served in the commandos with Lovelace."

That took Kieran by surprise. His black eyes flashed. "Why yes, he did do."

"Do you know how your father died?"

"In a live-fire accident at Achnacarry, during training. This isn't something we put about, of course, a bit awkward, isn't it?"

Cameron leaned forward just a bit, forcing Kieran to take a step backwards and bump up against Charlotte's pouter-pigeon chest. "Did you know your father died the same night Glendessary House burned down?"

"Did he? Well, well, well. Like Greek myth, isn't it, the man and his ancestral home are taken at the same time. Quite a story there, I'm sure. Is that why you're working hand in glove with the press?" Kieran, obviously deciding the best defense was offense, pointed toward Jean.

Charlotte picked up on her cue. "Considering what's happened in your own life, Chief Inspector, I'd think you'd prefer staying as far from the press as possible. But with your commendations, well, no doubt you have a very bright future ahead of you. A little publicity, however vulgar, goes a long way to helping one achieve his ambitions."

That was hitting below the belt, Jean thought indignantly. But Cameron merely lowered his head and in his best—his worst—stern voice asked, "Have you any further information to share about Lovelace's death? Any thought of who might have murdered him?"

"I should think it was perfectly obvious," said Charlotte. "I tried to warn Vanessa, as Rick was beyond reason—imagine hiring a criminal as a security guard! But no, Walsh got his hand into everything. One can only imagine what he discovered whilst poking about."

It was hard, Jean thought, to guard the body of a man who rarely left his house. No wonder Toby had ended up as jack-of-all-trades. General dogsbody, as Neil had said about himself.

Neil's father said condescendingly, "You understand, of course, Chief Inspector, that Walsh is trying to incriminate anyone around him, no matter how ludicrous the charge. But you're locking him away good and proper, aren't you? Good man. Well done. Now if you'll excuse us." Kieran seized Charlotte's wrist and dragged her out the door. A moment later the outer door slammed shut.

Jean leaned back against the wall, the paneling hard and cold against her shoulder blades. Cameron stood like an ice sculpture in the middle of the room. She could almost hear the crash of melting icicles, the long sharp kind that occasionally stabbed an unwary passerby to the heart. Melting icicles that hinted at a white-hot anger inside his cold shell. But then, he didn't waste that anger on just anyone. He saved it for the people who threatened him. That, too, she could sympathize with.

"So who's scamming who here?" she asked. "Whose idea was it to play to Rick's fantasies, George's or Kieran's?"

"I'm still betting on MacSorley. Although Lovelace was certainly not what we thought he was."

"Who is?"

Cameron's eyes turned toward her. He didn't need to answer that one.

"So now you've hauled Toby away again. Both times because of the MacSorleys. First the brakes on the car, now the burglary. Can you say 'scapegoat'?"

"I'm not disagreeing with you. But it's his word against theirs."

"And he has a record." Jean shifted her laptop and the album to her other arm. "I guess Toby wore gloves at George's house? He'd have some fingerprints there already, but surely not on everything."

"I reckon so." Cameron gestured toward the plywood-covered billiard table in the main room. "We've got one pair in evidence, although we picked those up before Walsh went out to Corpach."

Following his pointing fingertip, she walked out into the cooler air of the outer room. Other than the low hum of power, the room was silent. On the table cardboard trays held neatly labeled boxes and bags, including a plastic-wrapped pair of canvas gloves. "There are probably twenty pairs of garden gloves like this lying around."

"Oh aye," said Cameron from just behind her shoulder. His arm edged through her peripheral vision and his fingertips patted the plastic bag, making a tiny crinkling sound. "But these have got fibers from Lovelace's tweed suit and a couple of hairs from his head. As well as muckle pollen and bits of garden twine, although that's not saying a great deal. They were found in the shrubbery just outwith the back door."

"The murderer wore these when…." A chill tightened Jean's shoulder blades, and not because Cameron was standing so close to her. She extended her own hand for comparison. It was smaller than Cameron's, but not much smaller than the gloves. "They seem kind of little for Toby, don't they?"

"That they do, but they'd fit well enough if need be." His hand reached into a box and pulled out a bag containing a thick stick, indented slightly in the middle and stained with mud on one end. "This was used in the garden to prop up a plant. See how it's been pressed in? It's the stick that turned the garrote, most likely."

"Oh." Such an insignificant stick to take someone's life.

"The twine ligature—well, you're not after seeing that, I reckon."

"No, thank you," Jean said emphatically. "I saw it in use."

"Aye." Cameron made a sigh out of the word, so that his breath stirred the hairs on the back of Jean's neck.

With a shiver of something that she saw no point in acknowledging, she stepped away toward a row of larger bags. Each held a folded piece of MacLyon tartan. "What's in here?"

"Clothes."

"The kilts Toby and Rick were wearing at the time of the murder, right? Vanessa's kilted skirt. And Neil's and Fiona's clothes too, just to be fair."

"Just to be fair." Cameron tilted one bag toward her, so she could see the knife-edge pleats and buckled leather straps of one of the kilts. "Fiona's telling me each man's kilt and her and Vanessa's skirts were custom-made. Must have cost MacLyon thousands. No surprise he's the only man here with more than just the one."

"A properly-made kilt isn't cheap," Jean agreed. She'd priced them at the Texas Scottish Festival more than once, but could never convince Brad it would be worth the investment—even though, to his credit, he hadn't been given to cracks about guys in skirts.

"The football fans have taken to buying women's tartan skirts at Marks and Spencer. Works well enough when following the team."

"If not as classy."

Cameron's forefinger lifted the bag's tag with its careful listing of the chain of evidence. "Ordinarily we'd have collected bits and pieces of the Lodge members' clothing as well, but since MacLyon saw them off before we arrived, they had every opportunity to destroy anything relevant."

"Not that they had anything relevant to destroy."

"No." He let the tag fall soundlessly back against the plastic.

"You never collected anything of mine, either, except fingerprints."

"Oh aye. Bit of an oversight there, I'm thinking." His voice was even drier than usual.

"You never suspected me at all, did you? It was only Sawyer who did."

"I'll not be revealing trade secrets, Miss Fairbairn." With the least hint of a smile, Cameron took a couple of steps toward the smaller room. "I've got more reports and interviews to read through before MacLyon's command performance the night."

Jean took the hint. "I'll leave you to it, then. Rick said something about suitable clothing, I'd better go find out just what he has in mind for me. I see your outfit's already been delivered." She gestured at the kilt hanging from the rack. "That looks like an Argyll jacket, not a Prince Charlie coatee. Is Rick going semi-formal?"

"I've no idea how MacLyon's dressing himself. That's my own kilt and jacket. I had one of the lads bring it down from Inverness. The kilt-hire places rarely get the fitting just right. It's subtle, but it makes a difference."

Jean stared. Cameron? A Gaelic fashionista? But if he had any expression on his face at all, it was yet another variation of *Don't Tread on Me*. Don't worry, she wanted to tell him, she had as much intention of treading on him as she had of letting him tread on her. Neither of them, though, had to state the obvious.

TWENTY-SEVEN

ACCORDING TO THE CLOCK in the entrance hall, it was two p.m. From the kitchen end of the house came mingled female voices, Fiona's overridden by Charlotte's and both punctuated by Vanessa's questioning inflections that were not questions at all. Delectable aromas filled the air.

Jean's stomach was growling, but she figured it would be better to go to ground than brave the fray. She hurried up the stairs and unlocked the door to her room. Just as she was closing it, Clarinda came trotting down the hall, meowing peremptorily. "You, too?" Jean asked her. The cat slipped inside, leaped up on the bed, and started sniffing at the swath of MacLyon tartan that had magically appeared there since the morning.

The tartan sash was laid across the white blouse and black skirt that had been hanging in her wardrobe. A neatly-printed note read, "Please wear these clothes. Dinner is at seven. A lunch is on your desk. F."

Jean crumpled the paper and pitched it toward the waste basket, then had to walk across the room and pick it up. Good servants were supposed to do go through your things and make decisions about your meals, weren't they? As far as Jean was concerned, that was a good reason for being a member of the proletariat.

She opened the drapes, sat down at the desk, and lifted a starched white dish cloth from a tray. A ham sandwich sprinkled with cress, potato chips, two morsels of shortbread, and a bottle of Highland Spring mineral water. Okay, so Fiona had made a good decision about her meal. She picked up a sandwich-quarter and bit, wondering if Cameron were having any lunch. He had to live on something more than coffee; he wasn't as wispy-thin as Rick. Or as tall and slender as Neil. Not that his body shape mattered, she told herself firmly.

The day had turned into a beauty, the sky a fathomless blue, the mountains' harsh edges tempered by sunlight into Art Nouveau designs. Below the window, on the lawn beside the courtyard, Kieran was smoking and Neil was tuning his pipes, interspersing skillful runs of notes with the occasional squawk. By Kieran's insistent gestures Jean assumed he was offering advice. By the angle of Neil's shoulder she assumed he was rejecting it.

Clarinda leaped onto the desk, almost upsetting the tray. Laughing, Jean lifted the cat back down—she was one heavy animal—and bought her off with a bit of ham. Clarinda's sharp teeth snatched it up without biting the hand that fed her.

Once the plates were stacked back beneath their towel and Clarinda had settled down for a nap at the foot of the bed, Jean got out her notebook. She could get an article from the gold coin. She could get one from Archie's ghost. She could get one from the commando school. Whether she got anything out of George's murder, which tied all the other stories together but which was outside *Great Scot*'s jurisdiction, was something she'd have to discuss less with Miranda than with her own scruples.

From outside came the bravura strains of "Scotland the Brave." Instead of standing and saluting, Jean picked up the photograph album. The faded photos were stuck onto thick black paper pages with glue that had become brittle over the years and left little amber particles on her fingers. Each photo was annotated by a hand-printed label.

Among all the fresh, young faces she recognized George's and

Archie's. Several pictures showed them kidding around, grinning. Seeing the men young and vital emphasized the tragedy of their deaths, both of which had been premature. That was the horror of a ghost, the what-might-have-been of its life.

The last page of the album had come partly loose from the binding. It looked as though George had repaired it recently, the glue was still flexible.... No. Wait. This page was heavier than the rest, two sheets of the black paper stuck together. No wonder it had pulled loose. The question was, why would George glue two pages together?

Jean inspected the double page in the light of the desk lamp. The glue behind the photos on its front and back was also more recent than the crumbling glue of the other pages. And, she thought, carefully rubbing the paper between thumb and forefinger, this page was a bit thicker than any two of the others put together. Was something hidden between them?

She rummaged through her bag and pulled out her miniature Swiss Army knife. Carefully she worked the blade between the two leaves of paper, just far enough to slice them apart. She peered into the gap. Good God. Something white was nestled inside.

Her adrenalin surge was as strong as when she'd found George dead, like an electric charge exploding in her chest. Once again her idle curiosity had turned up the unexpected, although this time it wasn't the question, it was... George had told Ogilvy all the answers were in this album. He had not meant that metaphorically.

Her lip caught between her teeth; as though that somehow steadied her hand, Jean slit the pages far enough apart to work tweezers between them. There! She had it!

She pulled a sheet of white parchment paper from the book and spread it out beneath the lamp. At the top, in beautiful eighteenth-century script, was written, *"The Testament of George Albert Lovelace. At the end of a long life, conscience oft times comes to war with expedience...."*

"Good God," Jean said aloud. She leaped up, found the press kit Rick had given her, and dumped out the documents. Being copies, she couldn't tell whether they'd been written on the same paper with the same ink. But the page from the album had the same handwriting as one of the copied letters. And of the bogus registry entry, too, allowing for a curlicue here and there.

She read quickly through George's testament. Names, places, dates. How he had confessed his guilt to Kieran. How Kieran had manipulated him into forging the documents and including them in his perfectly honest work for Rick. How George, caught in a cleft stick, had "made a decision." Cameron himself couldn't have set down a statement this meticulous. The only data that weren't there was the full story of Archie's death.

Had George written this out and hidden it in the album on general principles? Or had he had some intimation of—well, not his death, necessarily, but trouble to come? Like an invitation to meet someone at Glendessary House during the Lodge meeting?

Exultant and impatient both—this was a major breakthrough, but it still didn't provide the all-important name—Jean tucked the new page into the press kit with the others. Closing that in the album, she headed for the door. No one was in the corridor or on the staircase. When she burst into the billiards room only one youngish guy was still there, staring vacantly at a computer screen. She didn't stop to exchange pleasantries or make excuses but went straight for the back room.

Cameron was right where he'd said he'd be, sitting behind the desk, papers spread out before him. He looked questioningly over the top of his glasses when Jean pelted in.

She extended the album toward him. "Look here. George's confession. What do you want to bet this is what Charlotte had Toby searching for? It was right in front of him the entire time. And of us, too. I picked up this album myself that day in Corpach. It was on George's coffee table. He got it out before he came to Edinburgh to see me, probably to hide the confession."

Cameron looked over the book and the papers, quickly but thoroughly. She could almost see the flow charts and subject outlines scrolling down his face. "This shops Kieran MacSorley right and proper, doesn't it?" he said at last, with that same quick, dry grin she'd glimpsed once before.

"It's still George's word against Kieran's. And it doesn't name the killer."

"Oh aye, but still, well done, Miss Fairbairn."

"You would have found it yourself eventually," she conceded.

"Perhaps." He shouted, "Shaw!" toward the outer room. When

the younger man appeared, Cameron ordered, "Bag and label this paper. Get it and the album to the labs in Inverness. Request a complete work-up: fingerprints, paper, ink, the lot. Compare it to the MacLyon documents."

"Yes sir."

"Phone D.S. Sawyer and tell him to give over the search of Lovelace's attic. Tell him to meet up with D.C. Gunn in Fort William and have another go at Walsh, then come back here."

"Yes, sir." Shaw carried the album and the papers away.

Cameron considered the photos in the press kit, then closed it and laid it on the desk. Taking off his glasses, he pinched the bridge of his nose.

"Headache?" Jean asked.

"No more than usual. I'm thinking it's not my eyes…" he held up his glasses, "…but my brain. Takes a lot more effort nowadays to get through the same amount of work."

"I know what you mean. Sometimes you have to fight your way through the neuron jungle with a machete." She didn't need to introduce the subject of burn-out. They were already on the same page, close to being in the same paragraph. Just as long as she didn't get personal. "I don't think George came out here Tuesday intending to stand up in front of the Lodge and blow the whistle. That's cutting straight to the chase. If he wanted to do that, he wouldn't have involved me."

"I'm thinking he came to meet his killer, who lured him here on some pretext or another."

"Pretty bold, with the house full of people."

"And every one of them a suspect, eh?"

"Well, yeah," said Jean. "So how many of the Lodge members thought Rick's pretensions were a great game, and how many swallowed the whole story?"

"Some of the latter are now claiming to be amongst the former."

"No kidding. But you've decided none of them could be the killer."

"No. Especially now that I've read through these." Cameron indicated the stack of reports. "You're wanting to know what's here, are you now?"

"Yes, please," she said, trying to look as guileless as possible. Judging by the glint in his eye, Cameron wasn't fooled. But he wasn't put off, either. Getting personal was not on the agenda. "You mind the clothes I was showing you? The shirts, the coats, the skirts and blouses were clean. But the forensics chaps found the same tweed threads, several more hairs, and muckle twine fibers on one of the kilts."

"Rick's."

"No. Walsh's"

"What? Toby really did kill George?" Jean shook her head, as though the negative motion would make the facts change themselves around.

"I doubt he was acting on MacSorley's orders, just as he was acting on Mrs. MacSorley's orders when he burgled the house."

"But breaking and entering is a far cry from murdering someone who helped out your family. Someone you liked."

"It is that, aye."

"Dammit, Toby's just too—too easy to pick on. Too cheap."

"That he is. But how else are you explaining the forensics?"

Jean could only shrug. She could have used one of those perceptual machetes.

"There's one thing," Cameron went on. "Lovelace's right jaw was bruised a bit, as though the killer bashed him one with his fist. Probably not hard enough to knock him out…"

"…but enough to make him woozy, so he wouldn't fight back. That fine old man…." She let her voice run down. Nothing she could say now would change anything.

Was that a gleam of sympathy in Cameron's eye or a twinge of pain? "The killer might could be left-handed. You've had more chance to take note of such things than I've done."

"Oh. Well." Jean raised her own hands, looking from the one to the other, visualizing everyone's gestures. "Kieran lighting his cigarette—yeah, he's right-handed. Charlotte pouring the tea, ditto. Vanessa fluffed up her hair and poured drinks. She's right-handed too. Rick was eating his dinner with his fork in his right hand."

"That's American fashion."

"But left-handed Americans usually hold their forks in their left hands, just tines up instead of down, like y'all do."

"Ah. I see."

"Toby was stirring the soup with his right hand. And…." Jean frowned, seeing Fiona's smooth white hand, the one with the wedding ring, stroking Clarinda's fur. "Fiona's left-handed. But you knew that."

His eyebrows rose a millimeter. "Can't say as I've...oh aye, you're right, I mind her signing her statement."

Men, Jean thought unfairly. Never notice anything. "That covers it, except for Neil. And he.... Oh. He was waxing Rick's car. He's left-handed, too, it's just that everyone plays the pipes right-handed, because of the design. But he couldn't have killed George, I heard him playing the entire time I was in the sitting room. I saw him walking around."

Cameron's brows were still off kilter, now indicating less puzzlement than thought processes at full-throttle. Like his were ever anything less, Fiona's handedness to the contrary. "How's this for you?" he asked. "Do you mind Hawley's car accident?"

"We were wondering if it really was an accident."

"One of the rocks from the MacSorleys' garden was found to have brake fluid on it. What if immediately after the accident MacSorley backed the car up to its usual parking place, drained the brake fluid, then bashed in the line?"

"So it would look like the fluid drained out by itself overnight. And then he rolled the car back down to the end of the drive and stopped it with the emergency brake, as though Charlotte had used the emergency brake when she almost hit the other car."

"And all the while Norman's drowning."

"Kieran thought Norman was a threat to the scam, because he'd overheard some important conversation with George."

"True enough, but I'm thinking something else just now."

"That Kieran and Charlotte took advantage of the accident to throw suspicion on Toby, being nothing if not opportunists. Because they wanted to protect Rick, do you think?"

"Or perhaps it was Neil who needs protecting."

Jean folded her arms defensively. *Neil?* He had a heck of a surface gloss, that was for sure, but that didn't mean he was rotten beneath. It didn't mean he wasn't, either. "You're right," she said with a sigh. "It could go either way."

"I'm not saying you didn't hear what you heard," Cameron said, spreading his hands placatingly. "I'm just..."

"...brainstorming. I know. Besides, if you've got the goods on Toby, there's no reason to try and break Neil's alibi."

"Walsh has the means and the opportunity, if not exactly a motive."

"Maybe you can prove that Kieran manipulated him into murdering George the way he manipulated George into forging the papers."

"Chance would be a fine thing." Cameron pressed his fingertips into his brow ridge, as though his brain was swelling and he was trying to push it back into his skull.

"Besides, under Scottish law you need two independent streams of evidence before you can bring anyone to trial, don't you?"

"Corroborative evidence, aye. Even Toby's kilt's not enough. As yet."

"Yeah." Jean felt a brief twinge in her left temple—his headache was catching. The breathless, stuffy feeling in her chest might be from the metallic odor in the small room, or might be a reaction to the electrical buzz in the larger one. Maybe she was merely anticipating Rick's dinner party.

Cameron looked up, one corner of his mouth tucked in, probably indicating frustration. "It's almost time for the dinner. We'd better be putting on our glad rags."

"I'll see you in a little while then." Jean headed back up the stairs to her room, informing herself that the weight in her chest wasn't anticipation but dread. No, she didn't want to play the decoy. But Cameron would be at the dinner, too. That thought was so reassuring it set her teeth on edge.

TWENTY-EIGHT

JEAN CHECKED HERSELF OVER in the mirror. The only pair of black shoes she had with her owed more to comfort than to style, her long, straight skirt was soft denim, and her white blouse was utilitarian. But the tartan sash, draped from her left shoulder around her opposite hip and caught back at the shoulder with a breathtaking Celtic-design brooch, was indisputably posh.

Her face was flushed, she saw, and her eyes dazed. She'd blend right in with the other inmates.

She shooed Clarinda into the hall and locked her door. Walking down the hall wasn't so bad—the skirt had a deep enough slit in the back she could almost take her full stride. But descending the staircase meant clinging to the banister with one hand and raising the skirt with the other. Not that fashion and comfort had ever coincided. At least Rick didn't want her to wear the hoop skirts of Charlie's day, so voluminous that one Jacobite woman hid her lover beneath them when the redcoats came to arrest him.

The dining room was perfumed by vases of flowers, most of them white like Charlie's cockade, although a few blue ones alluded to the blue and white of Scotland's flag. The colors complemented the MacLyon tartan runner stretching the length of the table atop a dazzling white linen cloth.

Crystal, china, and silver place settings were equally dazzling. Antique candlesticks repeated the intricate curves of the chandelier. Fiona, wearing a skirt of bright red and green Royal Stewart that was no doubt Rick's idea, was just lighting the candles. "Good evening," she said as calmly as though she'd been sitting zazen all day—until the match she was holding singed her fingertips and with an abrupt gesture she shook it out. Even Fiona, then, wasn't immune to the tension in the air, a faint squeal like the whine of a fluorescent light that had Jean clenching her jaw. *Contents under pressure.*

The door opened. Kieran ushered Charlotte inside. Jean quailed at the sight of his knobby knees below the hem of his kilt. Even so, there was something about a kilt that caused even a dinosaur to look dignified, although in Kieran's case the black vest, jacket, and bow tie made him look like a dignified butler. If only he'd lose the aftershave.

Charlotte's long kilted skirt and lace blouse might as well have the price tags on the outside. She looked Jean up and down, smiled her best Lady Gracious smile, and said, "Now that you know Rick's little secret, I'm sure you and dear Miranda will write a lovely article. Despite his eccentricities, Rick's risen above his upbringing and done so much for the community."

"You should write an article about Rick's philanthropic work," said Kieran, his tone of voice as peremptory as Clarinda's meow.

The MacSorleys had to know the jig was up on their Jacobite scam. They were trying to rescue something from the wreckage. No way would Jean let them make her part of the salvage operation. Smiling back, she said, "I'm sure Miranda and I can come up with something."

Cameron stepped through the door. The MacSorleys vanished from Jean's vision as though they'd burst like bubbles. A good thing her face was already flushed, because she could feel even more heat mounting into it.

There was something about a kilt that made even an ordinary man devastatingly handsome. The jacket and tie, the kilt in the dark red Cameron sett, the tall socks, fit his body to a tee. Firm, straight legs, broad shoulders, one strong hand still on the doorknob, the other resting on a modest leather sporran. Grave and yet keen expression on a face carved in fine-grained basalt. Eyes a quicksilver blue, like a loch beneath a clear sky…. His eyes were lit with a subtle amusement. He knew Jean was impressed.

He should be embarrassed by his vanity. Sending for his own kilt had not been doing things properly, it had been getting in touch with his inner peacock. She strolled away, remembering at the last second to take smaller steps. The kilt was no big deal, she told herself sternly. Unlike, say, jeans and a T-shirt, a kilt flattered every variation of masculine shape. Cameron was heavier and more solidly built than Neil, who with all his airs and graces was still heavier than bird-boned Rick. Neil was also the tallest of the men, having an inch or two even on his father. Toby was about Rick's height but had a linebacker's body—and he looked good in a kilt, too.

From outside came the first peal of pipe music. A flash of tartan behind the hedge became Neil, pacing up and down in the waning sunlight, his shadow keeping step and his kilt swinging fetchingly. Tonight, he, too, was in Royal Stewart. He would be handsome wearing a gunny sack, but as far as Jean was concerned, he was no longer a menu option.

A sudden pop made her spin around. Fiona had opened a bottle of champagne and was pouring it, frothing, into crystal flutes. Kieran picked up two and handed one to Charlotte. She regarded Cameron with the strained smile of someone who smells a fart. Cameron looked up at the picture of Charlie and Flora, eyes slightly crossed.

The door crashed open. Ah, the main characters, Rick and Vanessa. They made a grand entrance to the strains of "Scotland the Brave," Neil having nothing if not good timing.

Rick looked feverish, although he might simply be hot from the weight of the cloth and the knickknacks in the same over-the-top outfit he'd worn Friday morning. One slender hand was knotted on the hilt of his dirk, the other held Vanessa's in the air with a "now presenting Miss America" gesture.

Her black velvet skirt and vest, lace blouse, and MacLyon sash looked dull and plain next to Rick's splendor. Except for the glistening stones in her brooch, which Jean bet her next paycheck were genuine diamonds.

"Welcome," proclaimed Rick. "How good to see all of you on this important occasion, the beginning of a new era for Scotland."

Fiona handed Jean a glass of champagne. It was so light she almost fumbled it. She'd have to ask Miranda what brand of crystal was spun from wind and sea-foam.

"To the royal house of Stuart!" declaimed Rick, and swigged.

Jean took only a sip—now, if ever, she needed a clear head. The bubbles tickled her tongue, seeming to evaporate before they ever reached her throat. From the corner of her eye she saw Cameron swallow, then nod approvingly. Either he was also concealing a palate beneath his crust, or she'd noted a bit of poseur in his personality.... She really needed to stop paying so much attention to the man.

Jean was seated on Rick's right, next to Kieran, while Cameron was on Vanessa's right. This left Jean with a view of Charlotte across the table, who, judging by her lemon-sucking expression, was not at all amused by the interlopers getting the seats of honor.

Vanessa gestured as though throwing coins to the peasantry. Fiona opened the kitchen door and said, "You may serve now." A parade of white-coated servitors began offering soup. Prawn bisque, Jean saw, and took one ladle-full. The bread was brown soda with spinach and raisin.

Rick picked up his spoon, set it down again, and launched into a monologue about Charlie, charisma, and Stuart absolutism, which in his view—ignorance apparently being a valid viewpoint—became benevolence, tolerance, and the wellspring of democratic principle. Kieran and Charlotte threw in the occasional flattery. Vanessa looked either morose or resigned. She was no idiot. She knew it was over. The *Titanic* was sinking, no matter how hard they all tried to ignore the icy water washing across the carpet. But then, maybe Vanessa had intended all along to sink Rick's ship.

The second course was salmon salad with red peppers and artichokes. Very good, yes, but Jean couldn't force more than a few bites past the knot in her esophagus. It was her brain that was working overtime. She was squeezing it like Neil squeezed the bag of his pipes, although he was producing music and she was producing static.

Neil. A good-looking self-centered kid. A fine musician. Not a murderer, no. Drat Cameron, for planting that idea in her mind.

He sat scooping his food onto the back of his fork with his knife in good British fashion, eating some of everything, all of nothing. Self-disciplined? Repressed? Not nerveless. By the set of his shoulders beneath the epaulettes of his jacket she could tell he was ready to spring from the chair or dive under the table, whatever was required by…. By what?

Rick groped in his sporran, pulled out his cell phone, squinted at its tiny screen, and set it down on the table. A waiter whisked away his untouched plate.

Fiona opened two bottles of red wine. Italian, of the sort Charlie had drowned his sorrows in. Jean accepted another air-spun glass and again only sipped. Even so every object in the room, the candles, the gilded frames of the paintings, the silky petals of the flowers, seemed oddly distinct, fraught with significance. The pipe music resonated in her teeth and down her spine. Now was the time for the ghost of Archie MacSorley to walk through the room, like Banquo's ghost walking through the dining hall in *Macbeth*. But the moment was as much *Alice in Wonderland* as Shakespeare.

A hand set another plate in front of her. Haggis slices, sautéed in a batter light as tempura, served with horseradish sauce on a pedestal of turnips roasted to a caramel brown and frilled with mashed potato. Robert Burns would never have recognized his humble haggis, neeps, and tatties, the food of people who had to make do with what they could get.

"…and the loyalty of his people," Rick was saying. "There was a price of thirty thousand pounds on Prince Charles' head, a fortune, but no, none of his loyal subjects ever turned him in."

Not that quite a few of his disgusted would-be subjects wouldn't have wanted to. They just couldn't catch him. Jean tasted the haggis. Its cloying but meaty flavor was mitigated by its accompaniments.

"His loyal subjects turned out to help him, passing him from hand to hand…."

Like a hot potato. Jean caught a gleam from Cameron's eye and ignored it.

"…including the lovely Flora," Rick said, gesturing toward the painting with his fork. "A MacDonald, as is my wife."

Vanessa smiled with her red lips only, not her eyes.

"Prince Charles," said Kieran, "was betrayed by the disloyal, cheated out of his inheritance."

Charlotte nodded. "People of quality always have to guard against that stab in the back from the envious."

"No matter how threadbare and dirty Charles was," Rick said, "everyone still remarked on his bearing, his majesty. Blood will tell."

Yeah, right, Jean repeated wearily to herself. It was Rick's mantras that were getting threadbare.

The servitors were doling out dessert, stemmed glasses heaped with beige clouds. Jean licked a curl from the end of her spoon. Atholl Brose—oatmeal, honey, cream, and whiskey. Her stomach felt as tight as a snare drum, beating out the pulse of the music and of her heart as well.

Outside, in the gloaming, Neil played "Lord Lovat's Lament." Rick scooped his hair back from his glistening forehead and talked on, faster and faster, leaving out words and running the others together. "…Charlie—such courage—a prince living under such conditions…."

Better than being executed in as gruesome a fashion as the English could devise. Although if he had turned himself in, would the English have gone on rooting out what to them was a rebellion and sowing salt in its ruins?

What would have happened if George had turned himself in? He'd still be alive, for one thing.

Vanessa held out her glass and Fiona refilled it. Kieran and Charlotte ate with tiny, genteel bites. Cameron ate half his Atholl Brose and started sculpting the rest, hand steady, face set in neutral. But Jean could almost see each tendril of his hair standing up alert as antenna, taking in every nuance of his surroundings. He probably never relaxed, even off-duty.... He was still on duty, wasn't he? He didn't think he had the murderer. He'd said himself, the evidence of the kilt wasn't enough.

And suddenly she wondered, how did the police lab know that the incriminating kilt was Toby's, when they all looked alike? Was it simply Toby's kilt because it was in the bag labeled with Toby's name? What if the kilt with the threads and the hair and the fibers was actually Rick's?

That was the alcohol and the fat making her think she was clever. If she could question Cameron about evidence collection techniques.... *Oops.* She'd stared at him too long. He looked sharply up. With a shrug she looked back down at her dessert and took another bite. It melted in her mouth and left a satiny sheen on her tongue.

Rick threw down his napkin. "Okay," he announced.

Charlotte stuffed one last spoonful of Atholl Brose into her mouth, leaving a smear clinging to her lip. Vanessa stood up. "Coffee for the ladies upstairs, Fiona."

Jean wasn't surprised Rick insisted on that old custom.

"Bring out the Drambuie and the cigars," he ordered. "And some of the blackberry stuff Neil likes. Just like a kid, isn't it, to like the sweet stuff?"

Jean took that as a compliment. Pushing back her chair, she met Cameron's jaundiced eye and wondered whether he'd call Rick's attention to his—fraudulent—ancestor James VI and I's tirade against tobacco.

Fiona went into the kitchen. The pipe music stopped. Neil had impressive lungs—he'd played for over an hour. But Jean supposed he was used to that. He'd played a long time the day George was killed.

Vanessa opened the door. Charlotte got up. Neil came through the kitchen door, his fair skin glowing attractively, his hair tousled appealingly. "Music," Rick said to him. "Toby's not here. Fix the music." Bestowing a smile on each of the ladies, Neil brushed by Vanessa and out into the hallway.

Poor Toby, Jean thought, shooting one last glance at Cameron. His eyebrows registered concern but hardly remorse. One way or the other, he was only doing his job.

TWENTY-NINE

JEAN MINCED OUT into the corridor behind Vanessa and Charlotte. Funny how the floor seemed a bit unsteady and the mock candles even dimmer than usual. A nice bright light shone from a door at the far end of the hall, in the room across from the game larder. Vanessa had called that room Toby's office.

Jean had assumed, when she'd thought about it at all, that the intercom sound system was controlled from Rick's office. Apparently not. Now that she did think about it, she'd seen electronic equipment in that room moments before she'd seen George Lovelace hanging in the game larder, an image that had nullified all others.

A sudden burst of pipe music filled the air, either Pincock or Skelton, thank goodness, not more of the blandities. Neil walked out into the hall, bowed toward Jean, and strolled back into the dining room. Rick's voice called expansively, "Sit down, Neil. Have some of this cough-syrup stuff."

The blackberry and whiskey blend didn't taste at all like cough syrup, Jean corrected silently. It was sweet balanced with dry, something rarely done successfully.

Vanessa led the way upstairs, turning on lights as she went. Waving Jean and Charlotte toward chairs, she flopped down on the loveseat, next to windows opaque with the night. A moment later Fiona came gliding up the steps like a geisha. She set down a coffee tray, produced gem-like bottles of liqueur and crystal glasses from a nearby cabinet, and drew the curtains. "Will there be anything else?"

"Join the party," Vanessa answered, adding, "What there is of it." Skipping one caffeine-delivery system, she reached for another, a bottle of Kahlua. "Coffee? Booze? Help yourselves."

Fiona sat down on a straight-backed chair at the rim of the circle of lamplight, balancing on the edge of the seat, holding a cup of coffee but not drinking it. In the shadow her face was unreadable.

Charlotte served herself coffee and Amaretto, and began a monologue about a Labrador retriever Kieran once took to hunt grouse. What a shame some factions were trying to stop the hunting.

Some people were intent on depriving the cultured and sophisticated of the rewards they deserved, apparently for nothing more than existing.

Tuning Charlotte out, Jean drank a few sips of black coffee. It scoured the sweet cream from her mouth. By the time Clarinda came trotting along, whiskers at full alert, Jean's head had cleared a bit. But still her every sensation, every thought, left a wake across her mind, ripples that expanded further and further until they lapped up against memory.

The cat padded a sortie around the coffee table, making prissy feline faces at the smell of the liqueurs. Charlotte said cats were cold, selfish, and unfeeling. There was something to be said for not feeling, Jean thought. That could be an exercise in self-preservation. Been there, though. Done that.

From the courtyard came the sounds of voices, car doors, and engines. The caterers, presumably, packing up and moving out. Was Cameron the only policeman left in the house? Most of the others were in Fort William hounding Toby, the wild.... Well no, he wasn't a wild goose, the forensic evidence was conclusive. Wasn't it?

Only if the kilt in the bag labeled with his name was really his. She promised herself she'd mention her doubt to Cameron, even if she got a lecture in police procedure in return.

Vanessa poured herself another Kahlua. Fiona responded abstractly to Charlotte. The pipe music played on. If she was going to get drunk, Jean thought, it would be on that music, potent as whiskey, strong as death.

She'd only spent a few hours here when the infernal canned music hadn't been stuck in her ears like a pebble in her shoe. The only times she could remember not hearing it was late at night and when Neil was piping. It might be Toby's job to keep the music going, but tonight wasn't the only time Neil had put on a CD. Thursday night he'd put on Hugh's new album, right before Hugh himself told her that if Neil had played with Gallowglass at all, it had been in a recording studio....

Jean's stomach shimmied, sending a wave of cream and coffee and turnip into the back of her throat. Her cheeks went clammy and her hands icy. This must be was what Fiona felt, seeing a vision of the future. Except Jean wasn't seeing a vision. She was seeing the truth. Neil. A good-looking self-centered kid. A fine musician. Not a murderer…. *Oh God. No. Please, no.*

One small part of her mind whined, leave well enough alone. Let it go. Even if the kilt were Toby's, they couldn't convict him on that evidence alone. After a while the case would simply die away. And George's murderer would go free.

Most of her mind, the stubborn part she'd flexed so often it bulged like a muscle, knew what she had to do—prove her suspicions, one way or another. And if she found a whistle, she had to blow it.

"Excuse me," she said. Charlotte paused long enough to inhale, then went on. Vanessa stared at the door of Rick's study, her expression set in deep, almost calculating thought. Fiona watched Jean go, eyes hooded.

Jean found Clarinda outside her room, staring as only a cat could stare down the hall toward the black well of the back staircase. Opening and shutting her door loudly enough to reach the ears in the sitting area, Jean skirted around the cat and walked toward the stairs. She cast only one quick glance behind her, yearning toward the light—the cat's eyes made two golden gleams, like twin Louis d'Ors—and started slowly and carefully down, one tread at a time.

Being scared of the dark was as irrational as thinking there were monsters beneath the bed. She wasn't afraid of ghosts—she knew they weren't monsters. And yet there was something frightening about darkness, about the way ordinary objects changed form, about the way darkness could hide almost anything.

Charlotte's distant voice mingled with the amplified wail of the pipes. "The Flowers of the Forest." Neil had played "The Flowers of the Forest" the day George was killed, appropriately enough. But then, the MacSorleys knew how to act at good manners.

The air on the landing was arctic cold, thick with the scent of smoke. Keep moving, Jean told herself. Ghosts can't hurt you. Darkness can't hurt you. Living people hurt you. Stepping through the icy patch, she made it down into the back hall and looked right and left, up and down. Archie might be on duty, or standing watch, or whatever ghosts did, but he wasn't visible now.

A deep breath filled her lungs with cool air, not smoke. She started along the hall toward the far end. Rick's increasingly shrill monologue, cut with Kieran's oily bray, grew louder the closer she got to the dining room. Occasionally Neil's smooth murmur annotated a phrase. Once or twice Cameron's voice laid down a base line, like the drones keeping the music of the pipes tied to the earth and the truth.

She tiptoed past the dining room door, close enough to smell the smoke of the cigars, richer and sweeter than the eerie acrid scent of the burning house, and shut herself in the darkened office. Guided by the blinking lights of the various control panels, she found the light switch.

Bright light stabbed her eyes, but it took only a moment for them to adjust. When they did, she saw that the room looked like it had last Tuesday, littered with odds and ends, the electronics connected by a spider's web of cords. A blank monitor reflected her image like a fun-house mirror. The lovely melody of "Dark Island" echoed from the hallway outside, but now, here, Jean could hear the tiny whir of the CD player itself and see the display counting out the seconds.

Vanessa wanted to have a garden party. She'd said the lights and the electronics were all ready to go.... Yes. There was the switch, one side reading "Indoor Speakers" and the other reading "Outdoor Speakers." Jean patted it with her forefinger. Now it was set to "Indoor." All the time she'd been here it had been set to "Indoor." Except for that first day. No, there were no video cameras hidden beneath the eaves as she'd first assumed. What was hidden outside were speakers. She'd heard pipe music at the time of the murder, yes. But she'd only seen the piper after it was done....

No. Please, no. A stack of CDs sat on one corner of the desk. Her hands trembling, she went through them. Pipers. Dance bands. Throbbing tenors. Two of Hugh's recent releases. Easy listening from Yanni to Phil Coulter to Celtic mishmashes. A Gallowglass album. A couple of alternative rock, some pop, and a stray classical disc completed the stack.

Please, no. But if no, if Neil were innocent, then what? Jean started opening desk drawers. From down the hall, muffled by the door, came a gust of laughter. Just below that she heard footsteps. Vanessa thought the ghost was George because Archie had only become active at George's death. Ghosts were often sensitive to— well, a disturbance in the Force was as good a way of putting it as any. That was as good a description of what she'd felt in the sitting room when George was murdered as any, the groan of a spirit torn unwillingly from this plane of existence. She'd live with any number of ghosts if she had to, but she never wanted to hear, to feel, that groan again.

In a drawer, beneath a stack of brochures for everything from plant food to paint, lay several more CD boxes. The one next to the bottom held a silver disk marked in an ink-penned scrawl, "Demo. Neil MacSorley. Andy Renwick's 'Ferret' and other contemporary pieces. 53 minutes."

Gritting her teeth—*yes, no, yes, no*—Jean pulled out the bottom disk. "Demo. Neil MacSorley. 'Flowers of the Forest' and other moldie oldies. 58 minutes."

There it was. Her fingers spasmed on the plastic case. *Damn you, Neil!*

Means, motive, opportunity. He had them all. He'd even had the garden gloves, to protect his musician's hands when he'd punched an old man in the jaw and then tightened the garrote around his neck. An old commando trick, easy enough to learn when you've spent your life surrounded by stories of old commandos.

The pause followed by a squawk she'd heard the afternoon George died, that was when Neil had turned off the recording, darted the few steps out the back door, and begun actually playing. A few moments later he'd walked by the window of the sitting room and she'd had her first look at his enticing figure. *If only I had known,* she thought mockingly. But why should she have known? Even Fiona, with her second sight, hadn't known.

The murder had taken dexterity. It had taken intelligence. It had taken guts. Neil had all those. What he didn't have was one ounce of integrity.

Just one more thing. One more stream of evidence. Jean took a shuddering breath and commanded herself to stop trembling. Tucking the CD back into the box and the box into her blouse, so it would ride against her waistband—against the flesh Neil had touched—she turned off the light and waited until her eyes adjusted to the dark. Then she opened the door.

The door of the game larder just opposite wasn't quite shut. A chill, musty draft leaked from the darkness within, making her senses pucker. But physical darkness was what she feared now.

Again she tiptoed past the door of the dining room, beaming her desperation toward Cameron, trying to lure him out into the hall. He didn't hear. His voice said, "Lochiel wanted to keep on fighting. He had the men, he knew the country, he could have drawn Cumberland into a guerilla war. It was Charlie who abandoned his troops and legged it into the hills by way of saving his own manicured hide."

"The prince in the heather…." Rick began.

Jean stepped noiselessly across the tile floor of the entrance hall. Upstairs Charlotte's voice was still declaiming something about being cheated out of one's entitlements. And Jean was doing her best to get Charlotte's son, Charlotte's spoiled rotten son, shut up in prison for the rest of his life. He was certainly entitled to that.

The recorded pipes might just as well be squeezing her heart. Or her stomach, it was hard to tell. Had Neil ever really wanted her? Or had all his attentions been directed to finding out what George had told her, and if she'd seen or heard anything at the time of the murder? Neil had gone through her things. He'd rattled her doorknob in the middle of the night. If she'd let him in, he wouldn't have turned down a freebie.

Yeah, she'd gotten cynical about men. Her cynicism had served her well.

The sound of footsteps echoed down the hall. There was Archie, a shape in the shadows, trudging along toward the staircase. Jean edged around him—around his image—and opened the door of the billiards room.

A few LEDs gleamed, but no one was here. She turned on the lamps that dangled low over the billiard table, making an island of light in the darkened room, and starting pulling the plastic bags of clothing out of their box. Rick's jacket. Neil's jacket. Rick's, Neil's, and Toby's shirts. Neil had probably taken off his jacket before he jumped George, maybe rolled up his sleeves. Most butchers worked with their sleeves rolled up, didn't they?

Jean saw the scene in the corners of her eyes: The old man greeted Neil, a friend, a trusted colleague. Neil's fist shot out, suddenly, without warning. George staggered back. Neil threw the cord around his neck, pulled and twisted. George collapsed. Neil followed him down, still twisting. Only then did George's body—and Jean hoped that by then he was a body—fall against Neil's lap. Against his kilt.

She remembered Neil's hands, his slender hands, capturing and holding hers, playing them like he'd play the chanter. Her skin crawled. Thinking sex was cheap was one thing. But he thought life was cheap.

In the back room she found Rick's press kit just where Cameron had left it. She pulled out the photo of Neil posing with his pipes in front of the house. Yes, his kilt fit perfectly. She propped the picture against one of the evidence boxes and opened the plastic bags holding the three kilts.

She should be wearing gloves. She was contaminating the evidence. Cameron would demand to know why she hadn't waited. Well, she'd tell him.... The kilts were made of a very soft, smooth wool, the waists lined with broadcloth. High quality materials and beautifully constructed, the belt loops and the folds matched almost invisibly to the pattern, each pleat straight and sharp as the blade of a knife. Jean arranged the three kilts each on top of its bag. They'd been custom-made for their owners, right? For Rick, for Neil, and for Toby.

The fit, as Cameron had said, was subtle but important. A properly made kilt wasn't just a roll of fabric wrapped around a man's hips, like it had been centuries ago. The hem had to hit right at the wearer's kneecap. A too-short kilt looked like Bermuda shorts, a too-long one looked like a tablecloth. The apron, the flat part over the wearer's stomach where the two ends wrapped, had to be made of two equal widths of fabric so that the overlap met exactly. If the buckle that extended through a buttonhole from the inside edge didn't fasten to its external half just so, the two buckles on the outside edge would be off and the fabric would either bulge or bunch.

The kilt in the bag labeled with Toby's name had a smaller circumference by two or three inches than the one in the bag labeled with Neil's. It was also longer by a good two inches than the one in the bag labeled with Rick's name. That one was perceptibly, if not by a huge amount, smaller around than the one supposedly belonging to Toby.

Q.E.D., Jean told herself with a sigh that was almost a moan. The kilt labeled as Rick's really was his. But the one labeled as Toby's actually belonged to Neil. How Neil had managed to switch kilts Jean didn't know, but he was quite capable of a bit of sleight of hand in the chain of evidence. Especially when the only reason the police collected his clothes at all was to be fair. To stick to form. Not because he was a viable suspect.

It was her own testimony that had established his alibi. Just as it was her work that had encouraged George to set his plan in motion by bringing her the coin. Maybe he, too, knew her personal history, knew she couldn't leave well enough alone…. Don't flatter yourself, Cameron would say.

Now she had to go into the dining room and—no, she didn't have to denounce Neil to his face, she simply had to draw Cameron aside and show him the evidence. He was the pro. She'd done more than enough already.

Her feet weren't moving. She was still standing beside the line of kilts, the blues, greens, reds, and golds glowing in the lamplight.

This was no time to be giving Neil the benefit of the doubt. There could be no doubt. And yet…. If she just folded each kilt back into its bag and went back upstairs with her tail between her legs, would Cameron or anyone else think of trying the same comparison? *Trust me,* she thought, *to ruin another young man's life.* Throwing Neil to the wolves wouldn't bring George back. Protecting him would allow a fine young musician to—to live a lie. To get away with murder.

If it was too late for George, it was too late for Neil as well. She couldn't ruin the life he had already destroyed.

Footsteps came down the hall. Archie's feet, Jean thought, no matter how insubstantial, were going to wear a track in the carpet. But the steps didn't turn up the staircase. They came on, to the door of the billiards room.

You could see the light beneath the door from down the hall. Cameron must have finally escaped the dining room and come to see who was here. Amazing, what a relief it would be to see the man.

The door opened. In the gap between the lights and the equipment-strewn table, Jean could see the bottom of a jacket and the top of a kilt. A kilt in Royal Stewart tartan, not Cameron.

"There you are, Jean," said Neil's light, supple, seductive voice. "Whyever are you hiding yourself in here?"

THIRTY

OHGODOHGOD.... Jean's stomach bounced like a basketball into her throat and back down again. Act casual, she told herself, and said, "Oh! Hi!"

Damn, her voice squeaked. She stepped away from the row of kilts. If she started hurriedly bundling them back into their bags he'd notice her—well no, it wasn't her guilt that mattered here. But she bet she was the only one feeling any.

Neil started toward her, leaning over so he could see her face below the lights. His smile was broad and brilliant and just about as sincere as the smile on the face of the tiger. "Old Dour Cameron will be ticking you off right and proper if he sees you in here messing about with his bits and pieces. His evidence." His voice put quotation marks around the word "evidence."

Ohgod... She edged away, but not too far. She didn't want to look like she was frightened of him. She didn't want to be frightened of him, but she was. Give her an old familiar fear—a dark hallway, a newspaper headline.... She had to say something. With an effort she came out with, "I left the press kit Rick gave me in here. I came to get it."

"Oh aye. Poor old Rick. Barking mad. But you've noticed that. What are you after doing with his press kit, papering the loo with it?"

"That might work," she said, all too aware of the doppler effect in her voice.

He was halfway along the side of the table. While he might be a murderer, he wasn't stupid. He knew something was up. "Asking more questions, are you? Have you got any I could be answering for you?"

"I don't think so, no."

Neil reached the corner. He saw the kilts arranged in their row, each lying on top of its plastic bag. The bags labeled with the wrong names. Jean took two slow half-steps toward the opposite side of the table.

After a long moment his eyes rose to meet Jean's and his lips curved in a brave little smile, trying to hide his hurt and disappointment. She should have known he'd try a charm offensive. "All good journalists—and you're a good journalist, aren't you, Jean—know 'evidence' can be twisted about. Cameron and his lads, now, don't you know they're being pressurized into finding a guilty party. Any party will do."

"I'm sure they want to solve the case."

"Enough to cheat, Jean? Enough to find some poor muggins of an innocent bystander and fit him up?"

At least he respected her intelligence enough not to try the Toby ploy again. Jean closed her eyes. If she didn't look at that handsome face that had morphed into a murderer's mask and yet, horribly, remained the same, maybe she could think of something to say. But what came into her mind were Cameron's words, *killers of my acquaintance.*

She heard Neil's footstep and her eyes flew open. He'd come around the corner of the table and was two arm lengths away. The low lights painted his face with harsh downturned shadows.

Talking. Along with everything else he was good at, he was very good at talking. "That's a good photo of you," she said, pointing. "I bet you could use that for publicity when you go on the road. All the women will be throwing their room keys at you."

"Ah, Jean," he said, "I was thinking you found me repulsive."

"No way." *At least,* she added to herself, *I didn't used to.*

He shook his head sadly. "You're winding me up, Jean. All you've done is push me away."

She wished he'd stop saying her name. He sounded like a salesman. But then, he, too, was trying to establish a false intimacy.

"Or is there hope for me yet? I've done you no harm, have I, Jean? I've enjoyed chatting you up. A shame to leave it there. Come away with me. We'll drive west, to the islands. I know a small hotel on Skye, brilliant food, a view of the sea, soft beds."

"Just leave? Just like that?"

"Oh aye. We'll leave Rick and the polis behind. Disappear. Start over again. You did that yourself, when you left the States."

"Yes, I did." How long could she keep him talking before someone came looking for them? Before she saw a chance to bolt, bolting being a much better option than going off into some lonely place with him.

He was listing toward her, balanced on the balls of his feet. Great. She wasn't fooling him one bit. He was coming after her here and now. Although what he thought he was going to accomplish by attacking her with Cameron and the others in the house…. She already knew his mind didn't work the way most people's minds did. At least he wasn't going to take her by surprise, the way he did George.

"Or would you rather I went away on my own?" Neil asked. "Have you turned against me?"

Yes. God, yes. She leaned up against the table, the CD sticking to her rib cage. Funny how hot it was in here. The wool of the kilts prickled the palms of her hands the way Cameron's gaze pricked her skin.

"Is that it, then? You're that repressed you can't thole a man who's comfortable with his own sexuality? Is that why you're always doing over the poor young sods who never did you any harm?"

Of course he'd use that ploy. From his perspective she was betraying him, not the other way around. "There's harm, Neil, and there's harm."

"Ah, Jean, you've given me no choice, have you now?" He lunged.

And he hadn't given her any. Jean's hands closed on one of the kilts. She whipped it from the tabletop and across Neil's face, deliberately aiming for his eyes. His cry of surprise and pain told her she'd connected.

She wrapped the length of fabric around his head. Then she dropped it, set her hands on his chest, and pushed with all her adrenaline-pumped might. He fell backwards against the easel holding the chart. It crashed to the floor, Neil on top of it, clawing at his head and face, legs flailing. How about that. He wasn't wearing anything beneath his kilt.

Jean hiked her skirt up to her thighs and ran, blessing God and Naturalizer for sensible shoes. Into the chill air of the corridor. Past the doors of the drawing room. Past the media room. Into the entrance hall.

He was behind her, she could hear his steps, and the pipe music, and Charlotte's voice echoing down the stairwell, "A truly distinguished gathering, how honored we are to be included."

Jean sent the dining room door crashing open and catapulted through. No one was there. The table was littered with empty glasses, half-full bottles, and an ashtray like a miniature volcano emitting a tendril of sickly sweet smoke. The candles guttered in the sudden draft from the hall.

Shit! The gentlemen had gone to join the ladies upstairs; that was why Neil had come looking for her. She inhaled to scream. Surely, even in Glendessary House, someone would hear her scream….

A violent tug on the trailing end of her sash pulled her backwards, choking her cry in her throat. She glimpsed Neil, eyes red and watering, face contorted in rage, just behind her.

Jean twisted away, almost tripping herself up on her own skirt. Her blouse ripped, leaving him holding the sash and the brooch—damn, the sash was still looped around her waist—with a desperate wriggle and spin she was free. She hitched up her skirt again and sprinted for the kitchen door.

Swearing, Neil threw the sash onto the table. It knocked over a candle. A tiny flame started somewhere on the tartan cloth of either the sash or the runner, Jean didn't hang around long enough to see. Better and better, now the house was on fire. Again. There had to be an extinguisher in the kitchen….

Neil burst through the door behind her. The door into the garden was closer than that into the hallway. Without stopping she propelled herself toward it, praying it was unlocked.

It was. She threw it open and raced outside, for once appreciating the darkness. Plants grasped at her ankles and she felt her stockings rip but she kept on going. The bushes, the trees, the mountains were all indistinct smudges in the night…. The hedge. She dived behind it and crouched, pretending with all her might to be a rose bush, and dared a look back.

A slender, kilted figure stood outside the kitchen door, head turning right and left. He made a frustrated gesture and cursed, the word falling short and sharp into the cold night air. Jean had always wondered why a word describing the physical act of love also meant any number of harmful things. It showed you the ambivalence of sex.

Her heart tumbling in a syncopated rhythm, she gasped, exhaled, inhaled again. Maybe she could sneak around the corner of the house past the game larder, into the parking area. And then what? She didn't have her car keys or anyone else's. But a constable was stationed at the foot of the drive—unless he, too, had the night off.

She peered out between the yew branches. A twig scraped her glasses and another snagged in her hair. The house looked like a game board, each window a square of clear bright light against the shadowed stone. Except for the dining room window, where the light was a flickering smoky orange…. A smoke alarm started shrieking. At long bloody last! That should get everyone's attention.

Either Neil had gone back inside or he was sneaking up on her. With a yank on her hair she jerked away from the hedge, her eyes darting from side to side. The bushes and flowers shifted and rustled in the wind, in the darkness, but she saw no human figures. There were plenty of shadows large enough to hide one, though. As much as she'd like to light a candle, all she could do right now was both curse the darkness and use it.

Still crouching, she shuffled along behind the hedge until she came to its end. She peeked again. Through the dining room window she saw Fiona lifting a red fire extinguisher and letting fly with a stream of white foam.

Bent double, Jean plunged out into an open area. A sudden explosion pushed a squeak of terror from her throat. Convulsively she leaped and flattened herself in a flower bed, and only then remembered that some of the plants were supported on stakes. But it was the edge of the CD box that stabbed into her ribs. She hadn't impaled herself.

Neil was shooting at her, and not with a paintball gun, either. What, didn't he care how badly he incriminated himself? Or had he decided that since it was all over, he'd go out in that blaze of fury many men equated with glory?

Jean crawled through the flower bed until she came to another segment of hedge. She rose to her feet, folded her skirt up above her knees, and dashed for the corner of the house.

There were the louvered windows of the game larder. There was the back door, its indented porch a block of dense black shadow.... Something leaped from the darkness. An arm like a steel bar wrapped her waist and dragged her toward the house. A hand set itself snugly over her mouth. She emitted a terrified scream, muffled against those firm fingers. Part of her nervous system went limp as a noodle, but another part sent her elbows and knees flailing, twisting, desperately trying not so much to attack her attacker as to get free.

"Hush," whispered Cameron's voice in her ear, the word expelled on a gust of breath as her jabbing elbow found his solar plexus.

"It's you," she wheezed, freezing. His hand tasted of soap. His broad chest behind her back seemed steady as a stone wall.

"It's no one else, is it? I saw you from the window, reckoned you were heading round this way. Come back inside." Settling her back on her feet, he removed his hand from her mouth and his arm from her waist.

She turned on him, her hand pressed to her chest to keep her heart from falling out at his feet. "Inside?" she hissed in his face. "In case you haven't noticed, Detective Chief Inspector, I am now officially in danger."

"Oh aye, I've noticed." His breath was scented with single-malt but not with cigar smoke, thank goodness. "A proper hash you've made of escaping. Why didn't you fetch me?"

"I tried to! You weren't there!"

"I was taking a leaf from your book, paying a visit to the loo."

No, she was never going to live that down. Jean tried to pull together both her wits and the gaping tear in her blouse. If Cameron noticed she wasn't exposing a Victoria's Secret bra but a simple full-coverage number he showed no sign. Good. She liked a man who had his priorities straight. "Neil's the killer. He set up his alibi using a CD of his own piping. Here it is."

"So I was thinking." He took the CD and tucked it away in his sporran along with the cell phone she only now noticed in his hand. Then he peeled off his coat and held it while she slipped it on.

"No you weren't thinking that," she said, settling the coat's much larger shoulders over her own. "You didn't have a clue."

"I did so have a clue, I was locked down in the dining room with that blasted background music drilling a hole through my head."

"Well, you didn't try laying all the kilts out in a row, did you? Then you'd have seen that Neil switched kilts with Toby."

"Can't say I'd never have thought that hypothesis worth testing. I've seen muckle kilts round and about the night."

"So have you bothered to phone for help or would you rather critique the way I've been running for my life?"

"The cavalry's not so far away. Until then… ." He pulled something out of his sporran, something that gleamed darkly in the shadows.

"Oh. You have a gun."

"Not the sort of thing you'd be expecting a policeman to carry about with him, is it? Come along."

"I repeat. Inside?"

"If I was thinking you'd gone round the front, then so can he. And you can see who's shooting at you when you've got a bit of light. I'm sorry I've got no time to write it out and let you sign off on it."

Rolling her eyes as much in gratitude as exasperation, Jean let Cameron grasp her hand and draw her silently into the door and along the corridor.

Smoke hung in the air, but the alarm was no longer shrieking. Neither was any music playing. The office was dark. Somewhere male voices were shouting—Kieran restraining Neil, with any luck—and a female voice was scolding—Charlotte bawling him out, hopefully. Too late. Years too late.

The dining room door opened onto the wreckage of the feast: blackened tablecloth, broken dishes, flecks of white foam mingled with tumbled white flowers. The red cylinder of the extinguisher lay on the floor abandoned. If Fiona had any sense—and she had a lot—she was hiding somewhere.

The door of the sitting room stood ajar. Cameron pushed it open with his foot, slowly, then darted inside, gun at point, Jean jerked along behind. This room was also dark. She could see the furniture dimly outlined by the light from the hall. The glass covering Jenny's portrait reflected the glow, then went black as Cameron pushed the door back to its original position.

"Now what?" Jean asked, trying to see through the shadows gathered in the far corner, behind a chair.

"Go to the window, tell me what you see."

Jean released his hand, leaving her own feeling slightly scorched. With a sense of déjà vu that would have been unsettling had she not already been thoroughly spooked, she edged around the furniture and peered between the drapes. "Neil's out front, carrying a rifle or a shotgun. Waiting for me to come around the corner of the house, I bet."

"So I said," he replied, which was marginally better than *I told you so*. "Although he might could be watching for the constable to come up the drive as well."

"Will he come up the drive?"

"If he's following orders, he's behind the garage, waiting for reinforcements."

"And we wait to see who gets here first?"

"Oh aye, that's...."

In the center of the room something moved. Several somethings, shades of darkness, shapes in shadow, Cameron's face a pale blur beyond—no, through—them. She'd thought her senses were already at battle stations, but no. Now her sixth sense rose up like a commando out of deep water. Every hair on her body twitched erect. She forced her knees upright and into a locked position.

Several men leaned into the small pool of light cast by a lantern, their faces sharply etched, their backs dissolved into darkness. A young George, his arm in a sling, laid down his cards and picked up a large gold coin. Archie swore and threw his own cards down onto the pile of matches they were using as chips. He punched George's good arm. George punched back. They were laughing.... The scene wavered as though it were being projected on smoke. When it steadied again only Archie was left, hollow-eyed and blank-faced. The reek of smoke filled the air.

That was spectral smoke, wasn't it? It wasn't the fire in the dining room rekindling itself. Cameron looked toward the door.

"Maybe we'd better go check." Jean stifled a cough.

"No."

From down the hall came a nasal female voice. Charlotte's. "Smell that? The fire's started up again."

"Where's Cameron?" asked Kieran.

"Took to his heels, I expect. Trust Rick to invite a policeman to a formal dinner. He's never had one jot or tittle of class, has he?"

"Damned sneaky fellow, Cameron."

"Looked the sort to scarper. He's got his position by fraud and treachery, I expect."

Slowly the door opened. Cameron crouched, gun at the ready. With a friendly meow Clarinda trotted in the door. Then she stopped, staring into the center of the room. Her fur rippled as though in a breeze. Archie was still standing there. The air, like a sodden quilt, wrapped so heavily around Jean's shoulders that her knees cracked and bent and she sank down behind the chair.

Cameron lowered the gun and exhaled audibly, either because he'd almost shot the cat or because he knew a shot would have drawn unwelcome attention….

Too late. "The cat's just gone into the sitting room. I'll have a look." Kieran's statement was punctuated by the sound of the front door slamming open and then shut.

Cameron whispered, "I reckon Neil's just come back inside. Do you think Mum and Dad are after taking away his popgun?"

"I wouldn't bet on it." Funny how the darkness behind the chair had suddenly become friendly, not that several inches of leather and stuffing would be much protection. In his white shirt Cameron made an outstanding target. Too late to give him back his jacket, but then, it wouldn't be much protection, either.

Archie's ghost started toward the door, beginning his pre-programmed walk from the sitting room where the fateful game had been played down the hall to the staircase that had probably led to his sleeping quarters. Clarinda backed up, hissing, and bolted into the hall. A blast from the shotgun shattered the silence and Jean convulsed. *No! Not the cat!*

Charlotte screamed. "Bugger it!" shouted Neil.

The door of the sitting room crashed against the wall. Kieran stood outlined by the dim corridor lights, head thrust forward, arms outspread warily, whether serving as point man for Neil or trying to stop him from shooting Jean wasn't about to guess. She could just see Neil behind him, straining forward, shotgun poised. By the movement of the white blob that was Cameron's shirt, Jean deduced he'd gestured her to stay down. That's all right, she didn't have anywhere to go.

Archie's ghost walked toward the door. Kieran's eyes widened, the whites glinting around the poppy-seed pupils. His jaw dropped, almost unhinging itself. His moustache bristled. A shining strand of spittle ran from the corner of his mouth.

The spectral allergens were so strong, here, now, that Kieran could see the ghost of his father advancing toward him. The moment, Jean thought incoherently, was a cross between Darth Vader's *Luke, I am your father* and Hamlet on the battlements of Elsinore.…

Neil shouted to Kieran, "Get out of my way, you doddering old fool."

Archie kept on walking. With a cry of horror Kieran fell back into the corridor. Neil leaped past him. Then, also seeing Archie, he yowled and lurched back. Jean braced herself for another shot, but no, he jerked the gun up so that it was less a weapon than a shield held across his open-mouthed mask of a face. Archie walked right through them both. Charlotte screamed again. The sound broadened and lengthened into the wail of sirens.

A patter of feet and the front door opened. Jean spun around and jerked the drapes aside. Neil, having all the courage of his convictions that most liars had, ran into the night. And was pinned in the sudden glare of headlights coming through the trees.

He dodged toward the garage. A fluorescent yellow figure leaped out from the shrubbery and tackled him. Not an angel, but close enough—the gate constable in his reflective yellow coat.

Car engines roared. Voices shouted. Blue lights strobed across the walls of the sitting room. Cameron was on his feet and headed for the door. Jean scrambled up, caught her heel in her hem, dragged the skirt up to her knees and followed.

From outside came the report of a gun, something smaller than a shotgun. "Oh for the love of God!" Cameron exclaimed and charged off down the hall.

Jean's feet danced with indecision, her mind flipping through one image after another. Charlotte sitting on the bottom step of the main staircase, her face in her hands, rocking back and forth wailing. Archie disappearing down the far corridor. Kieran moving in slow motion toward the door.

Outside the dining room, Fiona crouched over Clarinda's body, clasping it tightly in her arms. Tears flooded down her face. But Clarinda's sleek striped fur was imperforate if rumpled, and her golden eyes peered past Fiona's arm, reflecting gracious tolerance of the embrace. Neil's shot had hit the wall, blasting a ragged hole in the plaster and exposing the lathes beneath.

"I was hiding myself in the kitchen when I heard her meow. I came to look...." Fiona's voice caught in a sob.

Suddenly the entrance hall was filled with people. Jean squeezed Fiona's shoulder and quelled any sarcastic thoughts about zen resignation. She plodded toward the front of the house. Her knees were so wobbly she could hardly walk, and rolled from side to side like a drunk.

There was Neil, handcuffed and held between two constables, the worse for wear but still haughty. He tried an occasional wriggle, as though the constables were nothing more than flies, but they held on.

There was D.C. Gunn, holding, appropriately enough, a shotgun. There was D.S. Sawyer, grasping Kieran by the scruff of the neck and replacing his own gun in the holster inside his coat. "You're lucky I'm a good shot, Sunshine. Could have had your boy's head off if I'd wanted. Didn't waste any time throwing down that posh Purdey, did he?"

"That's a quality shotgun," Kieran whined. "Have a care...."

There was Cameron, giving Sawyer a level stare that said as clearly as words that shooting off either weapon or mouth was out of line. Sawyer deflected that stare with a bellicose sneer.

A female constable lifted Charlotte off the bottom step and patted her down. "...under a great deal of stress recently," the woman was whining. "Very responsible positions here, terribly stressed...."

Cameron faced Neil. "Neil MacSorley, I arrest you in connection with the murder of George Lovelace. You are not obliged to say anything, but anything you do say will be taken down and may be given in evidence."

Charlotte gobbled indignantly. Kieran swore. Neil offered

Cameron a suggestion that was anatomically impossible. Cameron was unimpressed. "Take him…."

"Cease and desist at once," shouted an imperious voice.

Oh no. Jean stepped around the corner. Everyone looked up. *Oh yes.*

Rick, in full panoply of tartan and silver, stood halfway down the staircase, weaving slightly, his face flushed and his eyes blazing. He was holding his cell phone like a scepter. Behind him Vanessa grasped the banister with both hands, her chest inflating and deflating, her eyes so large Jean expected them to fall out and bounce down the steps.

"Stop this disturbance at once!" shouted Rick. "I command you!"

No, Jean thought, and forced her bone-weary body to take another step forward. No one had tackled Rick yet.

THIRTY-ONE

CAMERON MURMURED a few words and made several subtle gestures. The spear-carriers cleared out, relieving Gunn of the shotgun on their way, but they left the door open just in case. Sawyer took up a position between Kieran and Neil, ready to bring down the ham-handed arm of the law if necessary.

Fiona appeared beside Jean, her exterior calm again. A well-rehearsed calm, Jean thought. She offered her a sickly smile. Fiona smiled wanly back.

"Detective Chief Inspector Cameron," said Rick from his height. "What's the meaning of this?"

Cameron opened his mouth, but it was Kieran who answered Rick's question. "You stupid Yank. You bloody buffoon. Look where you've brought us, you and your delusions."

Rick drew himself even further erect, almost toppling over backwards. "I beg your pardon?"

"Playing at being gentry, and all the time the legitimate gentry reduced to scrabbling about amongst your leavings. Tell him," Kieran said to Jean. "Tell him what that old fool Lovelace did to him."

"It wasn't George alone who did it," Jean retorted. "It was your idea. You took advantage of George when he tried to do the right thing by you."

Neil was looking at her, eyebrows knotted, lower lip outthrust, as though she'd kneed him in the balls, gratuitously.

Jean turned the angle of her shoulder toward him and focused on Rick. "Those documents proving your descent from Bonnie Prince Charlie. They're fake. They're forgeries. They're bogus up one side and down the other. The letter saying they're authentic is just as phony. When Kieran told you he'd taken the documents to the Museum, he lied."

Sawyer stifled a snicker. Gunn looked blank, but still whipped out his notebook and pen.

"Hold on," said Kieran indignantly. "I never...."

Rick shook his head. "So you're part of the conspiracy, too, Jean. A respected journalist, corrupted by the Hanoverians. But you, Alasdair, you're a Cameron, surely you haven't fallen for this vile plot?"

"The documents are fakes," said Cameron. "You've been used. The MacSorleys here set up the entire story so you'd buy Glendessary House from them and they could embezzle the restoration funds."

Fiona crossed her arms protectively across her charcoal-stained blouse, dismayed but not surprised.

"It's only money," said Rick with a regal wave of his phone. "What's at stake here is principle. The truth of the secret history of the Stuarts. Are you telling me, Alasdair, that you've turned against that truth? That you're betraying your clan and all of those who died for me?"

Cameron braced one foot on the bottom tread of the stairs and set his hands on his tartan-clad hips. He seemed taller than Rick, even with Rick several steps above him. "No one's died for you. Because of you, aye. George Lovelace died for the truth. So did Norman Hawley, in a way."

Charlotte flinched at Norman's name and looked around at Kieran.

But Kieran didn't crack that easily. "Doddering old fool,

George Lovelace. I never thought him capable of making so much trouble. And Hawley, no better than a common yob."

"Never underestimate the malice behind a smiling face," Neil said. "Isn't that right, Jean?"

"You should know." She didn't even feel bitter or resentful toward him, she decided. Bitterness and resentment took caring.

Turning to Cameron, Charlotte explained, "George cheated us of our inheritance, then had the neck to brag to Kieran about it."

Cameron said nothing, simply watched her with his patented half-skeptical, half-menacing composure. Gunn scribbled furiously.

"We had to defend ourselves," Charlotte went on, indignant. Why wasn't everyone nodding in understanding and letting them go?

"Defend yourself from what?" demanded Jean. "Fiona's cat?"

"A man has to see to his family before anything else," said Kieran.

"Even when his son commits murder?" Sawyer asked.

Neil turned on him. "What are you calling murder, you witless oik? What would you know about loyalty? George was out to get us, just as he was out to get Archie. He wanted stopping."

"Are you confessing to the murder of George Lovelace?" asked Cameron.

"You execute traitors and murderers. You hang them. George was a traitor and a murderer. He murdered my grandfather."

"We used to hang murderers," Cameron told him. "I should think you'd be pleased that's one custom no longer observed."

Some of the color drained from Neil's face, but still he kept up his devil-may-care stance. His demonic self-assurance. But his gilded surface had been rubbed away to reveal a mind so abscessed it made George's guilt look no bigger than a pimple.

"Traitors?" repeated Rick. "Traitors?"

Vanessa was no longer hyperventilating, and her astonished expression had hardened into resignation. She set her hand on her husband's arm. "Rick, let it go."

Jean remembered the waiters removing his plates as full as they'd set them down. How much alcohol had he poured into an empty stomach? What was surprising wasn't that he'd slipped into total lunacy, but that he was speaking in complete sentences and standing on his feet to do it.

Rick's already flushed face went purple. He shook Vanessa's hand away. "Good God! To think I have lived to see this!"

In the immortal words of Charlie himself, advised not to march on Culloden.....

In one clumsy but effective movement, Rick dropped the phone, pulled the dirk from its sheath, and charged down the stairs. "You've cheated me, Kieran! You've cheated me of my inheritance!"

Kieran quailed. Charlotte squealed. Cameron spun out of Rick's way, then grabbed his shoulder. For a second Jean thought he was doing the Vulcan nerve pinch. But no, he was slowing Rick down so that Sawyer could step forward and twist the knife out of his hand. Rick shrieked in pain and rage, then buckled to the floor. If there had been any carpet he'd have chewed it, in the fine tradition of generations of rationality-impaired kings. Maybe he did have royal blood.

Vanessa hurried down the stairs and wrapped her arms about Rick's moaning form. "I'm here, baby. I'm here."

"Can we get on with it now?" Cameron asked, losing himself so far as to make a broad gesture that was part frustration, part disgust. "Take them all to Fort William."

Charlotte's voice reached a register only dogs could hear. "You don't understand, Chief Inspector. Neil was raised properly, he's never misbehaved in his life, always did his poor old mother proud...."

Constables surged back into the entrance hall. Gunn tucked his notebook away. Sawyer plucked up Rick and steered him out the door, Vanessa supporting him from the other side. Neil shot one glance back at Jean. "Look what you've done," he sneered, and then he was gone.

Cameron stood with Jean and Fiona alone in the midst of the battlefield. If he'd had a sword he'd have leaned on it. She wished she had something to lean on, and settled for the newel post at the foot of the stairs. Her voice seemed thin and reedy. "What have I done? I figured out that Neil used a recording of the pipes to set himself up an alibi and switched Toby's kilt for his own. Yeah, it's my fault. It's always someone else's fault, isn't it?"

"That's how he did it, then," said Fiona. "I've always thought Neil was too clever by half."

Jean had to ask, "Who did you think killed George?"

Fiona shook her head. "Rick, I suppose. In any case, I was living with a murderer."

"Was MacSorley storing his gun here?" Cameron asked her.

"Oh aye. He persuaded Rick that this was a hunting lodge, Charlie was mad for hunting, and the illegalities of it all be damned. Good job Neil's such a poor shot."

"A very good job." Jean took off the coat and gave it back to Cameron, even though a chill was starting to permeate not just her limbs but her bones. "Here."

"Are you all right?" He took the coat from her hands.

"No," she said. "But I will be. Thanks, Chief Inspector."

With a curt nod and the least trace of a smile, Cameron said, "Good night then, Miss Fairbairn. Fiona." He shut the door behind him.

"I don't know," Jean said, half to herself, "whether to kick him or kiss him."

Fiona started to say something, stopped, and settled for, "He cleans up right nicely, does Alasdair." Humor moved in her eyes, those eyes afflicted with second sight. Jean would have wondered just what Fiona was seeing now, what it was that amused her either about Cameron or about Jean herself, except for once she simply didn't want to know.

The first seven notes of "Scotland the Brave" sounded tinnily from the staircase. Fiona picked up Rick's phone and switched it off. Outside cars started up and drove away. Silence fell, broken only by the distant complaint of a bird and the wind in the trees. The house was empty, filled with nothing but shadow and the acid dregs of greed. Jean would have felt more at home in a carnival fun house.

Keep busy, she told herself, or else you'll think about it. "Let me change my clothes and I'll help you clean up the dining room."

"Thank you kindly," said Fiona.

Jean glanced back from the top of the steps to see Archie walking through the entrance hall. He crossed within a foot of Fiona, but she didn't notice. With all the strong emotion of the last few days, even Vanessa, even Kieran and Neil, had heard and seen Archie's phantom. But not Fiona. Given a choice, Jean would rather see the past than the future, be it amusing, tragic, or any combination of the two.

She went into her room. The toiletries ranged along the glass shelf above the bathroom sink looked just the same. Her reflection didn't. Her eyes were fixed and her face ashen with a shocky expression she didn't like, although maybe noticing it meant she wasn't going to faint. Her glasses had stayed on her face through it all.

Now she took them off and spent a long moment hanging on to the side of the washbasin, chills racking her body. It was over. Lives had been lost, families shattered, but for her it was over. Whatever effects would linger—and they would, she knew that—were of little import, considering.

At last she was able to wash her face and brush her teeth, willing the ordinary gestures to soothe the emotions she'd not only rediscovered, but exfoliated. She wondered if Cameron, wherever he was right now, was shivering in reaction too, then decided, no, he wasn't. He was still at work.

Her skirt and blouse were pretty much totaled. Pitching them aside, she dressed in jeans, a *Great Scot* T-shirt, a sweater, and athletic shoes. Downstairs she found Fiona, similarly dressed and similarly shocky-looking, collecting the broken dishes. Jean waded in. Clarinda did her bit by sitting next to her bowl in the kitchen and complaining until she got a well-earned extra serving of kitty kibble. The footsteps paced up the hall to the far end, again and again. Jean jerked around every time, fighting up through the dense, cold air, hardly able to breathe. Finally the dustpan clattered from her numb fingers and she knew it was time to act before she lost it entirely. Besides, in a way she owed something to Archie, too.

"He's restless, is he?" asked Fiona.

"Yes. Who can blame him? Come on, I'm going to try something. It's not like there's anything to lose if it doesn't work."

The women walked out into the corridor. Sure enough, here came Archie out of the sitting room door. Jean stepped in front of him. The reek of smoke filled her nostrils and throat. "Archie. Archie MacSorley. It's all over, Archie. You can go now."

The ghost stopped. The hollow eyes were still focused on the end of the hall and the deeply shadowed face, looking like Neil's in the billiards room, was still expressionless. Not Cameron's intelligent expressionlessness, but complete vacancy, no expression at all.

"Yes, Archie, George was here. But he's gone now. He's waiting for you. Your oppo is waiting. Go with him. Go together."

A flicker of comprehension trickled down Archie's face, no more than the shadows subtly shifting.

"Go home, Archie. It's all over. George is waiting."

And suddenly the figure wasn't there any more. It didn't fade away, it simply vanished, and with it the smell of smoke. Jean tried to clear her throat and ended up coughing from somewhere deep in her gut, down around her ham sandwich lunch. At last she stood up straight, into lighter, fresher air, and stretched some warmth into her limbs.

Fiona asked, "You've sent him away, then?"

"Maybe. Maybe not. I hope I've helped him, whatever happened. You'll have to wait and see."

"It won't be me seeing." Fiona turned toward the kitchen. "We could do with a cup of cocoa and a scone, I'm thinking."

A normality fix. Not to mention a fix of sleep-inducing carbs. "Yes, please," Jean said.

Sitting at the kitchen table they ate and drank and chatted about books and movies, each comment interspersed with long meditative silences. At last, yawning and pleased she was capable of yawning, Jean went upstairs, took a long hot shower, and sank into her pillow. Her brain jerked hither and thither and finally flatlined. The yew hedge. Cats. Kilts. But, thank God, no gunshots. She woke up abruptly at the sound of car doors slamming.

The sun was shining through the curtains. Voices echoed from the entrance hall. She crawled out of the bed, dressed, and staggered downstairs for the epilogue.

Fiona was carrying a tray into the library. Jean followed her through the door, and saw Cameron scouting along the bookcases. He was still wearing his kilt but without the jacket. The sleeves of his shirt were rolled up and its collar lay open, exposing his throat. The lines between his brows and bracketing his mouth were plowed deep. His skin had the pallor and his eyes the bruises of a sleepless night. Even his voice was scraped a bit thin. "I've brought Mrs. MacLyon home. She's upstairs having a wash. I thought you'd like a word or two about last night's interviews."

"How's Vanessa doing?" Jean asked.

"Well enough, I reckon. Rick's in hospital, heavily sedated."

"Pity," Fiona commented, which summed up the situation nicely.

They sat around a small table and shared out coffee and toast. No, it didn't taste of ashes. Feeling almost herself again, whoever that was, Jean leaned back with her cup balanced on her thigh. The tall windows gleamed, darkened, and gleamed again as clouds drifted across the sun. Clarinda dozed in a sunny spot with her paws tucked beneath her well-groomed breast. Jean was jealous.

"Well then," said Fiona.

"You've heard them talking, the MacSorleys," Cameron began. "I'll spare you the recriminations and excuses. I didn't hear one word of remorse, I'm telling you that."

"You suspected that Kieran had gotten someone else to do his dirty work," said Jean. "You thought it was Toby, though. Not Neil. But he took his family mythology like a drug, didn't he? The mythology that was his identity as a MacSorley, as his parents' son."

If Cameron caught the significance of her choice of words he didn't take advantage of the opening. "Like his mother, he was given to eavesdropping. He overheard Lovelace telling you, Fiona, about taking the coin to Jean. But Neil, being a bit of a liar and a sneak himself, decided there was more to it than that. Lovelace was after seeing a journalist, therefore he was after blowing the gaff on the entire plot: the forgeries, the embezzlement, the lot."

"Well he was, but not directly," Jean said.

"Neil felt he had to dispose of George before the journalist turned up for her interview. Then no matter what she was claiming Lovelace said, Neil's mum and dad could say it was all a lie."

"But George didn't tell me anything. All I did was put a dent in Neil's plans. He thought he'd have more time before George was discovered, so that the other people in the house could wander around and act suspicious. Instead I showed up and pinpointed the time of death. And since I wasn't doing anything else, I paid attention to his piping."

"You were a problem for him, no doubt about that." The coffee was drawing the color back into Cameron's unshaven cheeks. He even offered Jean a quick quirk of a smile on the word *problem*.

She'd give him that silent comment, along with a rather cramped smile of her own.

"It was premeditated murder, was it?" asked Fiona.

"Oh aye, that it was," Cameron replied. "Neil lured Lovelace here, on a day he'd normally not be here at all, by pretending he wanted to—well, he told us 'turn traitor as well,' but like as not he told Lovelace something different, something about doing the right thing."

"How did he manage to switch his kilt with Toby's?" Jean asked.

Cameron extended his cup. Fiona poured him more coffee. "He was never a proper suspect, mind. We're thanking you for that, Miss Fairbairn."

She had fallen into Neil's trap. Her, Ms Skeptic. It was little consolation everyone else had fallen, too. All she could do was grimace and say, "You're welcome."

"Sawyer told Gunn to collect the men's clothes. Rick went into his room and Toby and Neil into their rooms, which are at the opposite ends of the house."

"Gunn couldn't cover all three at the same time," Jean concluded. "Neil told Toby he'd take both their kilts down together. Toby trusted Neil—why shouldn't he? He didn't suspect Neil had switched kilts any more than anyone else did. I hope Gunn isn't in trouble over this."

"Not so much as he might have been, as otherwise he's conducted himself well. It's a fine learning experience for him, I'm thinking. For us all."

By the window Clarinda sat up, stretched, and then lay down facing the opposite direction. A cloud blotted out the sunlight. She looked up, annoyed, then when the sun shone out again settled down secure in her power.

"So you have a strong case against Neil," Jean said.

Cameron nodded. "Oh aye. Good job he never destroyed that CD, but then, why should he do? It was perfectly innocent in itself. Even now all it can do is throw doubt on his alibi. Taken along with the forensic evidence of the kilt, though, not to mention his confession of a sort, well then. I reckon he'll be sent down for life."

"Poor Neil," said a flat female voice. "Poor handsome, stupid Neil." Jean looked around, Cameron stood up, and Fiona reached for a clean cup. Vanessa walked down the spiral staircase from Rick's office. With her fresh-scrubbed face and brightly-patterned silk robe she'd look about fifteen, except for the worry lines faintly etched at the corners of her eyes and mouth. And there was a new tautness in her posture, too, as though laid-back didn't do it for her, not any more.

She accepted a cup of coffee and crunched into a bit of toast. "What's this I hear about George writing a confession about the forgeries and everything?"

"There was one hidden in his old photo album," Jean said.

"Norman said something about George saying something about 'writing up the truth,'" said Vanessa. "At the time I didn't think anything about it, Norman was always the know-it-all. I'm not surprised Kieran latched onto him, they were a lot alike."

"Maybe after Lovelace's death, Hawley saw his chance for a bit of blackmail," Cameron suggested. "But that's one area where Kieran's keeping his mouth tight shut, the accident when Norman drowned, and whether he and Charlotte planned to deflect suspicion from Neil to Toby. We may never know the truth of that."

"So Kieran and Charlotte didn't know Neil had killed George until the deed was done?" Jean asked "And the fact that they both had alibis was just coincidence?"

Cameron answered, "In a way. Mrs. MacSorley was helping Mrs. MacLyon prepare for the meeting…."

"Harassing me," interjected Vanessa.

"…when Mrs. MacLyon said something about Lovelace having been to see Jean. And Mrs. MacSorley drew the same conclusion Neil had done. She made some excuse and rushed off to Corpach to—she's saying persuade, I'm thinking threaten—Lovelace into changing his mind."

"But it was too late," Jean said.

"Kieran went jogging instead of attending the meeting, said he'd had his fill of Rick and his pretensions. Even though it was Kieran himself pushed Rick over the edge."

Vanessa snorted. "No kidding."

"And once I was on the scene," said Jean, "the MacSorleys and the MacLyons went into damage control mode. Sorry, Vanessa."

"That's exactly what we were doing," Vanessa returned, "and not just with the damage of poor old George being murdered, either. I figured, somebody was dead, Rick had gone far enough, it was time to bring down the curtain and douse the lights. It was time to get on with our lives. I wasn't intending for Rick to go completely over the edge, though. No way, no how."

"His fantasies were encouraged beyond all reason," said Cameron, and this time his eye did stray to Jean's face.

"Is he going to recover?" she asked, returning his look evenly.

"They've got him medicated up to the eyebrows right now, but as soon as I get him home…." Vanessa set her cup down with a ding. "I've got to call his clients, let them know he's going to be out of it for awhile. And the Popcorn Board. That's going to be fun. Fiona, can you fix me breakfast? None of this kipper or kidney stuff, you know, eggs and fruit and a bagel. Bring it into my office. Alasdair. Jean."

Both Jean and Cameron stood up, but before they could speak Vanessa was already gone. Her high-heeled slippers clicked across the tiled floor of the entrance hall and down the corridor.

"She's had no more sleep than I've done," said Cameron.

"She's young," Jean told him. "She's not far from pulling all-nighters in college. And what she's got up to her eyeballs is caffeine."

Fiona gathered together the cups and toast racks. "More coffee?"

"The lads will be along soon to break down the incident room," Cameron said. "I'd better be having my bath and a change of clothes."

"I'm going home," stated Jean, rather surprised that when she said *home* it was Edinburgh she meant. Her own space. Free air. "Unless you want me to hang around here and make another statement."

Gracing them both with a benevolent smile, Fiona left the room.

Cameron looked after her, his brows tilted up in the middle, registering puzzlement. *Don't ask,* Jean told him silently. *Don't tell.*

With a slight shrug, he turned to her. "We'll be needing another statement, aye. Could you come to Fort William on the Tuesday?"

"Sure. And you know where I am in the meantime; you have my card."

"Right." Cameron turned toward the door.

She watched him walk away, shoulders set, kilt swaying. No amount of disillusionment was going to spoil the inspiring view of a man in a kilt. A tingle ran down her body, commemorating Cameron's firm, matter-of-fact embrace—if you could call that grab and drag into the back door an embrace.... The name spilled from her lips, from her emotions, before her rational mind could dam it up. "Alasdair."

He stopped. "Aye?"

Go on, or you'll always regret it. "How about dinner Tuesday night?"

He glanced over his shoulder, blue eyes sharp and bright as the lights atop one of his own squad cars. He paused just long enough to make Jean wonder if she needed to start wiping egg from her face. Then he said, "Dinner? Oh aye, Jean, that's a grand idea."

"See you at the police station on Tuesday," she replied, but she wasn't exactly relieved.

"Oh aye." He shut the door quietly behind him.

Well then. Her pride—their pride—had gone down as smoothly as whiskey. She was even feeling just a bit dizzy.... With a rueful laugh, Jean turned and looked around the beautiful room. Heaven must look very much like a library. Books, comfy chairs, a cat dozing by a window overlooking a garden. No ghosts complicating matters. No....

But she wasn't sure she'd want a heaven without men.

THIRTY-TWO

JEAN GAZED OUT of the window of the restaurant at the yellow façade of the hotel opposite. Some pedestrians paused to read the chalkboard listing the day's specials. Others strolled on by, enjoying the rays of sun slanting between the buildings of the High Street. Overhead, gulls floated in a clear blue sky.

The waiter began clearing the table of its dishes—madras, raita, balti. Rich, greasy, spicy food that made her think vaguely Biblical thoughts about the fat of the land and anointing heads with oil.

Alasdair leaned back. "Coffee," he told the waiter. "Jean?"

In his resonant voice, her first name sounded odd, as though it had greater substance. "Sure. Coffee and kheer, please."

The waiter nodded and walked away. In the background a twangy Indian melody didn't quite hook up with her neurons, and therefore didn't distract her from the matter at hand. Who was looking at her with his usual cool curiosity. "All right then, what were you really wanting to talk about?"

"You did well keeping up the idle chitchat this long," she told him.

He didn't waste his time parrying that sally. "You'll be called to testify at the trial, right enough. The trials, Neil's and Kieran's as well."

"I guess they won't let Neil have his pipes in prison. What a waste." Jean looked out the window again. The sun's rays had crept a millimeter closer.

Alasdair said, "Rick's stabilized, I'm told. Vanessa's organizing his transfer to the U.S."

"He'll recover, then. Or at least be able to deal with reality again."

"Depends on your definition of reality, doesn't it now?"

"Yes, it does." They'd spent a good—a very fine—hour discussing literary and cinematic fantasy, the great stories, the ones that mattered. They weren't just in the same paragraph, they were in the same.... The dragons' fiery breath stirred the hair on the back of Jean's neck.

The waiter set down coffee cups and a bowl of thick, milky rice pudding. She ate a bite. Smooth, sumptuous. Sensual. "What about the house?"

Alasdair poured several drops of cream into his coffee and watched them swirl through the black liquid, taking its edge off. "Fiona tells me one of Rick's clients owns a hotel chain, is looking to buy Glendessary House as a country hotel. Should the deal go through, Fiona plans to stay on and help manage the place."

"She'll do a great job. I hope it works out. Does Toby have to go back to jail?"

"He's turned Queen's witness, which will mitigate. Fiona says he'll have a job at the hotel when he's released."

"Good," Jean said, exhaling in relief for Toby, the fall guy. "What about Rick's Jacobite collection? Would Vanessa consider selling or even donating that to the Museum of Scotland?"

"Ask her. Just now she'd be glad to let it go, I reckon. May I?" Delicately he scooped a spoonful of pudding from her bowl, ate it, and licked his lips, his tongue slowly tracing their elegant Gothic curve.

Jean quenched the flare in the pit of her stomach by looking quickly down into her pudding.

"Not bad," he said. "Oft times the kheer's too sweet and sticky."

"Does sweet offend your aesthetic sense the same way sentimentality does?" She scraped her spoon across the indentation his had made in her pudding, obliterating it.

"I suppose I mistrust them both, aye." He set his spoon back in the saucer. "By the by, Toby, of all people, was able to fill in the last gaps of Archie's story."

"Toby? Aha! His grandfather who served with Lovelace!"

"Got it in one. He was working as an orderly at the infirmary, and gambling with the others the night of the fire."

"So what happened exactly? Archie and George were roughhousing, shoving each other around like my nephews do, and they knocked the lantern over?"

"At the same moment Archie fell against the corner of the fireplace. Bashed in his head and killed him instantly."

"Oh no!" Jean set down her spoon.

"The lantern fell into the pile of matches they were using as chips for their game. Before anyone quite realized what was happening, the place had blazed up. They ran for their lives."

"And didn't have time to bring Archie's body out with them." Jean could see the whole awful scene, taste the smoke and the panic. "The authorities thought he'd died in the fire and staged a modest cover-up."

"When you go quick like that, all of an instant—well, it's no surprise Archie was still walking about, just as he would have done the night he died."

"You're saying 'was.'"

Alasdair nodded. "Fiona told me about your—not an exorcism, that's right uncharitable. Whatever you're wanting to call it, Vanessa says she's not heard Archie since the Saturday."

"And Fiona's never sensed him at all, but then, she only sees the future…." Jean tried another spoonful of pudding, hoping fat would make a good anesthetic.

It was Alasdair's turn to look outside. "Are you thinking Archie was waked up by George's death?"

"Called from whatever limbo or purgatory he was in, yes. Not just because George, his oppo, was murdered down the hall, but because Archie's own grandson did the deed. Avenging a crime that never happened. I said something to Miranda last week about wheels of fate and poetic justice."

"Justice is possible, if not probable. Look at George, gnawing his guilt long past time to bury it. But then, that's not so unusual."

She'd seen implacable profiles like Cameron's in medieval sculpture. "Guilt isn't distributed evenly enough. Some people don't feel it at all, others…" There was a point she didn't need to belabor. "I stopped by the Commando Memorial this morning and left some flowers in the Garden of Remembrance for George. I'm sorry I never got to know him. He was a lot more complicated than I'd thought. But then, I'm a little quick to judge sometimes."

"Oh aye, that you are." But he smiled when he said that, and turned back to face her.

"And you aren't?" she retorted teasingly. "What did you think of me when we first met?"

"Here's a conceited wee woman, right clever but with a chip on her shoulder, thinking she can't trust a man to take notice of her cleverness."

She'd give him that, too. Resisting any mention of the chip on his own shoulder, she asked, "And my, ah, sprightly genius and very agreeable conversation won you over? Broke through your shell?"

"Don't go breaking through my shell, woman, you might not like what's inside." His smile was more amused than bitter, repeated by the crinkle at the corners of his eyes.

She couldn't ask for a fairer warning than that. And yet she'd had a glimpse beneath his shell, just as he'd had one beneath hers. They couldn't pretend it didn't happen. Or could they?

Jean realized she was leaning across the table, into the faint prickle of electricity she'd associated with the incident room but now realized was Alasdair himself, who was leaning toward her as though he, too, sensed something strong. Something hazardous. "Why ask me to dinner?" he asked, voice quiet but perhaps, still, just a bit menacing.

"I needed reassurance," she said, giving him only part of the answer.

He knew it was only part of the answer. "I'm a policeman, not a psychiatrist."

"But you've been involved in a lot of criminal cases. Me, all I seem to do is destroy young men's lives. My history's repeating itself."

"Could you have lived with yourself if you'd not grassed up your student? If you'd let Neil get away with murder?"

"No. I had to do the right thing. Like George."

"There you are, then," Alasdair said.

"No matter where you go, there you are," she returned, deliberately light, and sat back, breaking that subtle attraction. "You solved a high-profile case, Detective Chief Inspector Cameron. This will be a feather in your cap."

He, too, retreated, his face suddenly weary. Either he was showing a lot more expression these days, or she had learned how to read him. "You did a fair amount of the work yourself."

"Happenstance. Dumb luck. Stupid luck, for that matter." She bit her lip. "Have you ever considered quitting the police force?"

Alasdair's brows rose at that, in what Jean interpreted as a mixture of surprise and resentment. "Every so often I feel Andy Sawyer's breath on the back of my neck, aye."

"Here's your chance to go out on a high note."

"What should I do with myself, then?" His voice whetted its edge.

Good question. One she couldn't answer. She looked out the window to see people were clotting into groups along the sides of the street. "It's Tuesday. The school pipe band's playing."

"Oh aye," he returned mildly, sheathing his vocal blade.

Jean signaled to the waiter. "Check, please."

"I'll get it." Alasdair reached for his pocket.

"No, this was my idea."

"All right, then."

She squinted at the chicken tracks on the slip of paper the waiter presented, decided the sum was close enough, and fanned several banknotes across the plate it rested on. Alasdair stood up. "You're away to Edinburgh the night, then."

"It's good to be back in my own flat. With my own stuff, pedestrian though it is, and my own cat, who's not even remotely pedestrian. With all due respect to Clarinda, she's a real lapful, but she goes with the big house. Dougie's the size of a teddy bear. He fits." She worked her way out from behind the table.

Alasdair didn't repeat his comment about the importance of fit. Neither did he volunteer any information about his own home—a semi-detached house near Culloden was all he'd told her earlier. He held the door open for her, saying, "You'll be writing more articles," in the same tone he might say, *You'll be lobbing more grenades.*

"I'll get several out of the last week. When those run out, Miranda's teeming with ideas. I just hope I don't attract any more conflicted people, but I suppose like attracts like…." She brushed by him into the street. He was doing it again, letting her rattle on until she revealed too much.

He said, "If you get yourself into trouble again, mind that you're now known to the police."

"I mind." In both meanings of the word, she added to herself.

The Lochaber Schools Pipe Band was formed down the street, all the young people, girls as well as boys, tidy in their green tartan kilts. Alasdair, Jean thought with an appraising sideways glance, looked good in his understated business suit. In his kilt, he looked…Would she have asked him out if he hadn't been wearing a kilt, his own kilt, one that fit properly?

And now what? What would she have done if he'd said, *Sure, break my shell open?* Would she have dared to expose the vulnerable creature inside? No. Dinner and conversation were easy enough, pleasant enough, when they mutually agreed to dance around the emotional elephant lying in the middle of the table. But that was all. She didn't need a reclamation project in her life any more than he needed one in his.

With a ruffle of drums the band began to play "Scotland the Brave." The kids came marching up the street, music echoing from the buildings on either side. "By any chance," Jean asked, "do you prefer light jazz?"

"Eh?" Alasdair grinned, every tooth gleaming. "Ah no, this is the music that stirs the blood."

The band marched past, drawing most of the crowd with it, leaving Jean and Alasdair standing on the curb like an island at ebb tide. Not that anyone was really an island.

He glanced at his watch. "Sorry, must run, media interview. Thank you for the dinner and the conversation."

She looked into his eyes, guarded still despite that almost congenial little crinkle at their corners. "Thank *you*." She extended her hand.

He took it in his firm but discreet grasp. Instead of shaking it he bowed, a la Bonnie Prince Charlie, and kissed it. His lips lingered, as cool and brisk on her skin as the wind from the sea. Something sparked in his gaze, like heat lightning on the horizon, and then chilled. "Cheers," he said, released her hand so abruptly he threw it away, and turned to go.

Jean's hand dangled in mid-air, hot and cold at once. No, she hadn't asked him whether he found emotional intimacy aesthetically offensive, or whether he found it frightening. She didn't have to. His answer would have been the same as hers. There might be some way of compromising between selling your soul and being lonely, but neither of them knew what it was. Which is why, she told herself as she made an about-face, she and Alasdair Cameron were walking away in opposite directions. Hail and farewell.

The band stopped in Cameron Square, in front of the West Highland Museum. After Culloden, the English had banned the bagpipes as instruments of war. Because their music went right to the core of your being and squeezed until your eyes bugged out and your mind reeled and your heart bled with passion that could never be expressed. Not safely, anyway. Not safely at all.

She wondered if Alasdair were making the same rationalizations. She wondered what she'd say to him the next time she saw him—at one of the trials of course, strictly business.... Smiling wryly, Jean leaned up against the cool stone of the Museum and tried to convince herself that it was the music and the music alone that pulsed dangerously in her blood.